Into the Arms of Danger

First Edition

Copyright © 2012 Lola S. Kohen

Published by
Journeys Press
1010 University Avenue #712
San Diego CA 92108
wwwjourneypress.com

Cover Art by Susan Burns
Author photo by Don Hoffman

Library of Congress Control Number: 2012948216

ISBN: 0-9882-6430-7
ISBN-13: 9780988264304

Into the Arms of Danger

A Thriller in Future Israel

Lola S. Kohen

2012

Dedication

Into the Arms of Danger is dedicated to Mayor David Bouskila and the brave people of Sderot, Israel, who live in the Negev Desert under constant threat from enemy attacks.

Acknowledgments

My deepest thanks go to my editors Syd Love, Dave Feldman, and Laura Merrill. I am also grateful to my review partner Glenda de Vaney, to those who helped critique my story, and to my friends and family who supported and encouraged me throughout the process.

"What happens today is a reflection of the past and a mirror into the future."

Commander Ari Alexander

chapter 1

IN THE LATE morning of a warm, clear spring day, the missile launched. It raced through the desert sky to plummet over a security wall protecting a community of three thousand people.

The shrapnel-filled rocket exploded through the roof of an ancestral home in a communal family neighborhood, called a *moshav*, killing a young couple and their three daughters. The last in their line, they once traced their presence in the Negev Desert, through the mother's lineage, to the time of Solomon's reign.

It happened at Kol Shofar kibbutz on the first day of Passover in the year 2045.

At the same time, military commander and leader of Kol Shofar Ari Alexander was speeding across the Mediterranean Sea with three others from his enclave in southern Israel on a fast luxury yacht-turned-cargo cruiser headed for Turkey.

Their destination, a secret international conference in the port town of Antalya, would bring them together with Jews from around the world to plan the defense of their homeland during the current Islamic civil war.

Ari checked his watch—they would arrive on schedule in the morning. He looked out over the railing as night descended slowly. The reflection of the full moon glistened like a handful of sparkling gems thrown across the surface of the water while the heavens blazed with stars in an ultramarine sky. He watched for a moment before turning to follow the others below deck.

For the long night journey, the captain had instructed his passengers, Ari's group and the eight delegates from Jerusalem traveling with them, to crowd into the lower cabin, away from the deck lights. Commander Ari, at six feet, ducked slightly to avoid a curtain hanging at the top of the cabin doorway.

The passengers settled in for the ride on padded benches built into wood-paneled cabin walls. After hours of traversing dark waters, Ari opened one eye to see his always-worried intelligence officer, Dove, gently nudge his silver-bearded explosives expert and Torah scholar, Zev, to stop his snoring. The ship lurched, abruptly changing Zev's position and solving the problem.

Ari turned to the fourth member of his group, Devorah. She moved her waist-length dark hair off her shoulders, glanced at Zev, and smiled back at Ari. The youngest of the community leaders at age thirty-six, the petite Devorah stood almost as high as Ari's shoulders. He admired her legendary close-contact fighting skills and considered her a valuable friend.

The overweight, unshaven captain appeared at the cabin doorway. He entered and came straight to Ari. "We may have trouble." Cap spoke in a low voice. "We've spotted an Islamic warship off our starboard."

"Who are they?" Ari asked quietly.

Dove leaned in to hear. He smoothed his curly brown hair, matted on the side from the uncomfortable napping position.

"We don't know." The captain bent closer. "The ship is unmarked. Could you come up? Take a look?"

Ari squeezed Devorah's hand. "It's probably nothing." He stood to leave with Cap.

Several passengers rubbed their eyes and starting talking. Devorah rose and whispered to Dove, "We should go too."

"I agree." Dove stretched his shoulders and stood with her.

The captain led the way up a narrow, heavily varnished wooden staircase to the upper deck, then up an outside, metal staircase to the second story. His operations room, situated over the wheelhouse, could be described as plush utilitarian.

"See for yourself." Cap took high-powered binoculars off a small sofa littered with papers and a tray of half-eaten food and handed them to Ari.

Ari adjusted the lens, looked through the large, round starboard window, and said, "It's an express-class destroyer." He handed them to Dove. "Look for the black shape prowling on the water."

Cap's dark eyes darted between Ari and Dove. "They probably won't harass us," he said nervously. "We're under a Turkish flag and our manifest says we're going to Egypt."

"Why don't we speed up?" Ari asked.

"I'm not giving them a reason to look at us." Cap nodded toward the wheelhouse. "I told the helmsman to take it slow."

Ari agreed. "Let's cruise past as if we have all night to get to North Africa."

Cap motioned toward the window facing the possible menace. "My first mate noticed them on the radar about an hour ago. They stopped moving north when we came into visual range."

Dove watched through the binoculars. "We're directly opposite now," he reported. "If they're going to make a move against us, this would be the time. They've launched no inspection craft, so I think we're in the clear."

Ari tilted his head toward the door and ran his fingers through his light brown, wavy hair. "It's about six hours to port," he said. "Let's get some sleep." He saw relief wash over Devorah's face.

Outside, a sudden roar caused Ari to rush to the window. He watched two underwater sub runners break to the surface on the starboard side. Floodlights from the runners came in through the porthole while a loudspeaker blared in Arabic. Dove slid through the open door and raced down the stairs so fast Ari hardly saw him go.

Staring through his telescope, Cap called out, "I see an inflatable speedboat coming off the warship. We can't outrun them. Men from the sub runners will hold us here until the inspection boat arrives. I've been through this before."

A large oak desk with drawers on both sides and a panel across the front sat bolted to the floor on one side of Cap's room. Ari rested his hands on Devorah's shoulders and gently pushed her under the desk. "Dove will warn the others," he told her. "Stay silent. We don't know what we're up against."

Cap shook his head when Ari removed a high-powered smart gun from a shoulder holster under his jacket. "Don't even think about it." Cap pointed to a gray metal trash can bolted to the floor next to the desk.

A thud echoed through the room when cables shot from the runners struck their hull. Ari hesitated, then lowered his high/low velocity gun into the can and placed crumpled paper on top. Next he slipped off his lightweight nylon jacket, tossing it under the desk. "Put it on," he told Devorah.

Cap gestured toward Ari's shoulder holster. Ari hesitated, then slipped it off, and stuffed it behind a sofa pillow.

Two muscular, black-hooded men with submachine guns entered moments later. They scanned the room and opened a closet. One man jerked his thumb toward the door and the other, a husky, swaggering man, left immediately.

All waited silently for the twenty minutes it took the inspection boat to pull alongside. Ari leaned toward the window and glanced out to see two men disembark the inflatable boat and climb over the rail.

A short man with a sparse beard, shoulder-length dark hair, black pants and shirt walked with a slender young man, maybe a teenager, wearing white clothing. Neither wore a hood or mask, but the slender one carried a submachine gun.

Minutes later, the short man dressed in black ascended the metal stairs and entered Cap's cabin alone. Ari could see he wasn't Arab. About thirty, obviously the leader, he held a nickel-plated revolver, and spoke Persian to the captain.

The other hooded man from the sub runner returned to the room shortly after their leader arrived.

The leader again said something to Cap in Persian.

Cap tilted his head toward Ari. "He wants to know who you are."

Ari stood a little straighter. "Turkish citizen," he said in English. Ari knew his Israeli accent was impossible to hide.

The leader looked at Ari and said in heavily accented English, "You are Jew." He slapped Ari's face.

Ari barely restrained himself. His hands moved forward, then stopped.

The husky hooded man stepped in front of Ari. He called the leader Tariq, and he pushed Ari away from the edge of the desk. The smaller hooded man held a submachine gun on Cap.

Ari stumbled, but caught his balance. Inadvertently, he glanced at the desk. *G-d help me,* he thought. *What have I done?*

Tariq saw the glance. He walked over, leaned behind the desk, and pulled Devorah out by her hair. She scrambled to lessen the pain. Tariq pointed his shiny Beretta at her chest, pushed her into the center of the room, and looked at Ari. "Yours?"

Ari didn't feel—he just calculated the next word, the next movement. "I don't know her." He scowled at Tariq. "But serious trouble will come to you if you harm her."

The three terrorists spoke back and forth in Persian and laughed. The husky hooded man said something that seemed to anger the leader.

"You are hiding Jews down below," Tariq shouted. He pointed his pistol toward Cap's feet.

A sharp crack permeated the air while the pungent aroma of spent gunpowder filled Ari's nostrils. The bullet hit inches from Cap's right foot.

Cap didn't move. His face paled.

"Jew bastards." Tariq took a step toward Cap. "Where do you take them?"

Cap didn't answer.

"We're Turkish citizens traveling under our country's flag," Ari said defiantly. He had the forged identification papers in his shirt pocket to prove it.

Tariq pushed his gun barrel against Cap's stomach. "You are smuggling Jews in international waters."

"No, I give you my word," Cap said. "I make no profit from them. I swear. I'm not a smuggler. They're just passengers while I deliver my cargo."

Tariq waved his gun in Cap's face. "You mean my cargo, don't you?"

"I don't understand your meaning," Cap pleaded. "I can show you a legal manifest. I can account for everything aboard. I'm expected in Cairo in the morning."

"Enough," Tariq shouted. "I seize this ship for the crime of smuggling Jews."

"Under what authority?" Ari asked.

"The Republic of Persyria," he snapped.

There was a moment of stunned silence. Ari regretted putting his weapon into the trash can. *Persyria*, he thought. *The fanatical new union between Iran and Syria. Breeding ground for the next bunch of terrorists.*

"But maybe we can make a deal," Tariq said. "I have something you want. I will sell them to you." He waved his Beretta toward the door leading below deck. "My man downstairs can kill them all. Or you can buy them."

"Okay, I will buy them," Cap answered quickly.

"Half million euros each. My man counted ten of them down there." Tariq pointed toward Ari. "I will throw this one in for free."

"I'm only a poor transporter," Cap sputtered. "I don't have that much."

The terrorist pointed the Beretta toward Ari, saying, "The boat, the cargo, your crew, the Jews—all for five million euros. This is a good deal. You disagree?"

"No, I agree with you," Cap whimpered. "I'm just a poor man."

"You are a lying, rich smuggler." The gun moved to Cap's head.

"Please," Cap sputtered, "we can work this out."

Tariq didn't move the Beretta. "Lucky for you I'm in a hurry. I will sell the Jews for two million. And I get to shoot one."

"Half million," Ari offered. "And no one gets shot."

"Maybe one million. And I shoot your leg." Tariq laughed. A nasty, growling laugh. He pushed his gun barrel against Ari's right thigh and moved close enough for Ari to notice the stink of garlic on his breath. "You admit you are a Zionist?"

Ari looked down into his eyes. "Unrepentant Zionist."

"So, you are Israeli military?" He pushed the gun in deeper. Ari's slender, powerfully built body was now against the wall.

"No, of course not," Ari answered without flinching. "I'm a schoolteacher."

"Liar!" Tariq shouted. "So, you have killed many of our innocent believers?"

Ari didn't blink. "Too many to count."

"I should kill you right now, to save my people." Tariq moved his gun a little higher, pressed it hard against Ari.

"And I should kill you right now, to save my people," Ari said calmly.

Tariq laughed and moved away. "I told you I would buy the Jews down there. I will keep my word to throw you in unharmed. One million. Now."

Ari motioned toward Devorah. "Including her."

The expression on Tariq's face became threatening again. "This one"—he looked at her—"maybe I keep for myself."

Devorah adjusted Ari's loose-fitting jacket over her cotton summer dress. She looked down and didn't speak.

The leader put his hands on her shoulders to remove the jacket. Ari struggled to remain calm. His mouth tightened into a thin line; his hands curled into fists.

One of the hooded men moved close to Ari, submachine gun inches away.

Tariq pulled the still-zipped jacket over Devorah's head, tossed it to the floor. He reached behind her and grabbed a handful of hair, close to her head. She put her hands behind her head to protect her neck as her head jerked backward.

Tariq held his weapon out. The short, hooded man who wasn't covering Ari stepped forward to take it. Tariq turned back to Devorah and slowly unbuttoned the top button of her dress, letting his hand slip over her breast.

Ari calculated the time and distance needed to take the weapon away from the terrorist near him, train it on the other hooded man, then take out Tariq. He was seconds away from springing into action when Devorah's voice startled everyone.

"Take your hands off me—you bloody terrorist." Devorah pushed him away with both hands on his chest. Tariq stepped forward and slapped her cheek hard enough to leave a red handprint. He turned to retrieve the pistol from his hooded companion, but Devorah pulled Ari's weapon out of the trash can and jammed it against Tariq's back.

"Easy, boys," she cautioned. "Everybody moves real careful, and everybody keeps their heads."

"My man downstairs will kill every cursed Jew on this ship," Tariq hissed.

That's the armed teenager I saw on the deck, Ari thought.

Devorah tapped the gun on Tariq's back. "You'll meet your maker at the same time. Tell him, Ari."

"If you don't order them to drop their weapons," Ari said, "we will let your men go home after she shoots you. They will tell everyone you were sent to hell by a woman. Your name will make people laugh. Your family will live in shame."

No one moved.

"They can't understand what I'm saying to you, Tariq." Ari's voice grew forceful. "Tell them to lower their weapons because we made a deal. You'll get money, but your men will leave without their guns. Tell them or die. You decide."

Tariq made a growling sound. "How much money?"

"Enough," Devorah answered. "Now tell them."

Tariq's eyes grew colder. He ordered his men to put their weapons on the floor. They hesitated, then slowly obeyed.

Ari picked up the Beretta and kicked the two submachine guns across the floor toward the desk. "Cap, get some cuffs on these thieves," he said, and gestured to the two hooded ones. "We've got one more down below."

Cap stepped to the desk and returned with two sets of cuffs. He handed them to Ari.

Ari held the restraints. "Is this all you've got?"

Cap nodded.

Moving close to Devorah, Ari slid a bracelet onto Tariq's right wrist, then pulled hard to bring his left wrist down to cuff.

"Good work," he whispered to Devorah. She kept the gun pressed into Tariq's back.

Cap took a pistol from the top desk drawer and motioned for the two hooded men to face the wall. When the second man refused, Ari smashed him in the face with the Beretta. The sound of the impact was followed by a low groan from inside the black hood. The man reached up to feel his shattered nose while Ari cuffed his other wrist to his companion.

"If they try anything, shoot them," Ari told Cap.

A crooked smile crept across Cap's face. "With pleasure."

Ari picked up the submachine guns and stashed them under the desk. He held the Beretta in one hand and with his other hand gripped Tariq's arm. "Cover Cap," he told Devorah, and nodded toward the prisoners. "I'm going for the fourth man."

Pushing Tariq in front of him, Ari descended the stairs to the deck, then to the passenger cabin.

Dove moved cautiously next to Ari as he entered.

Zev sat close by on the bench. Curly silver hair burst out from under a navy-blue cap with a short, slanted brim. His thick silver beard covered most of his face. Ari saw concern in his soft brown eyes.

Zev and the other passengers were looking at the teenager pointing a fully automatic Tech-9 submachine gun at them. "Tell him to drop his weapon." Ari pushed Tariq forward a step.

"It's not that easy," Dove replied quietly. "Look at the bottom of his shirt."

The boy, with a glazed stare, stood in the center of the cabin. He looked thick around his middle. Loose wires hung just below his white cotton shirt hem.

Suicide bomber raced through Ari's mind. His first instinct, to leap on top of the killer, filled him. But his desire to live paralyzed him for a split-second.

"Tariq's plan is clear," Dove whispered to Ari. "To collect ransom from us, return to his carrier with the two hooded ones, and leave the teenager to blow up with everyone on board."

Ari squeezed Tariq's arm and whispered in his ear, "Talk him down or die with him."

Tariq stood silently.

"Tell him," Ari said, "that you have to follow this Jew boat to Egypt to collect the big money."

Speaking in Persian, Tariq laid out the new plan. It took several minutes, but it looked like it was working. Ari told Tariq to tell the boy he would go home a hero, his family made rich.

The bomber laid his Tech-9 on the floor, and Zev stepped forward to defuse the bomb components strapped to his body. When Zev finished, he looked up and nodded.

Ari gripped Tariq's arm and said, "Let's go."

Dove took hold of the teenager. Zev picked up the submachine gun and followed them to Cap's cabin.

"Start moving south," Ari told Cap as they entered.

Dove found a plastic cord in Cap's desk and used it to tie the suicide bomber's hands behind his back.

Cap gestured toward Tariq. "What about him?"

"We'll dump the prisoners into their inspection boat and send 'em back to their warship," Ari said. He turned to Dove. "But first bring those two submersibles on board. Let's take a look at that technology."

"My first mate, Isyanov," Cap offered. "He'll help you haul them up."

"I'll photograph them," Dove said.

Cap grinned. "I'll keep 'em."

Ari whispered instructions to Zev, and he left with Dove.

Devorah held the handgun steady, pointed at Tariq. Ari could still see a red mark on her cheek. For a moment, he felt proud of her. And maybe more. *There will be time for that later*, he thought. He began watching the warship through the binoculars.

Twenty minutes later, Dove returned to Cap's cabin. "Ready," he told Ari. Zev pulled the hoods off the two handcuffed together while Dove snapped photos for later identification. Dried blood stuck in patches on the face of the one Ari hit.

"Stay here," Ari told Devorah, "while we take the prisoners back to their inspection boat." He led the way, holding Tariq in front, down to the deck. Isyanov followed, carrying the Tech-9.

Zev pushed Tariq, the two bound together, and the suicide bomber through the rail gate onto their craft. He leaned over the edge to set their engine on low throttle before he cut the line that secured their boat to cleats on the side of Cap's cargo cruiser.

While Isyanov and Dove finished hauling the sub runners on deck, Ari watched the would-be hijackers move across the dark water toward their warship. He tried not to think about the close brush with death, to push those thoughts out of his mind. He would forget, yet always remember.

Devorah descended to the railing and pointed to the black outline lurking in the water against the night sky. "It's like a creature of prey," she said. "Will we be safely out of big-gun range by the time they get back to their ship?"

Ari looked at his watch. "I told Cap to open his engines when we cut the terrorists loose. It's been about five minutes. They should be stopping anytime now."

Devorah grabbed the railing when the cruiser picked up speed. The salty air rushing past tangled her hair around her face. "Why would they stop?" she asked.

"Because Zev drained their main fuel tank." Ari pointed to the terrorists in their boat. "They have enough in reserve to get them maybe halfway to their ship."

Seconds later, the dying sputter of the inspection boat engine carried across the water.

"There it goes," Ari said. "It'll take them at least ten minutes to get a rescue boat from the warship to the inspection boat."

Devorah looked worried. "But Ari, ten minutes is still cutting it close, don't you think?"

"First you don't think I can take out Tariq, now you say I'm cutting it too close?" Ari moved past her. "I'm going up."

Zev and Dove exchanged looks and stayed.

Devorah hesitated, then followed Ari up the stairs into the captain's cabin. "Please, Ari, let me explain." Her voice trailed off as he turned to face her.

"Explain what, Devorah? I told you not to engage the enemy."

Her cheeks flushed red, her dark eyes flashed anger. "How dare you judge me," she said, tossing her long hair.

A message from Dove beeped on Ari's wrist com. "Let's go watch the fireworks," Ari said, starting for the door while she hurried to keep up with his long stride. In moments they descended the stairs and stood on the deck.

"You didn't really think I'd take a chance with our lives?" Ari looked hard at Devorah, then turned to Zev. "You got it?" he asked brusquely.

"Right here, Ari." Zev held up the detonator he'd removed from the bomber.

They took turns watching through Dove's binoculars while a rescue boat from the warship neared the stalled speedboat.

"I set the timer on the bomber's vest," Zev said. "It should be—"

Red-yellow flames shot skyward in a curling plume before he could finish speaking. The deafening sound of the blast followed a split-second later. Ari gazed out at the fireball rapidly filling the place where the rescue boat had stopped near the bound terrorists sitting in their inspection boat.

"We'll be out of big-gun range soon," Zev said.

The sky still glowed red. Burning debris drifted where the boats had been. Ari used the binoculars and saw what appeared to be a body floating among the wreckage. He looked away.

Devorah sighed. "It was their lives or ours."

"Of course it was," Ari said loudly. "They want to kill us because they want what we have. I had to do it."

"I don't think she disagrees with you," Dove told him.

"She's right," Zev said. "We made a choice. We chose life."

"And now it's over," Ari said. "So let's get back to the cabin. I want to watch from Cap's telescope." Dove and Zev started back, but Ari lingered. "I didn't mean anything by that, Devorah," he said softly.

"No, you're right. We don't want war," she said. "It's tragic that the rest of the world doesn't see what's really going on."

Her clear, sweet voice always reminded him of a harp playing dreamy music. "It's not profitable to see the reality of it," Ari said as they walked up the metal stairs to the captain's cabin. "Small-arms manufacturers in China, and the international bankers who broker the deals, would all be out of work."

They entered in time to hear Cap say, "We're six hours from the port near Antalya. We'll arrive at first light."

Devorah tugged on Ari's sleeve and he stopped. "Just between us, Ari, do you think we might lose this conflict? Give up our kibbutz and leave our homes?"

Ari shook his head. "If we keep giving up, we'll lose our way of life." He looked into her eyes. "A way of life worth saving."

chapter 2

THE CONFERENCE DELEGATES from Israel arrived at the farmhouse in Turkey as the sun splashed morning pink over the Mediterranean Lands. Billowy clouds looked like cotton candy during the first hour of light.

At the same time, an American woman disembarked at the Antalya airport a few kilometers away. Waiting most of the day to clear customs and answer questions about an accidently torn page in her travel visa, she grew tired. Rita Jordana, a stranger in a foreign land, tried explaining to airport officials that she planned to meet a friend and he hadn't arrived—she was not traveling alone.

The officials couldn't be persuaded. They offered her a small, sparse room with shiny yellow walls to use the inspector's telephone. Her cell phone had been confiscated in New York at JFK airport. She'd forgotten that recent laws made communication devices illegal inside any international airport.

Rita spent most of the day in the inspector's windowless office. She'd tied back her blonde hair, fastened the top button on her long-sleeved blouse, and the floral border of her navy-blue skirt almost touched the floor, but that wasn't enough. The airport officials wanted her kept away from the other travelers.

Every few hours she tried to call Jacob, the man she'd come to depend on for the last year. A security official questioned her again in the late afternoon.

"Why did you come here?" the slightly overweight official asked.

Rita kept her thoughts focused on her story, her finely angled face expressionless. She felt faint from the stifling heat inside the small room. Perspiration ran down her arms inside her blouse.

"He will be here soon," she said at the end of another round of questions. "And that's the truth."

The official finally released her just before sunset on the condition she stay overnight in town because regional custom forbade women to travel after dark. He arranged a taxi for her.

"Better that you should not return to this airport alone," the official told her when the taxi arrived.

The driver didn't respond to Rita's questions during the ride. He finally rolled to a stop on a wide, shop-lined boulevard in a commercial district of Antalya ten minutes from the airport. She saw run-down buildings and streets crowded with honking cars, but the sidewalks and buildings looked clean.

Rita clutched her heavy cloth satchel and stepped out.

"Thank you," she called out over her shoulder.

The taxi sped off, and the hotel she needed wasn't in sight. A store in front of her had an open door, but when she entered to ask for help the proprietor raised his fist and shook his head. She backed out and kept walking.

Streetlights came on a few at a time. Near-panic welled up inside her because women alone after curfew could be arrested. Airport authorities had warned her of this several times. Rita turned the next corner and hurried down a long sidewalk. The smell of car exhaust nauseated her. *I can do this*, she thought. *I have to.*

A large yellow building at the end of the street displayed a sign in front. "Hotel" was written in English beneath Arabic lettering that Rita couldn't understand. Relief flooded through her. "I'm doing something important," she reminded herself. "I have to keep going."

Rita adjusted the shoulder strap of her satchel before she made her way down the narrow sidewalk, crossed the street toward the tinted glass entrance door, and reached for the handle.

As her fingers touched the brass knob, a man's strong hand grabbed her left arm. She felt herself move backward as if in slow motion before slamming into the building. A small man with dark eyes turned her toward him, clutched her arms, and shook her.

Shouting "Whore!" he pushed her into a second enraged man. She lost her balance and stumbled into the second man's chest. He twisted her arm and flung her back against the attacker. Rita didn't have time to think, or feel.

"Help me!" she screamed.

The hotel entrance door swung open and a short, muscular man with graying dark hair and raised fists ran toward them. "Leave her!" he shouted.

The second man turned and fled. The one holding Rita clutched her forearm. In one smooth motion he drew a curved dagger from inside his belt and slashed her upper right arm.

Blood oozed as she drew in a slow, deep breath. White-hot pain tore through her arm. The world around her seemed to slow down as adrenaline accelerated her pulse. She crumpled to the pavement. The last thing she remembered was the hatred she saw in the attacker's deep-set eyes before he scurried away.

Rita awoke lying on a couch in a dimly lit room. A woman bent over her, jabbed a needle in above the bloody wound, pulled the thread across, and dug the needle in for the next stitch. In a fog of pain, Rita heard herself scream. The room around her began spinning out of control. Then nothing.

The next time Rita opened her eyes, she found herself on a small lumpy bed in a dark room. She sat up and let her eyes adjust before slipping out of her torn, stained blouse. The bag she'd dropped outside now rested against the side of the bed. She wrapped herself in a robe and drifted back into sleep.

A few hours later, sudden shrieking awoke her. Two men argued outside her window. Rita couldn't understand their words. She held her breath. Fear pumped through her body until the men took their disagreement out of earshot.

Rita exhaled slowly, reached out next to her bed, and felt a table. Her fingers slid up the base of a metal lamp until she found the switch. A table and padded chair sat under the window. She got up and pulled a clothbound book from her bag.

"I will write for as long as I can hold up," Rita wrote in her journal. *"My upper arm is covered with a bandage and the pain is continuous. It took me almost a week to get here. In Hebrew, the Mediterranean basin is called Agan Hayam Hatichon. I read one interpretation that it means Middle Earth."*

Writing for a few more minutes took tremendous effort, but she thought it important to chronicle her journey. *"Now we're just a few hours away from our goal,"* she wrote. *"The end of a year-long, nonstop effort."* She set the pen down and gazed out the window through the blinds. She added, *"Except Jacob's not here."*

Rita's arm throbbed with razor-sharp pain. She unconsciously touched the bandage with her left hand and winced. Glancing at a clock on the nightstand next to her bed, she changed her mind, and wrote, *"The morning sky is getting light. I can't miss the hotel breakfast, so I'll stop for now."*

In the distance she heard birds singing. The first hint of light stretched across hills covered with crowded, ancient buildings, forming a rolling landscape of old structures mixed with modern housing. For a moment, she could have been home in her comfortable bed, waking to bird calls from pinyon pines in the nearby canyons. *Ah, but I'm here,* she thought. *The Mediterranean Lands.*

Rita looked into a mirror next to the bed. She struggled to tie her hair into a ponytail while her mind replayed mistakes she made on this trip. *I should've waited for Jacob in Paris,* she thought.

The stitched-up knife gash across her upper arm made dressing an arduous process. Each blouse button could be fastened with her left hand only. Finally, Rita adjusted the waistband of her long, dark-blue skirt, tucked in her loose cotton blouse, and looked at her watch. She wanted coffee, and she needed a phone.

Rita grabbed her satchel, removed her heavy overnight case, took the satchel, and stepped outside. The distinct thud of an old-fashioned lock satisfied her. She watched for a moment to see who might be around. To go anywhere in public unaccompanied by a male was a dangerous flouting of local custom.

While the early morning still afforded some protection, Rita hurried down a short walkway across an enclosed courtyard and sighed in relief when she stepped into the lobby. She greeted the aging but muscular hotel manager who'd come to her assistance the night before.

"You should not be out walking around," he admonished her in English. "This is not allowed here." He stood behind a brick counter, the center of his little kingdom. "I told you I will bring morning food to you in your room." He shook one finger slowly back and forth at her. "It is still dark outside."

"Madame can dine with me this early mornin'." A deep voice with an American accent startled her.

Rita turned to see a man in his mid-forties with a round, well-tanned pleasant face and intense blue eyes. "Thank you anyway, but I'll take my meal in my room," she said, looking at him closely.

The mysterious man extended his arm. "You could wait all mornin' for that meal, or join me now while the dinin' room is empty."

Maybe it's worth taking a chance with a stranger to get breakfast, she thought. Rita wrapped her slender hand around his proffered arm and they entered the small, clean dining room through the lobby.

"We can have whatever they put together and call breakfast, or just coffee," the smiling American told her as they sat at a square table covered with a white cloth. "My name is Myrl and I'm from Texas, by the way."

"I'm Rita. From Arizona. Flagstaff." She started to relax for the first time in days.

"You're a long way from home, darlin'." He spoke with a slight drawl. "You travelin' solo?"

She studied the table top. "I'm here to see friends."

"Gutsy move." He raised an eyebrow and frowned. "By yourself?"

She waved in dismissal. "No, of course not. What's your reason for coming here?"

"My wife's Arab, from around here. We come for a month every year to visit her family. She's with them now."

Rita noticed he didn't wear a wedding ring.

"That's a nasty bruise on the left side of your face." Myrl pointed. "Not to mention the condition of your arm. I guess you know the meanin' of the word hostile."

"I guess I do." Rita touched the bandage on her right arm. She'd rolled her shirtsleeve above the dressing to prevent the seeping blood from staining her blouse.

The manager arrived with hot coffee in clear glass mugs. He set them on the table in front of Myrl and said, "Food is coming."

"He probably wants us out of the dinin' room before his other guests come to eat," Myrl said with a lopsided smile.

"Why?" Rita looked around at the other four tables sitting empty.

"Even American women are supposed to follow their strict dress code. You might cause some kinda international incident walkin' around dressed like that." He slid a cup of aromatic coffee toward her.

"I wasn't planning to come here until the last minute," Rita explained. "I thought it'd be interesting."

Myrl lowered his voice and leaned in. "*Interestin'*? This whole region is a powder keg waitin' to explode. Most folks think a major war here is inevitable. Could be a week away, or maybe a month, but it's comin'."

"Is that what you think?" Rita sipped her coffee.

"Doesn't matter much what I think." Myrl studied her face. "But you'd better come up with a better story. This so-called Islamic civil war has become a power grab between the most vicious warlords. With an endless supply of weapons, these guys will fight until they wipe each other out. That could take a while."

"Well," she said, "I'm just here to see a friend."

Myrl shook his head. "You're not tellin' the whole truth. Anyway, the point is, do you know what these people will do to you if they think you're a spy? Or a Western journalist?"

The food arrived after a second cup of coffee. In silence they ate pastries, bananas, and olives. When he finished, Myrl moved his chair back, scraping it on the painted concrete floor. "You can tell me what kind of pickle you're in." When she hesitated, he added, "It's obvious."

"Why do you care what happens to me?" she asked. "I'm nobody to you."

"You're a beautiful woman, and you seem nice enough. If my wife went somewhere unfamiliar and got herself into a barrel of trouble, I'd hope someone would help her out."

"I'm not in trouble."

Myrl tilted his head. "You never did say where you're headed."

Rita closed her eyes for a moment and sighed. "I don't know. My friend Jacob knows but he's not here. I need a telephone to find him."

"Well, you can't use a public phone in this town," Myrl said, "but I could use the lobby phone. If you give me the number, I'll make the call for you."

"Thanks. I tried the number yesterday from the airport. No answer. We were supposed to meet at de Gaulle airport in Paris. He got delayed and told me to wait a day, but things happened and I came here." A little warning voice began to go off in her head. Wondering how much to reveal, she stopped talking.

"I'd like to help you," Myrl said. "Unless you're some kind of radical zealot."

Feeling indignant at the inference, Rita tilted her head and looked away.

"This isn't a game and these people aren't playin'. I'd think after what happened to you"—he nodded toward her bandaged arm—"you'd realize that."

Foolish wasn't a strong enough word to describe how she felt. "We were supposed to meet friends at a large farm just north of Antalya. I don't know where."

"Why didn't you say so, darlin'?" Myrl's grin stretched across his face. "I'm familiar with the area, and I think I know the place. I can get you there."

Rita pushed her chair back and stood. "Thanks, anyway. I can manage."

"Are you naïve?" he asked in a tone that implied the answer. "No Muslim driver is going to take you anywhere. He might get killed by one of his own for fraternizin' with a loose American woman."

Rita blushed. "It would be foolish of me to leave with you," she said. "I don't know you."

Myrl stood. "It was foolish of you to come here in the first place." He looked at his watch. "We should get goin'."

Rita followed him through the empty lobby down a concrete walkway past a row of shabby doors. She went in, collected her overnight case, and they left in his rented car.

On the drive to the countryside, Myrl told her he'd overheard a conversation about a big family reunion at a farm on the outskirts of town. "Is that where you're headed?"

"That sounds right." She glanced at Myrl, raised her foot, and pointed to her sturdy sandal. "I can't thank you enough. I figured I'd have to walk."

They drove past the old part of Antalya where Alexander the Macedonian marched with his troops twenty-three hundred years earlier, and Rita felt a thrill when Myrl told her about it. Passing the crowded suburbs, the landscape changed to open, hilly farmland.

Myrl pulled up to a gate across a private dirt road leading into a rolling green pasture. Just beyond the gate, in a thicket of cypress, she saw a blue van parked among the trees. Two men got out and walked up to the car.

"This is a family gathering," one dark-haired young man said to Myrl.

"Yep, and this is one of your lost family members right here." Myrl motioned toward Rita. "Lookin' for a friend named Jacob."

The young man stepped back and spoke into a wrist com. He came around to the passenger door and opened it. "Rita?"

She nodded.

"Come with us," he said. "Jacob is here."

chapter 3

It TOOK A day for news of the missile attack against his community to reach Ari through a relay of encrypted phone calls. Caught off guard by the unexpected rush of anger flooding through him, he swore aloud as he paced back and forth in his second-story room at the Antalya farmhouse.

"Nothing we can do about it this morning," Dove reminded him. "It wouldn't change anything if you were home right now. Did you know the family well?"

Ari sat in a chair under a curtained window, pressed his lips together, and looked silently out at the landscape for a few moments before answering. "Not well. The father, Ben-Josef, was twenty-six. The mother, Eva—her family's lived in the Negev longer than anyone I know."

Dove looked at Ari's somber face. "Well, maybe now we'll get the military help we need."

Ari shook his head abruptly, tried to clear his thoughts. "We can't change what's already happened. Let's go to the meeting in the library. Devorah's probably already there waiting for us."

They stood at the same time, and Ari's eyes narrowed for an instant. "We have to answer this attack on our people."

Dove started for the door. "Yes, otherwise it'll be seen as a sign of weakness. Leave it to me."

They found the library on the first floor and joined three serious-looking young men sitting with Devorah at a large, wood-plank table.

A good-looking man around thirty years old spoke first. "I'm Marc Rosenthal." Close-cropped dark hair framed angular features. Light olive skin contrasted against his white shirt. "The purpose of this meeting is to arrange financial support for the defense of Kol Shofar," he said with a smile. "We can bypass your Paris supply account and provide you with military hardware. Smart weapons." In his expensive Italian suit, Marc looked like a businessman who'd never stepped onto a battlefield or held a rifle.

"Who are the actual fund-raisers?" Ari asked.

Marc smiled. "We are. This is Bobby and that's George." The other two Americans nodded. Bobby's shiny brown hair fell around his face in relaxed curls. George wore his silver hair slicked back.

"We worked on the West Coast while Marc handled the Eastern Seaboard," Bobby said.

"Of course," Marc added, "we have the support of synagogue and community leaders in New York. We've raised enough money to supply you, the people holding on in Eilat, and several other Negev communities with enough smart military hardware to get you through the next several months."

"This is extraordinary," Ari said. "If it's true."

"Believe me, it's true," Marc said with confidence. "The importance of your continued presence at Kol Shofar can't be over-stated."

For the next two hours they exchanged information about world events and the travel injunction against them. Devorah complained about tapped communication lines and constant harassment when they tried to use the media-net.

"Yes," Dove said. "Our hard-line and fax calls are monitored. Cell and wireless com are snatched right out of the air. Net calls can't be encrypted long enough to matter."

"Hold on a few more months," Marc told them. "We have a plan to connect your community with the rest of the nation through Jerusalem."

"We represent people in New York who want this to happen," George said. "People who are willing to pay for what they want."

Dove nodded. "It's only a matter of time before this Islamic civil war ends."

"First, as these gentlemen have pointed out," Devorah said, "we have to hold on for a few more months. That won't be easy."

Ari concluded the meeting and shook hands with the Americans. He spent the rest of the day in a room adjoining the farmhouse kitchen, talking on a secure line with other Jewish leaders in the Euro States while Dove went into closed meetings with Mossad intelligence agents.

Zev left in the afternoon with a youth wearing a fringed tallis, and a yamulka sat atop his shoulder-length brown hair. Ari never could figure out where Zev went, and didn't expect to see him again for the remainder of the conference. As close to being a biblical prophet as anyone Ari had ever known, Zev was also a mastermind about the subject of explosives.

Ari and Devorah enjoyed a cold buffet in the evening with some of the other delegates, then found Dove on the wide staircase leading to their rooms. A narrow hallway on the second floor separated bedrooms on each side.

A basket of fruit and a bottle of red Turkish wine sat on Ari's table. He uncorked the wine, poured a glass, and let it sit. A door connected his room to the adjacent one, Devorah's. After he picked up the conference schedule and put it down without reading it, he rapped lightly on the adjoining door.

"I thought we might have a glass of wine together," he said when she opened it. "I think I'm still too worked up to sleep. Zev and Dove are staying across the hall, but I'm sure they're already asleep."

Devorah stepped in. "I've just been organizing my things," she said with a smile. "I'm not sleepy either. I have to admit, hearing about the missile attack unnerved me."

He offered her the glass of wine he'd set out earlier and poured himself a glass. The room was large enough to include a small sofa, and Ari motioned toward it. Fresh purple grapes and the wine bottle sat on a nearby side table.

"Tomorrow the conference security council will announce." He sat on the faded green sofa and turned toward Devorah. "They'll recommend sending more troops into the Negev."

They talked for a while about the conference schedule. Ari filled their glasses again. "When we get back home." He cleared his throat. "Devorah, one of the contacts I spoke with today on the phone says he could take you from Kol Shofar through Jerusalem to northern Israel, where your cousin might be."

She sipped her half-full wine glass.

"Think about your niece," he said. "Maybe it's time to get the children out of Kol Shofar until the conflict ends."

Devorah's eyes widened. "Why would I leave now?"

"Our situation is deteriorating." His voice became strained as he continued. "Without operating funds, the smart weapons and equipment we ordered today won't do us much good. When we run out of money this time, our circumstances become desperate."

As if silently counting nail holes from absent pictures, she leaned back into the sofa cushion and stared at the plaster wall.

He rested his hand on her arm and said, "You don't have to decide anything this moment—we still have some time."

The first presentation started the following afternoon in the farmhouse great room, a large plastered room with unpainted walls and a row of wood-framed windows overlooking a vegetable garden. To Ari's surprise, Zev came to hear the speaker.

The presenter, Noah, a former rabbi turned military officer, wore tan pants and shirt, similar to the clothes Ari usually wore. His short, curly black hair framed his face like a halo when the overhead light illuminated him as he walked to the front of the room.

Noah outlined detailed plans for an operation centered on a fall campaign by Friends of Israeli Defense Forces. Made up of mostly European and American Jews, the Friends formed the largest independent army in modern Europe's history. Financed by wealthy supporters, the troops came equipped with sophisticated military hardware. Stationed throughout Europe, they protected Jewish assets in the Euro zone.

"I've given you this encouraging news," Noah continued, "because now I tell you what our recent intelligence reports indicate. A rolling war is expected in the Mediterranean Lands within the next year. It will start in a few hot spots and then spread to engulf the entire region."

Ari saw a few people exchange worried glances.

"I'm an IDF security advisor," Noah said, "And I can tell you with certainty that few countries around the world openly support the continued existence of Israel. If a major war breaks out, we'll be on our own."

Murmurs of agreement filled the room.

Noah cleared his throat. "The four superpower governments controlling the world's economies squeezed us into impossible wars with every surrounding Islamic country, then threatened any government who offered help to us."

"He's stating the obvious," Dove whispered to Ari.

"This time around, however, our enemy has high-tech weapons and huge armies. We can't get support from the North American Union or Europe until we agree to give up our sovereignty and merge into the European Union under the authority of the One World Government."

"That's never going to happen," Ari said loudly enough for a few people to turn and look.

"Before we close," Noah added, "Kol Shofar kibbutz in the Negev has sustained a missile attack. We have specific, credible intelligence which suggests imminent violence in our desert while the Israeli Defense Forces are tied up on the northern borders."

Dove whispered to Ari, "I'll get the complete report tomorrow."

Ari stood. His deep voice carried easily across the room. "I'm confident Kol Shofar can hold on until the fall," he told them. "We're outnumbered, but today we've placed an order for a shipment of smart weapons. If our enemy stays conventional, we can maintain the upper hand for several more months."

The hour was late and Ari wasn't in a good mood when the presentation ended. "Let's meet in my room," he suggested. "It's the largest."

On the way up the stairs, he told Zev about the Americans and the weapons order they'd placed. "The men we met are private fund-raisers," Ari said when they entered his room. "They understand the strategic importance of Kol Shofar."

"They're American Jews," Devorah added, "who watched their own country's sovereignty melt away when North and South America merged under the authority of the One World Gov a few years ago. They don't want to see that happen to Israel."

She sat on the soft green sofa with Dove. Ari and Zev sat in straight-backed chairs across from them with an unadorned coffee table in-between.

"This meeting will change our future," Dove said with a smile. "We should celebrate. At least now we have a fighting chance."

"You mean now we have a chance to fight," Ari answered. He left his chair, moved close to the window, and looked out. He felt something big coming. He couldn't explain it to himself, let alone the others.

Dove flicked a hand toward Ari. "Stop pacing. Come sit, have a glass of wine. You're making us nervous."

"Sorry." Ari accepted a glass of port from Dove, and glanced at Devorah. "What they didn't say at the briefing is that the Negev Muslims will soon receive a shipment of smart weapons. They've agreed to join the regional One World Government peacekeepers."

Devorah gasped and covered her mouth. "What will happen if they use the smart weapons against us?"

"They're forbidden," Dove answered quickly. "It's part of their agreement. If they violate the terms, their future shipments of high-tech weapons will be cut off."

"Well, that's the way it's supposed to work," Ari said. "Muslim rage is reaching a boiling point. Their common people are starting to realize they have no chance at a decent life while their populations explode into miserable, crowded masses. Who knows how far they'll go."

"The Islamic civil war is an excuse for them to spread into our land," Zev said. "Our enemies have brought the fight to us and we will fight."

"We have no other choice." Dove smacked the table with his open hand. "There's no safe place for Jews except Israel. It's our duty to defend her."

Ari started to pace again. "It's just a matter of time before we defeat our enemy. We always have and we always will."

Dove eventually finished his glass of port, and said he wanted to retire for the night. Zev agreed it was getting late. They stood at the same time.

Ari called out, *"Layla tov."*

"And a good night for both of you," Zev answered as the door closed behind them.

"I thought you were worried," Devorah said.

Ari's earlier mood of frustration quickly faded. "Dove's probably right," he said, changing his tone. "We have cause for celebrating tonight. This story is far from over. We'll find what we need—we always do."

She didn't reply and for a moment he thought about kissing her. Not the greeting-on-the-cheek kind of kiss, but this time—

A loud commotion in the hallway followed by a bang on the door startled them. Ari looked through the peephole before he opened it. Zev and two others followed Dove in and Ari closed the door.

"This is Jacob," Zev said. "Levi's brother."

Ari nodded. "Levi is one of my best soldiers. I remember you, Jacob. You left Kol Shofar with the first group out five years ago."

"Yes," Jacob said. "Most of us went to New York."

Ari blinked. He didn't want to be reminded of how his life changed the day that first group evacuated. One day he was engaged to be married. Then the first enemy missile hit Kol Shofar, and she left on a bus the next day. She'd tried to steal his most prized possession, an ancient gold coin. He felt the sting of betrayal whenever he thought about reaching into her purse to retrieve her ticket for her, the woman he loved with his whole heart, and finding his priceless coin instead. *I won't again make the mistake of showing it to the wrong person. Next time—*

"And who is this?" Devorah's clear voice cut across Ari's thoughts.

"She's with me," Jacob said.

"I'm Rita from America," the woman answered.

Ari looked her up and down. "I heard about you. The American who showed up at the farmhouse gate yesterday."

Rita smiled.

Ari didn't.

"Well, Rita from America, what do you want?" Devorah demanded.

Commander Ari folded his arms across his chest. "Yes, please tell us what you're doing here."

"I'm glad you speak English," she said. "You can't believe what I went through just to get here."

"She came to help us," Jacob added.

Ari looked at Jacob's round, soft face. "This is a high-security private gathering," he said. "I don't recall seeing either of your names on the guest list."

"Jacob's looking for Levi," Zev broke in.

"To convince him to leave Kol Shofar too?" Ari asked.

"No," Jacob answered, "to join him."

"With the travel restrictions around Kol Shofar," Zev pointed out, "he had no other way to get in. He had to come here."

Ari turned to Zev. "You knew about this?"

Zev shrugged.

Then Ari motioned toward Rita. "What about her?"

"She was supposed to wait for me in France," Jacob explained.

"And yet she's here." Ari raised his eyebrows and waited for an answer.

Jacob finally said, "Rishon at the corporation in Paris met with her while I traveled here to see Zev."

"And how do you know my cousin Rishon?" Dove asked.

Sounds of people running in the hallway caused Ari to open the door and look out. Eldad, a muscular man with thick black hair, tanned olive skin, and blue eyes, ran to Ari as several other guests hurried past.

"I've just arrived," Eldad said, entering the room. "We've come to get you out of here. Now."

"That's what I wanted to tell you," Jacob said. "The port is under attack from armed insurgents invading this town from the north. We should leave Turkey. Everyone's leaving."

"Eldad is a man I know and trust," Dove told Ari while Eldad moved Ari's bag next to the door. "He's a Druze from northern Israel." He lowered his voice to a whisper, and added, "Eldad's gathered sensitive information for us for years."

"Let's go home," Zev said. "We've already got more than we expected."

"I'll go with Zev and get my things," Devorah called out as she and Zev left the room.

Ari looked at Dove and swept his hand toward Jacob and Rita. "What about them?"

Dove turned to Jacob. "Come with us now to Kol Shofar," he offered, "or wait months for the travel injunction to be lifted. We'll take Rita to the airport on the way to the dock."

Rita cleared her throat. "I can't travel back alone from that airport," she told them. "Jacob has to come with me to Paris."

Jacob shook his head. "I'm not going back, Rita."

For a moment, no one spoke.

Ari finally broke the silence. "Well, she's not coming with us."

"Ari," Jacob pleaded, "what's she supposed to do?"

"She should have thought about that before she came here." Ari stepped forward and motioned toward the cloth satchel she held. "Show me your passport," he demanded.

Rita bit her bottom lip and rummaged through her bag. She held up a booklet for Ari.

He read it and stepped closer. "Is this information correct?"

"You don't understand," she said in a small voice. "These papers were made by the Paris underground so I could travel here safely."

He held the booklet. "Why would you need false identity papers?"

"When I left, my passport was about to expire in thirty days. I couldn't get a travel visa with it."

"Then why didn't you apply for a new passport in America?"

"The government has suspended passport renewals," she explained. "Now all passports in the Americas have to be issued from the One World Transportation Department out of the New York office."

"Yes," Jacob interrupted. "Even an unpaid speeding ticket or a bad credit report can prevent issuance of a passport."

Rita folded her hands and unfolded them. "I thought this might be my only chance to travel abroad."

Ari held up her travel permit and looked closely at the smudged expiration date. "What are you thinking?" he shouted. "This travel permit is only good for two days."

"That's all I could get." She glanced at Jacob.

Jacob took a step toward Ari. "I vouch for her. Isn't that good enough? The rabbi at San Francisco Chabad sent her here with the funds. He trusts her."

Ari shook his head. "You've been gone five years. And our communications are jammed on this side of the boundary line so we can't verify with Rishon or the rabbi."

"We couldn't get her back to the airport in time if we left right now," Dove said, looking at his watch. "We're running out of time."

Ari agreed. He put her travel document into his shirt pocket and looked at Dove.

Dove took Jacob into the hallway. Eldad closed the door behind them and stood next to it.

Turning toward Rita, Ari said, "If you're coming with us, you'll have to be searched." He put his hands on her shoulders, pressed her back against the wall and began to search, gently probing, feeling for anything unusual. He carefully avoided the bandage on her right arm. Deep bruises and scrapes along her left leg and hip from the altercation were sore to the touch because she flinched when his fingers ran along the backs of her sturdy, slender legs.

"You should tell me now what you're doing here," he said in a low voice.

She inhaled sharply when his hand slid under her blouse. He could feel the warmth of her breath on his face. Satisfied that she did not conceal a hidden weapon or explosive device, he stepped back.

"Why did you come to this conference?" He knew his demeanor suggested he would not wait long for an answer, and he saw how the unexpected search unnerved her.

Rita smoothed some flyaway hair back into her sagging ponytail before she glanced up at Ari. "I told you. I'm here to find Jacob."

Eldad finished inspecting the contents of her satchel and opened the door. Zev and Devorah entered with Jacob and Dove behind them.

"Let's go quickly," Eldad said. He picked up Rita's satchel, took Devorah's bag from Zev, then led the way down the stairs to the farmhouse kitchen. "You can't go through any checkpoints with her." He pointed to Rita. "Not without proper travel documents."

Ari nodded. "We'll have to walk from the shoreline to Kol Shofar."

Eldad opened a cupboard door exposing steps leading down into a dark passageway carved out of the earth and supported by heavy wooden beams. He pointed to a wooden ladder and said, "This way, no one sees who comes or goes. It leads to the barn where your van is parked."

They followed him for a half-kilometer until the passage opened into a basement. Concrete stairs led up into the barn where the vehicles were parked.

During the short ride to the dock, Eldad told Ari, "I return to my family in northern Israel after this conference. Sovereign Turkey is done. It's over here."

"What do you mean?" Rita spoke to him for the first time.

"The government hides inside their marble buildings in the capital while Islamic gangs control most of the countryside," he said, steering with one hand and gesturing with the other. "Greece is starting to grab part of the land from one side while Russia is spilling over from the other side. Soon, there will be nothing left called Turkey."

Dove patted his back. "You deserve a hero's welcome when you return home," he told him. "Your information's been of immense value to us."

"My family thinks I've been traveling and working in Europe all this time. They're probably still mad at me for leaving." Eldad glanced at Ari, sitting in the passenger seat. "When we park at the dock, move quickly. We've arranged a fishing boat with a trusted Greek skipper to take you home."

Ari and the others from Kol Shofar hurried Jacob and Rita from the van to the waiting fishing boat moments after Eldad parked.

During the uneventful night ride back to Eratz Israel, Ari napped briefly, then reviewed intelligence reports. They approached the southern shoreline near dawn.

The men inflated a motorized rubber boat and lowered it alongside when the skipper cut his engine. They said shalom to the crew and descended a rope ladder for the short ride to land. Ari climbed down first and held the ladder securely for the others.

Fresh salt air rushed past Ari's face as Zev guided the rubber boat skillfully through the water. Ari watched the sky change color minute by minute while the early morning sky lightened.

They beached inside a secluded cove. The engine was so quiet it hardly made a difference when Zev turned it off.

Ari stepped onto the sandy beach. He reached out to steady Devorah when she climbed over the side, followed by Rita, Dove, and Jacob. Zev got out last and pulled the boat above the high-tide line.

The men deflated and folded it before they trudged up the beach to a cave near their protected inlet. There a rock formation afforded protection for the entrance leading to their secret tunnel. Zev and Jacob hid the raft deep inside the cave.

"It's good to be home," Dove said.

They disappeared into the dark passageway which would take them past the town of Maccabiah—right under the dreaded checkpoints.

"We're not home yet," Ari reminded them.

chapter 4

THE TEMPERATURE IN the Negev rose steadily to a hundred and ten degrees Fahrenheit by late morning while Ari led his group through the dark, almost-cool tunnel running deep below the burning sand.

At one time it provided a safe route from the sea. Now it was a dangerous gamble to emerge near a town with both Jewish and Islamic neighborhoods during a conflict. Rita and Jacob walked a short distance behind the others. Ari glanced back several times and saw her struggle to keep up.

"My side aches from walking," she whispered to Jacob, "and I'm tired all over."

Jacob carried her satchel along with his own bag, and his flashlight. "It's not much longer," he told her in a low voice. "We've probably walked a good ten miles."

She breathed heavily as the group continued, and she now limped from a blister caused by her new sandals.

"We've walked thirteen kilometers—eight miles," Ari turned and called back. "To the end of the tunnel—three miles to go. Will the American make it?"

"What?" Rita whispered to Jacob. "Does he have X-ray hearing?"

"He does seem to have extraordinary instincts," Jacob whispered. "Never wrong. Seems to know everything."

Ari stopped, tossed his pack down, pulled a small box from it, and waited for Rita and Jacob to catch up. He removed a needle and thread from the box. Dove stepped forward and held his flashlight on Ari's hands while Ari threaded the needle. Ari looked at Rita, and said, "Sit."

Rita complied, sitting with her legs stretched out in front of her.

"What are you doing?" Jacob asked nervously.

"She's got a blister," Ari answered. "It has to be treated." He sat cross-legged next to Rita, unclasped her sandal, and rested her foot on his leg.

"Don't worry," Dove said, still holding the flashlight for Ari. "This won't hurt."

Ari carefully ran the threaded needle through one edge of the blister to the other edge, leaving the thread hanging out on each side about an inch after cutting off the excess. He repeated the procedure until three threads hung out from each side. "Soldiers get blisters all the time," he told her. "This is a little trick we teach each other in the field."

"It really works," Zev added. "By the time we get to the end of the tunnel, your blister will be gone."

Ari returned her foot to her sandal, and stood.

"Thank you," she said as Jacob crowded close and helped her stand.

The group walked the next three miles in silence except for Rita's panting. Ari's flashlight produced a powerful beam to light the way to the end of the tunnel.

From the darkness they emerged in the afternoon above ground into a narrow ravine, a wadi, to a sight so magnificent that Ari felt a sense of awe each time he saw it—the Negev in full spring bloom.

Ari was the first one out. It took a moment for his eyes to adjust to the bright sunlight. He looked around at the wildflowers, nourished by flash floods, growing waist-high on the banks. Sprays of compact little yellow flowers provided a stunning contrast to the sand floor and azure sky. Huge boulders lay strewn as if giants tossed them during play. At the far north end of the wadi the land sloped up.

Rita came out next and sat near a boulder casting shade to one side. She said she felt nauseated from the intense desert heat and lack of sleep.

Jacob sat next to her. "We're almost there," he assured her in a velvety smooth voice. "Just a few kilometers more to Kol Shofar."

Rita closed her eyes and leaned back against the boulder next to him. The hard stone, weathered by rain and wind, formed a smooth curved surface, almost comfortable.

"Let's rest fifteen minutes," Ari said as he set down the bags he carried. "Zev will keep one eye open here, and Dove and I will look around."

When Ari returned, he stepped in front of Rita to block the sun now burning on her face. She awoke with a start, and moved to the west side of the boulder, now in the shade, before looking at her watch.

Thirty minutes had passed. Ari and the others waited while Jacob handed Rita a plastic bottle of water. She took a long drink. Ari watched Jacob help her stand. Her face revealed the pain coursing through her body. She forced her right foot to step forward, then her left foot. He shook his head and took Rita's bag from Jacob. He tilted his head toward Rita. "You'll have to help her."

They made their way for the next hour across the sand floor in the heat of the desert sun. Finally, they stopped in front of a small cliff at the far end of the wadi.

A goat trail led up a steep path to level ground. Ari sprinted to the top, with Devorah and Dove behind him. When Zev climbed over the top and stood with Devorah, Ari hunched down and looked over the lip of the ledge. Rita was about half-way up, picking her way slowly with Jacob following in case she slipped.

Rita stopped to rest, breathing hard. She clutched her skirt and pulled it away from the rocks. When she neared the upper ledge, she looked up.

Ari had watched her climb, his face now a few inches away, his gray-blue eyes squinting in the sun. Tiny laugh lines around his eyes etched into his tan face. Perspiration glistened on his fore-head.

Ari swung his right arm down to the top of her shoulder. "Give me your hand."

She reached up, he grasped her left upper arm, and she held on tight. "Here we go," he said as he pulled her gently up over the edge. When she gained her balance, he gave her a little nod, released her arm, and stepped back.

A half-kilometer later, they stopped at the edge of a well-groomed peach orchard. Green trees on level ground presented a welcome contrast to the rocky terrain behind them. Many of the trees still showed fragrant white flowers alongside little green balls growing out along the branches. A few of last year's peaches lay shriveled and dry on the ground.

The desert sun beat down as Ari walked steadily forward in front of the others, using the trees for shade where he could. Breathing in the fragrance of the perfumed blossoms gave him a heady feeling.

Halfway through the orchard they stopped to rest briefly and drink water. Ari glanced at the American. In her wrinkled clothes, her face dotted with perspiration, her cheeks red from the heat, she looked miserable. Her skirt was cut from a heavy fabric and had a weighty embroidered hem. *Ridiculous,* he thought. He decided to ignore her.

Ari drank from his canteen, which was designed to keep water cool for up to twenty hours. Jacob and Rita were drinking out of plastic bottles. *That water has to be hot,* Ari thought. He sauntered over to where they stood next to a tree. Rita was quietly panting and Jacob looked helpless.

"Try to control your breath," Ari said. He handed his canteen to Rita. "We'll be home soon." She hesitated, then lifted the canteen to her lips. When she finished, Ari motioned with a nod toward Jacob.

When Rita began to breathe normally again, Ari led the group to the last row of fruit trees at the north edge of the orchard. Beyond fields green with young beet tops and cabbages stood the concrete security wall rising up out of the ground under a cloudless, pale-blue afternoon sky.

A worn dirt road ran from the orchard to a tall, barred gate, the only visible opening in the circular walled fortress. Ari walked to the center of the road and waved.

"We'll wait here," Devorah told Rita. "They'll come get us."

A few minutes later, two Israeli-made desert rovers sped toward them. Ari walked back to Devorah and stood with her.

Rita removed the scarf holding back her ponytail and used a corner of the cloth to wipe sweat from her face. She shook her head and her thick hair tumbled dramatically down her back. "Jacob," she said close to his ear, "is it okay for me to be here?"

Ari tilted his head to hear Jacob's answer.

Jacob wrapped his arm around her, draping it over her right shoulder. "Kol Shofar is my brother's home so you're welcome here for as long as you want to stay." Blood seeped through her bandage and she cried out. Jacob quickly removed his arm.

Ari, Devorah, and Dove entered the first vehicle to stop. Jacob helped Rita onto the front seat of the second rover. He and Zev climbed into the back.

After a short ride on the dirt road, the drivers slowed when they rolled through the giant gate onto a paved road inside.

Official buildings flanked one side of the road leading to an area of four-story apartment complexes with a spacious courtyard between the buildings. The other side was a parking lot with two rows of military trucks, desert-terrain rovers, and heavy-equipment vehicles parked near the wall.

They stopped in front of an L-shaped apartment building on the south side of the courtyard. "This is where Devorah and many of the single women live," Zev explained to Rita. The building dominated an entire block.

Jacob glanced around at the buildings and roads. "We had good times here." He helped Rita out of the rover. "I lived here for three years with Levi. I came to visit from New York and stayed until the conflict broke out five years ago."

Zev turned to Rita. "The good times ended when the Islamic civil war devastated towns in the Negev. The fighting dragged on year after year. You must've seen news reports about it in America."

Rita nodded. "Yeah, the news coverage was continual."

Four broad stone steps led to a heavy wooden entrance door. She placed her foot carefully onto the first step and stopped. Jacob moved close and she took his arm for support.

"Kol Shofar's security wall saved us from a similar fate," Zev said as Rita made it up the second step. "We were the end result of a government program around the turn of the twentieth century designed to populate the Negev with Jewish families."

Jacob smiled and helped her up the third step, then the fourth. "You know, make the desert bloom. A circular Garden of Eden."

Ari stepped forward and opened the door. They followed him through a vestibule framed with hand-hewn yellow limestone leading to a great room. One entire wall contained a huge fireplace faced with river rock. A wide arch revealed a large kitchen in the next room.

Rita looked around. "You could probably fit a hundred people in here."

"Easily," Devorah said.

Comfortable-looking sofas and upholstered chairs sat on a decorative tile floor. Thick, multicolored wool rugs lay scattered about. A dozen women sat talking with each other throughout the room.

Ari sat on a padded chair near a sofa and motioned toward Rita and Jacob. Zev, Dove, and Devorah joined them.

Rita hesitated, then brushed off her dusty, sweaty clothes. She lowered herself onto the sofa cushion next to Jacob.

Everyone started talking at once, except Rita, until Ari cleared his throat and they became quiet.

Ari looked at Jacob, then Rita. "Now you should tell us what you're really doing here."

"I came for my brother," Jacob said defensively.

"This one"—Ari nodded toward Rita—"has more to tell."

"I just wanted to help," Rita said, "after I met Jacob at Chabad House in San Francisco last year."

"What were you doing at Chabad?" His inflection made each word into a question.

"I often stayed with a girlfriend in San Francisco when I traveled there for business from my home in Flagstaff," she explained. "We went to Chabad for fun."

"Wait," Ari said abruptly. "What business do you have with Chabad?"

"No business," she answered. "Everybody went there. Jewish musicians, single women looking for Orthodox husbands, traveling rebbes from Morocco, and many others. The night I met Jacob—"

Ari smacked the coffee table separating them. "What business?" he repeated.

Rita jumped slightly. "I had a radio show based out of San Francisco for a couple of years. I got to know the people at Chabad during the two years I lived in the city. They were my friends. Before that I worked for a political strategist in Arizona."

"You left your job in San Francisco to come here?" Ari leaned forward. He wanted to end this nonsense and get some sleep.

"No, I quit the radio show about three years ago," she told him. "I got a death threat after supporting Israel during a call-in segment of my show. I've lived in Flagstaff on my savings for the last three years."

Ari waved his hand in a sweeping motion. "When you first met Jacob?"

"That night started out the same as any other," she said. "The dinner ended, several young men jumped up, right on top of the cleared table, and danced. Then a man named Marc arrived from the airport and everyone became serious."

"So you two met at Chabad House." Ari's voice echoed his impatience.

"Yes, and the rabbi told us the media doesn't report the full story of the conflict raging in our homeland. You know, people think the American press is so free, but it really isn't."

"What does any of this have to do with us?" Ari asked.

"Marc from New York said your kibbutz is now surrounded by mixed neighborhood towns." Rita moved her hands nervously as she talked. "He described some of the younger Islamics as hostile, even dangerous."

"And he told us," Jacob added, "about the teenage boy hitchhiking into Maccabiah last year. That he detonated a vest bomb at a gas station on the Jewish side of town. The family who gave him a ride and three others died with him that day."

Ari furrowed his brow and cocked his head slightly. "And this made you want to come anyway?"

"It made us want to do something," Jacob answered. "The rabbi reminded us that if Israel falls, Jews won't have a safe haven left anywhere in the world."

"And Marc told us money is the only way left to help," Rita added. "He knew people in New York and they contacted Rishon in Paris."

"Are you saying you came here to bring money?" Ari felt his irritation melt away at the thought.

"Well," Rita answered, "someone had to courier the funds to Paris because of the laws restricting the transfer of money. And Jacob wanted to find his brother. The rabbi in New York changed the money for bearer bonds to avoid the exchange rates."

"Wait," Dove interrupted. "Rishon put funds in our Paris bank account?"

"I'm coming to that." Rita paused. "You see, I just thought—"

Ari snapped his fingers. "You thought what?"

"I thought I could find Jacob at the conference," she said. "So Rishon introduced me to members of the underground in Paris. They helped me get a travel visa to Turkey."

Devorah shook her head. "Because you are in love with Jacob."

Jacob started to protest, but Rita spoke. "The hundred-year anniversary for the creation of modern Israel is only three years away. The rabbi said between now and 2048 is when our enemies will try to drive us out, before we pass the century mark as a nation."

"What can you do about it?" Ari asked. "And what do you expect us to do?"

"Too many Americans don't understand what's going on over here," Rita said. "If it's not reported in the American media, they simply don't believe it. Even other Jews, sometimes especially other Jews, don't make the connections. Most Americans have romantic ideas of Israel that aren't really true."

"That's America," Ari said. "I've been there many times. Even then, most Americans were insulated from world events, except what's selected for them to see on cable news. Nothing's changed."

"I changed," Rita said softly. "I felt alone until Jacob showed up. I really thought I could help."

Ari pressed his lips together for a moment, then asked, "How do you plan to get back to America?"

"Travel is restricted from this side," Devorah added.

"I'm so sorry." Rita shook her head. "I didn't realize."

"I don't believe this," Ari said. "With an expired visa you become a criminal, and we risk punishment for harboring you."

"I'll walk to the airport." She raised her chin and added, "Tomorrow."

"Great," Ari said loudly. "You walk back and you'll probably get killed. Or kidnapped, or worse, before you ever get close to the airport. And we'll be responsible for what happens to you."

"Now wait," Zev said patiently. "Nothing we can do tonight. We might as well get a good night's sleep and figure this out in the morning. This is what's in front of us, Ari. You can't change what is."

"Even if we do figure something out"—Ari waved his hand again—"it'll cost us bribe money. You know our general fund is depleted. We can barely feed ourselves since we've been cut off from the outside world for over a month."

"I told you I'm sorry." She spoke directly to Ari.

He couldn't decide if her eyes held tears. "Look," he said through a frown, "we're grateful for any money you gave Rishon, but four weeks ago the Islamic Coalition got the World Court to issue an injunction against us. We don't have immediate access to our account."

"Getting you back to France without a visa is a big deal," Dove said. "Very expensive."

Rita's face flushed with anger. "I'll pay for myself." She reached down into her bag, which Jacob had set on the floor next to her, and pulled out a small pair of scissors. She hiked up her skirt, and cut away at the threads next to a wide, mirror-studded hem.

Ari moved forward to stop her, but when he reached out to grab the edge of her skirt he ended up holding a packet of bearer bonds.

"That's right. This is the reason I left France." Rita cut more of her hem, and packet after packet of bonds fell to the floor around her.

Zev smiled broadly and called out, "Our G-d and G-d of the universe, Hashem, bless us. That decorative border conceals a fortune in the padding."

"Rishon told me"—Rita paused as the last packet fell to the floor—"the authorities in Paris tightened banking regulations and now he has a limit on how much he can deposit into your account. He gave me a choice to take the funds to you myself or leave them with him to deposit later. I didn't know what to do, and I didn't have anyone to ask."

Zev started picking up packets from the floor to stack on a nearby table. "How much is here?" he asked eagerly.

Rita pursed her full lips and looked at Ari. "About a million Israeli shekels," she said.

Ari locked eyes with her, already thinking through a plan to send her home.

"I know I should've told you," she said quietly. "I don't know whom I can trust. Rishon told me not to show the bonds to anyone but Dove. Not even Jacob."

Ari glanced away, then looked back.

Zev waved a fist full of bonds. "This is brilliant," he cried.

Rita looked at Jacob. "I'm sorry," she whispered.

A side door opened from the hallway and thin, delicate Batya entered. The lower half of her young face had a bloody wound, and her left hand hung bandaged at her side. Using a sturdy metal cane, she slowly limped across the floor.

Devorah stood and took a few steps toward the girl. "My darling, what can we do for you?" Her voice was soft, affectionate.

Batya smiled shyly. "Good evening, Commander Ari."

He smiled back. "Always good to see you, Honey."

Blushing, the girl turned away.

"I'll be right back," Devorah called out before they left through a side door.

Rita glanced at the door and cleared her throat. "What happened to that girl?" she asked. "Shouldn't she be in a hospital?"

Ari's expression changed from irritated to compassionate. "Batya's wounds are slow to heal," he explained. "Maybe we don't have the right medicine. Our hospital got bombed last year and the only remaining doctor works out of her home."

Zev slowly nodded. "It's been almost a month now since the attack. It was the middle of the day when Devorah's sister, Hannah, drove with her two daughters through the Islamic section of Maccabiah. She probably turned down the wrong street by accident. Three Muslim men shot the tires on Hannah's car, and the bastards dragged her out of the car when she stopped. Hannah was pregnant—they stabbed her to death. Batya was beaten and left to die."

Rita touched the bandage on her right arm. "What about the other daughter?" she asked in a whisper.

"They slit her throat," Ari said evenly, trying to block the anger that slowly filled him. "Her name was Miri and she was only fifteen. Three years younger than Batya."

Zev motioned toward the side door. "Batya's lucky to be alive."

"This is terrible," Rita said. "Was anyone arrested?"

"No," Ari answered, "and no one passing by came to their aid. Batya survived by lying still until the murderers left."

"Until," Zev said, "a woman dressed in traditional, required covering walked up to her, gathered her up inside a sweeping cloak, and whispered in Hebrew to be silent. The woman pulled out another cloak, covered Batya in the same traditional look, and walked her home."

"Zev was on guard duty that day," Ari said.

"And all I saw were two Islamic women rushing my position at the secret entrance in the security wall," Zev told her. "I got ready to fire. One woman made a shrill whistle and pulled their head cloths off."

Rita listened spellbound. "Who was the Hebrew-speaking Arab woman?"

Devorah returned through the inner door and handed a black plastic bag to Zev. "She was no Arab," she broke in. "My niece was rescued by one of the Mossada agents in disguise."

Zev started filling the bag with packets of bonds. "They're an elite unit," he explained. "Selected from the top of their class at Women's Officers School."

"Because of that incident," Ari continued, "we were blamed for provoking Islamic men. They accused us of aggravating violence by allowing women to drive in Arab neighborhoods. That's how they got an injunction against us. That's why travel outside our grounds is restricted until their court decides what our rights are going to be."

"I thought it was in the World Court," Rita mentioned.

"The World Court is their court—just take a look at the panel of judges." Ari's irritated tone returned. He shook his head.

"It's getting late," Dove said. "I'll take Jacob by the army barracks tonight to see Levi on my way home."

Jacob stood. "We'll talk tomorrow, Rita," he said on his way out with Dove and Zev.

They heard the sound of the kitchen door swing shut. Devorah glanced at Ari. "We should get the American settled for tonight."

Ari nodded. He was finished dealing with the foreigners.

Rita picked up her satchel, took a deep breath, and followed Devorah into the hallway to enter the world of the kibbutz women. She was beginning to think this was the longest day of her life.

"Welcome to my building," Devorah said as she led the way down a hallway of closed doors.

"Thank you for letting me stay," Rita said timidly.

"You American Jews," Devorah answered with a wave of her hand, "you don't know any conversational Hebrew. Thank you is *todah*. Now you know a word." She stopped and opened a door. "You can sleep in this room tonight."

Rita smiled. "Todah," she repeated.

A bed sat tucked against the wall with a side table next to it. A straight chair and wooden bench nearly filled the rest of the room. Rita looked through an open door connecting to an adjoining washroom. Exhaustion hit like a thundering wave and she wanted to collapse on the bed.

"If you're hungry," Devorah offered, "come down to the kitchen. We can fix something."

They said shalom and Devorah left. Feeling an almost overwhelming mixture of emotions, Rita sat on the edge of the bed and sighed. A few tears escaped down her cheeks until she forced herself to feel determined instead, a technique that had worked since childhood. Then she took a shower and changed her clothes.

At that moment, hunger became her priority, and she found her way back to the kitchen. Four gleaming stainless steel stoves lined the back wall with pots, lids, and utensils hanging over them. Open shelves along the opposite wall held all manner of jars, kitchen equipment, and dishes.

Batya sat at a long wooden table in the center of the room. In front of an empty chair next to her, Devorah set a platter filled with white cheese, matzo crackers, and a dish of crushed walnuts, grated apples, and honey. Seeing Rita, she waved her over.

Batya held a damp cloth on her chin to catch little drops of blood escaping from her cracked skin. She pointed to Rita's arm. "You got hurt too."

Rita nodded and sat. She tasted the crackers and realized how hungry she felt.

Devorah smiled for the first time. She placed a half-filled juice glass of deep red wine in front of Rita. "Here, this will help you sleep tonight."

"Did you come to our house with Commander Ari?" Batya asked.

"In a manner of speaking, yes, I guess I did," Rita answered between mouthfuls of food. "Do you know him?"

"I'm in love with him," Batya gushed.

"Don't say that," Devorah reprimanded. "The man is forty. Old enough to be your father."

"I don't care," Batya said in a high-pitched voice. "I love him. And someday I'm going to marry him."

chapter 5

ARI SLEPT SOUNDLY the night he returned from Antalya. His bedroom was soundproof and windowless, the perfect lair for a tired warrior. In the early morning, his bedroom phone rang three times before he jumped to answer it.

"We're ready to go out to the missile attack site," Zev greeted him. "You told Dove 'first thing in the morning' and we're already on the way to pick you up."

"Call the head of moshav security."

"Already done. Uzzi will meet us there."

Ten minutes later, Ari stood waiting in front of his building. Before long, Dove arrived in a desert terrain vehicle and Ari jumped into the front passenger seat.

"Shalom," Zev said from the back seat. "Moshe came with."

"What can you tell us?" Ari asked Dove's top intelligence analyst.

"Shalom, Commander," the young man said. "This attack appears to be an isolated incident. One low-level improvised missile. No one was inside the school at the time the missile crashed through Ben-Josef's house."

"Until last year," Ari reminded them, "we used insect-shaped nanocamera drones to observe a twenty-kilometer radius. Cameras shaped like mosquitoes that could land in trees or on buildings and send back images." He shook his head. "Now we have lookouts with binoculars."

Dove turned down the street where it happened. "You wouldn't have been able to stop this," he said, "even with surveillance."

"I understand this was a conventional missile unleashed from a mobile launcher," Ari said.

"That's right," Moshe answered. "They only have conventional."

Ari could see the destruction a few blocks ahead. They slowly drove by the site of the children's school. The ground looked chewed up around a massive cavity torn from the point of impact where the Ben-Josef family once lived. Damage to surrounding houses looked extensive.

A few people stood around, talking and pointing. Uzzi, a young father of four, raised his fist and shook it skyward when Dove drove past and parked. Ari leaned out the window and said, "I know, Uzzi, I know."

"He wants to kill them all," Dove said as he got out of the car, "those who cause this destruction in a family neighborhood."

Moshe stood next to the car. "Can't blame him. His two boys attended this school."

They walked around with Uzzi, shaking their heads.

Ari stopped for a moment, and the others stopped with him. "This may be intended to provoke us into a violent response before the court rules on the injunction against us," he said. "It's been five years since the other missile hit inside our walls. And that one landed in a field. Why now?"

Uzzi touched Ari's arm. "We need a missile shield. How can we protect our children this way? What if school had been in session?"

Ari agreed. "We do need surveillance."

"Why'd we stop using drones?" Uzzi demanded.

"The French," Moshe answered. "They perfected a drone-detection system and immediately sold it to Persyria. We couldn't outbid them."

"That's right," Zev said. "The Islamic civil war waged inside France left the country broke. The politicians had to raise funds fast or turn over control of the government to a victorious Islamic faction."

Dove agreed. "As I recall, a particularly severe group."

"Not to worry," Ari said. "Our top weapons engineers in Jerusalem are testing new technology for nanotech surveillance scorpions that are completely undetectable."

"We'll have the new surveillance drones soon," Dove added.

"Not soon enough," Uzzi grumbled, looking at the mountain of wreckage.

Ari didn't have an answer.

A quiet week passed and Devorah missed a required briefing. Ari called the women's building and left a message, then went to look for her. He entered the kitchen and greeted three women preparing food. "Why was Devorah absent this morning?"

"Batya's not doing well," one of the women told him. "The doctor can't figure out what's wrong and Devorah's a nervous wreck." She directed him to an outside area.

The courtyard garden was decoratively enclosed with lattice covered in fragrant jasmine, accented with shades of red and pink flowering succulents. Clay pots along the edges created a graceful backdrop. Grape vines covered a pergola in the far corner, where he spotted Devorah with Rita. He breathed in the mixture of sweet fragrances as he strode across a brick pathway to the women.

Ari moved a wooden chair from the trellised archway and sat across from them. "I heard about Batya. How's she doing?"

Devorah looked tired. "I stayed up with her all night. She felt hot with fever for hours. When I left just now, she was finally asleep."

Ari had known Batya's parents. He sat with Hannah for three days after an air raid killed her husband in Tel Aviv, two years before Hannah was stabbed. "What does the doctor say?"

Devorah shook her head. "Her internal injuries aren't healing properly. The doctor believes the skin rash on her face is a super infection, but she doesn't have access to a lab."

Rita stood to excuse herself, but Ari nodded toward her chair. "You can stay."

"Good," Devorah said. "She has unique ideas."

Ari glanced at Rita from the corner of his eye, then turned to Devorah. "I informed our community security council that I want them to consider evacuating the children to Jerusalem. The Islamics fighting each other do agree on one thing. They want to push us out." He smiled at Rita and added, "We won't let them—but that's a discussion for another day."

Devorah leaned forward. "You're serious about this. How soon do you want the children to leave?"

"Within thirty days."

"Excuse me," Rita interrupted. "Will Batya be better by then? She can't travel with an infection."

"I think so," Devorah said slowly. "Dr. Goldstein prescribed a dose of antibacterial medication. Batya should respond to treatment in a few days."

"Good," Ari said as he stood. "Ladies." He gave a nod before leaving down the garden path toward the buildings.

Springtime didn't linger in this desert region. The days quickly grew longer and hotter. The leaders of Kol Shofar applied to the One World Travel Department for a passport renewal for Rita through contacts in Jerusalem. The denial arrived two weeks later. They next applied for a residency visa.

Jacob, assigned to training at the soldier barracks, didn't call, and Rita settled into a routine without him while she waited for permission to leave.

Rita's morning started with her assigned chores. Around noon, she began filling the ritual hand-washing urns with purified water when her friend Tarah from synagogue prayer group stopped by the community kitchen.

"It's the end of your first month here," Tarah said. "We should have dinner tonight to celebrate. Have you met anyone interesting at the dining hall yet?"

"I usually have dinner in my building." Rita stopped filling the last urn, and looked at Tarah. "Why?"

Tarah laughed. "You're a beautiful woman. The dining hall is where the single men exchange glances with the single women. If you're not going to be a couple with Jacob, then you should go there often. You won't stay single long."

"I don't know how much longer I'll be here," she stammered, "before my travel permit to Jerusalem is approved and then, of course, I'll be returning to America."

"Well, let's not talk about that," Tarah said with a smile. "Local gossip is so much more fun."

That night, for the first time, Rita went to supper at the spacious dining hall with tall, pretty Tarah. They were the same age, thirty-two, and Rita felt comfortable with her easygoing nature. Rita enjoyed the exercise and the conversation on the walk across the courtyard.

The clatter of dishes and scent of fresh warm bread greeted her as she followed Tarah into the main dining room. They piled their plates high from the buffet of raw and cooked vegetables, roasted barley cakes, fresh fruits, olives, and cheeses. Tarah led the way to a long table in the back of the room with several chairs still empty. Devorah joined them and sat across from Rita.

Halfway through the meal Rita looked up to see Ari stride through the main entry. She hadn't seen him since that day in the garden. He looked over, and crossed the room toward her.

"Shalom," he said with an official tone. "I guess I should welcome you to our community. It looks like you may be here a few more weeks. Your temporary residency visa was approved today. But don't worry; we're getting your travel papers cleared so you can return to America as soon as possible."

He stood quietly for a moment until her green eyes gazed up at him. "I hope you're comfortable during your stay here," he said stiffly.

"Thanks," she said. "I'm sorry I caused you and the others trouble by coming here. I really didn't understand." Rita turned her head and her golden-blonde hair flowed gracefully around her shoulders.

Devorah reached over and patted her hand. "Sweet daughter of Israel, you have as much right to be here as any other Jew."

Zev walked up and sat with Devorah. He pointed to the last empty chair, next to Rita. "Join us for a moment, Ari."

"Can't—my officers expect me." Ari turned and went to the other side of the room to a table filled with military men and women.

"Was it worth it to come here, Rita?" Zev asked.

Rita put her fork down and took a drink of water. "I just wanted to help my people after meeting Jacob. In America, hate crimes against Jews are rarely prosecuted anymore. It's been getting worse for the last few years." She felt her throat tighten.

"You have to ignore it," Zev said.

Devorah agreed.

"I tried," she insisted. "But the news only reports the Arab and Slavic Muslim point of view. There's hardly any news about the Jewish side. Islam is taught in American public schools, but the *Shoah*, the terrible Holocaust, isn't even mentioned in the history books."

Her reference to the Shoah drew nods.

"Yes, we know," Tarah said.

Rita played with her napkin. "Then Jacob arrived and he woke me. He constantly talked about Kol Shofar." She looked down, no longer feeling hungry. "Jacob told me we'd be safer here than in San Francisco."

Devorah nodded. "The word 'safe' takes on new meaning here."

"Well," Rita said, "maybe things happen for a reason."

Tarah touched Rita's shoulder. "Whatever the reason, this is your home now, at least temporarily."

Rita fell silent for a moment, thinking about her worthless passport. "I have no way back."

Zev stroked his beard absent-mindedly. "Yes, maybe things do happen for a reason."

Rita finished her dinner, declined dessert and stood to leave. "I've got some reading to catch up on," she explained.

Tarah offered to walk back with her, and Rita felt grateful for the company. A light rain started to fall as they stepped outside. The summer air had a fresh, wet-hay kind of scent.

"Is something the matter?" Tarah asked. "You were quiet as Rachel's Tomb during dinner."

"I don't know why, but that man makes me feel nervous," Rita confided.

"Commander Ari?" Tarah laughed. "No wonder. He's about the most eligible bachelor in the community. Not to mention he's gorgeous."

Rita walked without speaking for a few steps. She pictured his sleek good looks, classic Mediterranean high cheekbones, distinctive nose, and deep-set, soul searching eyes. "I thought maybe Ari and Devorah." Her voice trailed off.

"They've been looking like they might be a couple for about the last five years." Tarah glanced at Rita. "But she's Traditional, so his only move is marriage. If he ever makes a move."

"I understand," Rita said.

"Too bad I'm already married," Tarah said through a grin. "I'd go for the commander myself. Just kidding," she quickly added. "My husband's a catch. I wouldn't trade him for a pile of gold." Tarah said shalom and headed home when they neared Rita's building.

Rita pulled her sweater a little tighter, and walked up the front steps feeling alone in a community bound together by devotion to their heritage and love for one another.

An uneventful week passed and Rita longed for company. After having dinner in her room, she went to the great room to meet Tarah. Devorah sat nearby reading.

Zev wandered in, handed coffee drinks to Rita and Tarah, and lowered himself into a chair across from Rita. "Since the World Travel Agency approved your residency visa, you're legal to stay for one year." He smiled. "So, what are your plans?"

Rita leaned back in an overstuffed green velvet chair. She looked at Zev. "But I can't leave Kol Shofar, right?"

"This is a first step," Zev assured her. "Next we apply again for a passport."

"Not that I'm in a hurry to leave," Rita quickly added.

Devorah put her book aside and moved her chair closer. "We'll use part of the money you brought to smuggle you back to Paris when the time is right," she offered.

"Sure," Zev said. "Even though it seems we are in the middle of nowhere, we are on the upper north rim of the Negev Desert. Just a couple of hours by car from Jerusalem."

"Except that the main road north got bombed last year," Tarah said. "Now it takes longer to get to the city."

Devorah's face tightened. "The road was bombed by Slavic Muslims, the same group who murdered those families in Samaria five years ago. A hundred and twenty people died."

Zev looked at Rita. "Bastards from Bosnia, most of them. It's easier to float a raft from Bosnia to our shores than it is to cross from Cuba to Florida. A bunch of refugees from Yugoslavia came here in the 1880s escaping trouble at home. More followed."

"They're here only a hundred fifty years and they call Israel their ancient homeland," Devorah said angrily. "My family has been here for over two thousand years."

"Two thousand years. You know this?" Rita sighed. "That's amazing."

"Of course we know." Devorah looked at her. "Don't you know your family line?"

"I guess, not like you. My mother's great-grandparents survived World War I in Spain. They lost most of their family in that war. Two survivors traveled to America in the 1930s when the political apparatus of Europe embraced fascism."

"Don't feel bad," Zev counseled. "Many families lost their way in the Diaspora. We take the memories we have and go forward."

Rita nodded. "My grandmother used to say, 'May your memories be a blessing.'"

Zev smiled. "Wise grandmother."

"Yes," Rita reminisced. "She made great cornbread too."

Tarah motioned toward Rita's upper right arm. "How is the wound? Does it still give you trouble?"

"It's healed fine. No trouble." Rita slid up her shirtsleeve to prove it.

Devorah looked at her arm and shrugged. "You like our strong-as-mud coffee, and you got a nice scar on your arm. You are practically an Israeli already."

"I would know how to use a rifle," Rita said, "if I were really Israeli."

Tarah's face brightened. "My husband, Eyal, gives weapons proficiency classes."

"What are you saying?" Rita almost dropped her coffee cup. "Can I take lessons?"

"Wait a minute," Devorah cautioned. "This is not a game, you know."

"I know." Rita glanced at Tarah. "I've practiced daily defense drills with the other women. I'm ready."

"Well," Zev said, "I guess now we know what's next for you."

Rita met Eyal in a field near the security wall the following afternoon. Five years earlier, an enemy sniper shot Tarah's husband while he was on border patrol. Rita noticed that he still limped.

Eyal handed her a military-issue rifle with a high-density steel barrel. "It's the latest model, delivered only two weeks ago. We got dozens of them, Galil ACE compact carbines."

"Todah," she said, reaching for it.

"It's fully automatic, or single shot, and uses a standard magazine. They're accurate at long range with very little recoil. Light as a handgun with a synthetic rubberized coating on the barrel. It won't get hot in the sun."

Rita held it tenderly with both hands. *My own rifle,* she thought.

"I've recorded the serial number under your name. Notify me or Devorah immediately if anything happens to this weapon." He handed her protective glasses and ear covers.

With a nod, she moved her braided hair behind her ears, planted her new boots on the ground, and eagerly waited for her first instruction.

Rita completed her daily lessons with Eyal three weeks later. The next afternoon he dropped by the community kitchen to offer his favorite student an advanced class.

"You could qualify for sniper class by fall," Eyal told her. "Mazel tov. You worked hard."

"By the way," Rita mentioned, "I've heard rumors that some of our military men recently deployed out. You always know what's going on."

Devorah arrived at that moment. "Ari and his officers left two weeks ago," she said, "to attend an important meeting in Jerusalem."

A freckle-faced young soldier stepped in and stood by the kitchen door. He nodded to Eyal and ran his fingers through his curly red hair. "Shalom, ladies."

"Samuel, what can I do for you?" Devorah asked.

"I came by to tell you central command called our reserves into service to defend the eastern border. Half our military men deploy tomorrow. And, well, with so many of the men already away on covert ops with Ari, the guard positions have to be filled by women again. At least temporarily."

"I was afraid we would have to resort to that," Devorah said with a sigh.

As casually as she could, Rita asked Samuel, "When will Ari—and the others—come back?"

"Soon, hopefully, next week."

"I guess I feel vulnerable with our men away." Rita immediately felt her cheeks getting warm after admitting in front of Eyal that she felt fear. "And, I thought Ari was at a meeting in Jerusalem."

Samuel broke out in a hearty laugh. "Ari? Sitting around talking for two weeks? Not likely."

Rita didn't say anything after Eyal and Samuel left.

Devorah excused herself to retire to her quarters. She turned to Rita at the door. "Meeting. Ops. What difference does it make? They are not here."

By the end of the next week the men were still away. Devorah's turn to stand perimeter guard came on Thursday afternoon, according to a roster posted on the kitchen bulletin board.

Rita hung her apron on a hook by the kitchen door and walked across the building to Devorah's rooms. She knocked, then let herself in. "They can't expect you to do this," she blurted out as she entered the sunroom. "Everyone knows you want to stay with Batya. You should be exempt."

Devorah greeted her with a half-hearted shalom, and sank into a chair under the window. The early afternoon sun streamed through lace curtains, causing floral patterns to splash across the wall.

"You're part of a family and I'm not." Rita sat on the sofa across from her. "I should be the one to go."

"Don't say that," Devorah said sternly. "And anyway, someday you will have children to worry about."

"I doubt that." Rita looked at her watch. "It's only two hours before your assignment starts. Please let me do this. Look how tired you are. You'll be up all night."

"I'm not a coward," Devorah insisted. "What do you doubt?"

"Of course you're not. But you're Batya's mom now. That must come first." Rita stood and looked at Devorah. "I don't plan to have children. I decided that a long time ago."

Devorah shook her head. "I am tired, but I wonder if this is a good idea."

Rita started for the door. "I've got to go change my clothes and get my rifle. You call the acting commander for reassignment."

"Only if you're sure," Devorah said.

Excitement grew in Rita with each passing moment. "Devorah, I've already made up my mind. I'm doing this." She waved and then practically ran through the door.

By the time the hour arrived for guard duty, Rita sat waiting to go in her place. She adjusted the rifle strap on her shoulder, looked at Devorah and said, "I'm ready."

They stood at the same time when they heard a knock on the open door. Devorah greeted the handsome, middle-aged Sephardic man standing there. Smooth, creamy skin and characteristic dark features referenced his heritage. He stepped inside at her invitation.

He nodded to Rita. "Shalom, I'm Bernardo." His voice had a slight Ladino cadence that Rita found soothing. "And I have news from the outside."

Devorah and Rita leaned closer.

"Word came in at the command center," he told them. "A car blew up in a neighborhood south of Jerusalem. It happened a few hours ago. No one was arrested."

Both women caught their breath.

Bernardo lowered his voice. "Eight people died. Five were children."

"That won't happen here," Rita said, gently squeezing Devorah's hand.

Bernardo followed Rita's gaze to Batya sitting in the adjoining room. "That's right, nothing like that will ever happen here." His voice sounded strong, confident.

Devorah looked upset, but she didn't say anything. Rita hated to leave her. Yet it was time. She glanced at Bernardo. "I'd better get going now."

Bernardo cleared his throat. "I thought Devorah had duty for tonight. I didn't know you are even on the roster."

"I got permission with the acting commander over an hour ago." Rita tried not to sound defensive. "I got my instructions for tonight direct from Special Squad Leader Daniel."

"I'm not questioning you. I think you're brave to do this."

Rita laughed nervously. "I don't feel brave."

"I'll tell you," Bernardo said, "no enemy has ever gotten through the secret entrance. They don't know it's there. It's hidden in a cluster of trees and bushes on both sides of the wall and it's protected by powerful motion detectors. But we also keep eyes on it every night as a security safeguard. It's the only section of the wall without nanowiring. The only place to go through without being electrocuted."

"It's rarely used," Devorah added, "except when one of our teams goes out on an operation. An enemy satellite watches our brightly lit main gate every night."

Bernardo smiled at Rita and held the door open. "I'll walk with you to the post."

Rita let go of Devorah's hand and followed Bernardo out to the front door. She heard the door latch fasten, stepped down the front stairs toward her first official assignment, and looked out at the horizon while another hot summer day gradually released its grip.

He set a good pace crossing a field toward the perimeter wall. Gravel crunched under her boots as she walked on a worn path alongside him.

"Anyone on guard duty for the first time should have a veteran backup," Bernardo mentioned.

Rita loosened her rifle strap. "I guess this night is different."

"Yeah, I suppose no one wants to see Devorah on guard duty while she's caring for Batya."

They neared some tall trees, and she saw the security wall standing majestically beyond the trees. He stopped near a cluster of bushes at a gray stone bench. "I could stay out here with you, if you want."

She considered his offer. "How long have you been on duty already?"

Bernardo shifted from one foot to the other. "About fourteen hours."

"I'm well-rested and I have my coffee for backup." She held up a fabric bag with a stainless steel thermos peeking out the top. "I can do this." Rita hoped her voice displayed confidence she didn't feel.

"This area used to be swampy after the rains," he told her. "Mosquitoes were the problem so they planted eucalyptus trees and these bushes here to soak up the standing water. Anyway, the main gate is about a kilometer down the wall, and two guards are always posted there. You've got your wrist-com with you?"

She patted the front of her bag.

Bernardo smiled. "Shalom then, and have a good night."

A bright orange sun sat low on the horizon in a purple-streaked sky while she watched him walk down the path through the green fields. The scent of eucalyptus infused the warm air.

In the growing darkness, she pulled a cushion out of her bag, sat on the stone bench, and remembered Devorah's advice. *This is merely a precaution so relax. Nothing's going to happen tonight.*

For the first few hours she felt alert and ready. Then she stretched, yawned, and poured a cup of coffee.

The moon was full enough for her to see clearly, so she didn't turn on the night-vision feature in the large lens installed to serve as a giant telescope through the six-foot thickness in this section of the wall. Everything looked normal in the fields beyond the wall. Nothing moved. The night seemed peaceful and blissfully quiet. Tree frogs serenaded each other in the nearby eucalyptus grove.

She returned to the bench after checking the computer monitor installed in the wall and placed her weapon next to her. "Devorah's right, nothing's going to happen tonight," she repeated over and over.

In the middle of the night a different sound caught her attention. Rita sat still. Her heart started to pound as she reached for her rifle.

With shaking hands she picked it up, moved the safety off, and waited in the dark. Hearing a rustle in the brush set her heart racing. Her legs trembled when she stood. She shook her head to clear her mind, flexed and relaxed her muscles, and forced herself to breathe.

Agonizing minutes passed.

A faint "coo" sound echoed through the trees and she froze. Then rustling. Thick bushes stood between her position and the hidden entrance. She heard a muffled click. With her senses on alert she prepared to defend the post. Leaning forward, she fingered the trigger on her rifle.

Rita hid in the darkness behind a eucalyptus tree.

And listened.

chapter 6

COMMANDER ARI HEADED home after a three-week operation designed to keep the area around the secret cove free of enemy intrusion. For security reasons, Ari traveled alone after covert ops, and would arrive home a day ahead of his team.

He was tired—he'd been up for thirty-six hours by the time he crossed the fields surrounding Kol Shofar and slipped into the eucalyptus grove outside the secret entrance.

Ari placed his hand on the wall where he knew the unmarked biometric keypad was situated. A sliding door disguised as part of the wall slid open, and he made his way inside the nearly invisible entry. The molded inner shield on either side contained nanosensor wires embedded in a spider web grid pattern. Except at the entrance gate, and this secret opening, the electrical web made any intrusion deadly. A low-level electromagnetic pulse protected the wall from above. As he stepped silently though the final inner security shield and clicked it closed, he sensed something was wrong.

Nothing looked unusual, but it was quiet at the post—too quiet. Ari crept into the bushes and moved silently around the edge of the trees. The outline of a person became visible as he moved in from behind.

He inched forward and reached his arm around to secure the rifle. "What are you doing here?" he asked in a low voice. "Holding a loaded weapon."

Rita didn't move, didn't answer. He came around and faced her directly while maintaining his grip on her rifle. She looked terrified. He gently unclasped her fingers from the trigger with his other hand without looking at the rifle, moved the lever onto safety, and leaned it against the tree.

She stood straight, but he could see her tremble. "I wanted to help," she whispered.

Ari reached out to steady her. "Everything will be all right now."

She sniffled and took his hand. He pulled her close, felt her heart beat against his chest. Tears ran down her cheeks onto his shirt.

"I couldn't shoot it, the rifle." She choked back tears. "If it wasn't you."

"It is me," he whispered as he stroked her hair. "And you're braver than the man who let you come out here alone. This is obviously your first night out here."

She nodded, still crying.

"I'm furious a man would let you replace him on guard duty." He spoke in a low, even voice.

"Most of the men are gone and the ones still here are exhausted," she said. "The reserves left a few days ago for the northeastern border. You must know this."

"I didn't." Ari pressed his lips together and tried to think. "Outside Kol Shofar our communications can be picked up so we don't transmit sensitive information." They stood pressed together while Ari listened to the sound of her breathing. "The reserves weren't due to be sent out until the end of this month," he finally said. "Something must have happened."

"I don't know," she said. "I took Devorah's duty tonight so she could stay with Batya."

"Well, it doesn't matter. I'm here now." Ari felt her relax in his arms. "And hundreds more are coming in soon with the Israeli Defense Forces from Haifa."

Rita inhaled deeply. "You smell like the ocean on a happy summer day."

"I came in on a Greek fishing boat." Ari let go enough to remove his backpack. "With a good skipper. He got me close, but I still had to swim to shore."

She released his shirt and leaned against a post next to the stone bench.

He removed his .45-caliber Glock from his pack and checked it. "It's been a while since I've guarded the perimeter," he said with a chuckle.

"You're too important to stand guard on the fence line." She wiped her shirtsleeve across her runny nose. "But I'm glad you're here."

They sat on the bench and talked quietly for the next hour. She shared her coffee with him and he checked the computer monitors installed in the wall.

Ari leisurely sipped a second cup of her strong coffee, and set the thermos cup on the bench. "Thanks for the caffeine," he said without taking his eyes away from the cutout view on the wall monitor. "It's a good thing you have some left because I've been without sleep for a while."

For a moment, Ari let his mind float back to the long walk from the coastline to Kol Shofar. The last thing he expected to find on his arrival was this foreign woman guarding his home. He glanced at her. *I guess this is her home now too.* Ari brought his mind back to the present. "Have you thought about returning to America?"

"I don't think it's the right time to leave," she stammered.

"You might be safer in my war-torn nation facing impossible odds than you would be in the United States." Ari shook his head. "Imagine that."

After a long silence she asked, "Are you trying to tell me something?"

Ari looked away. If the night wasn't so dark she might have seen him grimace slightly. "Rita, we could get you out. Eldad can arrange passage on a ship bound for the East Coast of America."

"What about my expired passport?"

"Dove can buy fake identification papers." He felt the strain of too many sleepless nights, and said what was on his mind. "Look, Rita, you've done more for us than I can ever thank you for, but our position is weakening. I don't want you to risk your life for us."

She set her coffee on the bench. "I'm not sure what I want."

"Just think about it. It might be better for you."

"I'm not ready to go back yet," she finally said.

He looked directly at her. "Don't you understand? Lives are going to be lost. This is normal for us here in Israel. We live with a daily stress that would paralyze most people in America. We live to survive each day. I don't want this for you."

"What do you want?" she demanded.

He didn't answer.

Rita stood and faced him, her body almost touching his. "Do you want me to leave Kol Shofar?"

Ari fell silent for a moment, then took a deep breath, and let go. "I don't want you to go anywhere." He stood slowly and she didn't move back so he reached down and took her hands, interlaced his fingers with hers.

He breathed in the scent of amber fragrance she rubbed in her hair.

She looked up and smiled. He looked into her eyes, and for a moment, he experienced a feeling that he'd known her forever.

With the scents of eucalyptus and amber fused in his mind, he stepped back, still holding her hands, until his back rested against the security wall.

After five years of being alone, he felt desire slowly flooding through him. He pulled her against him, wrapping his arms around her. She took a deep breath and he could feel her pulse race. He brushed her hair away from her face, touched his lips to her cheek, then the corner of her mouth. He thought he heard her sigh.

Ari cupped the back of her head with one hand and let his other hand slide down to the small of her back, moistened her lips with his tongue, and pressed his mouth against hers.

When he finally pulled away, she said, "What about Devorah?"

Ari held her close. "No, Honey, that never was. And since I have no way of getting you to Jerusalem right now I guess you're going to have to stay here with me for a while. Until things change."

For Ari, things were already changing. For the rest of the night he watched the grounds, and he watched Rita.

With dawn approaching, her guard duty ended. Ari tried not to question what had happened or how comfortable he felt with her. They sat on the bench while he drank the last of her coffee and she put her flashlight into her bag.

He would see to it that she never went out on perimeter guard duty again.

Time went by quickly for Ari after his return. A week passed before he finally made time to see Devorah and check on Batya.

In the late afternoon, Dr. Sasha Goldstein arrived with flowers at the same time as Ari. Sasha had fled to Israel from Russia with her boyfriend, Medad, during the "Time of Terror" in the months following Israel's initial military victory over Egypt five years earlier. Bright blue eyes and high cheekbones in a flat, round face revealed her heritage at a glance. Speaking only Russian upon her arrival, she learned Hebrew and some English from her wounded patients.

"Batya's injuries are more serious than we realized," Devorah told Ari. "Dr. Goldstein comes every day to check on her, but the prognosis does not encourage."

Sasha nodded. "Correct. She does not improve."

Devorah got a vase for Sasha's yellow and white daisies. "Come, we can sit in the sunroom while Batya sleeps."

They sat by a window and the doctor shook her head. "She is so young," she said.

That night, Ari made calls to request an emergency meeting with the community security council. They met the following day in the moshav community room.

"The doctor informed me that Batya may not make it through another month without proper care," Devorah told them. "She has serious spinal injuries and needs surgery. And her skin infection can't be treated here."

Sasha raised a hand. "Batya puts on a brave front, but the pain is considerable. Without properly equipped surgical hospital, we may lose her."

"No, that can't happen," Zev insisted. "She's only eighteen."

"Our resources here are limited," Sasha reminded them.

Ari looked around at the others. "It's time to act. We should send her to a hospital in Jerusalem or Tel Aviv."

"Yes," Dove agreed. "We have the money now to send her to an intensive-care clinic. There is one in Paris that specializes in treatment of spinal injuries."

"That's good." Devorah finally sounded hopeful.

"What are her chances of survival," Dove asked, "if we send her to the clinic in Paris?"

"Not good," Sasha replied. "Worse if we don't send her."

They spent the next few hours discussing ways to transport Batya into France. By early evening they developed a plan to get Devorah and Batya out of the country without going through checkpoints or airport security.

"As far as we know," Zev said, "the Muslim Brotherhood still has a death contract out on Devorah. We can't put her name on travel papers."

"At least now we have a plan," Sasha said.

The others agreed, and the meeting ended.

Ari took Dove home a few minutes later, and parked the car.

"So, how's Rita?" Dove asked.

"What do you mean? Did she say something?" Ari ran his fingers through his hair. He looked at Dove. "What?"

"Nothing, I thought that you're seeing her."

Ari stared out the side window. "I've been really busy. Things piled up while I was gone, you know. And who said I'm seeing her?"

Dove looked hard at Ari. "You told me that her lips are the color of pomegranate."

"That doesn't mean anything." Ari gave a quick glance. "Anyway, I haven't talked with her since I got back from the op."

Dove's eyes widened. "That's been over a week."

Ari smoothed his hair. "Really? It's been a whole week already?" He got out, followed Dove inside, and hung his jacket by the door. Through an archway framing the living room, he watched Rita enter with Dove's wife, Naomi.

"Shalom, ladies," Ari said warmly.

Naomi returned his greeting and turned her attention to Dove.

"I have to get going but I'd like to talk with you later, Rita," Ari said as he pulled his jacket off the hook. "I didn't know you knew Naomi."

Rita smiled. "We became friends at morning prayers."

He looked back and waved before he slipped out the door.

Later that night, Ari arrived at Rita's room and invited her to go for a walk. She felt her pulse quicken, and longed to be alone with him again. *The waiting is over,* she thought.

They strolled to the garden under the soft light of a nearly full moon. "I've missed you," she confessed.

"I've been really busy." He cleared his throat. "So much to do since I've been back."

"I knew you'd call as soon as you could." Her voice was soft, eager.

"Rita, I think we should talk. I don't want us to have a misunderstanding."

"I know how important your time is. I can work around your schedule." She saw his lips press together. "Oh, Ari. What's wrong?" Her mouth went dry.

"I made a mistake by kissing you, Rita, and I don't know how to make it right." He sat on a bench under a night-blooming jasmine vine.

She felt the energy in her body drain into the ground.

"I have to leave Kol Shofar for a couple of months." He stared down. "It wouldn't be right to involve you and then leave you here alone."

"You're already doing that."

He didn't answer, he just stared straight ahead.

She took a deep breath and changed her tone. "I don't regret what happened. We got carried away. It's not your fault."

He looked relieved. "To tell the truth, I was afraid you might make a scene. I should've known you'd understand. I apologize, Rita. I really can't get involved right now."

"Nothing to be sorry about." She blinked, and her eyes glistened.

He stood. "Let me walk you to your room."

"I assure you, I can find my way home." Rita said it without emotion, turned, and walked away without looking back. She felt her heart close down a little with each step, but she kept walking.

News of Devorah and Batya's impending trip spread through the building and, on Sunday before they left, Rita decided to see them off. She didn't mention Ari to anyone or allow herself to think about him. She felt humiliated and foolish every time he crossed her mind. *It's time to put this behind me and move on,* she thought.

Devorah's rooms were down two long hallways. Rita smoothed her dark green skirt, adjusted the stiff collar of her turquoise cotton blouse, and walked over. She found Devorah in the sunroom and sat with her under the window.

"I heard you and Jacob are not together," Devorah said, after they greeted each other. "He's such a soft-spoken, sweet man. Maybe things will still work out. I heard he wants to have lunch with you."

The rooms were on the south side of the building and light poured through the windows. The sunlight glinted off Rita's eyes. "How could you hear anything?"

"The grapevine," Devorah answered with a laugh. "Dove told me this morning. His wife, Naomi, knows everything."

"Like I told Naomi, I don't think it's a good idea." Rita shook her head. "I've already made up my mind. I don't want to make another mistake."

"Bring a box of your almond cookies and, for sure, you'll get a second date," Devorah teased.

Rita made a face. "It's not really a date and anyway, I'm not going."

"You deserve to be happy. Jacob is handsome and intelligent. He is your age, thirty-two. Perfect for you. Of course you're going." Devorah raised her eyebrows. "Do you still long for Jacob?"

Rita gazed out the sunroom window. "I don't long for anyone."

"He looks like the kind of man who usually gets what he wants," Devorah said. "Give him another chance. I know I would."

"Give who a chance?" Batya asked as Dr. Goldstein pushed her wheelchair into the room.

"You know Jacob, don't you, darling?" Devorah asked.

Batya nodded. "He's very handsome. Not as fine-looking as Commander Ari but nobody is."

Rita winced at the mention of Ari. "Jacob is only a friend. And speaking of friends, you have many people here who are going to miss you terribly while you're away."

"I know," the sweet-voiced Batya said. "I'll miss all of you too."

"Did you get travel visas approved?" Rita asked.

"Batya and I have special medical passes to go to Jerusalem," Devorah explained. "The airspace is protected for medical helicopters. From there we sneak out across the border from Tel Aviv into the Med. We're booked on a steamer headed for Nice."

"You're not traveling by yourselves?" Rita glanced at Batya.

Devorah's face brightened. "Ari's going with us. Well, at least to Jerusalem. He insisted."

Rita's head felt hot. A wave of emotions poured through. She looked away so the others wouldn't notice.

"We should go to the transport," Devorah said to Sasha. "Ari will be waiting."

Sasha looked at her watch. "In a few minutes." Then she took Devorah aside for a private conversation.

Batya motioned for Rita to come close. "I'll be gone for several months. Please," she whispered, "don't let Commander Ari marry anyone until I get back. I can't talk to Aunt Devorah about it because she gets mad at me."

"Sweetie," Rita said in a quiet voice, "I don't have anything to do with him. I wouldn't know what he's doing."

"Please, you can help me. You hear things from the women in the kitchen."

"Batya, I couldn't."

"But I don't have anyone else to watch out for him," Batya pleaded.

"Trust in Creator," Rita said gently, "to bring you together with your soul mate at the proper time. There's nothing you have to do but be ready."

"Are you sure, Rita?"

"I'm sure, Honey."

Rita hugged Batya and then Devorah. Moments later, Dove's aide Shoshona arrived with a van to drive them to the transport.

Rita sighed. "I already miss them." She pushed aside thoughts of Ari traveling with Devorah.

"We all will, of course," Sasha said. "Devorah's a strong voice on our security council."

Two weeks passed quickly and Rita still felt alone. The phone rang while she rearranged the clothes in her closet for the third time.

Naomi dispensed with the usual greeting. "You're still coming tonight for Shabbat dinner? Dove has a late meeting and I'd so appreciate your company."

"Yes, of course."

"Excellent. See you in a couple of hours."

Rita finished dressing and went to the kitchen. She pulled a loaf of herb bread from a shelf above the stove and chose a blue-patterned cloth to wrap it in before starting the walk to Tarah's house to borrow her car.

The solar electric car Rita borrowed from her friend responded to her voice commands. In minutes she arrived in front of a modest-looking stucco house with a small, unkempt front yard.

Inside an entryway, she found the front door ajar. "Shalom," she called out.

Naomi stood inside, smiling and waving her in. Tight dark-brown curls framed her round, pretty face. Sparkling brown eyes welcomed Rita from underneath dark, perfectly shaped eyebrows.

"Finally." Naomi pulled Rita into a bear hug. "You're almost late."

Rita followed her into the kitchen and gave her the bread.

She found her friend eager to share. "Dove just told me, before he left for his meeting. Devorah and Batya are now on their way to France."

Rita sat at the kitchen table. "This is great news. How'd they do it?"

"They bribed people," Naomi said as she set the bread on the kitchen counter. "It's easy."

"Who's taking them?" She caught herself before she asked about Ari.

"Devorah's a trained fighter," Naomi answered. "Believe me, they'll be safe by themselves."

"Kol Shofar feels different with so many of our men away." Rita didn't want to admit she felt out of place now in this tight-knit community after the break-up with Ari. "And now Devorah's gone," she said wistfully.

With a satisfied smile, Naomi set another plate on the table. "Well, we're having a guest for dinner tonight and that will make us all feel better."

"Oh no," Rita moaned, "not another single man."

Naomi placed dishes of food on the table. "Look, just because the other one didn't work out doesn't mean you quit trying."

"I'm not trying." Rita tossed her head sharply and her hair flew out around her shoulders. "You don't seem to understand. I want to be left alone."

Naomi placed a basket of bread rolls on the table. "Of course you don't want to be alone and you already know this man."

Beginning to dread the evening ahead, Rita tried to think of a way out of this unexpected obligation, and figure out who'd been invited. Too late to act, she glared at her friend when the doorbell rang.

Naomi moved to answer it while Rita disappeared into the back room to tell the children dinner was ready. A few minutes later they piled into the kitchen.

Rita stopped when she saw Jacob seated at the table.

"Hello, Rita." He stood and walked around to move a chair out for her. "Thanks for asking Naomi to invite me," he whispered.

She'd forgotten what an exceptionally handsome man he was. His tousled brown hair framed a distinctive face, one with deep-set, velvety brown eyes and high cheekbones. Her shalom was barely audible as she slid into the chair Jacob held. She noticed the vase of fresh flowers on the table and smiled.

"Your food looks wonderful," Jacob told Naomi. He glanced at a plate of sliced raw bell peppers and cucumbers.

Naomi moved from the stove to the table placing a baked squash-walnut loaf and other dishes in the center. "Tonight, Rita will say the blessing," she announced, placing two white candles in front of Rita.

Rita stood and lit the candles.

Jacob watched as Rita, Naomi, and the girls waved their hands through the air to gather the light and bring it to their closed eyes while Rita said, "Blessed is our Creator, Sovereign of the Universe, who sanctified us and commanded us to kindle the Shabbat lights."

The children giggled when Jacob winked at them after the prayer. "You've grown much bigger since the last time I saw you." Naomi's brood included four girls and her youngest, a boy. "Don't tell me." Jacob held a finger to his lips. He smiled at each child and recited their names, "Leah, the twins Rachel and Revka, Sara, and Little Ben."

"I'm not little anymore," Little Ben blurted out. "I'm six!"

"My mistake," Jacob said. "Let me make it up to you. I'll tell you a story." True to his word, for the next hour he engaged them all with tales of Jewish history from Torah while he ate a soldier's portion of food.

"We're having fun," Leah chimed. "Please, Jacob, please tell us one more."

Naomi pushed a platter of roasted vegetables closer to Jacob. "Let him eat."

Jacob shook his head. "Really, no more." He took a last dinner roll before Leah began clearing away the empty dishes.

"I can help," Rita said as she stood, and took a plate from Jacob.

He flashed a smile at her, and Naomi grinned when Rita smiled back.

The children waited while their mother measured out a half cup of freshly ground dark-roast beans into a glass pitcher and poured in boiling hot water. She strained the steaming hot coffee into three glass mugs, placed a spoonful of fresh-whipped cream on top, picked up a little metal grinder and gave a half turn over each cup. The spicy aroma of fresh nutmeg filled the room.

Naomi put one cup in front of Rita and one in front of Jacob. She brought out a dessert and placed it on the table. "My chocolate pie," she said with pride.

"How'd you get coffee?" Rita asked.

Naomi smiled at Jacob. "You can thank our guest."

"Thank you, Jacob." Rita leaned closer. "Is that your ration for the month?"

"My absolute pleasure," he replied. "And, yes, it is."

They enjoyed the pie, and then Naomi sent the children to their rooms to prepare for bed. She brought out a dessert wine and a plate of purple grapes and set them on the table. "A little dessert nosh for you," she said with a smile.

"I can't," Rita moaned. "I've had too much already."

Jacob laughed and accepted a glass of the dark red wine from Naomi. "You go ahead and nosh while I check on the children," she added.

Rita and Jacob talked and laughed together while Naomi tucked the children into bed and read them a story. Jacob poured the last of the wine into Rita's glass. "It's probably time for me to leave now," he said reluctantly. "When can I see you again?"

"I don't know."

"Have lunch with me next Friday before Shabbat," he offered.

Rita shifted in her chair. "I might have some obligation I'm forgetting, or something. Do you think this is a good idea?"

"It's just lunch, Rita."

She closed her eyes and took a deep breath. "I suppose lunch would be all right."

Rita spent the next few days trying to convince herself that Jacob could make her happy. By Friday, she was ready to give him another chance.

chapter 7

THE DAYS GOT shorter as summer turned to fall in the Negev Desert. Intoxicating showers left the air full of moisture. Rita saw black-trimmed, iridescent blue butterflies soar by in large groups on their way south for the winter.

With Ari away on a secret op, Dove conducting training in the north, and Daniel on special assignment, Jacob had a relaxed duty schedule with enough free time to become a frequent dinner guest at Naomi's home in the weeks following that first lunch with Rita.

On the Friday evening after the autumn equinox, Rita arrived early to help Naomi prepare dinner. They set the table and Rita sank into a chair. "Do you think Jacob's getting serious?"

"Jacob is a Traditional," Naomi reminded her. "He's playing for keeps. And he's undeniably interested in you. He said it plainly last Shabbat."

"But I've been seeing him for almost two months and he hasn't even kissed me goodnight," Rita told her.

"I just told you, he's become a Traditional, same as his brother. Like the Orthodox, he'll probably propose marriage first. Ask for an understanding. That's why he comes here to see you. He doesn't try to get you alone out of respect."

"I thought Traditionals are Orthodox."

"Similar." Naomi covered the bread basket with a cloth and joined Rita at the table. "But we keep Jewish Law the way it was before our Temple was destroyed, when women enjoyed equal status with men. And, of course, the Orthodox eat animal meat and most of us don't. I think Traditional men make the best husbands and fathers. That's why I married one."

"I was wondering, is Ari a Traditional?"

Naomi laughed out loud. "Heavens no. Ari's as secular as you can get."

Rita thought for a moment. "That makes sense."

"Where do you fit in?" Naomi's perfect eyebrows arched while she waited.

"I don't know. Kinda lean toward Traditional, I guess."

"You'll find your way." Naomi patted Rita's hand. "Jacob will accept you no matter."

At that moment, Jacob poked his head through the doorway. "Did I hear my name?"

"Yes, we were talking about you," Rita teased.

Jacob stepped inside and greeted her warmly. She'd changed from her usual plain skirt and blouse to a flowing green floral dress that hugged her figure. He raised his eyebrows and smiled.

Naomi motioned toward an empty chair. "I'm explaining the difference between Orthodox and Traditional."

"Come to think of it." Rita smiled up at Jacob. "When we visited in New York last year I did see Orthodox men wearing black coats with the black felt hats. But I haven't seen any here."

"They prefer to live closer to Jerusalem," Jacob said. "We only have one synagogue here—it's not strict Orthodox—so they won't attend."

"Remember," Naomi said, "when that guy flew over the Temple Mount in 2020 and dropped that bomb on the mosque that was built over the ruins of our ancient temple? Orthodox from all over the world applied for Jewish citizenship, *aliyah*, to move here. They filled the suburbs around Jerusalem so they could help rebuild our Temple."

Rita unconsciously wrapped her hair around her finger, and asked, "What happened to that guy?"

Jacob grinned. "They never found him. He flew over, dropped the bomb, and escaped out over the Med. That happened twenty-five years ago. The Orthodox are still waiting to rebuild while the government tries to decide what to do about it."

Naomi moved Rita and Jacob into the living room before she went to check on the children.

"Since battle tensions have escalated," Jacob said as he sat on a sofa across from Rita, "women have been removed from perimeter guard duty. It's too dangerous. I guess I'll have less free time to spend with you, but it's okay with me to take more duty. I'd rather not see women do it."

"What do you mean by escalated?" It was a pleasant evening and Jacob didn't seem to be worried, but Rita felt her pulse quicken.

Naomi entered the room and put her hands on her ample hips. "Tell us what you know, Jacob. Please—five children are playing in the back rooms."

Jacob looked up at her. "You're the first house on this side of the fields, closest to the wall. It's important your house be protected, so two guards are stationed outside for tonight. Just a precaution, of course."

Rita and Naomi looked at each other, speechless.

Naomi sank into the sofa cushion next to Rita. "Before Dove left he set up alarms at the edge of the field to alert us of anyone approaching. Is there anything else we should do?"

Jacob pointed toward the picture window. "You have bullet-proof windows, don't you?"

Naomi's eyes widened. "Yes. We were going to put in metal doors. But we ran out of money."

"What else can she do to protect her house?" Rita asked. The thought of having guards outside sent flutters through her stomach.

"Levi told me this," Jacob said. "Military teams install nanotech netting, thin as a spider web, over the roof and house, down to the ground. It's cut away around the windows and doors. You'd never know it's there."

"That netting was invented a few years ago by an Israeli," Naomi told Rita proudly.

"Yeah," Jacob said, "and the inventor could have won fame and fortune for it, but the government classified it top secret. That stuff will repel bullets and even minimize the damage from rockets."

Rita shook her head. "I don't understand the physics."

"It's produced by carbon-to-carbon bonding at the molecular level, called Heck coupling," Jacob explained. "Projectiles can't penetrate it. A rocket will still collapse the roof, but it won't shatter. And even when the rocket explodes, the damage is less because the shrapnel is contained. Sometimes safe room walls are covered with it."

Rita turned to Naomi. "Have you and Dove considered putting in a safe room?"

"Of course. We talked about it after the rocket hit inside the moshav last Passover."

"If we really think something's going to happen," Jacob reminded them, "they'll open the underground shelter for women and children."

"Jacob," Rita asked, "could the teams put in metal doors for her?"

"I'll ask Levi when he gets back. In the meantime—"

"Please," Rita interrupted, "tell me this isn't serious."

"Unfortunately, we have to treat any threat seriously," he said. "Warlords from the Sinai sneak across the border. They like to attack when the men are away. And anyway, by next month our commander and the others should be back."

"But you don't think we have anything to worry about now?" Rita sat on the edge of the sofa, her hands clasped together, and ignored the reference to Ari.

"No, I really don't." His voice softened. "Now will you ladies give me your word that you won't worry?"

"Yes, of course," Rita said. "Let's change the subject and find something to celebrate over."

Naomi sprang from her chair and headed for the kitchen. "I'll make a nosh before dinner for us," she called out over her shoulder.

Rita turned to Jacob. "Maybe you could come over tomorrow night too."

"That depends. Will you be here?"

"I told Naomi I'd make the dinner tomorrow."

He tilted his head a little as he spoke. "Well, I could be back around meal time. If it's okay with Naomi."

"Absolutely. I'll tell her." Rita allowed herself to feel something close to happiness, an unfamiliar feeling.

"Maybe we can talk after dinner," Jacob said quietly. "Something I'd like to ask you."

"I told you we need our men," Naomi said from the doorway. "Doesn't it feel better when Jacob's here?"

Rita winked at Jacob. "Yeah, it does feel better."

Naomi sat in an overstuffed chair under the window, across from Rita and Jacob. She opened her mouth to say something at the moment the moshav warning siren sounded.

Jacob rushed to the window and peered past the side of the blackout curtain. A floodlight on a fig tree in the front yard illuminated a large area.

"My children!" Naomi started for the back of the house with Rita and Jacob following. Leah stood holding Little Ben when they entered the girls' bedroom. The twins ran to their mother. Little Ben started crying.

"Come, children," Jacob said in a firm voice. "This is what you practiced. You know what to do."

Leah called to the children and took them to the windowless playroom in the center of the house. "I am right here with you," she reassured them. "We're having a sleeping party. We'll rest here on our sleeping bags and tell stories."

Jacob nodded to Leah. "You're in charge here. Keep them on the floor."

He took Naomi's arm and guided her back into the main room with Rita following. "Naomi, do you and Dove keep weapons in the house?"

Naomi's face paled, but her voice stayed steady. "A Galil assault rifle."

"Get it, load it, bring it here."

A knock at the back door caused Rita to move toward it, but Jacob stepped in front of her. "No, Rita, I'll check it."

Two men stood at the door when Jacob answered it. "We live down the street," one man said. "We came to help Naomi."

"I know them." Rita nodded. "They're friends."

Jacob pulled the door open and they entered.

"I'm Eitan, this is Davi," the first man in said.

"Good that you carry rifles," Jacob noted.

"We're part of the moshav security force," Eitan said, closing the door. "Davi also has a handgun with him."

"I'm Jacob. Thanks for coming." He led them to the living room where Rita and Naomi sat on the sofa.

Naomi's phone rang and she put it on speaker. "Uzzi here. My boys spotted enemy men in the north fields outside Kol Shofar. Maybe a hundred of them. Gotta go. Uzzi out."

Naomi's face paled as she loaded a magazine into the rifle and used the corner of her apron to wipe the sight clean.

Jacob motioned for her to set it behind the sofa.

Naomi stashed the rifle and headed through the arch. "I'm going to my children."

"Stay down, Naomi," Jacob called out after her.

Rita picked up Dove's rifle from behind the sofa, checked the mechanisms, and looked through the sight.

"Can you shoot that?" Jacob asked from across the room.

She looked up. "I can."

Jacob went to a tan square on the living room wall next to the picture window. "This looks like an electrical source box, but it's called a cutout." He pulled off the metal cover to reveal a small hole with a telescopic wide-angle lens above it.

"I know." She inserted the rifle through the opening. "I've been on guard duty."

Then he spoke in a tone of voice she'd never heard him use. "Shoot anything that moves in that field. You understand?"

She nodded.

"Eitan, you and Davi go watch out the back-room windows," Jacob ordered. "Call out if you see anything."

Jacob picked up his assault rifle from where he left it by the front door and took it off safety. He moved near Rita. "I won't let anything happen to you," he whispered.

Rita gritted her teeth and took a deep breath.

"Is this your first battle?" he asked. "What we're facing now?"

She heard her voice in a distant fog say yes at the same time the phone rang.

Jacob took the call for Naomi. "Oh, Rita," he said when he finished, "the enemy is getting closer. They're outside section N-16."

Rita's face paled, her hands became clammy. "That's the secret entrance."

Naomi rushed in and went to Jacob. "Is the shelter open? Is it safe here? What should I do?"

Rita thought of the children crouched under blankets in the center of the house. "Creator, guide us to protect these innocent ones," she prayed.

An explosion above shook the house with a deafening roar, and Naomi screamed.

"Eitan, Davi," Jacob shouted in the direction of the arch.

Both came running.

Jacob pointed toward the front window. "They're using grenade launchers—stay away from the windows. Davi, go find out what's happening and report back. Make it quick." Jacob nodded toward the back door and Davi disappeared.

Jacob put the next call from Uzzi on speaker. "They made it inside! Armed men are coming through our eucalyptus grove toward the moshav. The guard posted there doesn't respond."

Rita listened for threatening sounds from outside. She couldn't distinguish anything unusual. She pushed her fear aside and gripped her rifle.

Jacob went to the archway and removed the curtain obstructing a clear view to the back of the house.

Eitan ran to open the dead bolt when Davi came to the back door, banging and shouting.

"The enemy is pushed back," Davi said, running into the room. "Moshav security formed a line of engagement at the edge of the eucalyptus grove." He glanced over at Naomi. "Women with children are going to the underground shelter."

"That's us, we're fighting back," Jacob called out to Rita over the muffled sounds of rapid gunfire. He ordered Naomi to gather her children and leave immediately.

While Naomi and her children fled out the back door with Davi, a couple in their early thirties entered. They identified themselves before Jacob closed and bolted the door. The man, Saul, was part of moshav security. The nicely dressed woman was his frightened girlfriend.

"Lilith doesn't want to be alone," Saul explained. "And I gave my word to Dove I would come here if we got trouble in the moshav."

They walked quickly to the front room.

"Where's your weapon, Saul?" Jacob asked.

"I gave it to my sister to take to the shelter." Saul looked toward the back of the house. "Dove keeps an extra rifle here I can use."

"Can Lilith shoot?" Jacob asked. "Does she have any kind of training?"

"She can't really do anything." He shook his head. "Lilith's a lawyer."

"Eitan." Jacob pointed. "Stand on this side of the archway and give your pistol to Saul. Rita and I will take the cutouts. Saul, stand on the other side of the arch."

Time seemed to slow down while Rita waited. She felt calm, and for the first time in her life felt she had a purpose, a reason for being right where she stood.

Jacob returned to the window near her. She noticed him looking and managed to smile back. He'd hinted the day before that he wanted to talk about something important. And he mentioned it again before the siren.

"Thank you for getting Naomi and the children out," she whispered.

Jacob lowered his rifle and moved close. "If you want me to get you out of here, tell me now. You still have time to go."

Rita shook her head. "I'm here for the duration."

"It's going to be a long night," Lilith said from across the room.

"I pray we make it through this night to another morning," Jacob whispered to Rita.

Fifteen minutes later, the phone rang and Rita clicked the speaker button. "Uzzi here. They broke through our ranks. Too many to hold. They're making it past us. Get ready." She felt her chest tighten and forced herself to breathe.

Saul went to Jacob and whispered something.

Lilith started to cry. Jacob told her to get behind the sofa next to the windowless east wall of the living room. He motioned to Rita. "You stand next to me. Give your rifle to Saul."

She wanted to ask questions but didn't want to distract him. She handed her rifle to Saul and moved close to Jacob. He touched her hand. "We're going to make it," he said through gritted teeth.

Rita felt the tension in the room. She closed her eyes for a moment and tried to control her breathing.

"This won't last long," Jacob called out. From under his vest he withdrew a small, sheathed dagger and extended the handle to Rita. "Take this." His voice was low.

She shook her head.

"Take it," he repeated. "I know what we're facing. You don't."

When they heard screams from the backyard, Rita instinctively moved behind Jacob. Without thinking, she did what she was told. She took the dagger and set it on the window sill next to her. She felt numb.

"Get ready," Jacob called out. He aimed his rifle at the archway past Eitan and Saul.

Two simultaneous explosions rocked the house. Rita heard glass breaking as concussion grenades flew through the bedroom windows. The noise shattered the silence the way rolling thunder closes in before a storm. Frozen with shock, Rita watched dust pour into the living room, bringing with it the acrid smell of burnt powder.

The back door suddenly broke open and crashed down. Three men stood firing submachine guns into the room.

Eitan and Saul crumpled to the floor.

Before Jacob could shoot back, the three staggered forward and fell, shot from behind. Blood slowly pooled around them.

Rita heard excited shouts outside. Peering though the side window, she saw enemy men dressed in long tunics running past the house as though being chased. From the backyard she soon recognized shouting in Hebrew, G-d's own sweet words.

chapter 8

JACOB GRABBED RITA by the shoulders to get her attention as bursts of gunfire erupted outside Naomi's house. "Stay away from the window," he shouted before he rushed out through the back door, leaping over the three enemy bodies lying there.

Crouching behind the sofa with Lilith, Rita felt her heart pound like a war drum against her chest. Her ears hurt and her eyes burned.

"What's happening?" Lilith cried out.

"The fighting's moving back." Rita cupped her hands around Lilith's young face and looked her straight in the eyes. "Don't move from behind here, and don't look out for any reason."

Lilith's eyes widened in her already pale face. "Why not?"

"It's not safe. Give me your word."

"Okay." Lilith pressed against the back of the couch.

Rita tried to make her legs work but she felt weak all over. She crawled to the front of the sofa and pulled herself up onto the cushions to look around. Rifle fire popped and crackled in the distance. Everything seemed to be happening in slow motion. She noticed Jacob's handgun by the front window and crawled the short distance to retrieve it.

Sitting with her back against the wall, and her legs straight out in front, she checked the pistol to make sure it was loaded.

Using both hands, she held it on her lap, pointed at the archway. She tried not to look at Eitan and Saul, or the dark red blood slowly surrounding their bodies.

Two moshav men came to the back and pulled the dead attackers away from the doorway. They approached the front room with weapons drawn. One man asked, "Is everyone all right in here?"

Rita nodded.

"It's over now," he said when he saw her.

She laid Jacob's pistol on the floor next to her. One man stayed with her while the other went into the back rooms. He returned with blankets to cover the bodies of Eitan and Saul in the archway.

Lilith peeked out and started crying.

The man with Rita, his hand on the gun at his side, looked at Lilith. "Are you hurt?"

"She's not hurt," Rita answered for her. She pointed to Saul on the floor and motioned toward Lilith.

The two men moved toward the back door. "We have to go now to inspect the next house," one called back. As they left, a dozen neighbors entered, a few at a time, through the broken back door into the living room to check on Lilith as word spread about Saul and Eitan.

Jacob walked in behind them. Blood stained his face and shirt. He extended his hand and pulled Rita up. "It's over now. The murderers are gone." He put his arms around her and hugged her.

Closing her eyes and melting against his chest, she felt calm next to his muscular body. Remembering the blood on his shirt, she pulled away.

Shoshona, with some of the neighbors, brought Lilith out from behind the sofa. Rita heard her sobs turn to a sad wail.

Jacob directed two men in the room to get stretchers for the dead. "We have to get them out of here before Naomi returns with her children."

The two men left. A short time later they returned with Davi and two lightweight aluminum stretchers. People in the room gathered around to sing a prayer of remembrance for the two fallen warriors. Rita felt grateful that she knew the song from synagogue services as she solemnly joined the voices filling the room.

Osay Shalom bim romav
u'ya say Shalom aleinu
vi'a kol Yisrael.
Veim aru, veim aru amain.

"Jacob," Shoshona said quietly, "we have no team available to make certain Eitan's and Saul's blood stays with their bodies. We can't move them."

"We'll do it ourselves," Jacob told her. "The *Za'ka* teams will be busy all night."

Davi stepped forward. "I've done this before. In the field." Davi took Shoshona aside and they spoke for a few minutes. Then they cleaned around the men thoroughly before lifting them gently onto the stretchers. Shoshona placed the blood-soaked cloths, to be buried with each man, on the stretchers next to them.

Jacob stepped forward next to Rita and raised a hand. "These courageous men gave their lives willingly for our lives to go on. Our gratitude to them is boundless. May the Source of their courage inspire us."

Others murmured their gratitude while Lilith continued to sob.

"Please join me now in the *Mourners Kaddish*." Jacob looked around the room before he spoke. "*Vit kadal, vit kadash . . .*" He led them through the familiar final prayer.

Rita said the words along with him. Four men picked up the two stretchers. Silence filled the room as they left with a weeping Lilith following.

All the explosions and the blood left Rita feeling sick to her stomach. Jacob found a small bottle of grape juice in the kitchen. She finished it.

"The children are asleep in the shelter," Jacob told her. "Naomi decided to bring them back in the morning."

A few more people stepped in from outside. Naomi was moshav leader, so her house became a natural gathering place. These last arrivals seemed to buzz with excitement—something about Ari.

Rita listened, but couldn't hear what they said. "What did Ari do?" she finally asked Jacob.

"Commander and his men brought me one more night of precious life," Jacob answered. "With you."

Then Ari walked in. The people around her cheered. She felt numb.

Jacob brought two chairs out from the kitchen. "Want to stay for a little while, Rita?"

She sat in the chair he offered.

Jacob extended his hand when Ari approached. "Well done, Commander."

"Todah." Looking past Jacob he said, "Shalom, Rita."

She cleared her throat. "Shalom, Ari."

"Ari," Jacob asked, "is my brother with you?"

"Yes." Ari looked away from Rita to Jacob. "Levi's at the shelter helping the women."

"Commander," Davi called out from across the room, "tell us how you stopped the enemy."

One of the men brought a chair for Ari. The blackout curtains remained drawn tight, as always at night. Shoshona lit candles and placed them around the room. Electrical power was out.

Eli, an older man who looked the part of a seasoned warrior, sat next to Ari. "We were en route here on a troop carrier. Your commander organized an advance group."

"About eighty men came in with me," Ari added.

"You tell it." Eli thumped him on the shoulder. "You deserve the credit."

Ari shook his head. "No. The men deserve the recognition. And praise to Hashem who led us to this triumph over our enemies."

People murmured agreement throughout the room. Some called it a miracle.

"We brought the carrier *Sharon* down from Haifa," Ari told them and a hush fell on the room. "We were sitting about four hours from shore awaiting orders when word came in through our communications relay."

"From our satellite network," Jacob whispered to Rita.

"Muslim Brotherhood soldiers pouring in through a rupture in the security wall along the Sinai border were attacking towns in the Negev," Ari told them. "When we observed a flash of light on the shoreline, we boarded a transport and put the engine on full throttle. Levi connected loudspeakers to the engine room to make us sound like a whole fleet coming in."

"That was Commander's idea," Eli broke in.

"We pushed that ship hard," Ari continued. "We made it to the beach in about three hours, jumped off, and ran in without using the tunnels."

"Didn't you run into anyone on the way in?" a man behind Rita asked.

Eli chuckled. "We ran over anyone in the way."

Ari joined in the laughter with many others.

"Tell us more," a short man wearing a skullcap called out.

"Well," Ari said, "we spread out as if leading a company into the olive grove. We caught armed Bedouins in the eucalyptus trees outside Kol Shofar. We killed them. The secret entrance stood open—more Bedouins were inside the wall. We took care of them and then fought our way through the moshav." He looked over at Rita when he finished.

She lowered her eyes and rested her hand on Jacob's arm. "Did the underground shelter hold up?" she whispered.

"Yes," Jacob answered and covered her hand with his. "During the night they ran right over the top of it. Our camouflage worked."

From the corner of her eye, Rita watched Ari move toward them.

"I want to go home now," she told Jacob.

"I could take you home," Ari offered.

She pushed her chair back and stood. "What about Naomi's door?" she asked, trying to change the subject. "We can't leave it gaping open."

Ari gestured toward the back. "My men will board it up tonight before they leave, I assure you."

Jacob stood, almost between them. "I'll take her home, Commander."

Rita mumbled shalom and walked to the front door with Jacob. She could feel Ari watching as she left.

The next day Rita learned from the kitchen grapevine that the invaders blew up a few buildings and roads, but overall damage had been minimal. The telephone cell tower and electrical generators for the moshav were down.

Officials lacked a casualty total, but everyone knew someone killed or wounded. A chill went down Rita's spine when she saw Uzzi's name on the list of the dead. She hadn't known him well, but she'd seen him and his wife at synagogue services.

Rita took a fresh loaf of challah down from a kitchen shelf and covered it with a cloth from a nearby drawer. "Why so many extra loaves of bread today?" she asked a woman standing by the main stove.

"Shabbat is tomorrow, and we have almost a hundred extra soldiers to feed at the dining hall. You know," the woman said with a big smile, "the men who came in last night during the moshav attack."

"Of course," Rita said on her way out the door.

Relieved to find that the solar-powered car she borrowed from Tarah was available, she drove to the moshav in the late afternoon. No one seemed to be home at Naomi's. She parked the car at the curb and walked up to the front entryway to be sure.

A soldier walked by with a rifle slung over his shoulder. Rita recognized him from a silver-framed photo she'd seen. Jacob's younger brother.

He smiled and walked over, saying, "Hi, my name is Levi." With his rosy cheeks and curly brown hair, he looked more like a college student than a highly trained soldier.

"Shalom, I'm Rita. I'm looking for the family who lives here."

He motioned toward Naomi's door. "I shot the attackers here last night."

A shiver went down her spine as she remembered the door breaking open. "I'm grateful you arrived in time," she said.

"I only got one of them," he clarified. "Commander Ari shot the other two."

She couldn't think of anything to say. *He doesn't seem to know who I am. That I'm seeing his brother.* "Here, take this," she stammered, "for Shabbat." She handed him the bread, and he gratefully accepted.

"Anyway," Levi said, "Leah and her family went to stay with relatives on the other side of the moshav. I could take you there, if you want."

Rita shook her head.

"Well then, good Shabbis." Levi waved and walked away.

Rita returned the borrowed car and started the kilometer-long walk home. What Levi told her ran through her mind with every step. *Ari saved my life.*

She arrived home to find Jacob waiting in the great room. With a warm smile, he placed his hand on her right arm and leaned close. "You look beautiful tonight," he whispered.

"It's good to see you, Jacob." She managed a smile, her thoughts still on Ari.

"I have to go soon," he told her. "Shabbat notwithstanding, I still have duties. So, when can I see you again?"

"I don't know. I can't think clearly right now." Her cheeks felt flushed, hot. "I think I'm coming down with something."

"I understand. I'm sorry you went through that ordeal. Take some time. You'll call me when you're ready."

Ari stood in the doorway. He cleared his throat and they noticed him.

"Commander, are you looking for me?" Jacob didn't move an inch from Rita, and he didn't move his hand from her arm.

"It can wait," Ari said abruptly. He spun around and left.

chapter 9

ONE THOUSAND TROOPS disembarked from the Israeli Defense Forces troop carrier *Sharon* a week after Ari and his men saved the moshav. Half the men were assigned to the military barracks. The others were invited into homes throughout the community. Ari felt a new surge of confidence with their arrival.

Days after solemn burials for the victims of the attack, men from the moshav began to rebuild. Hundreds of IDF soldiers joined the effort, and neighborhoods soon buzzed with energy as teams cleared the wreckage and brought in supplies. The soldiers wielded hammers during the day. At night they ate home-cooked meals and flirted earnestly with the single women. Ari drove by the moshav every evening to view the progress. What he saw pleased him.

Dove slipped in late one night a few days after the *Sharon* arrived. Two days later, Ari called an intelligence meeting for a dozen people.

At Ari's request, Dove asked Rita to attend in Devorah's place. "We always include at least one woman from the community—it's part of our culture," he told her on the phone. "Shoshona will be there as well."

The following morning Rita arrived early for the meeting at Ari's compound. She stepped through the entry doors to be cleared by the guard inside. Two men stood talking in a hallway outside the conference room adjacent to Ari's quarters. About a dozen people filled the room, standing in groups. Dove, standing near Shoshona, looked over and crossed the room toward her when she entered.

"I'm sorry about the condition of your house," she said.

"The house—it doesn't matter. My family is safe." He touched her arm. "I understand you helped keep them from harm."

"I didn't do anything," she protested. "Honest."

"You stayed with them, and that's something."

Everyone sat around the conference table when Ari rapped on it to begin. "First," he said, "a welcome to Yalon, who speaks for Captain Baruch of the carrier group."

Yalon, a large polar bear of a man, sat straight and carried an air of authority. Closely cropped thick white hair framed his deeply wrinkled face. A scar ran down his cheek from just under his right eye to his chin. He nodded, and said, "Please continue." His gruff voice matched his demeanor.

"What we went through the other night," Ari told them, "could have been much worse. Intelligence reports indicate the Islamic Coalition is planning to ignite an EMP over the Negev. They've already tested it, and they failed."

Several people in the room chuckled nervously.

Rita tugged gently on Dove's arm.

"That's a special nuclear bomb," he whispered.

"This type of Electro Magnetic Pulse bomb," Ari told them, "is a small nuclear device exploded in the upper atmosphere directly above the target population. It's designed to immediately disable all electronics, including communications."

"The effects are devastating to the target population," Dove added. "An EMP would be similar to a major solar flare hitting the earth." He motioned toward his first officer, Moshe.

"Car engines won't start and planes would drop from the skies," Moshe explained. "Power generators would fry, along with equipment and devices wired to source energy plates. Our electronic command center would be useless, except as a bomb shelter. An atmospheric explosion would damage our satellites beyond repair."

"What about our defensive missile shield?" Daniel asked.

"The shield will be rendered inoperative, and our smart weapons won't launch," Moshe answered.

"In other words," Zev said, "we'll be instantly thrust into the same level of technology as our Israelite ancestors. The Israelites against a madman with a nuclear bomb aimed at us."

"Do you mean the Babylonian madman, or the psychopath ruling Russia?" Ari asked.

Several people around the table chuckled at his reference. Ari noticed that Rita wasn't one of them.

"This might be the beginning of a much larger offensive," Dove suggested. "From the com chatter alone, intelligence suspects an impending attack."

"The failed EMP may have been another test," Ari said. "They could perfect their delivery system while we wait. In the meantime, our defense forces are pushing back along the Jordanian border."

"That's good news," Shoshona said.

"Unfortunately," Ari continued, "that means the men who arrived on the carrier are needed in the north for the fight heating up on the border with Persyria."

"Commander," Daniel said, "Yalon and the carrier group haven't even been here for a month."

"Eight hundred troops are expected in the Negev soon from Eliat," Dove reminded them. "They'll replace the soldiers going back to Haifa."

Shoshona held up her hand. "When are they expected to arrive?"

Ari looked around the table. "In two to three weeks. But the carrier group has to deploy north in five days."

Shoshona's eyes widened. "Can you delay them?"

"You realize," Daniel broke in, "that leaves us vulnerable. A troop carrier is too big to hide. Shoshona's right. You should keep them here another week."

Ari looked at Yalon. "Tell them."

"This deployment order is not the decision of my captain. Captain Baruch protested, to no avail."

"Obviously," Ari added, "we are susceptible to an attack from the time the *Sharon* leaves until reinforcements get here. We have to hold out until they arrive."

"We should have evacuated the children," Shoshona said loudly.

Everyone began talking until Ari banged the table with his fist. "Now, you're going to hear ways to increase community security, so pay attention." He gestured abruptly to Dove.

Moshe handed Dove a list of suggestions an intelligence analyst prepared.

Dove took the paper and read: "Kol Shofar leadership should require all perimeter buildings to install motion-detection lights facing the security wall. Each household should store six liters of water and enough dry and canned food for five to ten days for each person. Additional water and food for pets and livestock should be included as necessary."

Zev said, "We should allow each household to pick up a case of bicarbonate of soda from the community warehouse for their first-aid kits."

Ari nodded. "Add it to the list."

"Baking soda?" Rita asked.

"Very useful," Zev answered from across the table. "We used to make soap from the roots of certain plants. Now we recommend using baking soda in place of soap to save the water we used to produce the plants. People use it to brush their teeth and wash clothes."

"And it's great for treating the children's rashes and insect bites," Shoshona added. "We make a paste using aloe juice, or even water, and apply the paste over the rash or bite."

"If you're finished with your first-aid seminar." Ari cleared his throat and the room went silent as Dove continued.

"Keep a good supply of candles and lighters handy in addition to solar flashlights. Leave boots and a change of clothes next to each person's bed." Dove laid the paper on the table. "That's about it. We can include instructions to set up safe rooms with rolls of plastic, duct tape, water, and emergency supplies."

"I can provide a copy to the group leaders for community-wide distribution," Shoshona offered.

Ari nodded toward Moshe. On a wall map, Moshe outlined recent Islamic uprising locations in Turkey and North Africa. Zev gave a brief report about the high cost and difficult logistics of attaining smart weapons.

"We'll have a new intelligence report at next week's brief," Ari said. "In the meantime, stay sharp and take care." With that he closed the meeting.

Rita, her face tight with worry, caught up with Zev on his way out. "Is this as bad as it sounds?"

"We can't live in fear, Rita. We're Jews. We have to do what we think is right and pay with our lives if necessary. But believe me when I tell you that Ari is the best there is. He has the heart and mind of a hero. As long as we have him, we have a chance to prevail."

They started to go out the door together but Ari walked over. "I need to speak with Rita for a moment," he said.

Zev said shalom and left.

"What do you want?" she asked.

"I just want to talk." He leaned closer. "I could walk you back to your quarters."

She turned and stepped into the hall while he locked the door.

"It's over half a kilometer to your building," he said as they went down the front steps. "I'll get a car if you'd rather drive."

She didn't answer right away. The late-morning sun had started to scorch anything not in shade.

Ari looked around. "It's going to be a hot one—strange weather this time of year." Motioning toward a car at the curb, he walked over and opened the passenger door. She got in and said she was grateful for the ride.

They drove in silence for the few minutes it took to reach her building. He turned off the motor and looked at her. "Don't be mad at me, Rita." His voice was soft.

"I'm not mad. You don't know anything." She opened her door and stepped out.

He scrambled to get out and came around to her side.

They walked into the courtyard leading to the garden. Stone benches sat under the pergola, now covered with fragrant winter jasmine. Dried purple grapes hung on a nearby vine.

"What's on your mind, Ari? Did you come here to apologize again?" She sat on one of the benches.

Ari sat on the other bench. "The truth is that I miss you, Rita. You were on my mind while I was gone. Three months is a long time to think things over." He looked down briefly and then met her gaze directly. "I know I've made mistakes."

She looked into his eyes. "Is that what you wanted to tell me?"

"What I want to know is," he leaned closer, "do I have a chance?"

She studied the vines growing along the pergola. "I don't know anything anymore. I thought I was going to die when those three murderers burst through the back door. Then I found out it was you who saved us."

"I'll only take the credit if it means you forgive me." He studied her face, wondering how this small, intense woman could cause such a cascade of emotion to pour through him.

Rita stood and put the strap of her bag over her left shoulder. "I have kitchen duty today." She looked at her watch. "I'm probably late already."

He walked with her to the building entrance. As she started to move up the front steps, he touched her elbow. "Will I see you again?"

She stopped, and turned to face him. "We live in the same compound, Ari. You'll see me again."

A smile spread across his face before he turned and went down the steps.

For the next week, the *Sharon* prepared to leave for Haifa. Ari went to the carrier to meet with Captain Baruch, a short, stout man in his fifties who looked like he could easily pick up a small car. He had kind gray eyes, and Ari liked him.

"I wish you could stay longer, for obvious reasons," Ari said.

"I'm leaving a hundred of my best men with you, including Yalon," Baruch told him. "That's all I can spare. You understand."

"I'll take what I can get, Captain. A hundred men will help us. Two hundred would help more."

Baruch's expressionless face softened. "Yes, of course. But sometimes we have to look at the reality in front of us and just accept it."

Ari frowned at the thought.

The night prior to the carrier departure, Ari drove to Dove's house without calling. His stomach felt tight—he wanted to relax and get his mind off Baruch leaving.

Dove answered Ari's knock. "Anything wrong?"

"No, sorry. I was out driving around."

Dove opened the door wide. "Rita's here with Naomi, and Levi helped us move our stuff back home, so he's here with Jacob. Come in, join us."

Ari followed Dove into the kitchen and sat across from Rita. He sighed inwardly, remembering the fragrance in her hair.

Naomi brought a platter of sliced raw vegetables, grapes, and dates to the table. She placed them next to a basket of flat-bread with a bowl of garbanzo bean garlic spread, set out napkins, and insisted everyone should eat more.

"Do you mean right now," Dove teased. "Or that people should eat more in general?"

Naomi laughed. "Both," she cried out.

Her answer gave everyone a good laugh.

Dove brought out two bottles of homemade pomegranate wine while Naomi went to a cupboard and pulled out wine glasses. She arranged the glasses while Dove opened the bottles.

"I was explaining to Rita why our taxes used to be so high," Naomi said with her hands dancing alongside her words.

Dove looked up from filling the glasses with sparkling red wine. "To pay for the other Garden communities." He poured grape juice into the last glass and handed it to Leah when she joined them at the table. Slim and delicate-looking, Leah moved gracefully into her chair. Dark brown hair like her parents' framed her sweet, sixteen-year-old face.

"Are there more villages built like this one?" Rita asked.

"Kol Shofar was the first in a promised series of ten walled communities," Dove explained, "each covering approximately six square kilometers."

Naomi nodded. "They were going to be connected to each other with new roads. We paid taxes for the roads, but they never built them."

"The people waited almost five decades for the other nine to be constructed," Levi added. "It never happened. Ancient artifacts were found at the site for the second project and construction stopped."

"What kinds of artifacts?" Rita asked. "I love hearing about this."

Leah smiled broadly. "I know the answer," she said eagerly. "Pottery pieces and metal tools dating back almost three thousand years were uncovered at the construction site. But other artifacts date back even further."

Rita encouraged her to continue.

"My schoolteacher says that ancient Negev Hebrew is the mother tongue of human language. Old stone tablets with Hebrew names were found at the place where the Sumerians lived six thousand years ago on the plains of Nineveh. But the oldest artifacts are objects with proto-Hebrew letters found forty years ago at Gobekli-Tepe in Turkey. They date back almost twelve thousand years."

Rita praised her knowledge on artifacts. The others agreed. Leah was becoming an expert.

"I took a semester at school on this subject," Leah told them proudly.

They talked about everything except the carrier group departure. The wine and nosh were finished after an hour.

Jacob and Levi stood at the same time and Jacob motioned toward his brother. "I've got to get this soldier back to barracks. Commander, could you see Rita home for me?"

A smile crept across Ari's face. "Sure."

Naomi looked at Dove, but he kept his gaze fixed on Ari.

Rita stayed seated at the table until Jacob sauntered off with Levi. Then Ari said shalom and stood.

Without thinking, he slid his hand around her waist as he walked her to his car. The short ride to her building was quiet until he parked, turned off the motor, and looked at her. "Rita, are you sorry you came here?" His voice was low. "To Kol Shofar?"

"Most of my life," she said quietly," I didn't think I belonged anywhere." The corners of her mouth turned up slightly. "Kol Shofar is more than a community. It's a dream—a place to repair the world. And it's my dream too. This is my home now."

Ari slowly opened the car door. For once, he didn't know what he was feeling and he didn't want to think about it.

The next day the carrier *Sharon* departed. Ari went to the underground command center in the early morning to begin defense planning with Moshe. They reviewed intelligence reports for most of the day while Dove and Zev coordinated logistics for the carrier group.

Streetlights twinkled in a dark, moonless sky when Ari emerged. He phoned Zev from his car and drove directly to his house. Zev sat waiting while Ari walked into the living room and handed him a report.

Zev read it and looked up. "This is serious. Does Dove know?"

"Yes," Ari said. "I left a message earlier."

"I'll try again." Zev phoned Dove, spoke, and hung up. "He's coming right over. With Jacob."

Ari sat on a sofa and spread papers on the coffee table. He looked up. "Why is Jacob at Dove's house?"

Zev glanced at Ari. "Don't know."

A short time later, Dove arrived with Jacob and Rita.

Ari gave a curt nod and started talking as they entered. "We've just learned that fighting has broken out in some of the mixed neighborhoods in Samaria and Judea. And a terrorist plot to bomb Ben Gurion Airport was narrowly averted."

Dove sat in one of the upholstered chairs ringing one side of the coffee table. "This morning's intelligence report indicated that Persyrian battleships are moving into the Mediterranean Sea."

"Moshe showed me that report." Ari pressed his lips together. "This is going to be a waiting game. And the wait won't be long."

Rita sat next to Jacob. "What does this mean?" she asked.

Ari met her gaze, then looked away. "It means we are going to initiate operations at the underground command center." He turned to Dove. "Start calling your people tonight. I want personnel to staff the center by the end of the week."

Zev leaned toward Rita. "I'll explain the function of the emergency command and control center. It's located next to the underground complex where Naomi and her children went during the moshav attack. We built it in the middle of our community as part of our defense strategy."

While Zev explained, Ari took Dove to the kitchen for a private word.

"Rita has clearance now as an intel analyst and I want her included in the staffing of the command center," he said.

Dove nodded. "I'll see to it."

"We expect an attack within the month." Shadows under Ari's eyes told of a string of long days and sleepless nights. "I'm giving the order to distribute weapons to the families staying above ground."

"Approximately four hundred women with children will be notified to report to the underground safe complex," Dove confirmed. "Everyone without safe basements will be ordered to evacuate to community shelters. I'll tell Shoshona to alert the squad leaders."

They joined the others in Zev's living room in time to hear him tell Rita, "The immediate threat comes from local Bedouin groups fighting each other and the Egyptian Arabs for control of supply routes from the Sinai through the Negev over to the Jordanian border. Our towns and roads keep getting caught in the crossfire of their human-trafficking business."

"That's right," Dove said as he sat across from Ari. "And we believe the Bedouins to be armed with second-generation weapons. The Egyptians have better munitions."

Rita shook her head slowly. "I don't understand why Islamics won't allow us to live in their midst. Even in our own country."

"They can't," Jacob said. "It's cultural, not religious. They treat women as property, we accept women as equal citizens."

"Yes," Zev said. "And they teach their young that these are Islamic lands and that we are invaders. It starts with the children. They grow up hating us and refusing to accept Jewish authority over Jewish lands."

Ari felt anger rise up inside. "That's the root of our current dilemma. They believe these lands belong to them because they claim they once conquered this region."

"That's right," Rita said. "That's what the head security official from the airport told me." Her eyes glistened with tears. "He said they'll never stop."

Jacob turned to her. "It's getting late—we should leave now."

"Rita," Ari said when she stood, "don't worry. We'll make it through this."

chapter 10

For Ari, the week following the carrier departure was filled with briefings and meetings during the day and reviewing intelligence reports at night.

On Saturday night, workers draped mirror-net camouflage over a walkway trellis outside a community room, disguising the entrance to the underground complex. An hour later the exodus of women, children, and elders began to those subterranean quarters. By dawn, nearly one thousand would be settled in safety, sequestered deep below the community greenhouse.

After the successful relocation of the community's most vulnerable, Ari turned his attention to staffing the command center. He called Dove the following afternoon and asked him to stop by.

"I'm taking Rita home," Dove told him. "She helped Naomi get ready to go to the shelter."

"You should come here first." Ari didn't give a reason. "I'm in my conference room at home."

Minutes later, Dove and Rita arrived. "What is it, Ari?" Dove asked. "We came right over."

Ari shuffled through some papers and motioned for them to sit. "I don't have a good feeling. I need you to tell me how long we can hold out."

Dove sat in a chair across from Ari. "You've seen Moshe's estimates."

"Perimeters are too broad." Ari motioned toward an empty chair at the table for Rita.

"I'm due to go down to the com center." Dove looked at his watch. "Do you want me to delay? Try to rework the estimates?"

Ari looked at Rita. "You did statistical analysis for the election campaigns of several American politicians, so you can do this for me. Yes?" He noticed stress lines around her eyes.

"Sure she can," Dove said. "And I can go to the com center." He stood and threw a hand up in the air as he went out the door.

Ari took a stack of papers and slid them across the table. "This is a list of our available weapons and where they're located."

She read over the papers. "What do you want me to do with it?"

"The next paper is a diagram of our community showing where our men will be stationed during an attack. I need you to put that together with the ammunition inventory and tell me how long we can defend ourselves."

"This will be a rough estimate." She pulled blank paper and a calculator from the center of the table, took a pen from her purse, and started to work.

Ari watched her for a few minutes before going to an adjoining room to make phone calls.

Three hours passed before he came out to see her still working and sat across from her. "How long?" His voice lacked discernible emotion.

She finished writing and set the pen down. "The variables are based on how intense the assault is and how long it takes the soldiers to get here."

Ari nodded. "I understand. I need an educated guess."

"Two days, maybe three."

He swore softly in Hebrew.

Rita stretched her shoulders. "The tension in the air feels like static electricity before a storm."

"Most leaders feel charged up and restless before a big battle," he told her. "But not me, I feel calm and ready."

She looked at him for a moment, and smiled. "I should go," she said. "Dove told me to report to the community room tonight, and you probably have things to do."

"You'll be assigned to Dove's staff for the next three days," Ari told her. "But you'll report directly to me. How soon can you be ready to go?"

"I'm ready now." She sounded confident, even excited.

"Good." He stood and picked up a bulletproof vest from the edge of the table. "Rita, you have to prepare both physically and emotionally for what is surely coming."

She paled. "Is this really necessary?"

He set the vest down and held her hand for a moment. "Fear can creep into your veins like a sedative you can't control. I've seen what's left after a successful enemy attack on families with children. No matter what you see on television, nothing can prepare a person for the shock of seeing it for real. You must be ready."

Rita took a deep breath and tried on the vest.

They crossed the room to the archway leading to the outer door, where they paused. Moved by sudden impulse, Ari put his arms around her shoulders. "Military custom, you know, before a battle begins." He leaned in slowly and kissed her.

She relaxed in his arms. "So you think it starts tomorrow?"

He gazed off into the distance, still tasting her on his lips. "Yes, I think it starts tomorrow."

A soldier knocked on the open door. "It's getting dark out, Commander. Time to leave."

Ari let his arms drop away from Rita. He pointed to his brown canvas bag by the door for the driver. "Rita," he said quietly, "you might as well report for duty now. Come with me."

The driver stopped by Rita's building on the way to the community center. She ran up the front steps in the winter cold, and went in for her overnight bag.

They arrived to find the community room filled with people waiting near the front door for an elevator to the underground command center. Ari led Rita to the back wall where he entered a number code into a biometric keypad. He placed his thumb over the top, a door opened, and they stepped inside.

"We don't have to wait with the others," he said. "This is for officers and the intelligence staff."

The elevator descended several floors before stopping. Then the doors opened with a swoosh into a large room with futuristic decor. Everything from the lighted wall panels to the utilitarian molded furniture was designed to facilitate ease of operation.

Ari greeted a dozen people in an open area of the center before taking Rita to the main operations room. He sat in front of a monitor and smiled. "What do you think?"

Rita sat in a comfortable padded chair next to his. "It's amazing down here."

On the opposite side of the room, two analysts on roller chairs watched banks of holographic images covering every angle of sight into the community grounds. They greeted their commander warmly, then turned back to their displays.

Ari motioned toward the east wall. "On the other side is the underground shelter. Over there is the lifeblood of our community, the women and children."

"Commander, you're needed in the back," a woman with fine features and large hazel eyes said as she approached.

Ari stood. "Rita, come with me." He smiled. "You can take the vest off now."

She quickly unbuckled it, set it on the back of a chair, and followed Ari down a corridor illuminated by yellow battery-powered lights.

The woman walked next to Ari. She turned to Rita and said, "Shalom, I'm Monica." Short, smooth auburn hair framed her face.

Ari glanced at her. "What is it?"

"Increased activity early this morning in the Maccabiah town square, Commander."

"How could you know that?" Rita asked.

Ari walked faster. "We have two microscopic cameras hidden in the main enemy neighborhood."

Monica turned to Rita. "You know about the Mossada?"

Rita nodded. "They no longer patrol the Islamic parts of Maccabiah dressed like their women," Monica explained, "because any unaccompanied females walking around became targets. One of our agents was caught a month ago. Her battered body was found a few days later dumped on a main road outside Jerusalem."

"The surveillance patrols were terminated immediately," Ari added.

Rita was almost jogging to keep pace with Ari and Monica. "That's terrible."

"Before the other agents left our area," Monica said, "they hid the cameras for us."

"That's not all they did." Ari stopped in front of a door and leaned close to an eye scanner. "Under the guidance of Zev, they also set up remotely controlled explosives."

The door opened and they entered a large room. Aerial and ground maps lined yellow painted walls. Yalon paced while Dove and Moshe waited at a table.

Yalon started in the moment Ari entered. "The communication relays are still inoperative? Is this true?"

"Our satellites have been off-line since yesterday," Ari said.

Yalon frowned as he sat with the others. "So, the only intelligence you have rests on the two surveillance cameras in the town square?"

"Not necessarily." Ari took a chair across from Yalon.

Yalon sat straight. "What are you thinking? We need more surveillance."

"I'll decide what we need," Ari said. "Our satellites will self-repair and be back on-line soon."

"That's right," Dove said. "Our communications satellites are vulnerable. The Islamic Coalition knocks them off-line occasionally whenever they test some new missile. Nothing we can do about it."

"Of course we can do something," Zev broke in. "Israel has two fully cloaked surveillance satellites in orbit. We need to launch more."

Ari shook his head. "Not at a cost of a hundreds of millions of shekels each. We'll have to wait."

"Crews are working on restoring the com lines now," Dove reported. "They won't be down long."

Yalon slapped his hand on the table in front of Ari. "This is unacceptable!"

Ari folded his arms across his chest and stared at Yalon.

Dove cleared his throat. "We have to report to our assigned stations now." Dove looked at Monica. "Yalon needs a tour of the operations room."

"Come with me," Monica said in a voice as smooth as Moroccan silk. "It would be my honor to show you the way."

Yalon slowly smiled and followed her out the doorway with Moshe.

Dove chuckled. "Monica's good. She could be a field agent."

Zev entered and sat at the table. "The detonation triggers for the bombs are ready."

"You can set them off from here?" Rita asked.

Zev nodded. "Once we send the remote signal, the main square where they gather and distribute weapons will be destroyed in seconds."

"They'll never know it was us," Ari said.

"Hopefully," Zev agreed, "they'll think it's another one of their stupid accidents."

Ari turned to Dove. "What about the increased activity in that square?"

"Several important-looking men have made appearances there in the last hour. More than the usual crowd seems to be hanging around. Maybe they're waiting for something. It does appear to be their main gathering place."

"Watch 'em closely." Ari stood. "Rita and I will be in the officers' quarters."

She walked next to him through a long corridor until he stopped to open a door marked "Officers." Four closed doors dominated two of the walls in the room. An archway in another wall opened into a dining room where a plain brown table sat surrounded by tan chairs.

Monica entered and greeted Rita. "That's our room." She pointed to one of the four doors on the far wall, and led the way into a room they would share.

Ari peeked through the open door to see Rita's bag on one of two twin beds in the small, square space she would call home for the next three days. Then Rita and Monica followed him to the dining room to join the others seated around the table.

Ari listened on his headset to Levi's report. He sat across from Rita and briefed them. "Levi's unit protects the center of the kibbutz next to the giant community greenhouse. Two of his soldiers are stationed at the top of a concrete block grain tower. They report no movement outside the wall."

"Listen up," Dove said, cupping his hand over his headset. "Surveillance monitors indicate new activity in east Maccabiah."

"What are they doing?" Monica asked.

"Distributing weapons," he answered. "If they're coming in with a ground assault, we can expect them in the morning."

"We're expecting this, no?" Moshe asked.

"What's wrong?" Yalon's booming voice caught everyone off guard.

"Nothing," Dove was quick to interject, but everyone looked at Ari.

"We should've at least evacuated the children to Haifa," Yalon said. "We're risking our lives to defend a piece of land. We shouldn't risk the children."

Ari opened his mouth to say something, but Yalon interrupted.

"It's just that I've seen this once before. The children died with their mothers."

Ari could see Yalon's eyes glisten as he held back tears.

Yalon slowly shook his head. "You can't imagine."

"Yes, I can," Ari said.

"Let me go out." Yalon became the warrior again. "I'll lead a team. We'll keep going until we get a message out to Jerusalem."

Ari shook his head. "We've done everything possible to prepare." He nodded toward Rita. "Our weapons analyst told us we have to hold our ground until reinforcements arrive. So we will."

"I agree," Dove said. "It's too risky to send a team out."

Ari stood and started toward the door leading to his quarters, then looked back at the others. "And remember, we're not fighting over land. We're fighting for our right to live as free people."

chapter 11

THE ATTACKERS ADVANCING toward the kibbutz arrived with the early morning sun behind them. A buzzer went off inside the officers' quarters at the time of the sighting. Soldiers guarding the entrance were the first to see them.

Ari sat in the operations room reviewing the main monitor and directing the action over his headset by the time Rita hurried in next to him. Without looking up, Ari pointed to the monitor. They watched the enemy rushing in on foot by the hundreds. Ari's eyes narrowed as the invaders entered the fields toward the front gate. He knew that the ground they crossed, covered in dew with little green plants poking up, would soon become a bloody battlefield.

Monica sat at the station with Ari when Levi's voice came in over a speaker phone near the monitor. "My brother's with me. We watched the first line of enemy fighters trample the cabbage fields on their way in."

"Hundreds of them, Ari. Egyptian Brotherhood troops." Jacob's voice crackled over the line. "They're coming right at us."

Ari studied the images on the screen. "You decide when to blast them, Levi."

"Now," Levi ordered.

"This is the beginning." Ari said to Rita. "Now it goes loud." His body tightened with anticipation as the explosives team detonated successive charges under the cabbage fields. Noise blasted through the speakers with each detonation.

On his monitor, Ari watched the invaders stop their advance amid the confusion. Blood-soaked bodies lay strewn on the ground. Black smoke clouds filled the air. Enemy wounded ran screaming with hands, arms, or parts of faces blown off. Blood pooled into the shallow irrigation ditches. He saw Levi signal the snipers stationed at cutouts on either side of the entrance gate to begin their work.

Ari asked Rita to take a shift on the split-screen monitor across the room. The large flat display streamed twelve images from cameras situated throughout the grounds.

"Thanks." Monica handed the headset to Rita. "I need to meet with Moshe. This set goes straight through to Commander Ari."

Rita put on the headset and adjusted it. She watched the fighting at the front entrance on the center screen.

"Are you sure you can do this?" Looking over her shoulder, Ari asked for the second time.

She assured him she could.

Ari returned to his desk to watch his monitor. Around midday, Zev reported in from the observation room. "We see mobile launchers coming in behind the foot soldiers. We count four. They're at the main road outside our fields."

Yalon entered and stepped close to Ari. "Did you anticipate this?" he demanded. "The rocket-propelled grenades on launchers?"

"Yes, we knew. Our soldiers are in position to launch counter-lasers set up behind our inner wall."

"How did you know?" Yalon was quick to ask.

Ari's eyes never left the monitor. "One of the cameras we installed in east Maccabiah showed the launchers moving through.

We're still watching—that's why I haven't blown the town square yet. We need the view."

Over a speaker, Ari listened while Jacob gave orders to his men. "Calculate the distance and commence firing in a random pattern," Jacob said. "Make 'em think we have mobile launchers too." Ari watched the monitor at Rita's station while their new smart rockets shot over the wall. One hit in the middle of the advancing army.

At least fifty fighters in front of the destruction continued their advance. Their black and olive-green uniforms distinguished them as the Brotherhood Front Guard, known for their cruelty to prisoners.

The next smart rocket hit the launchers. One was obliterated while the explosion tore the other launcher apart and blasted shrapnel into the dead and dying. In years past, this forceful volley would have ended the battle. These attackers, trained by the American CIA, were fierce fighters and they kept coming.

"How long can you defend?" Yalon asked, crowding close to see the screen.

Ari didn't answer. He continued staring straight ahead.

Monica gently took Yalon's arm. "Step back, please. I'll answer your questions." She led Yalon to a table nearby where Ari could overhear.

"We only fire one rocket from each location so the enemy won't get a fix on our launch positions," she told him.

"How can you be sure?" Yalon folded his beefy arms across his chest.

"We know the British and American weapons sold to our enemy are second-generation at best," she explained patiently. "Same for the Russian weapons."

Yalon didn't look convinced. "So, you believe we can win because of superior weapons?"

She smiled. "That's precisely what we believe."

Ari switched to his headset in time to hear Jacob say, "Get ready, Levi, the next wave's coming." Reaching for another cup of coffee, Ari braced himself.

Sporadic fighting continued until late afternoon when an alarm sounded inside the main operations room signaling a major attack. Ari watched green images of the fighting men flash across the screen, except the few times it lit up with the eerie orange light of exploding rockets.

The battle raged for the next hour. Then evening came and the fighting dwindled to sporadic gunfire. Ari walked to Rita's desk and tapped her on the shoulder. "You've been on shift all day."

Rita took off the headset and sank back into her chair as the monitors automatically switched to night vision. "I watched Jacob get hit by grenade shrapnel," she said in a weak voice. "He's wounded."

"I saw it too. Don't worry, he wasn't hurt bad. I assure you, he'll be back in it tomorrow."

The next report came to Ari thirty minutes later. "The enemy pulled back when the skies turned dark, as we expected," Daniel told him. "Lookouts reported the retreat."

"Surveillance cameras confirm," Ari answered.

An hour passed without incident, and Ari gave the order to stand down. He rose to address the personnel in the room.

"Thank you all for your diligence today. Be proud of a job well done. Our work, however, is not over. Stay on four-hour shifts through the night. And keep positive thoughts." He looked around the room, then headed to the officers' quarters with Rita.

Ari sat at the head of the table while an aide to Moshe passed around foil-wrapped dinners. During the meal, everyone talked and made jokes, except for Ari. He was lost in his own thoughts.

"What's wrong?" Yalon asked gruffly.

"Nothing," Dove said. "We're all tired."

Ari looked at the faces around him. "We were tested today. We'll get more tomorrow. A real fight."

Dove agreed. "I think they'll come early, fight hard, and stay late."

"What's the status of our weapons inventory?" Yalon asked.

"We used about what we expected for the first day," Dove said. "Our communication relays are still down. We have no word yet when reinforcements will get here."

"What if they don't come in time?" Yalon asked. "What if we run out of ammunition?"

Dove waved a hand as if to silence him. "We have adequate inventory to support this defense."

"We better," Yalon grumbled.

Ari turned to Rita. "What do you think?"

"I tried to recalculate our inventory every hour. I should check my numbers to make sure."

"Just tell us, Rita."

"We used about half of what we had."

Moshe whistled. "If the fighting is heavier tomorrow we won't make it."

"Yes," Dove said abruptly, "we know what it means."

"He's right." Rita gestured toward Moshe. "Most of our artillery ammunition will be gone before reinforcements arrive if we endure another sustained attack."

"If they arrive," Ari added.

Dove picked up a piece of paper. "Our last outgoing message stated our situation. Without help, we will fall."

Rita looked at Ari. "Do you think other towns in the Negev are under attack?"

"What's going on out there is simply a guess," Dove answered.

Ari's face looked taut, and dark circles colored the skin under his eyes. He reached for another coffee. "We're the ones with the security wall. They want to make an example out of toppling us."

"If we ration the ammunition tomorrow our losses will be staggering," Monica said. "If we use the same amount as today, we'll be finished off by the time our troops find us."

Dove nodded. "We have to let each day stand alone."

"Nothing more we can do tonight," Ari said. "Let's get some rest." He took a long look at Rita as she left the table. *I should've gotten her out of this mess when I had the chance,* he thought.

Rita sat on the edge of her bed talking with Monica about the first day of battle when they heard voices outside their door. Dressing quickly, she stepped out, saw a glow in the officers' dining room, and headed toward the light with Monica right behind her.

Dove, staring at a photo, sat at the table with Ari. Without looking up, Dove said, "It's a first-generation mobile launcher. We spotted it on the town camera screen a few minutes ago."

Rita sat next to Dove. "Is this bad?" she asked.

"We don't know," Ari said. "Dove's best weapons analyst is working on it now."

"What are you thinking?" Monica asked. "That it's been modified for biological warfare?"

"Yes," Ari answered.

Rita didn't react. She watched Ari's expression and tried to determine what this new threat meant.

"We have approximately eighteen hundred of our people still above ground," Ari continued. "Most of the basements and shelters don't have filter systems advanced enough to keep those people alive in the face of this kind of attack."

"I hate to say it." Dove shook his head. "But Yalon's right. We have to send someone out to investigate."

"I'll think about it," Ari said.

Zev entered and joined them at the dining table. "The tunnels are loaded and ready."

"Do you mean the tunnel that goes under the checkpoint out to the cove?" Rita asked.

Zev shook his head. "No, that's our escape tunnel, constructed five years ago. With the funds we received at the Antalya conference, we purchased special digging equipment in the Euro States and had it delivered under camouflage at night. When it arrived we took it underground immediately. We're certain enemy surveillance never sighted it."

"It took a year to dig out the escape tunnel to the shoreline," Ari remembered aloud. "This project Zev is talking about took us only one month."

"We burrowed under the fields," Zev continued. "Most of the dirt road and a good portion of the main town road are now riddled underneath by tunnels."

"What did you do with the excess dirt from digging?" Rita didn't know whether to feel hopeful or frightened. She searched Ari's face for a clue, but he looked unchanged: determined, focused, and tired.

"At first we brought it above ground at night to scatter around," Zev said. "Then we filled an unused escape tunnel. And now the new tunnels are loaded with explosives, something the enemy will never expect."

Monica said, "The blast might affect the stability of the perimeter wall."

"It won't." Ari shook his head. "I'm sure because Zev is sure."

Dove looked at his watch, then at Ari. "We should try to sleep for a while." He stifled a yawn. "It's after midnight."

"What about the missile?" Rita asked nervously.

"We don't know what it is," Dove reminded her.

Ari stood, signaling the end of the meeting. "We do know one thing for certain—surrender is not an option. Today we were lucky. Tomorrow we must be clever."

Rita, wondering what would happen the next day, returned to her room. *I should've given Ari that second chance,* she thought. *I hope it's not too late.*

An hour before dawn—day two of the siege—Ari's wrist communicator beeped. On his way to the corridor, he saw a light from under Rita's room door.

"It's almost morning," Ari called out at the door. "Let's go to our stations."

Rita's muffled voice came back a second later. "Five minutes."

He made his way to the operations room, and a few minutes later, Rita slid into a chair at the multi-screen station. Then Monica appeared with coffees and pastries for everyone.

A sudden cry from the courtyard crackled over the room speaker, and Rita's screen went blank. She looked at Ari. "What happened?"

"I don't know," he shouted across the room. "I lost my com channel to Daniel's command post. I'm going to find out." He jumped up, ripped off his headset, tossed it onto his desk, and sprinted to the elevator.

The moment the elevator doors opened in the community room, Ari ran to the front door and into the courtyard. The early morning sun felt warm on his face. Elongated shadows fell across the ground in front of the buildings. A dozen men stood by a lattice wall. Daniel's short, muscular body set him apart.

"The signal flares are blue," Daniel yelled as Ari ran to him. A distant blue light rose straight into the north sky like a tiny missile.

"Affirmative," Ari cried. "We're being warned. Coalition troops have crossed into the Negev from Jordan."

Daniel pointed toward the community building. "You're supposed to be underground at the command center. Until the Forces arrive."

"I know." Ari looked around the courtyard. "I thought I should be here since the com lines are down."

"You can watch everything on the monitors." Daniel tapped his headset. Curly brown hair wrapped around the metal band holding the receiver. "Sorry. I accidentally switched you off. It won't happen again."

"This second day determines our future, and I'm going to give my men the support they deserve." Ari lowered his voice. "Don't worry, I'll go back underground in a bit."

Daniel walked with him to the post, a fortified concrete storage room.

"I feel optimistic," Ari said, "even with the odds stacked against us."

"Because Moshe doesn't think the SCUD II is bio?"

"It's a good place to start."

They stepped through the metal door of the post. "We used too much of our armament yesterday," Daniel said as he closed the door. "I think today we'll face an even stronger volley."

"Yes, they'll try to break us today. But we have a surprise for them."

"Did Zev load the new tunnels?" Daniel almost smiled.

Ari nodded. "Even so, we can expect the enemy to come at us hard today."

Flares went up in the distant skies to the south, interrupting their conversation.

Ari pointed to the window. "Blue again. Coalition troops are crossing the border into Israel."

Daniel handed Ari a vest and a helmet with an embedded headset. He took a call and looked at Ari. "Spotters see them coming in on foot. They think, about half an hour."

"What side are they coming in on?" Ari put the vest and helmet on.

"North, to Levi's side."

Ari shook Daniel's hand, stepped into the courtyard, and moved cautiously along the inside wall. Levi and his men greeted Ari twenty minutes later.

They waited while a long hour passed.

Ari hoped the spotters were wrong. "Maybe the enemy backed down," he told Levi. "They should be here by now."

"No, they're up to some trick, but they're coming." Levi glanced at his commander. "This is sport to them. Why wouldn't they come?"

Before he could answer, Daniel called. "Commander, hundreds more are approaching the front wall in the south. Spotters see them now."

Ari clicked his headset to the command center and found Zev. "They're preparing for a combined blow."

"Affirmative," Zev said. "And our cameras picked up two Egyptian tanks. We watched them position on the main road at our dirt-road juncture."

"Get the coordinates to the Special Squad boys," Ari ordered. "Tell them to take the tanks out with Jericho II missiles."

"Will do," Zev said. "Are you coming back now?"

"Soon." Ari returned to the field command post moments before two white streaks flew overhead. The men cheered when the deadly projectiles struck their targets with a boom. A black cloud of smoke slowly rose over the destruction and billowed up into the sky.

Daniel returned and directed Ari's attention to a monitor covering the secret entrance. They watched enemy shrapnel bombs, packed with glass marbles, whiz over the wall near the troops defending the rear entrance. Levi held his soldiers out of range during the bombardment until an explosion blew a cavernous hole in the security wall facing them.

Levi barely had time to call it in. "Section N-16 down!" he shouted. "Attackers streaming in firing Russian assault rifles."

The moshav security force arrived as Levi ordered his soldiers to advance. A hundred moshav men walked behind Levi's soldiers. The front line with Levi discharged their high/low velocity smart guns into the approaching attackers.

Levi reported casualties after the firefight ended. "At least two dozen of our men are dead. Ari, we lost Eli. He's gone. And we have at least fifty wounded. Several critical."

Ari ordered a crew to the scene of the break-in to repair the rupture. Snipers covered them while they attached a metal grid over the opening and wired it with a deadly electric charge.

Daniel and his men exchanged gunfire with the attackers at the entrance gate while the sun rose high. Ari stayed at the field control center, and Daniel called during a lull. "Why don't you blow the road, Ari? We're losing too many men."

"I'm not ready yet. That tank group won't be the last." The line went dead. Ari grabbed the binoculars and ran to the door. He watched a sudden explosion blow the entrance gate inward with such force that Daniel's men scrambled to take cover from concrete pieces raining down on them.

Ari watched, jaw clenched. One side of the metal entrance crashed down, then the attackers broke through. The battle raged for almost half an hour until the enemy at the gate was pushed back. Ari checked his headset. The line was live again. He set the binoculars down, and turned on a camera monitor covering the front gate.

Several armored vehicles with steel plates fixed to the fronts sat in the parking lot. Daniel's men held the line while designated drivers ran to the trucks and drove to the opening. They parked the vehicles close together to form a solid barrier across the front.

A short time later, Daniel called Ari. "More are coming. Too many to halt. Please advise."

"Zev, are you getting this?" Ari shouted into his headset.

"Yes, I'll take care of it. I've got the coordinates. Get ready."

Ari switched channels. "Levi, Daniel, pull back. We're going loud."

"I'm here," Zev said when Ari switched back.

"Blow the bastards," Ari said.

The plastic explosives under the fields blew up in succession. The kibbutz men held their ground while the earth shook and the air burned as the fields collapsed into misshapen mounds of earth mixed with enemy bodies. Ari watched it on Daniel's monitor, then walked back into the courtyard.

"Ari," Zev said into his headset, "from what we can see, breaches are secured. Our line of defense is holding. Our casualties now number over a hundred. It's afternoon. When are you coming back?"

"I'm on my way now." Ari stepped into the elevator and pushed the button.

Sporadic gunfire from the enemy continued throughout the day. Then two enemy grenades sailed over the wall near Daniel's men at the gate. One grenade exploded upon impact.

Ari moved close to the monitor covering the front entrance. He rested his hand lightly on Rita's shoulder. "Brace yourself," he said quietly.

"One man dead," Daniel called in to Ari. "Two others badly wounded."

"I see it." Ari watched the medical response team rush out to the scene. The second grenade exploded with full force, killing two medics while they leaned over to transfer a soldier onto a gurney.

"Now we have five dead instead of one," Daniel reported. "They're using time-delay grenades to hit the medical teams."

Ari grimaced. Two of the dead were women. "I've seen enough death today," he said under his breath.

"We all have," Daniel answered. He called for another medical team to come out.

"Are you okay, Rita?" Ari asked.

"I'm okay," she said, her voice choked with emotion.

Jacob broke in on Ari's call. "They're bringing in a line of tanks on the main road. My spotters on top of the wall see them. They might be decoys."

"We see them," Ari confirmed. "We count five."

"Enemy tanks are lining up," Jacob reported.

"Watch them and advise of any movement."

"Will do. Jacob out."

Dove entered the operations room and went directly to Ari. He spoke in a low voice. "Our ammo supply is low, Ari. Two, maybe three hours left."

"We have to outmaneuver them." Ari's jaw tightened. "Get me some options."

"They have an endless supply of young men," Dove reminded him. "They'll use up our bullets and when our ammo's depleted they'll come against us hard."

Before Ari could answer, Levi broke through on his headset. "Commander, I put spotters on the top floor of the grain storage tower. They report a jet coming in high from the west. It's friendly."

Daniel reported enemy tank guns being aimed up. Toward the jet.

"Get ready to blast the road under those five tanks," Ari ordered.

"Say again. Do you want us to blow everything we have under the road?"

"Affirmative. Blow everything underneath them. Whoever this pilot is," Ari added, "we're going to give him every opportunity to complete his mission."

A few moments later the ground shook from the massive explosions. A cloud of smoke filled the late-afternoon skies and floated eastward.

"All tanks destroyed or disabled," Daniel reported.

"Confirmed," Zev broke in. "That pilot is flying deep into enemy territory. At least now he has a chance."

"The road's now an oblong crater filled with twisted metal," Daniel continued. "Enemy foot soldiers can't cross. The sides of the crater mounded up into two gigantic barriers."

"Stay sharp." Ari's voice grew crisp. "This lull may be temporary."

Enemy gunfire through the front gate continued sporadically for the next hour, then an alarm sounded in the olive groves outside the north wall.

Ari's headset sputtered. "Commander, Levi here. Our spotters say maybe two hundred, armed with rifles and swords, coming through the olive groves toward the damaged secret entrance."

"Wait one." Ari changed his headset channel. "Zev, are you there?"

"I'm here. What are you thinking?"

"How many missiles do we have left?"

Zev cleared his throat. "One."

"Get your special-squad boys to put it in the middle of the olive grove."

"Got it. Zev out."

Ari clicked his headset channel to Levi. "Get your men back. Zev's sending a missile into your grove coordinates."

"Will do. Levi out."

Minutes later a white trail streaked high into the sky and arched into the center of the olive grove. The perfectly placed rocket formed a small crater in the center of the olive trees as the blast radius spread in all directions. Trees growing closest to the explosion were uprooted and flew out against the subsequent rows of trees, and against the enemy men hiding behind them.

Few shots were fired for the next hour, then a brilliant sunset layered through smoke-filled skies. Ari breathed easier when the spotters reported clear perimeters an hour after that. Before he removed his headset, he ordered the men to stay alert.

The personnel cheered when Ari stood and ordered night watch. Dove saw the look on his face and motioned for Rita to join them when Ari headed toward the officers' quarters.

Ari and the others gathered at the familiar dining table.

"Our casualties are substantial," Dove said. "The ammunition inventory is running low. Still, we had enough to make it through the second day."

"I'm worried," Ari told them.

Dove nodded. "We all are."

Ari looked past Rita. "Our ammunition is virtually gone. We have maybe two hours of bullets left."

"Yalon suggested we deploy a commando force," Rita said, "to look for signs of our troops coming in."

Dove shook his head. "We have our surveillance people watching the two town cameras for incoming troops. Whatever information scouts bring back won't change the outcome."

"We need another day," Ari said. "And I don't think we're going to get it."

chapter 12

DEEP UNDERGROUND IN the command center, Ari sat in a corner of his dark room. He'd miscalculated, and he knew it. The third day would dawn soon. The enemy would attack with the arrival of the morning sun. Without ammo his people would be reduced to throwing rocks. *And that won't last long.* He shook his head to clear his thoughts.

The phone rang. For a split second he felt tempted to turn it off. "Shalom, Zev." Ari did his best to hide the frustration creeping into his voice.

"I've got an idea." Zev sounded so excited he almost stumbled over his words. "What about the people still in their homes? They know how to make Molotov cocktail grenades."

Ari sat up straight. "What are you thinking?"

"That we enlist every available person still in their homes for immediate weapons detail. All they need are glass bottles, dish-soap, and any kind of alcohol-based fuel. Even lamp oil will work. Seal a cloth stopper in place with candle wax and a formidable weapon is produced."

Ari paused for a moment. "We can manufacture thousands through the night. But even with an added cache, we only extend the fighting a short time."

"And the alternative?" Zev asked.

"Make the necessary calls to get it started." Ari set the phone down and pushed a call button for Dove. A short time later he called out "Enter" to the knock on his door.

Dove stepped in and closed the door. "Maybe the Forces will arrive in time."

Ari's head hurt. "I don't think we should count on it."

"You used much of what we had left to protect that pilot," Dove reminded him. "We don't know what he's even doing. Is that what's bothering you?"

"That I may have cost the lives of many to protect the life of one pilot?" Ari asked. "Yeah, that bothers me."

"What's left to discuss?" Dove tapped the coffee table. "We fight as long as we can. We'll make it or we won't. If you have something else on your mind, Ari, tell me."

Rita arrived in time to hear Ari say, "We should use the tunnel."

She closed the door behind her, sat next to Dove, and tapped her wrist communicator. "You called for me?"

Dove left to help Zev, and Ari turned toward Rita.

She sat on the edge of a chair close to Ari. "Are you thinking it's time to evacuate?" she asked.

Ari rubbed his forehead. "I don't know."

"Well," Rita said, "when will you decide?"

"If I knew for sure when reinforcements will get here, I could make it through the morning." Ari's voice took on a more confident tone. "If I had a drone." He looked at his watch and touched his wrist communicator.

A few minutes later Dove returned. "Production of the Molotovs is in progress. The mobile launchers will adapt easily to let 'em fly."

"Good," Ari said. "But that's not why I called you here. Time to take Yalon up on his offer."

Dove sat on a chair opposite Ari and Rita. "You're going to send out a reconnaissance team?"

"The choices are clear," Ari said. "Bluff or evacuate."

"Or both," Rita added.

Ari nodded. "What's not so clear is which path to follow. Our com lines are still down. I'm thinking a team can stealth outside the jam zone, get an urgent message out to Jerusalem."

"Why Yalon?" Dove asked.

"Captain Baruch trusts him," Ari said. "That's good enough for me. I'll put Levi second in command. Probably a six-man team. Yalon and Levi can pick the other four."

"Sounds right." Dove said. "Give me the word. I'll contact Yalon and Levi right now."

"What do you think, Rita? You are my weapons analyst." Ari turned to her and their eyes met.

"You have to," she said.

Ari turned to Dove. "Make it happen. And get Levi in here."

Levi was brought into the command center from his ground post to meet with Dove, Yalon, and Moshe. Within half an hour, four others were notified to prepare for the operation. Ari met with Yalon and Levi while they waited.

"We're very close," Ari told them. "We can prevail over this enemy. But without immediate help, our lives will be lost. You've got seven hours until dawn to complete your operation. Press hard. You should reach a safe town by then. Beyond that, you'll be visible to the most rudimentary surveillance. Get to Jerusalem if you can."

Yalon asked, "And what do we do in Jerusalem?"

"Await orders," Ari answered.

No one spoke for a moment until Levi asked to see Ari privately.

"Of course, Levi, what do you need?" Ari walked with him to a corner of the room.

Levi took an envelope out of his pocket and offered it to Ari. "Will you hold this note for me until I return?" The envelope had a Hebrew *lamed*, the letter L, scrawled across the front.

Ari accepted the envelope. "What's this about?"

"Commander, please give this note to Leah. If I don't make it back."

"Leah?"

"Naomi and Dove's daughter. Leah."

A smile crept across Ari's face. "I will. But you'll return and deliver it yourself."

"Is it true, Commander, what Dove said? That Kol Shofar could be overrun?"

"It is." Ari saw something like panic in Levi's eyes. "This is classified," he whispered, "but if you're going to become part of the family then you should know. We made evacuation plans for some of the command center personnel and their families in the event the soldiers don't arrive in time. You can be sure that Leah and her family will be in the first group to leave."

"Commander, if the enemy penetrates our defenses, how will Leah's family get out? And where will they go?"

"Levi, trust me. I've already said more than I should've. We have a way."

"I didn't mean to question you. Thank you, Commander."

Ari put his hands on Levi's shoulders and looked into his eyes. "It's important for you to stay focused on your assignment. You do your part and leave the rest to me."

They shook hands and walked back to Yalon.

"Is your team ready to go?" Ari asked.

The four expected soldiers entered, and Levi waved them over.

"It's twenty-three hundred hours," Ari told the team. "Yalon has your route. Go to the designated safe house if you need to."

The men said shalom and followed Yalon out the door to the elevator.

Ari wanted to lead them. Instead he would look at his watch every hour after they left and try to mentally calculate their location. But for now, he had to concentrate on the next priority.

He went to his washroom and splashed cold water on his face while his inner circle assembled in the map room.

Rita slid into a chair next to Monica, took a glass mug from the center of the map room table, and poured coffee from an insulated carafe.

Ari entered, sat, and looked at the others. "Time to make a plan," he said.

"How many can we evacuate?" Monica asked.

"Theoretically," Dove said, "we could evac everyone. Even if they storm our wall and take over the place, it would take several hours to penetrate our underground shelter, including this center. We can move thousands through the tunnel in one night."

"But that's not the problem," Monica said.

"No, it isn't." Ari tapped the table. "We don't know how far women, children, and elders can walk."

Dove pointed at a map spread out in front of him. "It's four miles to Maccabiah; fifteen miles to the coast."

Ari shook his head. "Maccabiah has mixed neighborhoods. We don't know what's happening there."

"Better than letting them die here," Dove said under his breath.

Zev said, "At least it's a place to start."

Ari nodded. "Okay, Dove, work something up with Monica."

Dove and Monica began planning as they headed out the door.

"I'm beginning to realize," Rita said, "it's possible we may lose this fight. Israel will continue on, but without us."

Ari started to say something, but he pressed his lips together instead and looked at Zev.

"It's sometimes difficult to face what's in front of us." Zev's face took on a soft glow in the low light as he spoke. His silver hair gave the illusion of an aura around his head. "We'll take this day that's coming hour by hour. And remember, this too shall pass."

Ari suggested they go to the operations room to wait for morning. He moved ahead through the corridor.

Rita held back and walked next to Zev. "Will Ari evacuate with the others?" she asked quietly.

"Rita, he is Kidon." Zev's eyes narrowed briefly. "Do you know what that means?"

She shook her head.

"A unit in military intelligence. Formed after the Shoah to hunt Nazis. Now they pursue and eliminate enemies of Israel." Zev lowered his voice to a whisper when they entered the operations room. "Kidon are fearless warriors. Ari will be the last to leave."

Rita moved a chair close to Ari's desk. "Anything yet?"

Ari shook his head. He barely glanced up from staring at the monitor covering the courtyard. *But we won't have long to wait*, he thought, watching the sky lighten over the grounds.

A quiet morning came and Ari's hopes rose with the new day. Then he saw movement on Rita's monitor. He clicked his headset to open all channels. "Get ready!" he ordered. "Here they come!"

Heavy enemy gunfire suddenly erupted through the damaged secret entrance. Ari clicked his headset. "Daniel, tell the men to spread out and stagger their return fire. We have a plan—just buy us some time. The next few hours are critical."

The first infantry assault at the north gate lasted fifteen minutes. Dove entered the operations room during a lull in fighting, then left with Ari into a private room. Behind closed doors, they made a plan.

"Time to get them out," Ari said. "Have you notified the ones chosen?"

"The group leaders know." Dove said. "They'll tell the others just prior to departure."

"Dove, you have to go with them. They'll need a leader." Ari's voice showed the strain he felt.

"You know I'll follow your orders," Dove said. "We don't have time to argue anyway."

They walked to the door. "Do I have to say it?" Ari pushed it open. "Make certain Rita's in the evac group."

"Already done," Dove said as they stepped into the corridor. "I'll notify her myself when the time comes. We leave on your command."

They returned to the operations room in time to see enemy troop press forward toward the shattered front entrance. More enemy fighters wore the distinctive black and olive-green uniforms than the dark blue cotton shirts and pants of the regular Egyptian army.

Ari listened on his headset while Daniel ordered his men to load Molotov cocktails into the adapted shoulder launchers. The bullets were gone.

The defenders held out until midday, until the grenades and cocktails ran out. Ari called Daniel. "Tell the men to get ready for hand-to-hand combat." Before he took off his headset he added, "Take out as many as you can."

Ari slumped in his chair. His hand, reaching up to remove the headset, stopped in midair when he heard Daniel's excited voice. "Wait one." Then, "It's a drone coming in low. It's a bomber. It's ours!"

Ari strode to Rita's station in time to see Daniel, on the multi-screen, run into the courtyard and point in the direction of the Med. They watched the drone fly in fast.

With precision the silver bird swooped down to dump its package on the advancing Islamic fighters. Concussion bombs flew out in all directions. A moment later, the small, oblong devices hit the ground and exploded with such force that enemy bodies were blown into the air with the debris.

A cheer went up in the courtyard after Daniel shouted, "Our soldiers are coming in!"

"That has to be it," Ari said to Rita. He stood, legs apart and arms folded across his chest, staring at the screen. "Those drones have a limited range."

Zev's voice echoed over the loudspeaker ten minutes later. "Battle's over. Lookouts report full enemy retreat in progress."

Dove called Ari. "It's time. If you want us to evac, we should start now."

"Stand down," Ari told him. "This battle is over."

"I'll notify the others," Dove said. "It got close, but we made it."

"We're not safe yet." Ari's jaw tightened as he said the words. He ordered Daniel, Jacob, and Levi to keep the men on alert.

For the next hour, he paced in front of the monitor and talked with Rita.

Zev called in the early afternoon and simply said, "They are here."

By the end of the day, nearly twelve hundred IDF soldiers marched through the damaged entrance into Kol Shofar. The command center personnel closed their stations and emerged above ground to greet the reinforcements.

Before he went up, Ari looked around for Rita.

"She left," Dove said, pointing to the elevator. "As we should."

Ari turned for a last look at the operations room.

"Are you satisfied?" Dove asked.

"I am." Ari pushed the elevator button and the last group to leave the center ascended.

"I received a call from the first officer," Dove reported as they walked into the courtyard. "They're setting up a camp inside our wall. We'll meet Commander Binyamin at first light tomorrow."

Ari looked at his watch. "Suits me. I'm ready to go home." *I wonder if it's too late to call*, he thought.

Zev pulled up in a desert rover and offered to take them to their homes.

As soon as he got out in front of his building, Ari pulled out his cell phone. *Cell towers are down. No service.* He pressed his lips together and tried to shake off his desire to see her. The glass protection panels of his building's front doors seemed cold and uninviting.

Ari stepped into the hallway leading to his quarters. Rita stood leaning against the wall next to his door. His step quickened when he saw her.

"Shalom, Ari. I thought you'd want to see the initial damage report as soon as possible." She held up a folder.

He placed his hand over a lock pad and pushed the door open. "I definitely want to see that report." Motioning for her to follow, he opened the door.

She followed him into his private quarters, the inner sanctum. He rarely extended an invitation to these rooms.

Two sofas faced each other with an ornate glass table, circa 2020, between them. Rita sat on a light-green sofa. Tan venetian-plaster walls gave the room an ambiance of being in a cozy, well-lit cave. A marble-faced fireplace took the chill from the room moments after Ari lit the gel cans contained inside.

Ari stretched and yawned. "It's been a tiring day." He flipped through the quickly compiled initial assessment Moshe had prepared. It didn't tell him anything he didn't already know.

Ari removed a bottle of bold, deep-red port and two glasses from a cupboard. He set them on a counter separating the kitchen from the living room. "This is the last of my wine from Gamla." He held up the bottle for her to see before he uncorked it.

"You mean the southern part of Lebanon that Israel annexed ten years ago when Syria invaded from the north? Up there?"

Ari nodded. "Some of the best wines in the world now come from Gamla." He poured and extended a full glass to her.

"Well, maybe I'll stay for a minute." She removed her coat and laid it on the back of the sofa before accepting the wine. "Ari, do you believe the legends of an ancient Gamla are true?"

He gazed at her. Just for a moment. He took it all in—her face, her hair, her style. And those mesmerizing green eyes. "I can prove ancient Gamla once existed." The corners of his mouth turned up when he saw how his boast interested her.

She set the wine glass on the table, clasped her hands together, and leaned forward. "Okay, what do you know?"

"It's what I have." He went to his locked gun box on the fireplace mantel, unlocked it, and removed a small brown cloth sack with a pull-cord closure. He sat next to her and, opening the bag with a flourish, he pulled out a gold coin, extensively worn, and held it up for her to see.

Rita took the coin and examined it. "This looks like a museum piece."

"Yeah. I found it in southern Lebanon during the war of 2030. In a cave."

"Ari, this is exquisite."

He showed her the Hebrew markings. "See, here near the wheat sheaf it says 'Gamla'." He turned it over. "It's worn down but it says 'Jerusalem Forever' on this side. It's dated 67, the last year the people in Gamla survived against the Romans."

Rita looked at him. "I wonder what our ancient relations, the Israelites and Gamleans, would think of us modern Israelis. Is that how you say it? *Gamlean*?"

Putting the coin inside the velvet bag, Ari laid it on the coffee table and shook his head. "Hashem protect us. Yes, that's right."

Staring at the bag, she asked, "How many people know about it?"

"Only a few close friends know." Ari smiled. "And you." He stood, and moved toward the kitchen. "Let's see what we have in the refrigerator." After inspecting the meager contents, he cut two figs into halves and soaked them in heated port wine before offering the dish to Rita.

She sampled one of the figs and gave the other one to him.

Ari sat across from her and raised his wine glass. "To life." He leaned in and touched her glass with the edge of his.

Rita repeated the toast and sipped her wine while Ari drained his small glass with one swallow. They talked about the extraordinary events of the past three days. Another hour and another glass of port later, she said, "I should go now. I really wanted to thank you for getting us though this terrible time."

"We did it together, Rita." His voice was low. He moved next to her and sat close.

"I'm leaving, Ari. I'm going home." She said the words but she didn't move.

He touched her arm. "Rita, I'll tell you anything you want to hear. Answer any questions you ask. If you'll stay."

"And tomorrow?" She pulled away saying, "You hurt me."

"I'll say it all over again. I want you to be with me. Tonight, and all the nights to follow." Having said it clearly, he looked at her, waiting.

"I want to believe you," she whispered.

Ari pulled her close. He brushed his lips across her cheek and whispered in her ear. "These last three days showed me how much I have to lose." He breathed in the scent of her. "Accept me or reject me. I don't want to wonder anymore."

"How do I know you won't change your mind again?"

"Because, I got this for you." Ari stood, and reached into his pants pocket. When he sat, a solid gold, hand-fashioned Star of David necklace rested in his hand.

Rita held her breath for a moment. Then she let go and said, "It's Rosh Hodesh, the new month. New moon, new beginning."

He still held the necklace in his outstretched hand.

A smile crept across her face. "Is this an understanding?"

Ari put it around her neck and fastened the clasp. "It's whatever you want it to be." He rested his hand on her shoulder. His life was finally coming together in a way that he'd wanted for a long time.

In the morning, Ari arrived early at the soldier encampment next to the barracks. A temporary building the size of a small house served as headquarters.

The leader said he was ready for his meeting with Kol Shofar's famous Commander Ari, as he put it. Ari didn't respond to the remark. The two men sized each other up. Binyamin stood as tall as Ari, was broad-shouldered, and he looked seasoned. Perfectly combed, wavy gray hair framed his handsome round face.

They talked for a while and congratulated each other on the saving of Kol Shofar.

"We're lucky," Binyamin said. "Other than the security wall, the infrastructure damage looks minimal."

"Luck has nothing to do with it." Ari grimaced. "They want our assets, our beautiful property. They're willing to murder every one of us to get it. Their goal is to eliminate us and then move in."

"Leaving the property intact, of course," Binyamin agreed.

"Our fields and orchards outside the wall are destroyed," Ari said. "We'll have to make immediate arrangements to bring in extra food from the outside for your troops."

Binyamin nodded. "In the meantime, each soldier carries four days' rations."

Ari smiled for the first time. "That takes some pressure off."

Binyamin slowly stood. "It's good to be here. And mazel tov, I'm happy for you that your community is saved."

Ari stood, extending his hand. "A rabbi once told me, 'We are an ancient people and our collective heart still beats strong.' Our community stood together, and we prevailed."

"I guess that's true," Binyamin said.

"It is true." There wasn't a hint of doubt in Ari's voice. He thought of Rita, and a warm, pleasant sensation filled him. He savored the rare moment on the way home, hoping the conflict would end soon, and he could start thinking about a family.

chapter 13

RITA FINGERED THE gold star hanging on the woven gold cord around her neck, then tucked it out of sight inside her blouse. Every day for almost a week she touched it to make sure it was really there. And every day, it was. It'd been a long time since she felt so confident, almost lighthearted.

She rushed through her duties in the community kitchen and went to her room to await Ari's call. He hadn't wanted to tell people they were together officially because he didn't like that sort of drama. He'd said he had good reasons, and they'd discuss it soon. She didn't care that he wanted to wait for them to move in together.

The phone rang and she reached for it eagerly. "Shalom," she said warmly.

"Shalom, Rita. It's me, Jacob. It's good to hear your voice. I have some time, and I thought we might get together and talk. If you're free now."

"Oh, Jacob, it's good to hear from you." The smile on Rita's face froze. "I guess we could talk now." *Might as well get this over with,* she thought.

"I'll come to you," Jacob said.

Rita sat with the phone in her hand for a moment before she set it down and went to the foyer. The wait wasn't long.

"Hi, Rita," Jacob called as he stepped through the front door.

They went to the great room to talk, the gardens being too cold now for walks. "A lot of news going around," Jacob said on the way.

"So, you've heard?" Rita sat near the rock fireplace where a lingering morning fire still smoldered.

Jacob laughed and sat across from her. "Who hasn't? And by the way, you look great."

"I didn't know it was common knowledge." Rita's cheeks turned a slight rosy color.

"Probably mostly among the military personnel," Jacob assured her.

"I'm sorry, Jacob. I should've called you." She closed her eyes for a moment, feeling the guilt of hurting him already working in her heart.

"No matter. I've been on sixteen-hour daily shifts getting the Forces settled in their camp."

"So, what are the military men saying?" Rita looked down after asking.

Jacob grinned. "That Binyamin wants to abandon Kol Shofar and Ari wants to stay. Everyone's talking about it."

"What?" Rita asked in disbelief. "That's what you heard?"

Jacob leaned forward and gently rubbed her shoulders. "I'm sorry, Rita. I didn't mean to upset you. Don't worry, Ari will stand his ground." Jacob chuckled at his own joke. "Seriously, we'll replant the groves and grow old here along with the olive trees."

"Jacob, there's something I should tell you." She looked away, unable to face him. "I don't know how to say it."

"Whatever it is—" Jacob's wrist communicator sounded. He looked at it and said, "I'm sorry Rita, this is urgent." Jacob stepped away to make his call.

Rita didn't answer.

"I'm sorry to keep doing this to you," he said as he put his phone into his shirt pocket. "I wanted to spend this afternoon with you but something's come up. I have to report immediately."

"Jacob . . ." was all Rita could say as he turned and almost ran. He threw a kiss back and disappeared through the great room door.

Ari called in the early evening. Rita told him she didn't feel well and didn't feel like talking. "Shalom then, Rita. I'll call later to see how you're doing." He set the phone down. Something didn't feel right.

Twenty minutes later, Rita answered Ari's knock on her door. He could see she'd been crying. He stepped inside and closed the door behind him. "Rita, what have I done?" His voice held a mixture of anguish and bewilderment.

She sat on her bed and put her face in her hands. "Nothing. It's not you." Her tear-stained face looked up at him.

Relief washed through Ari. He took her hands in his and kissed the back of each. "C'mon, Honey. Let's go to my place and get some dinner." He pulled her up and put his arm around her shoulder on the way to his car. Street lights flickered on as evening deepened into night.

They arrived at Ari's to find Binyamin walking up the front steps. They exchanged quick greetings. Binyamin said he remembered Rita from an earlier briefing.

Ari checked his wrist com. No message. "Do we have a meeting scheduled that I forgot about?"

Binyamin shook his head and Ari saw the look of concern on his face. He opened the door and led the way to his quarters. They went directly to the living room.

"Speak freely," Ari said, offering Binyamin an upholstered chair near the sofas.

"Well," Binyamin said as he sat across from Ari and Rita, "my first officer Chaim is meeting this afternoon with your Dove and Moshe. He says you have a man out."

Ari blinked hard. "I have six men out. Team leader Yalon is the one who contacted central command in Jerusalem."

Binyamin leaned forward. "We received no such contact."

"Wait," Ari said, "then how did you know to send in the bomber drone?"

Now Binyamin looked confused. "You must've seen the recon jet fly over the day before. That pilot risked everything to get those pictures. He transmitted digital images to us and we programmed the drone coordinates."

Rita smiled at Binyamin. "That was you?" She glanced at Ari.

Ari shook his head. "I gambled with the lives of six men for nothing."

"You can't blame yourself," Binyamin said. "I would've taken the same course. Sending them out was right."

"I don't know what to think," Ari admitted. "Yalon's experienced. I can't imagine him losing a whole team."

"Why now?" Rita asked Binyamin. "Why do you ask about the team?"

Binyamin didn't speak for a moment.

Ari nodded slightly, and Binyamin answered. "One of our intelligence analysts managed to hack into someone's keyhole imaging satellite. We think it's Chinese." He pulled a folded paper from his shirt pocket and set it on the coffee table.

Ari's strong hand swooped up the paper for a closer review. "You have an open com line I don't know about?" Ari waved the paper. "What is this?"

Binyamin smiled. "Give me some credit." His words flowed with the smooth charm of a politician's. "Look at the time stamp. It's from yesterday."

"How'd you get it?" Rita asked.

"Our troop carrier in the Med." Binyamin pointed to the paper. "The com tech on the *Gilad* took this to his captain last night. He thought it important enough to send a courier in a speedboat to the base camp on the beach this morning. It got to me about an hour ago."

Ari relaxed. He studied the fuzzy images on the photo printout. Without looking up, he told Rita, "Call Dove."

"No need," Binyamin said. "Chaim's working with him right now to project the necessary coordinates to extract."

Ari handed the paper to Rita, and pointed. "That has to be them."

"How soon can you ready an extraction team?" Binyamin asked.

"A couple of hours."

"My men are ready now," Binyamin offered.

A moment of silence passed before Rita asked, "What's Dove say?"

At the same time, a beep-beep emitted from Binyamin's communicator. He looked down to read the tiny screen on his wrist. "We're about to find out."

"Who is it?" Ari asked.

Binyamin read the text message from Chaim. "All's well for tonight. See you tomorrow." He looked at Ari. "Chaim dropped me here while he went to meet with Dove. This means he's on his way over to pick me up. It's our code."

Ari stood directly across from Binyamin. "What's going on?"

"We'll know soon enough," Binyamin answered.

Ari went to his outer door, unlocked it, and called the building guard to clear Chaim's entry.

Five minutes later, Dove and Chaim walked through Ari's door and into the living room. They skipped the usual pleasantries. "We can't do it," Dove said.

Chaim agreed.

Ari moved to sit next to Rita and nodded to the empty sofa across from him. "Make your case."

They sat across from Ari. "We don't have a clear picture of what's happening out there."

"This intel is too old to be of any real value," Chaim added.

"Okay," Ari said. "What do you recommend?"

Dove took a topographic map out of his pocket, unfolded it, and placed it on the table in front of Ari. "If these are Yalon's men and if they are here last night." Dove pointed to the topo. "The team will be forced to move west and south to make it back."

"Your soldiers," Dove said to Binyamin, "have established a safe travel corridor southwest to the beach from Kol Shofar. Yalon's going to have to make it around the enemy camp on his own."

Chaim held up a hand. "Our team will be waiting for them at the edge of the safe zone."

"If they make it that far," Binyamin reminded them.

Ari shook his head. "Unacceptable. My men will go out and find them."

"We'll know more in twenty-four hours when we get new images," Dove said. "We waited this long. It means sitting out one more day."

"I know what it means," Ari said, trying to dismiss the irritation he felt.

"If we get lucky," Binyamin pointed out, "we can task the keyhole satellite over the same area tonight from the *Gilad*. We'll have it in our hands by tomorrow morning."

Ari felt relieved. "That's much better than waiting twenty-four hours."

"I agree," Dove said. "We can't risk the lives of another team."

Ari stood and walked across the room.

"Does he want us to leave now?" Chaim asked.

"No," Dove answered. "He's just thinking."

Binyamin stood. "Well, I'm ready."

Ari turned. "Todah," he said warmly. "I understand. We really have to wait."

"Oh yeah," Dove said to Chaim with a nod toward Ari. "He's good at that."

Binyamin glanced in Rita's direction. "We'll drop Dove off on our way."

"Shalom then," she said as Ari walked them to the door.

Ari came back and sat next to Rita. He tried to shake off the concern he felt for his men and focus only on her. "What was it you wanted to tell me about earlier? Something upset you?"

"I can't even remember it now," Rita lied. "It seems so long ago."

"I'm sorry, Honey," Ari suddenly remembered. "You didn't eat dinner."

"It's okay." Rita smiled. "It's a little late now."

"We'll find something to nosh." Ari smiled back, forcing himself to relax. "It's never too late for something good."

Sometime in the early morning hours, Ari's emergency phone rang at the same time someone pushed his door buzzer. He pulled himself awake to answer the phone. The caller said one word—yes—and hung up. Ari rolled over and whispered to Rita, "It's Yalon. They've found him."

Ari threw on some clothes and hurried to the outer door. Seeing Dove's face on the security screen, he unbolted the lock and opened the door with one movement.

"Where is he?" Ari pulled Dove inside.

Dove's face looked pained. "Here, we have him. With two team members."

They moved into the living room.

"Only three made it back?" Ari felt a momentary wave of anxiety. "What happened?"

Dove didn't answer until they sat. "I got a call from Daniel about thirty minutes ago. He has men stationed along the wall at all times. One of them saw movement among the trees in the nearly destroyed olive groves outside our rear entrance. It was Yalon and two others. They made it all the way to the groves in the back."

Ari grimaced. "They're in bad shape?"

Dove nodded. "Medics are taking them to the temporary hospital we set up in that empty house in Goldstein's neighborhood. The one we used after the moshav attack."

"Right," Ari said. "Let's go. We should talk to them right away. Get the details."

"They're barely conscious," Dove said patiently. "Slow down—we'll go in a few hours."

Ari stood. "Goldstein can tell us how soon. I need to know how bad they're wounded."

"Okay, I'll drive," Dove looked at Ari's feet. "Go put some shoes on."

Ari pointed toward the door. "I'll meet you in the front."

A few minutes later, Ari and Rita met Dove at the outer door. They moved quickly to Dove's car.

The lights were on when they arrived. Two guards stood outside. One of them opened the front door as a nurse peeked out one of the bedroom doors. She stepped into the main room to talk.

"Commander, your man's in bad shape. He's refusing pain medication."

"Yalon?" Ari asked. "He's awake?"

"Yes, but we don't know how he could be. He sustained multiple stab wounds in his arm, neck, and thigh. Two gunshot wounds, one in his shoulder, that one went straight through. The other bullet entered his side and lodged near his spine. It doesn't look good."

Dove stepped forward. "Will he make it?"

"Too soon to know. I can tell you that he applied field dressings to his own wounds and to the soldiers with him. He saved their lives."

"A field dressing?" Rita asked.

Ari nodded. "They carry an emergency kit in their side pockets. He probably packed activated charcoal powder into the wounds, then covered them with special retracting bandages."

"Otherwise," the nurse said, "he would have bled out."

A loud commotion in the other room caused Ari to start forward. Dove and Rita followed.

The nurse walked toward a door and pointed. "This way."

Yalon lay inside on a cot. Wrestling with a nurse trying to hold his arm steady so the doctor could inject him, he called out as Ari rushed to his side.

"You're safe now," Ari said. "We've got you."

Yalon's voice was loud and agitated as he cried out, "It's madness out there." He clutched Ari's hand and took several breaths.

Ari leaned in close to Yalon's face. "Tell me what you know," he said softly. "I'm here. Tell me."

"They're fighting." Then Yalon screamed out in pain.

The doctor stepped forward with the syringe, but Ari waved her back.

"Who is fighting?" Ari leaned in closer. "Stay with me."

Yalon's eyes fluttered. "Everyone, all of 'em. Fighting." He screamed again and closed his eyes. He lay panting wildly.

Ari turned to the doctor. "Give him something. I need to hear this."

"Commander, he needs a morphine stabilizer. We need to operate."

"Give him enough to get him talking. Now."

Dr. Goldstein hesitated. Yalon jerked, and then opened his eyes when she inserted the needle.

Ari smiled at him and continued to hold his hand.

Yalon took several breaths. "We went to the safe house, we went there like you told us. We got there to meet our contact, we went there, it was empty, he is gone. We try to make a plan." His voice trailed off as the morphine started to take effect. "I told them, I said no morphine—I have to tell."

Ari watched him try to hold onto his thoughts.

"The explosion." Yalon rose a little and his eyes opened wide. "Everything lit up—there we were. And I said no morphine, the medic he gave me the shot and I told him to tell you, I have to tell you . . ."

The nurse looked at Ari. "He's going under."

Ari let his hand go and turned to the doctor. "How long before he wakes up?"

"Several hours. If he wakes up." Dr. Goldstein motioned to the nurse to attach an intravenous drip bag to Yalon's arm.

"What did he say when they brought him in?"

"He cried out something about not leaving him behind because he's not dead. I assured him that two others were brought in with him. I don't know which one he's talking about."

Ari walked to the door. "Where are the two others?"

The doctor pointed to another room. Rita and Dove followed Ari in. A woman bent over one soldier whose clothes were cut away to expose his wounded chest. The other man lay unconscious on a cot.

"How is he?" Ari asked.

The nurse looked over. "Commander. Well, he's aware of his surroundings. The pain is nauseating him."

Ari saw the hypodermic needle she held. "How much did you give him? I mean, how long before he goes under?"

"Commander, he begged me to wait. He heard you come in." She lowered to a whisper. "Talk fast, he's slipping in and out of consciousness from pain and trauma."

The nurse moved aside and the young man saw Ari. He tried to sit up.

"Relax, Samuel," Ari said soothingly.

Rita leaned forward for a good look at the wounded soldier. "I know him," she whispered to Dove.

Ari spoke in a low voice to the nurse. "Forget anything you're about to hear. Understood?"

The nurse nodded and looked away but stayed close to her patient. Dr. Goldstein went back to Yalon.

Ari turned his attention to Samuel. "Tell me about the others."

Samuel spoke slowly. "Ambushed. I think a grenade went off. Then I'm on the ground face down. Two of our team are dead. I can't breathe at first. It's night and men came over this wall we're behind. Ten maybe, I think. I couldn't move. I think Yalon killed them. About ten," he repeated.

Samuel closed his eyes. His face contorted. Tears ran down his cheeks. "I'm sorry," he murmured. He turned his face partway into his pillow.

"Commander, might I give him something for the pain now?" The nurse spoke in a low voice.

Ari nodded.

She inserted the needle into Samuel's arm.

Ari stroked Samuel's curly red hair, now matted with blood. He gently wiped Samuel's freckled cheek with the bed sheet. "It's all right," he whispered next to the young soldier's ear. "We've all been there. Believe me, you're safe now."

Samuel visibly relaxed as the opiate flowed into his veins.

Ari looked at the nurse.

"A few minutes," she said.

"Samuel," Ari asked, "what happened after the explosion?"

"More came." His words began to slur. "Yalon told me get Isaac out. I don't know, then screaming. Me and Isaac crawled away. Yalon fought them. They had knives and handguns and Yalon, he shot them. Then he found us. We lay there behind something. Me and Isaac got stabbed. We heard screams." Samuel shuddered. "Terrible screams." He closed his eyes.

Ari looked at Dove and Rita.

Samuel started to babble, but Ari leaned close enough to hear him.

"Yalon," Samuel gasped. "He said we have to go back, we have to get him. Isaac couldn't walk and then Yalon told us . . . we have to get . . . something . . . help."

"Help for whom? For Isaac?" Ari leaned close to Samuel. "Isaac's right here. He's safe."

Samuel's voice could barely be heard as he mumbled, "We left him. We had to. They got Levi."

chapter 14

NEWS OF LEVI'S capture spread through the community the way mist works its way slowly up a hill to the top and then rolls quickly down the other side. By late afternoon of the following day, Ari knew he had to deliver Levi's note to Leah. He dreaded the task.

"Rita," Ari said, "it might be easier if you're with me. Leah might take it better if you're there."

"Of course." Rita went into Ari's bedroom to get her coat from the closet. A small section was now reserved for her, and she felt at home.

Zev and Binyamin arrived at Dove's house a few minutes after Ari and Rita.

"Naomi's in with Leah," Dove said as he took their coats. "We can meet in the kitchen."

Ari pulled the envelope from his pocket with the Hebrew lamed, the letter L. "I have to give her this note."

Dove shook his head. "I told you, she's too young to be romantically involved. I won't allow it."

Ari glanced at Rita, then at the kitchen door. "You three go ahead. I need a private word with Dove."

Zev and Binyamin followed Rita into the kitchen.

Ari stood holding the note. "I gave that soldier my word," he said quietly. "Stop wasting time and let's get this over with."

The two men stared at each other, then Dove threw his hands into the air. "She'll probably find out about the note anyway, and she'll hate me for interfering. Fine. Go ahead. Give it to her."

Ari walked down the hallway in the direction he heard crying. Naomi opened the door a crack to Ari's knock. He handed her the note.

Naomi's eyes held tears. "I'll see she gets it."

Ari made his way to the kitchen and took a seat with the others. They heard Leah sob.

Zev cleared his throat. "Tell us what you know, Ari."

"Yalon, Samuel, and Isaac are badly wounded. Isaac hasn't yet regained consciousness. They each lost a substantial amount of blood. Yalon is scheduled for surgery tomorrow."

"Will Samuel recover?" Zev asked.

"They don't know yet. Goldstein's hopeful."

"What about Levi?" Binyamin asked.

"Levi is probably dead. But we don't know that for sure." Ari pushed his emotions deep inside. He would not allow himself to feel. That would come later.

"We don't even know exactly where this happened," Dove added.

"If Levi talks." Binyamin leaned forward. "If he tells them our situation. How vulnerable we are."

"If Levi talks, if he doesn't." Dove slowly shook his head. "What's the difference? We can't get to him, and we don't even know if he's still alive."

"Isaac was shot in his leg and chest," Ari told them. "Yalon took one in his side. He still carried Isaac home."

"But they wore Dragon Skin body armor," Zev said. "Made from ceramic and titanium. What could get through that?"

"Armor-piercing rounds?" Binyamin asked.

"Yeah, but like nothing we've ever seen." Ari inhaled deeply. "This was more than just depleted uranium with steel jackets."

Rita looked at Ari. "What will happen to Levi? If he's still alive."

He didn't want to tell her. "It's unlikely he lived through the night," he finally said. "Levi was bleeding from his neck and unable to walk when Yalon tried to drag him back behind some rubble. Two men wearing tunics with rope belts ran up and pulled Levi away from him. Yalon went back and hid with Samuel and Isaac. They think they heard Levi scream."

"Did they hear him scream after he was taken—or before?" Dove asked. "This is important."

"They don't know for certain," Ari admitted. "They think it was after."

Zev stroked his beard. "What are we going to do, Ari?"

"What we always do. Wait."

Days passed while Ari struggled with how to ascertain the fate of Levi.

Dove dropped by daily to see Ari. Occasionally they discussed Levi. Usually they did not.

One cloudy cold day, in the late afternoon, they sat in Ari's living room. Dove got up to pour himself a cup of coffee. "I do have some concern over the community finances, Ari."

"We have more reserve saved than in times past," he answered confidently, although he wasn't feeling as sure as he sounded.

"Ari, these shipments of food are not inexpensive. And we still have one more payment due for the smart weapons."

"Can't Rishon make the weapons payment?" Ari felt his stomach muscles tighten.

"Maybe. My cousin and the others give us almost everything they make. His employer in Paris pays well but most of it goes to our suppliers. Rishon says the French economy shows signs of real strain. He thinks they're facing economic collapse in the near future."

"In a few weeks it'll be spring and our families can plant gardens for food. You worry too much." He intended to work himself into a better mood, and Dove wasn't helping.

Dove shook his head. "Maybe so, but it will take years to replace the groves and fields beyond our walls."

Ari thought for a moment. "We'll start to repair them in the spring, after the rains."

"No, Ari. It's not safe for us to go out beyond our walls, won't be for a while."

Rita arrived at that moment and let herself in the front door.

Feeling grateful for the interruption, Ari turned the conversation to a casual nature until Dove left a short time later.

Rita sat next to him. She leaned close, and pressed her cheek against his. "Any news of Levi?"

"No," he whispered.

Rita's wrist com beeped. She looked down at the screen, and her face paled.

"What is it, Rita?"

"Nothing." She looked up. "It's only Jacob."

"Why's Jacob calling?"

"I think he still cares for me," she said hesitantly.

Ari blinked. "Well, I'll have to tell him then."

"I feel I owe him an explanation." She glanced down at the screen again.

"Why would you owe him anything?" Ari took a deep breath. "You weren't seeing him, were you?"

"No, of course not." Rita's fingers felt the star beneath her blouse. "A few dinners with friends—Jacob happened to be there."

"Dinners? Then you were seeing him." Ari wasn't worried. He knew Jacob was no competition.

"I didn't even know he'd be there." Rita coughed. "The first time."

Ari smiled. "Don't worry about it. He's still got a crush and he'll have to get over it." He patted her hand affectionately. "It's nothing."

After an early dinner, Rita turned her wrist com to silent, and opened a book detailing the archeological digs under the Dead Sea while Ari spent the evening in his office making phone calls.

Late that night a loud banging on the outer door woke Ari with a start. He saw his phone light blink and picked up the receiver. "Commander, it's the guard downstairs. Levi's brother passed through a few minutes ago demanding to see you. He's agitated."

Ari put the phone down. "It's Jacob, he's outside." Ari got up, pulled on his pants, and grabbed a T-shirt.

Rita sat up and wrapped the bed sheet around her. "Jacob is more serious than I thought," she said.

"You stay here," Ari said. "I'll take care of this." He closed the door behind him.

Jacob was shouting by the time Ari reached the outer door. He unlocked the latch and opened the door wide. "What is going on?" Ari's frame filled the doorway.

"I have to talk to you." Jacob's voice sounded excited. "By the way, do you know your phone's off?"

Ari moved back and Jacob stepped inside. "I didn't know. But couldn't this wait until tomorrow?"

"I thought you'd want to know right away, Commander. Yalon's conscious, and he remembers details of the attack. I just left the temporary hospital." Jacob was panting from running up the stairs and down the hallway.

Ari invited him into the living room. He pointed to one of the sofas and sat in the other one. "Tell me what you know."

Jacob sat with a satisfied smile. "Yalon came to, and recalled hearing the attackers say something about taking Levi. He's certain he can lead a reconnaissance team to the exact place where the abduction happened."

"I'm not sure how this helps us," Ari said. "Yalon's condition is serious. He can't lead anyone anywhere."

Jacob sat forward. "Yalon's convinced that Levi's alive."

"But we don't know where he's being held. If he is alive."

"It's more than we knew before. At least it's something."

Ari shook his head slowly. "It's not much."

"He's my brother," Jacob insisted. "If it were you instead of him, no one would give up until we knew for sure. We owe him that much."

"I'm not giving up," Ari said quickly. "I don't know what we can realistically do about it, though."

Jacob sat silently, looking miserable.

Ari glanced at his watch and stood. "Dove's awake in a few hours. I'll talk to him."

"Thank you, Commander." Jacob stood. "The only thing Levi has to hold onto is the belief that we'll come for him."

Ari nodded, and walked him to the outer door. "Anything else on your mind, Jacob?"

"No, and thanks for seeing me. I guess I should've waited." He flashed Ari a smile and started out the door.

"You did the right thing to come to me. Shalom, Jacob." He closed the door and returned to the bedroom to find the door open a crack. "It's not what you think," he said.

Rita sat up and clasped her hands together. "I know, I heard. Are you going to attempt a rescue?"

In the glow of the nightlight, Rita took on a radiant look. Ari cleared his throat. "We have no idea where he is. Maybe Dove can figure something out." He crossed the room and sat on the bed facing her.

"Will Naomi know about this?" Rita leaned back against a pillow.

"No. Discuss this with no one. Understood?"

Rita smiled and raised an eyebrow. "Of course, Commander."

Ari relaxed, took a breath, and gazed at her. "The others will know only if the operation is successful. You understand, don't you, Honey?"

Rita brushed her fingers across his chin. "I believe you'll be successful and then everyone will know what you did."

"If I knew for sure where the boy is being held, I'd go get him myself."

"I know you would," she whispered.

He wanted to shake Jacob from his mind, from her mind. He wanted to stop thinking about Levi. Ari reached over to the nightstand to turn off the light, then stopped. "I don't want you to feel upset." He leaned close and kissed her neck. "Let me massage your shoulders."

The morning was unusually chilly when Ari left at dawn for Dove's office. Rita left to attend morning prayers an hour later. She planned to spend the day at the women's building catching up with the other women after prayers. Since moving in with Ari, she'd taken herself out of the daily work schedule, and she missed the interaction with the other women.

Around midday, while chatting with friends in the community kitchen, Rita got a call from Dove. She stopped cutting vegetables and picked up the phone.

"Rita, we're at Ari's. He sent a driver over to get you. Can you meet him outside?"

"What's wrong, Dove?" Rita pressed her lips together, and tried not to worry.

"Nothing, just some holiday plans."

He sounded too casual. "Okay, see you in a few." Rita set the phone down and hung up her apron, her mind racing with possibilities on the way out the door.

When she arrived fifteen minutes later, Ari, Dove, Zev, and Daniel sat staring at each other in the conference room. She sat in a chair next to Dove and asked, "What's this about?"

Daniel gestured toward Ari. "We have a plan to find Levi. Ari doesn't like it."

Rita looked at Dove. "Your plan?"

"Well, not really. My team identified the most likely places where Levi is probably being held. Four, maybe five locations. All of them deep into enemy territory." Dove paused. "We should take the intel to Mossad agents in Jerusalem. Let them decide if it's feasible to plan a rescue."

"That sounds right," Rita said, enjoying her new role as mediator.

Daniel shook his head. "They'll take too long trying to negotiate first. He could be dead by the time they decide."

"Daniel wants us to go," Zev explained. "He wants to lead a Special Forces team to the most probable location and then, well, he wants us to storm the place."

Rita raised an eyebrow and looked at Ari.

"See," Ari said. "I told you the plan is insane. It's a suicide mission."

"We have to try," Daniel said. "We left him there."

Rita liked Daniel. Always first to volunteer for risky operations, that's what Ari had told her. "Daniel," Rita said gently, "if you were being held, you know you wouldn't want your brother Jews to die in a desperate attempt to prove their loyalty to you."

Daniel closed his eyes. "I should've been the one to go. I'd trade my life for his."

"We all know you would," Zev said. "But this is not your choice. It's not up to you to decide. Hashem has brought us to this moment. This isn't over."

"He's only a boy," Daniel said.

"He's a soldier," Ari replied. "A defender of Israel. Don't take that away from him, Daniel."

"We have to approach this with reason," Rita added. "We don't want to try and fail."

"We must have the exact location before we do anything," Dove said. "Communication relays are operational again so we scan satellite images daily in the five probable locations."

"Unless they move him," Ari said, "we have nothing more."

"It's unlikely they'll move him because they know our 'sat' eyes are watching," Zev said. "We need to gather our intelligence another way."

Ari turned toward Daniel. "Let's think on this awhile. But we won't rest until we figure something out."

Dove agreed. "And my tactical team continues to work on this."

They said shalom while Rita stayed at the table, and Ari walked them to the door. Returning to Rita in the living room, he sat shaking his head. "I should've been easier on Daniel."

"If you could determine Levi's location," she asked, "what would you do?"

"I haven't thought that far ahead, I guess." He moved closer. "Like Dove said, it's doubtful we're going to get any leads on this one. We'll concentrate on identifying his location. We'll get it eventually."

"Ari, how far are you willing to go?"

"What do you mean, Honey?"

"All this sounds risky." Thoughts of Ari going off in the night, leading a team on some rescue op terrified her.

Ari took her hand. "I am willing to risk a great deal for this. If we can somehow get him back, it'll boost the morale of this community as no other single act could."

"Any attempt will anger the group who has him," she reminded him. "And the Islamic Coalition that funds them."

"Good," Ari's hand tightened around hers. "If we get him it'll send a message to our enemies that they can't break us. And they can't break me."

chapter 15

IT WAS LATE Saturday morning, and Ari finished his second coffee with Rita. He set the cup on the table and his wrist com buzzed. "It's Zev," he said. "He's on his way here."

Rita set her cup on the kitchen table. "What's this about?"

"I don't know." Ari went out to unlock the door. A few minutes later, he returned with Zev.

Zev entered the living room, saying, "Shabbat Shalom. We have a plan."

Rita moved to a cushioned chair and offered him the sofa.

Zev smiled broadly. "Dove has three agents with mixed heritage. Two have relatives in Arab towns and one has ties to a Bedouin tribe living in the Sinai."

"We used to have operatives in several Islamic towns," Ari said. "We haven't had that kind of access since the conflict intensified."

"That's good," Zev replied. "Our enemies won't be expecting this kind of bold move."

Ari studied Zev for a moment. "So, what's Dove's plan?"

"Well, maybe it's time for those three agents to visit their distant relatives. We'll dress them appropriately and they'll go out under the cover of darkness."

"Forget it," Ari said. "I'm not letting anyone else walk into an enemy ambush."

"Of course not," Zev said, "they'll drive cars."

Ari shook his head. "That's not what I meant."

"How will they get back?" Rita asked. "What if they're found out?"

"Well, getting them back is the tricky part, but Dove's analysts are working on several possibilities." Zev stroked his beard. "They should get what they need in a few days. They'll each have a car with them to get back independently."

Ari sat across from Zev. "Their only objective is to identify Levi's location and get back here undetected. Is that right?"

"First we have to know he's alive and where he's being held. Then we can decide how to proceed."

Ari relaxed against the sofa cushion. "Do you realize what this will mean? If we get Levi back?"

Zeve smiled. "It will be a miracle if we can accomplish this. Everyone in our community will know Hashem is with us."

"What about Levi?" Rita asked. "If you get him back, he may not be able to recover from this ordeal."

Both men sat silent for a moment.

"We won't know until we can bring him home," Ari admitted. "He has a chance of regaining his life."

"Levi is young and strong," Zev said. "And he'll have Leah's love to help him heal. I believe we're getting him in time. Oh course, that's if we can find him."

Worry creased Ari's forehead. *Oh, we'll find him,* he thought. *I just hope we find him alive.*

The following evening, Ari invited Rita to accompany him to Dove's office for the team's operation briefing with Moshe. The chosen spies, dressed for their part, sat at the conference table.

Moshe paused when Ari and Rita entered the briefing room with Dove.

"Please, continue," Ari said as they sat.

"I'll begin the cover story now." Moshe nodded toward the operatives. "These men are not happy. They want to be on the winning side."

"Your greatest challenge," Dove said to the three men, "will be convincing your distant relatives to believe you. Don't investigate until you have their trust."

"At that point," Moshe said, "you will inquire discreetly about the fate of the missing soldier. Don't attempt anything. Your sole objective is to get information and bring it back to us. When you get the info, each of you will go off somewhere to stage a fatal accident of some kind to slip away from your relatives without causing them to face retribution. Otherwise, your disappearances might be viewed suspiciously."

Dove said, "You'll change your identities at that point to make your way back here. Your cover story when you travel will be that you are searching for a lost family member."

"Remember," Ari added, "you men are chosen to go for a reason. We have complete confidence in you."

Dove looked at his watch and stood. "Let's let Moshe work out the details with the team. I have to check on Yalon."

Ari and Rita followed Dove to his private office down the hall.

"Yalon?" Ari asked. "Did he have a setback?"

Dove opened his office door. Yalon sat in a wheelchair behind Dove's desk, outlining on a map.

Yalon smiled as they entered. "Ari," he cried out affectionately, "we're going to find him."

Ari turned to Dove. "What is he doing here?"

Dove smiled, and pulled out chairs for Ari and Rita. "Goldstein approved it. Reluctantly, but we have her blessing. Yalon's providing detailed descriptions of the area where they last saw Levi."

"I'm okay, Ari. And they need these maps. They need my memory. It's crucial for the operation." Yalon turned to Rita and lowered his voice as if they were sharing a secret. "I can't go with them. I'd be a burden to the unit." He looked down at his map and resumed drawing.

"Is this team prepared to leave in a few hours?" Ari asked Dove. "I want this to work."

"Moshe thinks they are. He's usually right. These men are fluent in Islamic dialects and fully knowledgeable about their customs," Dove said. "They'll have to provide false intelligence in exchange for acceptance, of that you can be sure. But we're counting on their distant relations to be eager to take them back. They should have no trouble slipping away when they get the information."

"What if the ruse doesn't work?" Ari asked. "How can you prevent them from disclosing anything real about our situation? We're vulnerable here. We can't let that be known, or even suspected."

Dove rubbed his chin. "There is a town in Judea named Efrania. They're constantly under enemy fire. We'll get our agents near Efrania and stage from there. It makes their story more credible."

Yalon looked up from his mapmaking. "It's true. Anyone living there might be tempted to save themselves by leaving."

A few hours later, the operatives were ready. Ari and Dove joined them for a final word while Rita hung back at the door.

Ari spoke first, warning them to take care with their own lives. "We may find Levi, and we may not. We may have already lost him. Our community can't afford to lose you, so take no unnecessary risks. Let the information come to you. Don't try to seek it out aggressively. If you can't get anything, or if you feel at risk, slip away and return to us."

"We'll have no contact," Dove reminded them, "while you're engaged in your operation. Listen to your commander's words. Take care."

"We're taking them down the supply line in a van," Moshe said. "The soldiers arranging the cars along the supply route don't know what it's for."

Ari nodded, and the team left with Moshe for the base camp. He didn't feel right about this operation. The risks were always high—it wasn't that.

On the drive home, he tried to explain it to Rita. "If these men are captured, they'll probably be publicly executed. That would affect more than our community. It will distress the entire nation."

Ari had serious concerns about this rescue attempt. He knew he should've cleared the operational protocols with his superiors in Jerusalem. But he also knew they never would've approved it. He was risking Dove's career on this plan.

Every night Dove reported details from the daily intelligence reports about the rescue operation. On day five of the operation, Ari phoned Dove in the evening. "Are you coming over later?"

"Yes," Dove answered, "I told Naomi I had to go out."

Ari heard Dove tell Naomi, "Ari's experiencing some difficulty and I thought I should drop by to see him. He needs someone to talk to."

"That's right," Naomi answered clearly. "I know all about what's going on. I finally got a call through to Rita, and she told me everything."

Ari listened carefully as Dove asked Naomi, "Then you know all about it?"

"Yes, of course I do," Naomi said. "I tried to tell her not to see Jacob and Ari at the same time. But she wouldn't listen to me. Now everyone's unhappy."

Dove said, "Better not wait up, Love. This could take some time." Then, "Ari, I'll be right over."

By Sunday night, eight days in, Ari felt edgy. Dove dropped by after dinner, and Ari finally relaxed after they talked for a couple of hours.

"I hate this part," Ari said. "The waiting."

"The timeline for the operation is tight, but it's too early to start worrying yet," Dove reminded him. "I've never seen you like this."

Ari's jaw tightened. "Yeah, I have a bad feeling. I can't explain it."

"What's the soonest they might return?" Rita asked.

"They're going to have to work fast," Dove answered. "We allowed two days in, four to six days in the villages, and two days back."

Ari slowly shook his head. "I sure hope their cover stories hold."

"We worked out the details they'll need. Have some confidence."

"You're right." Ari smiled at Rita. "These guys are the best."

Dove chuckled. "You say that every time a team goes out."

"And every time, I'm right."

"The hour's late," Dove said. "Naomi may still be up."

"Yes, of course." Ari stood and motioned. "I'll walk you to the door."

A few minutes later, he sat with Rita and held her hand. "I'm sorry we haven't spent much time on anything except the operation. I know we said we'd talk. It's just that—"

"I know," Rita said. "I'm happy the way things are."

Ari smiled, almost sheepishly. "I feel a need to be discreet, and I guess I do prefer to keep my private life separate. I've always been this way."

Rita smiled. "I guess I feel the same. I'm happy," she said softly. "Really happy."

On the tenth day, Ari almost regretted his decision to allow the operation. "I should've listened to my instincts," he told Rita.

She put their half-eaten dinners away, and they sat together in the living room until Ari's wrist com beeped. The message read, "Dinner in 5 min. I'm on my way." He sprang up. "C'mon, Rita. It's code. They know something."

A few minutes later they were in the car with Zev, headed for Dove's office. Zev knew only that one of the operatives made contact.

"How's this possible?" Ari asked Dove as he walked through his office door. "I thought we'd have no communication until they were back."

"One of them made it in. Inside Efrania."

Ari and Rita followed Dove to the briefing room. Moshe, wearing a headset, sat at the table. Daniel entered a few minutes later, followed by Binyamin.

"This is what we know," Moshe said. "We received a message using our operation code word from a soldier in the town. One man arrived alone. He is wounded, and he has critical information to deliver."

"From the description," Dove added, "we think it's Agent Shlomo."

Monica entered and slid into a chair. "I heard from the guard outside. Shlomo made it back to Efrania."

"Can we get him here?" Rita asked.

"We can't drive him," Moshe said, "that would be dangerous. We're going to fly him in a helicopter with two escorts."

Shoshona entered and handed a piece of paper to Dove.

Dove looked up after reading it. "We estimate three hours before we get him here."

Everyone had questions.

"We don't know the extent of his injuries," Dove said. "We'll meet back here in three hours."

The others left, but Ari and Rita stayed seated with Dove. Moshe closed the door and returned to the table.

"Does Yalon know?" Ari asked.

Dove shook his head. "No. By the time Agent Shlomo gets here it'll be the middle of the night."

"Yalon's too emotional about this to bring him in now," Moshe added.

Ari took Rita home to wait, his mind racing with questions that couldn't be answered. The minutes slowly passed into hours. He looked at Rita, sitting silently with him. *All she's been through,* he thought, *and she never complains.*

She saw him looking and smiled. "I'm here, if you need me," she said.

He nodded. "I know."

Finally, Ari got the call. He grabbed Rita's coat, and handed it to her on the way to the front door.

Zev took them straight to the briefing room when they arrived.

"They landed without incident," Dove told them when they entered. "They're on the way here."

"Is he conscious?" Ari asked.

Dove shrugged. "We don't know."

Moshe entered wearing his headset. "They're here," he reported. "The two medics with him have top-secret clearance."

Fifteen minutes later, the medics wheeled him in. Everyone gathered around.

"Can you tell us what happened?" Dove asked tenderly.

Shlomo stared up with a silly grin. Slowly he focused on Ari while the grin turned to a grimace. "I'm the Bedouin," he slurred.

"What about Levi?" Ari asked.

"It was easy," Shlomo said. "They were happy to see me. Another two weeks I'd be married off."

"Levi?" Dove repeated.

"I know," Shlomo said with a rush of words. "They're talking about him. I don't have to ask. They're laughing at him. I couldn't let 'em know how I really felt. I pictured in my mind what we'll do to them for torturing Levi." Shlomo's eyes filled with tears.

"He's alive?" Dove leaned close. "Are you certain?"

"Yeah, they're bragging about it. Having him." Shlomo's eyes closed. His face relaxed.

Ari asked the medic, "How was Shlomo injured?"

"A grenade was apparently thrown under his car as he drove into Efrania. The people who helped him said he's lucky to be alive."

Ari folded his arms. "His cover must've been blown."

"It wasn't. The soldiers indicated that he dressed wrong." The medic shook his head. "Attacked for being in the wrong tribe."

Rita cleared her throat. "Which groups are fighting?"

"All of 'em," Moshe said.

Shlomo opened his eyes and saw Dove. "We have to get him. They say they're cracking the Jew prisoner like a walnut."

"Tell us and we'll go." Dove spoke like a mother asking her child where it hurts. "Where is he? Do you know?"

Shlomo closed his eyes. "The stone fortress. In the Sinai." Then he lost consciousness.

"He's not hurt bad," the medic told them. "Torn flesh, a few broken bones."

"This is worse than we thought," Moshe said.

Zev nodded.

Rita touched Ari's arm. "Why? The medic just said he'd recover from his injuries."

"No, Honey, he means the stone fortress. It's a former Knights Templar castle."

Dove stepped back and said, "The borders are closed, the airspace is guarded. It sits at the far edge of a vast desert controlled by fanatical Islamics." He took a breath and let it out. "It'll take an army to bring Levi home."

Ari slowly shook his head. "I agree," he said quietly. "It's impossible."

chapter 16

A GRAY SKY dumped torrential rains over the Negev following Agent Shlomo's return. No word from the other two operatives came in, and Ari's mood began to match the weather. To make matters worse, Daniel and Jacob asked to see Ari for personal reasons.

The next afternoon, Ari told Rita he had to go out. "An hour at the most," he assured her. "I'll be at Dove's office."

Daniel and Jacob were waiting with Dove when Ari arrived. He pulled a chair away from Dove's desk and sat. "Let's have it," he said.

"We want to be in on it," Jacob began eagerly.

"What you're working on about Levi," Daniel said.

Ari looked at Dove. "What makes them think this?"

Jacob shrugged. "It's obvious."

"Did Yalon say something to you?" Ari asked.

"He might've mentioned something about it," Jacob admitted.

Daniel leaned forward. "We want to go when the time comes. I should lead the team."

Jacob pointed to himself. "It should be me because Levi is my brother. Besides, Daniel got married a month ago."

"Yalon told them we know where Levi is," Dove said.

Ari took a deep breath. "Yalon doesn't know anything. We can't get to Levi even if we knew where they took him. We don't have jets and armies to cross the desert wasteland to get him, and then cross it again to bring him home. I'm sorry. Levi is gone."

Both men started to apologize, but Ari shook his head. "Look, we're all under pressure. But understand, this is not to be discussed with anyone. This can't leak outside our walls."

Jacob and Daniel promised to help quash any rumors about Levi among the enlisted men before they left.

The door closed behind them, and Ari glanced at Dove. "Zev approached me about using the ancient Metzada tunnel to attempt a rescue operation. It runs southeast through the Negev into the Sinai and ends near the stone fortress."

"I know. He told me too."

"We have no way to verify." Ari shook his head. "We can't send men into that tunnel. It may be collapsed in places. Underground air vents might be blocked. Or worse, they could surface into a terrorist camp instead of the desolate area Zev described."

"We don't have good choices," Dove pointed out. "Each rescue scenario is high-risk. My people are running out of options."

Ari paused. "Have you discussed Zev's idea with Moshe, or the others?"

"Of course not." Dove shook his head. "No one knows about this tunnel except the four of us."

"Good," Ari said. "I'm not doubting you. I just need to know."

"Ari, if we divulge the existence of this site to our own population, our enemies will surely hear about it. If Islamics find it, they will destroy our ancient tunnel. Any evidence of our former presence will be wiped out. Do we have a right to decide this for future generations?"

Ari didn't answer for a moment. Then he said, "Islamics could stumble upon it any time. Our tunnel, and anything our ancestors left inside, would be destroyed. If we knew for certain he's really there it'd be worth exposing."

"The men who rescue him have a choice to go or not," Dove reminded him. "Levi's being tortured unmercifully every day and every night in captivity. We all know it. If we're going to go, we should start planning. We can't afford to wait."

"I know," Ari said. "Would your men try to penetrate the prison by stealth, or force?"

"We can't buy him out or trade for him, so we either go in and get him or abandon him to unspeakable suffering. I think a small, covert team. Sneak in and grab him."

Ari thought for a moment. "Our information about the fortress is old, and sketchy at best. But how long would it take?"

"A week to plan, another to execute. Ari, do you think he's there?"

"Zev does. He saw Levi's face in a blue flame spiraling around the stone fortress. In a dream."

"So," Dove asked, "are you authorizing me to put a planning team together tonight?"

"Yes. We should start tonight." Ari stood. "Your best tactical analysis team on this. For planning only."

"Of course," Dove answered. "Right away."

Ari noticed the clock on the wall. "Oh, no. I told Rita I'd be home in an hour, and it's been four."

Dove chuckled as Ari left.

When Ari arrived home, he found Rita sitting at the kitchen table. "Honey," he said.

She looked at Ari's face and hers lit up. "You're going to send a team to get him, aren't you?" She smiled. "I have a good feeling about this."

"Yes, I think we're going to try." Ari poured two small juice glasses of sweet red wine. "We should celebrate tonight, and stay positive."

"It's difficult to think about poor Levi, though." Rita accepted the wine.

He picked up the other glass and they moved into the living room. "Right now I can't do anything more about Levi. Or anything outside this room," he said. "So I control my thoughts until I can concentrate on what's here. In this moment, in this place—with you."

Rita sat next to Ari on the couch. "Not me. My mind wants to go back and think of what I could have done. Or what I should do next."

Ari sipped the wine. "I don't analyze the way you do. Discipline is simply a way of life for me. Always has been. Dove's putting together a preliminary plan now, so we'll know something in a few days. If we can risk it."

With a clink of her wine glass against his, she said, "This is so exciting. But, how can you do it?"

Ari sipped his wine, then set the glass on the coffee table. "Besides me, only Dove, Zev, and Devorah know about a secret tunnel Zev found when he put in the Maccabiah tunnel. When we constructed that tunnel he discovered an ancient tunnel built around the time of the standoff against the Romans at Metzada in the year 73."

"Is it still usable?" Rita leaned closer to Ari.

"The Metzada tunnel's in remarkably good shape. It goes east for a considerable distance then continues into the Sinai and ends near an old oasis."

"Who'll go and get him?" She finished her wine and set the glass on the table next to Ari's. "Has Dove decided yet?"

"Daniel wants to lead. Dove thinks he'll send Jacob on the team." Ari set his glass down when he saw a look of anguish cross Rita's face.

"Ari, I've never really asked you for anything. Never questioned you."

"That's true, Rita." Ari paused. "Is there something you want now?" With some uneasiness, he realized he would give her anything she wanted.

"Yes." Rita's voice faltered momentarily. "I want to ask a favor."

In Dove's office, Ari authorized the final rescue plan when Moshe presented it a few days later. "This is going to work," Ari said as he handed the confidential folder back to Dove.

Daniel reported to Dove's office to learn he'd been chosen for operation leader. Six other team members began training with Daniel that afternoon in an empty grain warehouse near the barracks. In five days, they'd have to be ready. Jacob wasn't one of them.

Two of Binyamin's men fashioned a false wall to hide the opening when Zev blasted a section of the Maccabiah tunnel to reveal a short passageway to the secret Metzada tunnel.

Ari dropped by daily to observe the team's progress. On the last day of the training, Ari addressed the men before they left around noon. "This ancient tunnel is a gift from Hashem," he told them as they gathered around. "There's a reason we found it."

Ari said shalom to Dove and Moshe, and headed home feeling the usual rush of adrenaline from the start of an operation. He didn't want to admit it, but he wished he were entering the tunnel. *Whatever's going to happen is up to Daniel now*, he thought.

chapter 17

SPECIAL SQUAD LEADER Daniel drove the team to the beach camp. They gathered inside the transportation tunnel while Binyamin's two men removed the false wall covering the new entryway.

Daniel reminded the team to switch on the photovoltaic lights embedded in their helmets.

The false wall, guided into place by Binyamin's guards on the other side, closed off the secret entry after the men stepped into the 2,000-year-old passageway.

Each man carried a heavy backpack through the winding darkness of the tunnel. The ceiling extended to a height of eight feet at the top of the arch. The floor and walls consisted of hardened sandstone. In some places they could see etch marks left by the original carvers.

Debris piles from partially collapsed walls slowed their progress for the first two hours. Daniel spoke words of encouragement to his men. They shared their experience of moving backward through time as they walked forward toward their goal.

After five hours, the men halted for food and rest. "We'll take a four-hour break," Daniel told them.

The soldiers ate energy bars and consumed the first of many protein drinks. Daniel waited until they settled down before he arranged his own pack. He calculated the progress made and the requirements of the following day, closed his eyes, and fell asleep.

Exactly four hours later, a series of beeps from their wrist coms brought the men to their feet. Yosiah, the medic on the team, approached Daniel. "This is a daring rescue attempt for a man we can only hope is even alive."

Daniel nodded. "We are the ones who will settle this. We'll bring resolution to our community. However this turns out, to start the healing process, our people need to know Levi's fate."

The men voiced their agreement and shouldered their packs.

The team followed Daniel through the tunnel's twists and turns for the next three days. On the fourth day, they advanced a short way to discover that the tunnel opened into a large, carved-out room.

Daniel pointed. "This cavern is close to our destination. Look for a way up."

Yosiah found steps in the section he was clearing with his hands. He called out for the others, and they came running, calling out, "Mazel tov."

For the next hour, by the lights on their helmets, the men cleaned rocks and debris off gray and tan stone stairs.

"You go first," Yosiah said to Daniel. "It's only right."

One by one, behind their leader, the men climbed the smooth, level steps into a small cave. Boulders and rocks blocked the exit. They could see daylight between the boulders.

"We don't know what's out there," team member Tikhon said.

Daniel turned, his helmet light flashing across the rugged cave walls. "It's midday," he said. "We'll wait the day out in the cavern room going over details of the rescue. Tonight, we'll remove a few rocks at the top and crawl out."

The men returned to the cavern room to wait.

In the afternoon, they ate a meal of canned fruit and protein bars. "Who do you think carved this?" a large man nicknamed Pybar asked while they ate.

"One of your ancestors," Yosiah answered.

Pybar raised his eyebrows. "Could be, I guess."

When the time came, the men slipped out into the evening air. Enough ambient light lingered to give Daniel his bearings as he looked around. The narrow valley they surfaced in appeared to hold only a few scraggly trees and the usual desert wildlife—scorpions, wild goats, and even an occasional llama escaping from the IDF special desert forces.

The sky darkened to a deep purple while they walked east for the next hour. The men put on night-vision goggles when they moved into uneven, rocky territory. Another hour of crawling, crouching, and searching passed before they located the target.

Daniel pointed. "We have it."

"Affirmative," Yosiah whispered back. "It looks to be maybe two clicks out."

They crawled the two kilometers. The muscle of the operation, Pybar and a man next to him called Smasher, moved close to Daniel as they neared their destination.

The uneven ground sloped up to a thick, four-foot-high stone barrier around the prison. The team moved in and crouched behind it. Daniel didn't see any posted guards while they waited. He gave a nod and they followed him over the barrier to land quietly on a stone walkway next to the 15th-century stone walls of the prison.

Team members Gabriel and Matan stepped forward. Gabriel quickly set explosive charges along the base of the prison wall. Matan took out a laser cutting tool. As quiet as a whisper, it cut through old metal bars covering the only visible window on the first floor of the two-story prison. Each bar gave way after only a few minutes. Once the last bar fell into his hand, Matan looked at Daniel and nodded.

One by one, the team went through the window and landed on a stone floor corridor weathered by centuries of use.

"We're in it now," Daniel whispered.

They moved single file down a hallway until Daniel stopped suddenly and held up one fist. The men behind him halted. He crept forward to hear faint sounds of Arabic coming from inside a room. Prison guards, eating and talking. He moved backward and the team proceeded in a direction away from the guards.

A dank odor eventually led to the prison basement. The team crept down stone stairs, following the smell. Around a hallway corner they observed a lone guard sitting with his back to them near an old wooden door with a round iron lock.

Pybar waited for the hand signal. Two of Daniel's fingers pointed forward. Pybar moved around Daniel and advanced toward his intended target. From behind, he reached one hand over the guard's mouth, and with his other hand he jerked the guard's head to one side. The sentry slumped to the floor with a broken neck.

Smasher found the wooden door easy to force open. Inside, a young man in a ragged, blood-stained caftan lay crumpled on the floor. Yosiah was the first one in. He dropped his kit and knelt next to the prisoner. Daniel leaned close.

"It's Levi," Yosiah confirmed. "He's barely conscious."

Yosiah prepared a field dressing for Levi while Smasher pulled the dead guard inside the cell.

"We're here, Levi," Daniel said. "We've come for you."

"He's in a fog," Yosiah told him. Matan and Gabriel formed a chair by interlocking their forearms. Smasher gently lifted Levi into their waiting arms.

"We have you, Levi," Daniel whispered to him.

Levi moaned.

"Let's go," Daniel commanded.

Pybar led the team up the stone steps to ground level. Matan and Gabriel carried Levi, with Yosiah next to him. Daniel, Tikhon, and Smasher brought up the rear.

They cautiously returned to the cut prison window.

Daniel went through first and fell to the ground, followed by Yosiah. Then Gabriel lifted Levi through the opening to Tikhon and Yosiah. Pybar and Smasher made it through, and the team withdrew to the outer barrier.

Alarms went off as they reached the four-foot-high stone rampart. The men flopped like fish over the side, pulling Levi with them. Crouched in the shadow of the barrier, they waited while a searchlight cut trails across the darkened desert floor.

"We can't stay here," Yosiah whispered. "They will find the window."

They inched on their bellies to the end of the barrier. While two searchlights crisscrossed the ground, they crawled first to an outcropping a few meters from the stone barrier. Levi groaned as they pulled him on a sleeping mat along the hard ground.

"We're going to make it," Daniel whispered as they hid behind a boulder.

Armed prison guards ran into the outside corridor as Daniel spoke. The guards swore loudly and ran about.

"We need a diversion now," Yosiah said.

Daniel clicked a button on his wrist communicator. The string of charges set by Gabriel went off in succession. Part of the prison wall exploded. Flying bricks became deadly projectiles.

"Use the boulders for protection," Daniel told his men. "I'll stay here until the last minute to cover you."

Gabriel wrapped his hand around the shoulder strap of Daniel's pack as it slid off his back. Then Gabriel pointed three fingers forward, the signal for the men to stay close. He crawled ahead toward the wadi. The team advanced behind their new leader each time the searchlights moved away.

Daniel, watching his team depart, sat with his back against the boulder, listening to the guards search the perimeter. He wore civilian clothes, no jewelry. Like the other team members, he didn't carry identification.

Searching guards came close. He held his breath. He'd squeezed into a dark crevice on the north side of a rock formation. Not even the array of brilliant stars above cast light on Daniel.

Guards with flashlights searched the area surrounding the prison for over an hour. Eventually fewer and fewer guards remained outside. Daniel breathed easier after two close calls.

Another hour passed and Daniel didn't move. Finally, he slowly unfurled himself from his rock-shelf hiding place. He moved a few inches back, stopped, waited. The next large boulder outcrop looked to be ten to twelve meters away.

The searchlights finally ceased their hunt for the intruders.

Daniel crawled a short way and stopped. Resting his ear to the ground, he heard no sounds.

Fifteen minutes passed before he crawled forward another meter and stopped. He continued until he rested safely behind the protection of the next rock outcrop. An hour later, he was halfway to the narrow valley.

He leaned close to the ground and stepped forward into the darkness toward the ravine. Another step, and then another.

A searing blue flame entered Daniel's right thigh. His leg stepped forward, and then it wouldn't move. A moment passed before his dark red blood spilled out. He grabbed his wounded thigh with both hands and forced himself forward toward the protection of nearby rocks. The next sniper bullet lodged deep in his left calf, shattering the fibula.

Daniel lay face down on the ground for a moment before lifting up enough to rest on his elbows. Using his forearms, he crawled behind the rocks. He'd made it at least two kilometers away from the prison, he calculated.

For a few peaceful moments, Daniel leaned his head on a rock and gazed up at the stars. A shooting star flew out and he was overwhelmed by the beauty of it. The earth beneath hummed a sweet song for him.

"My Creator, and Creator of my ancestors, accept my prayer," Daniel whispered. He carefully removed a small black bundle from his side pants pocket. "Guardian of life, protect my beloved family, for my life is bound up in their lives." He unwrapped the package and removed a motion-sensitive detonator. "Let my death serve as atonement, and pardon my shortcomings."

He could hear footsteps and shouting in the distance now.

"Creator Adonai, I place my spirit in Your care." Daniel found the set switch on the detonator and turned it. He had a minute now, before it activated. He breathed in the sweet night air. "You have redeemed me, Adonai, G-d of truth."

Daniel closed his eyes. "*Sh'ma Yisra-el* . . . Listen."

Somewhere in between the songs of the earth and the brilliant stars, Daniel crossed over.

Once inside the narrow valley the team members retraced their path. The men were almost to the cave entrance when they heard the explosion. Stunned for a moment, they stopped and listened.

"We don't know for sure that it's Daniel," Matan said.

"Yes, we do," Gabriel answered. "The sound signature is unmistakable."

The men said a prayer for Daniel, then continued the short distance to the cave. The team moved quickly to the entrance once they spotted it. Yosiah whispered prayers of thanks as Smasher and Pybar cleared the brush. Pybar moved the last rock aside, the team went in, and the ground swallowed up the grateful men with their wounded hero.

Smasher held up emergency flashlights and they laid Levi gently onto a blanket. Yosiah began a closer examination while Matan cut away his filthy clothes.

"The damage done to his body is extensive," Yosiah reported. "Surface torture wounds, infected bullet hole in his right arm. Knife wounds on left side of his neck. Extensive bruising."

"Clean him and apply dressings," Tikhon ordered. "We don't have time for more."

Yosiah worked quickly. Then he dressed Levi in a loose cotton tunic. Matan and Gabriel assembled a field stretcher at the same time. In less than an hour, the team stood, ready to move out.

Yosiah held up a hand. "Someone has to stay. Gabriel is at the cave entrance setting up a powerful motion-sensitive explosive. If an innocent person accidentally finds the entrance, they could easily set it off."

"I'll stay," Matan said. "I don't have a family."

Gabriel returned. "We'll draw lots," he said. "I've written numbers on pieces of paper. Each man draws except the medic. He'll be needed. The lowest number stays."

"We should get moving," Smasher grumbled as he reached for his lot.

Gabriel held up his slip of paper. "One. It's me."

"Time to move out," Tikhon ordered.

Yosiah and Matan lifted Levi onto the stretcher. Pybar looked at Smasher. Each took an end of the stretcher and started walking forward. The others followed.

"This is merely a preventative measure," Tikhon told Gabriel.

"Of course. I'll wait two days and make my way back."

They locked eyes. "I know," Gabriel said. "Now go on, get out of here."

chapter 18

"I'M ON MY way, Ari," Dove said into the phone receiver. He tossed the phone down and started out the front door over his wife's protests. Calling out, "Soon, my love, you'll know everything, but now I have to go out because Ari needs me," he rushed out the door.

"I have an idea," Ari said as soon as Dove arrived.

"Yeah, I figured. Let's have it." Dove poured a glass of water in the kitchen and joined Ari in the living room.

"Daniel and the team are due back anytime. We didn't use the tunnel runners because we couldn't risk the vibrations being detected above ground. But maybe now, they'd be so close, it might be worth it."

"I don't know about using the tunnel runners, but a two-man recon team isn't a bad idea." Dove looked at Ari's beaming face. "Oh no, forget it. You're not going."

"It's not dangerous," Ari said through a smile.

"Of course it is," Dove shot back. "For all we know, Daniel and his men have been discovered and murdered. Armed Bedouins could be moving toward us through the tunnel right now."

"Not likely. And anyway, how far in is the nanocamera?"

"A few kilometers." Dove thought for a moment. "If anyone passed it, we'd know."

"Well," Ari said, "the recon has to be someone who already knows about the Metzada tunnel."

"Binyamin's guards in the supply tunnel know. The two of them could go in."

Ari picked up his phone. "They're needed where they are. I'll call Jacob."

An hour later, Dove drove Ari and Jacob down the supply line to the Maccabiah tunnel entrance station. They walked down the underground ramp into a dimly lit room, and spoke with Binyamin's guards briefly while the secret entrance was opened.

"Do you think they'll make it back okay?" one guard asked.

"Yes," Dove answered. "The enemy has to believe the prison attack was perpetrated by one of their own. They won't figure out how we could get in that deep without being seen."

"Ready, Commander," the other guard said. The faux rock wall slid open on a hidden ground rail.

Ari stepped forward, then turned to Jacob. "We're going in hot. We don't know what to expect."

Jacob nodded, unclasped the strap over his sidearm, and moved the safety off. He followed Ari's lead and switched on his helmet's night vision light.

Ari walked in silence for the first two kilometers inside the ancient pathway. Only the muffled sounds of their boots on the sand floor and the surreal glow from the night-vision lights illuminating the carved limestone walls kept them company.

He picked up the pace for the next several kilometers with Jacob following close behind. Finally, they stopped for a moment, both breathing hard. Ari stood straight and listened. "I heard sounds farther down, he said."

"It's them!" Jacob shouted.

Running forward a quarter kilometer, they saw flashlights flickering.

"We got him," Tikhon called out as they approached.

Ari felt his heart swell with gratitude. He knelt over Levi and touched his cheek.

"He's in bad shape," Tikhon said quietly. "We stopped only briefly. We should move fast."

Ari motioned to Jacob. They each took an end of the stretcher. The team jogged behind them for the few kilometers to the transportation tunnel entrance. The wall swung open when they neared.

Binyamin's two guards gently took the stretcher. They hurried with Levi and Yosiah through the remainder of the tunnel to an ambulance waiting outside for them.

"You're short two men." Ari looked around in the dim light of the transportation tunnel. "Where's Daniel?"

Tikhon's haggard face gave Ari his answer.

Jacob looked away, shook his head.

Ari closed his eyes and fought back the emotion he felt. *Another good-hearted man lost to the world,* he thought. He looked at Tikhon. "Gabriel?"

"Guarding the tunnel exit. Two days—then back."

They walked the short distance through the transportation tunnel, and emerged above ground to find the afternoon sun low in the sky.

Ari blinked and took a moment to let his eyes adjust as soldiers gathered around and congratulated the team. Word of Levi's rescue was spreading.

Ari shrugged off the attention and walked over to a temporary supply building. He leaned against it and turned away from Jacob to dial Rita's number. When her anxious voice came on the line, he said, "It's done, we're good."

"Come home, Ari. Tell me everything."

Levi was in surgery by the time Ari and Jacob returned to Kol Shofar. Ari parked in front of the barracks entrance, but Jacob didn't get out. He turned to Ari. "I'd like a word on a personal matter."

Ari stared straight out the windshield. "It's about Rita, isn't it?" He glanced at Jacob. "She's with me now."

Jacob turned toward Ari. "You don't know what you want. I've heard about you."

Ari searched for the right words. "Jacob, it's too late."

"I brought her here. She's mine." Jacob's voice held a tinge of frustration.

Ari tilted his head and looked sideways at him. "Shame on you. She doesn't belong to anyone."

"I know what I want," Jacob pleaded. "I'm in love with her."

"It's not that simple." Ari's hands still gripped the steering wheel.

"Yes, it is. I'll pursue her properly. Unlike you."

"Jacob, I have an understanding—"

Jacob interrupted with a tirade. "You don't even know what that means. If you'll back off, I'll have a chance. No, she'll have a chance at having an honorable life with me. Not a dirty little affair with someone like you."

"That's enough." Ari's restraint showed in his voice.

"As my commander, I respect you. Levi says you have a brilliant tactical mind. That your instincts are rarely wrong." Jacob sat silent for a moment. "Not a person anywhere would doubt your courage."

Ari tried another approach. "We've become friends, Jacob."

"Leave her alone, Ari."

"I can't. I've asked her to marry me."

Jacob cleared his throat. "You don't deserve her," he said angrily. "She accepted?"

"She's thinking it over. She will."

Jacob didn't look at Ari. His hand moved slowly to the door handle.

"Do I have your blessing?" Ari asked.

Jacob opened the car door, but stayed seated. "You really want to put us all through this?"

"What's your meaning, Jacob?"

"Sure, Ari, you have my blessing. For as long as it lasts. I'll be there waiting when you've had enough. Again."

Ari's knuckles turned white. He swallowed hard and thought about hitting Jacob, punching him right in the face. But, he also felt sorry for him. And tired—he wanted to go home. Home to Rita.

Ari touched the ignition pad with his thumb and the engine started.

Jacob got out, closed the door, and walked to the barracks.

Excitement over the rescue of Levi swept through Kol Shofar like a wave, followed by collective grief over the loss of Daniel.

Ari spent two quiet weeks with Rita after the rescue. Shabbat was a day away, and Rita invited a few friends to celebrate the recent success. He didn't feel comfortable with the idea, but he wanted to make her happy.

Saturday arrived quickly, it seemed to Ari.

By early afternoon, Rita said she felt ready. "Our first social event." She looked around the carefully arranged living room and smiled. "You know, at our house. Do you think Jacob will come?" It was the first time she'd mentioned him since his brother's rescue.

"I don't see why not." Ari kept his voice soothing, reassuring. "He gave us his blessing, like I told you."

Dove and Naomi arrived first. Zev and Monica entered a few minutes later, followed by Shoshona with her husband, Zachariah. Moshe and his girlfriend, Kani, stepped in before Zachariah closed the door.

Rita hung their coats in a closet while Ari poured wine.

Platters of breads, olives, garlic hummus, and cheeses nearly filled the coffee table. Another plate of greenhouse cucumbers and yellow bell peppers gave the arrangement color.

A vase of pomegranate greens sat in the middle. Fresh flowers weren't grown in the greenhouse anymore.

Naomi picked up a plate and filled it with a little of everything. "Levi is getting better," she told Rita.

Monica moved close. "That's good news."

Rita stopped setting out more glasses and looked at Ari. "That's wonderful."

Ari nodded his agreement.

"The doctor allows Leah limited visiting time with him," Naomi said. "But no one else."

Monica sipped her wine. "I wonder if he'll ever fully recover."

Rita closed her eyes for a moment. "He has to."

Ari moved close and put his hand on Rita's shoulder. He gently hugged her and whispered, "He will."

"We don't know." Naomi shook her head. "And Dove's in a bad mood."

"Why?" Rita looked across the room at Dove. "He didn't want to come?"

"No, he's in a bad mood every day because Leah spends all her time at the hospital."

"The doctor's optimistic?" Rita reached for a glass of wine.

"She thinks he's got a fifty-fifty chance to recover. He's coming out of the coma."

"Is he talking?" Ari asked.

"Oh, no. Maybe in a few days if he continues to progress. I get a daily report."

"Naomi, how do you feel?" Rita asked. "About Leah and Levi. Do you think it's serious?"

"Oh, I do," Naomi said wistfully. "The note he left made his intentions clear. 'If I am able to return to you I will profess my love' is how it started out."

"Maybe we shouldn't hear this," Rita said. "It sounds so personal."

Naomi laughed. "He anticipated the family would hear. Otherwise, well, we're Traditionals and it wouldn't be right. He should've discussed this first with me and Dove. But since he's a soldier, and he went out on a hazardous operation, he had to do it this way."

"He proposed?" Rita glanced at Ari as she asked.

Dove broke away from his conversation with Moshe and turned toward Naomi. "He did not," he said loudly.

"Rita," Naomi said, "a proposal is a promise and you know we can't pretend to know the future, so we don't make promises. The usual way is for the couple to become engaged on the morning of their wedding because that's a promise he can keep."

"I thought an understanding is an engagement," Rita said.

Ari gave her a wink and moved closer to Dove.

"I was explaining to Rita," Naomi said, "that an understanding really means an intention to marry."

"I wouldn't really know about all that," Monica answered. "I don't care. I'm secular."

"Well, the note from Levi had a message to me and Dove asking us to allow him to make a life with our daughter." Naomi wiped a tear from the corner of her eye. "'Leah is my *basheret*.' That's what he wrote."

"That means soul mate," Monica explained to Rita.

Dove's face turned red, Ari smiled, and Naomi nodded so hard that the curls around her face bounced. "Everybody knows what that word means," she said.

"It sounds so romantic, and proper at the same time," Kani said.

"She'll be seventeen next month," Naomi said proudly. "I was seventeen when Dove asked me for an understanding that he could talk to my parents when I turned eighteen. He was twenty." She blushed. "He asked my cousin Reuven to ask me if I was interested. If I felt ready."

"And you told your cousin?" Kani asked.

"I practically pushed poor Reuven down the steps of my parents' house. 'Hurry,' I called out after him."

Zev laughed and said, "I remember, I was there."

Dove's face relaxed. "I guess she didn't want to give me time to change my mind."

Naomi picked up another plate of food and said, "This is for Dove," before she walked across the room.

"That's not why Dove's upset," Monica said quietly.

"He doesn't like Levi?" Rita asked.

Monica shook her head. "Levi's twenty-two. Leah is only sixteen and Dove doesn't want her to marry yet. What Naomi didn't say is that when a couple has an understanding, a wedding doesn't have to take place for a legal marriage to occur. Once a ring or necklace is given and accepted, they're engaged. When the couple has sexual relations, they're legally married. And he did send her the necklace."

"Really?" Rita took a plate of olives and began munching. "But it works that way only for Traditionals?"

"How would I know?" Monica popped an olive into her mouth, and reached for another.

Ari turned up the music. Dove's perpetual negative mood was starting to make sense.

Monica leaned close to Rita. "The war of 2030 broke out and Dove was in the tank group that held southern Lebanon until Israel annexed it. Leah was born six months later. I don't know why Dove's upset."

Rita looked around. "Maybe we shouldn't talk about this."

Monica laughed. "We're a community. Everyone knows everything."

The gathering took on a festive air when Ari turned the music selection to instrumental Israeli folk songs. He opened two more bottles of wine while the afternoon wore on. "Let's have another toast." He filled Dove's glass, and then his own.

"You're in a defiant mood," Dove observed.

"We're beyond their reach." Ari held his glass high and addressed the room. "We can feel proud. We've outmaneuvered a formidable enemy."

Everyone in the room cheered.

Dove clinked his glass against Ari's. "To our success for the greatest raid since Entebbe."

They sipped the wine and observed a moment of silence to honor the soldiers who had saved the 1976 hijacked Entebbe captives sixty-nine years earlier.

"Military academies around the world still call it the greatest raid in history," Moshe said.

Rita offered a tray of olive-filled pastries around the room. "I wonder what they'll say about this one."

"Outside a handful of people, no one will ever know." Zev shook his head. "It's a shame."

"No one will know about Daniel's sacrifice?" Rita asked.

Ari shook his head. "For Daniel." He raised his glass again. "Another quiet, unsung hero for Israel."

"Yes," the others agreed in unison.

The guests prepared to leave as evening came on. Everyone wished each other layla tov, a pleasant night.

Ari picked up empty glasses and followed Rita to the kitchen. They gathered the dirty dishes together—he washed and she dried—then they relaxed in the living room. Ari turned on a gel fire in the fireplace and sat next to Rita.

"For the first time in a long while I feel confident." He placed his arm around her shoulders. "We're almost at the end of this conflict. We were right to wait it out. Some of the others wanted to abandon Kol Shofar but I knew we could keep her."

"You're optimistic."

"It finally feels like we're winning."

"I wish I shared your good feelings," Rita admitted.

"You don't?" Ari gently turned her to face him. "Levi? You don't think he'll recover? Did Naomi say something?"

"No, I think Levi will make it. Naomi said he's doing better each day."

"What could possibly be wrong?"

"I don't know how to explain it," Rita said slowly. "I'm worried."

Ari went to the kitchen to prepare two strong cups of coffee. "Keep talking," he said over his shoulder. "I can hear you."

"Well, it seems out of character for the Islamics not to seek revenge."

He brought the coffees and sat next to her. "I want to know your thoughts on this."

"They have to know we have him back, don't you think?"

He took a drink of the coffee. "Not necessarily. I think we can keep this quiet. Dove's people are watching the area around the prison via satellite every night. Moshe's certain our escape route hasn't been detected. Gabriel made it back two days after we came out with Levi. He reported that no one came close to the cave opening while he guarded it."

Rita sipped her coffee. "How can you be sure no one is looking now?"

Ari's jovial mood began to fade. "They won't look for it. Daniel stayed behind to make sure." He gritted his teeth. "They'll find whatever's left of Daniel's body, and they'll think he was Levi trying to escape. They have to think that. Nothing else makes sense."

"Can't they identify . . ." Rita set her cup down.

"The type of explosive Daniel carried wouldn't leave much to identify. And desert Bedouins certainly lack the technology to test anything."

"Maybe I'm wrong." Rita shivered. "I just can't seem to shake this foreboding feeling. We made them look like fools."

"That we did." Ari set his cup next to hers on the coffee table. "We snatched Levi right out from under their grasp. But even if they figure out we have him, our enemies have other things to worry about. Like the civil war they're fighting."

Rita leaned against Ari's shoulder. "I'm sure you're right," she said softly. "I just don't feel it."

Ari kissed her forehead. He didn't want to think about the consequences if the rescue became public knowledge. He went to sleep that night holding her close, hoping she'd feel different in the morning, and knowing she wouldn't.

chapter 19

IN THE WEEKS following the daring rescue of Levi, Dove's agents examined the international media daily. Keyhole satellite images provided detailed surveillance over the Sinai every night.

Binyamin stopped by Dove's office occasionally to review the intelligence reports. His negative opinion on the stability of Kol Shofar grew into a source of friction. Ari began to avoid him whenever possible.

Levi continued to improve, Samuel made a full recovery, and so did Isaac. Ari felt confident, but Binyamin groused regularly about wanting to leave for higher ground.

Ari put his concerns on hold and prepared to leave the office early on the first Wednesday of the new month because he'd made dinner plans with Rita. She liked observing Rosh Hodesh and, even though celebrating the new moon each month held little meaning for him, it was enough that it pleased her.

On his way out the door, Binyamin stopped him. "Let me remind you, we can't exist here without outside help. You may be able to feed them, and even that's doubtful. But you can't pay for their defense. Like it or not, you're living on donations. The charity of others."

Ari hoped this now-familiar discussion would be a short one.

"The time is fast approaching," Binyamin said, "we'll soon be completely surrounded by fanatics engaged in a deadly civil war."

Ari leaned against the wall and folded his arms. "We have the underground aquifer. We can grow enough food to stay and wait it out."

Moshe walked up and nodded his agreement. "If we can hold this ground and refuse to become a mixed neighborhood town, then we've achieved something remarkable."

"At what cost?" Binyamin's words stung Ari.

"When would you propose moving the community?" Moshe asked.

"Let's go on Passover." Binyamin paused. "We'd get world-wide media attention. That's the best protection we can hope for."

"Out of the question," Ari said quickly. "Our enemies wouldn't dare attack as long as your forces are here."

"Passover's a couple of months away, the end of April this year," Moshe said. He saw Dove down the hall and waved him over to join the conversation.

"We could develop a contingency evacuation plan," Dove offered when he joined them. "What could it hurt?"

"Why wait until it's too late?" Binyamin asked. "Leaving is inevitable."

"Nothing is inevitable," Ari shot back.

No one spoke for a minute.

Ari unfolded his arms and stood straight. "Anything else? Anything relevant?"

"No," Dove finally said. "Nothing more. See you later."

Moshe said shalom, and Binyamin nodded.

Ari looked at Dove. "You might have your people work up a risk assessment. It couldn't hurt. Indicate the trigger points."

"Okay," Dove said, "but the report might find it's not feasible to evacuate at this time."

Binyamin glanced at Ari. "I doubt it."

"We'll know soon enough." Ari said shalom and left for home.

Rita called out from the kitchen when he arrived. "We have fresh goat cheese. Tarah's neighbor gave it."

Ari shook off his day and kissed her. He sat at the table while she prepared the evening meal. "I know it's hard," he said. "Soon we'll have fresh spring produce. Things will get better."

Rita turned from the sink and looked at him. "What if they don't?"

"Oh no, not you too." Ari rapped his fingers on the table. "I know our situation is precarious."

"Ari, some of the families don't have enough food."

"Our relations are buried here," Ari said. "It's impossible. We can't leave."

"Would you bury us along with them?" She immediately started to apologize.

"No," Ari said slowly, "you're right. Dove's working on a plan, in case it comes to that."

"Oh Ari, that's good." Rita leaned against the counter and smiled. "We'll probably never have to put it into action."

"That's right." Ari's good mood returned. "The communities living south of us need us to stay. We can't give away any more land. Israeli Jews have sacrificed enough."

Rita served a simple meal of steamed quinoa grain, sunflower seeds, and spinach greens with the creamy feta crumbled on top.

The phone rang seconds before they finished dinner. Ari spoke briefly with Dove, and hung up. "I'll turn on the monitor. Dove says a special One World news report is about to air."

Rita started clearing the dishes. "Naomi showed me a copy of the latest Euro newspaper downloaded from the One World Net. The Net came through for a couple of hours yesterday. They're talking about bringing the military force of the One World Gov to Jerusalem."

Ari flicked his hand. "Arabs and English royals. Same evil bastards trying to take Jerusalem for the last two thousand years. So what?"

"So?" Rita stopped midway to the sink with a glass in each hand. "It's fanatical. They can't get away with that."

"They already have." He leaned back against the counter. "Don't you remember your history? Fifty years ago your President Clinton bombed Serbia, and delivered the capital city, Kosovo, to the United Nations."

"Vaguely." She nodded slightly, and set the glasses on the counter.

"Well, Kosovo was Serbia's Jerusalem. It broke the hearts of the Serbian people to lose her. The UN, before it turned into the One World Gov, got jurisdiction over Kosovo as an international city."

"That's the way the UN gave the British jurisdiction over Israel and Palestine after World War II, by calling it a mandate," she said. "Then they changed the name of Palestine to 'Jordan' and carved a new Palestine out of Israel."

"It's the same," Ari said. UN officials looted artifacts from Kosovo's archaeological sites during the thirty years they governed her. Imagine what they could do if they got control over Jerusalem."

Rita closed her eyes and slowly shook her head. "I can't bear the thought."

He kissed her cheek. "Don't worry, Honey. The rabbis say, 'Help from Hashem can come in the blink of an eye.'" Instead of her usual fiery passion, he saw that her eyes held tears.

"This coming war is the one which will decide the fate of Israel," she said, her voice choked with emotion. "We don't want it, but we're sliding into it against our will."

"No matter," he said confidently. "They'll never take Jerusalem because there's one thing in their way. A few million of us Jews." He nodded toward the living room. "It's about to start."

Ari carried walnut muffins for dessert and Rita brought coffees to the table in front of the sofa. He pushed a button on the remote and the TV screen lit up.

"Now don't get upset because this program will likely be biased." He sat next to her. "It's something you have to get used to."

The program host smiled and introduced an international panel to discuss the latest crisis in the Middle East. A picture of a dead Bedouin girl lying crumpled on the ground outside a tent filled the screen for a moment. Her blood-stained clothes clung to her lifeless body.

> *"This is the tragic incident which set off the latest deadly cease-fire violations."* The host turned to one of the panelists. *"You interviewed the family and neighbors of this poor murdered girl. What happened?"*
>
> *"Thank you, Graham,"* the journalist replied. *"They described how an Israeli soldier named Levi drove into the Bedouin camp and shot the seven-year-old girl. Apparently, for no reason."*

"That's crazy," Ari shouted. "Liars! That village is on the other side of the desert."

Rita set her muffin back on the table. "Why don't they ask why a small child played outside alone in a war zone. Why don't they ask us what happened?"

> *"What happened to the errant soldier?"* asked the announcer.
>
> *"He escaped,"* the second journalist answered, *"to a Jewish settler camp not far away. When the Islamic Coalition asked for the*

*soldier to be turned over to them for trial, Israeli
authorities refused."*

The third panelist, a sharply dressed woman
with champagne-blonde hair, started in next.
*"Yes, and it would have ended there. But the Jew-
ish settlers taunted the Bedouins as they grieved.
As you can imagine, the poor girl's relatives lost
control and attacked the settlers."*

"They called us settlers," Rita said. "Why?"

"They're idiots," Ari answered.

They watched in stunned silence while the screen rolled
footage of the latest attack against their community. The view
looked fuzzy, and distant, but the explosions showed clear flashes
of light.

"Extraordinary," the host proclaimed.
"Where's the criminal Levi now?"

"Alleged criminal," the first journalist corrected. *"Although, we got several eyewitness
reports. There really can't be much doubt what
happened."*

*"He may be hiding out at a Zionist camp in
the Negev Desert,"* the woman panelist broke
in eagerly. *"But trustworthy sources say he was
fatally injured when the relatives retaliated."*

"Ah," said the host. *"So a bit of justice has
prevailed after all."*

*"What's it going to take to bring peace to
that troubled region?"* the woman panelist asked
plaintively.

Ari and Rita watched in silence as the first journalist
explained in great detail why the One World Government should
declare Jerusalem an international city so both sides would quit
fighting. The other panelists nodded their agreement.

Ari raised his fist to the screen. They sat for a moment after the broadcast. He slowly turned to look at Rita, and their eyes met.

"Yeah," she said, "they know we have Levi."

Ari swore under his breath as he turned the television off.

Ari contacted the Kol Shofar security council the day after the special news program.

A day later, the community quietly went on Stage One alert. That afternoon, Zev called Ari at home. "You're needed at Dove's office. Just some routine reports need your signature. Won't take long."

"Trouble?" Rita asked when Ari clicked the receiver off.

"Must be." Ari stood. "I don't sign Dove's reports. You better come along. This could take awhile."

Ari and Rita walked into Dove's office fifteen minutes later. At the same time, Binyamin entered.

"What's this about?" Binyamin asked.

Ari shrugged. "We'll find out together."

Dove, Moshe, Monica, and two analysts waited for them in the briefing room.

"Take a seat," Dove said from the conference table. "We're waiting for an intelligence report."

Zev entered quickly through the doorway. "The motion sensors in the Metzada tunnel have alerted," he reported.

Ari whistled softly. "We have intruders."

"I thought Gabriel wired a motion-sensitive explosive to the cavern entrance," Rita said. "Why didn't it go off?"

Ari touched her hand. "I thought you understood. He wired it and guarded it for two days in case the enemy followed the rescue team and discovered the cavern. He disarmed it at the cave entrance when he left."

"Then the killings would've been justified," Zev told Rita as he sat across from Ari, "if it went off while Gabriel guarded the team's escape. But we couldn't leave it hot, even in enemy territory. What if children discovered it and set it off by accident?"

Rita nodded. "I understand."

Ari looked at the two analysts. "Give us the room."

The two young women left and closed the door behind them.

"Beyond top secret," Zev said. "Gabriel set up smart explosives in two places deep inside the Metzada tunnel. Before and after the camera location."

"I'm sorry," Rita said, "I thought you said you couldn't allow explosives to go off."

"Smart explosives," Zev explained. "Harmless without the right detonator code."

"Could an animal somehow trigger the alarm?" Monica asked.

Dove shook his head. "It's motion-sensitive. We set it too high for an animal to trigger it."

Ari rapped the table. "Let's see the nanocamera footage."

"They're not in camera range yet," Moshe explained.

Ari glanced at his watch. "How much time do we have?"

"When the second motion-activated alarm sounds in the monitor room, we can calculate their pace," Moshe said. "And verify they're headed this way."

"Commander," Monica said, "we have to stop whoever's coming."

"Affirmative, Monica. We will."

They sat waiting and talking for the next two hours until Ari finally asked, "Should the second alarm sound by now?"

Moshe shrugged.

"What if it doesn't go off?" Rita asked.

"Then someone found our tunnel and went back out the way they entered," Dove said.

Ari turned toward Dove. "Could be a recon unit."

"We're not out of trouble," Zev said. "We've clearly been discovered."

Ari stood and held out his hand for Rita. "Keep watching and call me the minute you know anything. We're going home to wait."

"Sounds right," Binyamin said. "We should all take a break."

They started for the door when Zev's wrist com beeped. "This is it," he told them.

Dove led the way to the operations room. Within thirty minutes they saw shadowy figures moving toward them on the screen from the tunnel camera. The forms slowly took shape as twenty men neared the nanocamera.

Ari caught his breath.

Dove gripped the back of a chair.

"One World Gov uniforms," Moshe said quietly.

"Heavily armed," Binyamin noted.

"Who are these guys?" Dove looked at Ari. "They should be regional forces. I don't recognize this unit."

"Commander," Monica said. "You can't allow this."

"How long before we have to decide?" Ari felt his stomach tighten. "To blow the tunnel or not?"

Moshe calculated. "At their current pace, two hours, maybe more."

"They're a hostile force advancing on our position," Monica said. "My opinion, take them out before they destroy us."

Dove looked at the others. "What do you think their objective is?"

"They're coming to solve that Jew problem in the Middle East," Zev said. "You heard that news report. We're the Zionist camp in the desert. And now we're harboring a criminal. They're coming to arrest the leaders of this rebel band."

"And anyone who tries to stop them," Monica added.

Ari sat studying printouts of the images. He cleared his throat. "These guys look like Spetnatz. A brutal Russian special forces unit."

"What will happen if we resist?" Rita asked anxiously.

Ari looked at her. *I'm not going to let anything happen to you,* he thought.

"Don't worry," Dove said. "We can handle these guys."

"They probably have shoot-on-sight orders," Monica said.

"I'm not going to be arrested." Binyamin folded his hands. "They'd murder us in custody anyway. We'd never make it to a court of law alive. We might as well try to defend ourselves."

"This is a political move," Dove said. "If these guys are Russian, they're allies to Persyria."

"If we let them come in, they will arrest us. Or kill us," Binyamin said. "The people remaining here will be evicted, probably without protection. The ones who make it north will be abused along the way."

"If we're going to do it." Ari smacked the table with his open hand. "We'd better blow this tunnel and hope to the heavens the rest of the world thinks it's an accident."

"Is there any way to negotiate with them?" Rita asked.

Ari almost snorted his answer. "They're not coming here to talk."

"We can't give them a way in," Moshe said.

"No turning back from this." Binyamin looked at Ari. "If we're caught, we'll be treated like international outlaws. Terrorists, for G-d's sake."

Rita's lower lip quivered. "Do we have any other options?"

"They'll probably take you into custody too." Monica looked at Rita. "You lied on your entry visa."

Rita's face paled. "I've heard stories."

"Probably all true," Monica said.

"Probably not," Ari countered.

Zev sat stroking his beard. "They don't know we have the camera, or the sensors. We should deny involvement."

"Listen to me," Ari said. "We take this to our graves."

"I give you my word," Rita said solemnly.

The others nodded. In a chorus they said, "Agreed."

Ari took a deep breath. "Anyone who doesn't want to be a part of blowing this tunnel before those so-called peacekeepers get here should leave now."

"You insult us," Dove said. "No one's leaving."

Ari looked at Binyamin. "I was thinking of you."

"He's right," Dove added. "You could truthfully deny having any knowledge of what happens next if you leave now."

"This is retaliation for us snatching Levi." Ari shook his head. "You're not a part of this."

"I was born part of this," Binyamin said.

"Good enough for me." Ari picked up the printouts and studied them. "And when the conflict ends we'll make a place for you here."

"Todah, but I've got my sights on Jerusalem."

"Political aspirations," Ari said.

"No, I've been a widower for many years," Binyamin told them. "Alone too long. I'm Orthodox, and it's easier for me to find a wife in the capital."

"Well then we'd better make sure you're not arrested." Ari turned to Zev. "Get it ready."

When the time was right, Ari gave the signal. Gabriel's string of domino charges stretched over two kilometers.

Ari knew the heat signature in the night sky would be seen on satellite images around the world, and that pressure from the detonation would pulverize everything in the blast radius. What he didn't know, what kept him awake at night, was thinking about the retaliation that could follow—if the explosion were traced to him.

Ari asked Dove to contact Rishon the following day. Dove exchanged news about the family and, between words and sentences, told him in code to falsify records. The purchase of the still-experimental explosives material must be covered up. Untraceable. Rishon indicated his understanding before ending the phone call.

For a week, Ari went about completing his usual day-to-day responsibilities. Each day he persuaded Rita not to worry about the horrors of an arrest.

The expected media coverage regarding the massive tunnel explosion never materialized. Only a brief mention appeared of a weapons cache accident in that area at that time.

"We're not going to be blamed for the detonation," he told her repeatedly. "It would've been in some news report."

Day by day, Ari found new ways to calm Rita's fears. He avoided thoughts of the tunnel explosion and stayed positive.

"Passover is here in a few weeks," he told Rita over afternoon coffee. "It'll mark a year since you, well, showed up." He'd taken a break from reviewing reports in his office-conference room, and wandered into the kitchen to find Rita reading a science journal at the table. She assured him she'd finished reading and wanted some coffee.

"Sometimes it seems like only a week has passed." Rita sipped the coffee she'd just prepared.

"Other times?" Ari waited, his cup halfway to his lips.

"Like I've been here for a lifetime." She smiled. "In a good way."

"Things will get better," he assured her, "from this time forward. Home gardens are starting to appear now to replace the greenhouse."

"Ari." She said his name softly. "I thought we were going to think about leaving Kol Shofar for a while. Until the Islamic civil war ends."

Ari sat straighter. He moved his empty cup back and forth on the kitchen table. "I can't give up and walk away from everything I've spent a lifetime building."

"What would it take?" She paused. "For you to consider leaving as an option."

"I don't know. I guess I never thought of it that way. One day at a time and all that." Ari's brow creased slightly as he pushed thoughts of the future aside. "We're here to stay," he told her with a confident smile. "No one's going to push me out."

chapter 20

TWO WEEKS AFTER the Metzada tunnel explosion, Dove dropped by unannounced one evening at Ari's. The building guard barely had time to call it in before Dove stood knocking at Ari's outer door. Rita joined them in the living room.

They sat on the two sofas facing each other with the coffee table in-between.

Dove looked down. "I have terrible news."

Ari braced himself.

"Rishon is missing," Dove said. "And it's my fault."

"This is bad news," Ari said. "What happened?"

"I don't know. Only that the French police are looking for him and he's not returned to his apartment."

"Do you know the charges?" Rita asked.

"They say he stole sensitive materials and falsified the records to hide the theft."

Ari glanced at Rita. "Serious charges."

"Yeah, I hope he's got somewhere safe to go," Dove continued. "He's my only family member left in France. But the reason I came here is to tell you the emergency evacuation plan for Kol Shofar will be ready tomorrow."

"What will it say?" Ari braced himself again.

"That we're surrounded by people hostile to us," Dove answered without hesitation. "That the fighting that started in Egypt and spread north to engulf southern Israel was contrived, that the so-called Islamic civil war is funded by Western elite. We're against an enemy who will stop at nothing to eliminate us."

"Always have been," Ari said.

Dove looked at Ari. "We could travel north to Jerusalem. Our population would strengthen the city."

Ari shook his head. "Just head north? That's your plan?"

"Well," Dove said, "if we leave, we'd be better off going north."

"That's right," Rita said. "We could go to Haifa."

Ari shook his head. "No room for all of us in Haifa."

"Okay," Dove said. "So maybe you want to sail out the straits to India. We could go join the Zoroastrians."

Ari let out a deep breath. "No need to get sarcastic. I really think we should consider all options."

Rita said, "If we find we must do it, we should face it before we come under attack again. We can't move and defend our families at the same time."

Ari shifted his weight away from Rita on the sofa. "No," he said, "we can't give up everything."

Dove looked at his watch and stood. "This isn't cut in stone. It's only a preliminary report."

Ari stood and walked with him to the outer door. "I don't want to be the one," Ari said quietly, "who goes down in history as the man who lost Kol Shofar."

Smiling, Dove said, "On the contrary, you'll be credited with saving three thousand lives by leading us out in time."

"We would have to leave our buried here," Ari reminded him. "You know what Islamics do to Jewish graves. They desecrate them every time we leave our lands. Our enemy wipes out every trace of us so we can't reclaim our homeland." He shook his head. "I really don't see how we can leave."

"At least we don't have to decide tonight." Dove barely got the words out before his wrist com sounded.

Ari's wrist com went off and the alarm inside the building blared at the same time.

"We're under attack," Dove shouted.

Ari ran back to the living room. "C'mon." He took Rita's hand and started toward the door. They ran with Dove to the rover parked in front. Ari opened the passenger door and practically pushed Rita onto the seat. He got into the back and Dove started the motor.

"We don't have time to make it home," Dove said. "My office."

Fireworks lit the night sky as they turned the last corner. Dove slammed on the brakes and they slid to a stop in the driveway.

Dove led them through the office complex to the basement control center stairs. Moshe was already inside. A shattering boom echoed directly above them. Ari bolted the inner basement door.

"What about Naomi?" Rita asked Dove as she rushed down the stairs behind him.

"We put in an underground safe room after the last attack," Dove shouted over his shoulder. "Com lines are down, but I'm sure my family's safe."

Moshe greeted them from across the room. "A night attack," he said loudly. "They're trying to hide what they're doing."

"They came in fast," Ari said. "The alarms barely went off before they hit us." He pulled out a chair for Rita, then sat next to her at the conference table with Moshe.

"Doesn't sound good," Dove shouted as another blast nearly drowned out his words. "I think they're using smart weapons." He checked the blank monitors across the room before joining the others.

"Are they going to get us?" Rita asked.

"No," Ari answered quickly.

"They can't get to us in here." Moshe waved his hand. "This place is state of the art."

"They're going for the infrastructure." Dove looked around the room. "Probably using a space-based circumnavigating radio signal to trigger the explosions."

"They got our com line generator," Ari said.

Sonic booms followed strange whistling sounds.

"Who is it?" Rita finally asked.

Ari looked at Dove. "This has got to be funded by the Islamic Alliance."

"I agree," Dove said. "Rivals to the Islamic Coalition. The hardware must come out of Persyria."

Another boom sounded farther away.

"Is this about . . ." Rita's voice trailed off when she saw Ari's expression.

"Levi?" Ari's eyes narrowed. "Absolutely. And no, I'm not sorry we got him."

"It's not one way or the other," Dove said. "We found Levi and brought him home. If this is the consequence, then so be it."

"They think they can get away with it now," Moshe added. "They'll call it an eye for an eye. But what they really mean is, since we dared to save a life, they're entitled to destroy an entire city."

The bombardment above them drowned out their voices for the next hour. Then it ended.

They waited another hour in the silence.

"Let's see it," Ari said. He went up the steps to the metal door leading to ground level. Rita, Dove, and Moshe followed.

Ari threw open the reinforced door and they emerged into a pile of rubble that was once Dove's office building.

Rita gasped.

Ari strained to see in the dim light.

They stood in the rubble of the destroyed office complex watching flickering little lights move about as people in the distant neighborhoods searched for those in distress. By the soft light of a quarter-moon and the ever-present backdrop of star clusters, Ari made out more of the devastation around him.

Dove stood staring in the direction of the moshav. "It may not be as bad as it looks," he said. "I can see buildings, I think." With a flashlight, he pointed at his car. It lay smashed under concrete chunks.

"Emergency generators aren't coming on," Ari said. "It's dark as far as I can see."

Rita looked around. "What can we do?"

"Area search and rescue teams are already in place," Dove assured her. "Nothing more we can do tonight." He turned in the opposite direction and started the long walk home.

"I'll go with you," Moshe called out, moving carefully toward Dove. "I'm part of moshav security, and Kani's probably worried."

Ari took Rita's hand and led her through the twisted wreckage toward the damaged main road. He listened for sounds of people shouting, crying—anything—but only an eerie silence surrounded him. Some buildings, barely visible in the night sky, stood undamaged next to piles of rubble.

"We'll confirm in the morning," he told Rita as they walked. "I can't really tell, but it looks like a good number of structures made it."

Rita aimed her wrist com light on the ground. "Ari, will this attack be our downfall?"

They walked to a section of undamaged road, and he quickened his stride. "Of course not, Honey. This isn't as bad as it looks. We'll rebuild."

They walked in silence on the remnants of the main road. Then Ari stopped. He let go of her hand, and pointed. "See. Our building made it, and so will we. We'll start over."

The next morning, Ari awoke feeling ready to survey the damage. Kissing Rita's cheek, he gently woke her.

They got up and she brewed coffee. "Here," she said, handing him a cup. "I'll stay inside and appreciate our windowless living room. I don't want to see it."

Ari sipped the coffee and set the empty cup on the table. He crossed the room to stand next to the fireplace. "The morning's cool enough to justify lighting the gel cans." After lighting the fire, he moved to the door.

Watching the flickering flames, Rita waved from the sofa, still in her robe. For a moment, he thought about staying home with her in front of the fire. He said shalom, then he went out.

A desert rover sat parked outside his building, and he borrowed it. He drove out to the main road and found most of it still intact. He headed for the center of the grounds, to the greenhouse.

The giant greenhouse lay smashed. Shock over the magnitude of the destruction hit him hard. Broken glass covered the ground with metal frame parts protruding out at odd angles like arms reaching for help.

Ari drove to where two grain towers had collapsed into a heap of broken bricks. Beyond the towers stood the moshav. About half the neighborhoods sustained severe damage from direct mortar hits. He said a prayer under his breath when he saw that Dove's section escaped most of it.

The parts of the security wall he could inspect looked normal. He said another prayer and headed home.

On the way, he drove by the soldier barracks, destroyed by the attack. A third of the military housing lay in ruins nearby. He drove on, parked the rover where he found it, and entered his apartment. After he sank into a chair in the living room without speaking, Rita prepared an espresso. She pressed her open hand tenderly against his cheek for a moment, and handed him the cup.

An hour later, Dove and Zev arrived. "Shalom, Ari, shalom, Rita," they called out at the living room door.

"The wall," Ari said as they entered. "Do we have any reports indicating the extent of the damage?"

Dove nodded and sat across from Ari. "Not as bad as you might think. It is damaged at the main and secret entrances, but the conductive polymer nanowire in the wall is intact. The military barracks above ground were destroyed, but the underground bunkers were shielded from the blasts. And most of the men made it underground in time."

"They want the wall," Zev said. "If they're planning to take this place over, they'd be fools to destroy a billion-shekel fence."

"Oh, they're fools," Ari said. "But their overlords probably arranged it this way."

Zev rubbed his chin. "If we give up this town to Islamics, where will we go?"

"If we decide to abandon this shining star of Israel," Ari answered, "our leaders in Jerusalem will have to decide where to send us."

Rainstorms blew in, one following another, for two weeks after the attack. When the rain let up, the wind took over. Ari explained to Rita that a *khamsin* is a hot, dry wind that blows hard across the Middle East.

Each day for a week, Ari settled into his living room and studied damage reports. The final number of dead from the attack was ninety-six. He felt the loss of each name on the list.

On Friday morning, a week later, Ari heard from Zev that the community security council would vote to contact Jerusalem for transfer assistance. He bypassed Dove's office and drove home.

"They expect us to forsake our homes," he told Rita as he walked in the kitchen. "They're going to relocate us."

"It's not up to only you, Ari. It's a group decision, and it's probably temporary anyway." She quit putting clean dishes away and sat with him at the table.

He studied her face. "You're not upset?"

"I'm not so emotionally attached to this one piece of land as you are," she said softly. "As long as we're all together, and we're in our homeland, I guess I really don't care where we live. I'm sorry."

"Don't be." He looked into her eyes. "You see, the worst part for me is the feeling that I'm letting my people down. Not just the people of Kol Shofar. But people throughout the Negev."

Rita sighed. "I've wanted to tell you how I feel. Every few months a rocket comes over the wall and terrifies all of us. The women are afraid to conceive because pregnant women can't run to save themselves during an attack. And everyone thinks the constant threat of violence is traumatizing the children. They don't play outside anymore."

At that moment, Binyamin buzzed at the door. Ari brought him into the living room and nodded toward a sofa. He put his concerns on hold and asked Rita to join them.

"I heard the security council's decision," Binyamin said, sitting in the padded chair. "You must've expected it. We lost a hundred people in the revenge attack."

Ari shook his head and briefly looked away. "I know."

"Good men and women," Benjamin said. "All of them."

Ari looked up. "Our dead will be airlifted to Jerusalem for burial?"

"Yes," Binyamin confirmed. "Outside the old city walls, you understand. But technically, they'll be inside the extended city border. Does that help ease the pain of losing so many?"

Ari closed his eyes briefly before he answered. "I don't think about it. I tie it off inside my mind and let it go. If I allow myself to dwell on it, I'll want revenge. I'll want to kill them all."

"I understand," Binyamin said. "Believe me, I understand."

When Ari's wrist com beeped, he looked at the tiny screen. "Zev's coming."

"That's what I've come to tell you," Binyamin said. "An envoy from Jerusalem is here to meet with us. We're about to find out what our political leaders think."

Ari checked his watch. "When's he expected?"

"Right now," Zev said as he and another man entered through the unlocked door. The dark-haired man who arrived with him stood slightly taller than Zev. Thin and wiry, dressed in casual clothes, he carried himself like a military man but flashed a mesmerizing smile like an elected official.

"This is Moti"—Zev waved a hand—"here from Jerusalem. And this is Commander Ari, and Rita. And you know Binyamin already."

Ari stood and shook his hand. Nodding toward the sofa, he said, "Welcome to Kol Shofar."

"First of all," Moti said, "we're all very sorry for your tragic loss of life in the recent attack. Our leaders asked me to express that to you."

"Todah." Ari's jaw tightened.

Moti leaned forward. "And the soldier Levi? Will he recover?"

"He's making a rapid recovery," Ari answered. "He may have brain damage from repeated head trauma. Too soon to know."

"We think," Moti said, glancing at each of them, "that if you're going to move, probably better to do it sooner than later. We know you wanted to hold on until fall, but we no longer think that's feasible."

"We agree." Ari nodded toward Rita. "My tactical strategist advised me today that it's time."

Moti looked at Rita and the corners of his mouth turned up slightly.

"Really?" Zev asked. "I told Moti this was going to take most of the night."

"It's not my choice," Ari said. "But I understand it."

"Our culture is under attack," Moti pointed out. "This is a time for us to pull together. You're making the right decision."

"Where will we go?" Rita asked.

"We'll house you in Jerusalem until we can figure things out."

"The community stays together," Ari said tersely.

"Of course," Moti assured him. "Believe it or not, we do have some options for you to consider. But first, we have to get you there."

Ari shook his head. "It almost overwhelms my mind to think of it. Kol Shofar started with such high hopes for a bright future."

"This isn't over," Binyamin reminded him. "You may be able to bring your people back through a political agreement."

Rita quickly agreed.

"It doesn't matter," Ari told them. "Our emphasis has to be on preserving life, not protecting property."

"We've survived worse than this as a people," Zev added. "We'll survive this."

"We have the soldiers here," Ari said.

Moti looked at Binyamin and blinked. "You didn't tell him?"

"Under the circumstances, I thought it could wait until you got here."

"Ari," Moti said, "Jerusalem has recalled the troops. People living along the Jordanian border are in the fight of their lives. If we lose the Judean Hills, we lose the high ground surrounding our capital. We fear they'll attack the Samarian Hills next. The heart of Israel."

"My parents live near the old city walls." Ari felt a twinge of remorse for not seeing his parents for so many months.

"Then you understand." Moti leaned back against the sofa cushion.

"We'll need three months to prepare and international protection during that time," Ari said.

"You have three weeks." The smile left Moti's face. "Each family can take only what they can carry in their car, or cart, or suitcase."

Ari sat on the edge of his chair. "You're planning on using us as a buffer to protect Jerusalem."

Moti shook his head. "Not really. Not that it would matter. You'll go where you're told."

Ari and Moti locked eyes for a moment, then Moti looked away.

"We're pulling the soldiers out in three weeks," Moti told him. "If your community remains after that, your people would probably be massacred."

Rita looked at Ari. "Three weeks? We can't do it."

"Sure we can." Zev's eyes twinkled. "Don't give our enemies time to think about it. We'll leave before they expect it. We can do it."

"That's the way," Moti said as he stood. "I'd like to conclude now, unless you have something else."

Ari stood. "It's almost sunset. Has your lodging been arranged? Do you need anything?"

"Todah, but my wife's cousin Shoshona lives here in the moshav. I'll be staying with her and Zachariah. I'm scheduled to fly out at first light Sunday morning."

"Shabbat shalom," Rita told him. "And if I don't see you before you leave, good journey."

Zev raised a hand and said, "May Hashem be with you."

"And Shabbat shalom to you." Moti nodded, then turned to Ari. "One more thing. The One World Government wants a look. Expect an OWG representative to make an on-site inspection. Expect him sometime next week."

Moti walked with Ari to the door while Zev stayed and talked with Rita. Ari put his hand on the latch, but didn't unlock it. "What did Jerusalem get for giving us up?" He lowered his voice to a whisper. "Why three weeks?"

Moti looked at Ari. "Israeli access to Internet media is blocked under internal conflict provisions," he explained. "The legal case to restore access is making its way through the One World court system. It could take years."

"You traded us to get electronic media?" Ari folded his arms and waited.

"Do you have any idea how important it is for us to get our story out to the world?" Moti said. "To receive communications without interference? You were going to have to move anyway."

Ari turned and opened the door. "We could've made it until fall."

"Look, Ari, what you've done here is truly heroic. Don't think for a moment that we're giving up. Your community is being relocated to a more defensible position, that's all."

"We have been isolated here," Ari said. "It would feel good to stop fighting for a while. Let the children recover."

"Good." Moti smacked Ari on the shoulder. "You get your people ready. We'll do the rest."

"I don't like the plan." Ari leaned closer. "But we have to present a unified front. We can't let anything divide us. Our strength is our ability to organize and support each other."

"We'll take care of you, Ari. Trust your leaders in Jerusalem."

Ari didn't answer.

Moti stepped out, then looked back toward the living room. "Your strategist is sharp. We could use someone like her in Jerusalem."

"Shalom," Zev said as he walked to the door. "I'll catch a ride home with Moti."

Ari felt confident when he returned to the living room until he saw a distressed look on Rita's face.

"Your parents?" she asked as he sat next to her. "You never mentioned anything about them."

"I guess you never asked. I figured it'd come up sometime, and now it has."

"I thought maybe . . ." Rita sputtered. "So many people don't talk about their families because they died. How could you not mention your parents?"

"Well, you haven't told me about your family. Except for the Ladino great-grandmother from Spain. Someone in America must be worried."

"My mother died when I was twelve. I lost my father a few months later." Rita shifted in her chair. "My life in America seems like a million miles away."

"I'm sorry," Ari said. "I didn't mean to bring up a painful subject."

"She died giving birth to my younger brother, and he died three days later," she said quietly. "There was nothing I could do. It broke my heart."

Ari stood, took her hands, gently pulled her up off the couch. "Well, I'm your family now." He kissed her right cheek, then her left. "We'll be in Jerusalem in three weeks with my parents. You'll meet them when we get there. Sarah and Avraham."

chapter 21

A FLOOD OF regret and denial surged through Ari when the re-alization sank in that Kol Shofar would be abandoned. The an-nouncement to the stunned community resulted in altercations among the grief-stricken people as the pain turned to anger.

Ari couldn't go anywhere without having to console some-one or answer a series of heated questions. But the worst hap-pened when the moshav security team formed a committee with a spokesperson to challenge his decision to move the community.

After the first week, he rarely left his compound. He put his feelings on hold, assigned logistics details to Shoshona, and met daily with Dove and Moshe in his private conference room to plan the move.

Rita spent most of her time packing her meager possessions into a cargo van Ari would drive on the fateful day of departure.

"You know," Ari told Rita one early morning, "I'm not giv-ing up. There is a reason this is happening."

She stopped making their breakfast and looked up. "What are you saying?"

He shook his head. He wanted to tell her what he knew, but he held back.

"Don't worry," she said, "everyone feels the same. Kol Sho-far will not become a mixed neighborhood town."

Ari shook off his bad feelings. "You're starting to sound like me." He almost smiled as he sank into one of the chairs at the kitchen counter.

The aroma of leftover vegetables and fresh garlic cooking in olive oil filled the room while he watched her brew the coffee. For a moment, a rare feeling of contentment relaxed him. He let himself almost forget what was about to happen.

A few hours later, Ari asked Rita to accompany him to Dove's makeshift office—a previously empty house in the moshav. The front room was filled with people when they arrived, so they went into Dove's private office, the former occupant's master bedroom.

Ari gestured toward the front room after he closed the door. "What's this?"

"Shoshona's organizing the animal arrangements," Dove explained. "The poor creatures subjected to this human folly."

"Will the animals be transported with us?" Rita looked at Dove. "You won't leave them here?"

"Never." Dove shook his head. "We wouldn't do that to an animal."

"Any problems?" Ari asked as he sat in a chair next to Rita.

Dove smirked. "I hear the dogs seem to enjoy the preparation activity, but the cats are sulking. The goats and horses are going to be transported in covered trucks."

"Anything else?" Ari sat back in his chair, and looked at the clock on the wall. He felt uneasy and couldn't figure out why. A familiar feeling these days.

"Well, Naomi says the mothers and fathers struggle to explain to their children why this is happening. Even my own children seem to be confused by this sudden move."

"I understand," Ari said, "but what can we do?"

"It will make this forced move easier if you could tell our people where we're going." Dove glanced at Rita. "Naomi says the uncertainty is harder for the women."

"Ah yes." Rita nodded. "Hashem knows the state of the world by counting the tears of women." She turned to Ari. "We only hear we're going to Jerusalem. But no one thinks they can accommodate all of us. People are scared."

"I see. The truth is, we don't know yet."

"That's right," Dove broke in. "We're trying to do better, but it looks like they'll put up a tent city for our military and some of the families. Most of our people have friends or relations they can stay with. Our community leaders will be given apartments in the military quarter."

Rita's face brightened. "That's not so bad. The important thing is that the families don't want to be separated from each other."

They heard Yalon in the front office demanding to see Dove. Shoshona tried to be diplomatic, but to no avail.

Dove opened the door and waved to Yalon.

"We're at war," Yalon's voice boomed as he rolled his wheelchair in and closed the door. "Those murdering fanatics paralyzed my legs," he shouted. "Cost me my military career, and I want revenge."

"Oh, Yalon." Rita touched his arm. "What are you talking about?"

Yalon pointed at Ari. "I heard he won't wire the buildings."

Ari nodded. "That's right. It's an act of random violence to leave something hot where innocent people could find it. We'll blow the buildings as we leave."

"Not good enough," Yalon thundered.

"We can't risk retaliation if anything goes wrong," Ari said. "We're traveling with women and children. You can't put them at risk because you want revenge."

"Yalon," Dove said quietly, "we got our boy back. You paid with your legs but the enemy paid with their lives. I understand you took down a dozen fanatics."

"Oh, that's not true," Yalon protested. "I only got eight of them. Wounded two others."

"A change of subject," Dove said. "International media coverage on us increases each day. This will protect the families all the way into Jerusalem."

Shoshona knocked and opened Dove's door. "The OWG guy is here to meet with you."

Dove looked at Ari. "A day early."

"That's okay. Let's get this over with."

They stood when Shoshona brought him in, a prickly looking man with thinning straight brown hair and sharp, cynical gray eyes. *Reptilian*, Ari thought.

"You can call me Hancock," said the man with an obvious British accent. "I'd like to look around for a bit before we meet."

"Of course," Dove said. "We can arrange something."

Hancock started toward the open door, and said over his shoulder, "No need. I have people with me. We'll meet back here, say an hour. Cheerio."

Dove called Moshe in and closed the door.

With a look toward the door, Ari said, "Follow him, Moshe. Keep eyes on him."

Moshe nodded and left.

"Hancock's obviously British intelligence," Ari said. "They've been funding the Islamic 'uprisings' for decades." He picked up the phone. "Let's call Pybar and Smasher to sit in."

Dove smiled. "My thoughts exactly."

Rita shivered despite the warm room. "Do you expect trouble?"

"Did you see that guy?" Ari's voice was low. "He wants something."

The meeting started in the front room at Dove's office at sunset. Pybar and Smasher sat in the far corner, nearly out of sight. Ari sat at a dining table in the middle of the room with Rita, Dove, and Zev.

Hancock walked in, tall and thin in his perfectly tailored suit, and sauntered to the empty chair at the table across from Ari.

"What do you hope to accomplish here?" Ari asked him.

Hancock sat back with a narrow smile. "I represent those who wish to make you a cash offer in exchange for leaving the property undamaged when you vacate. You must agree not to leave anything hot. Or damaged."

"We'll consider it," Ari said. "Your next point."

"I don't think you understand," Hancock said. "This is the point. My client doesn't want you to destroy the assets they intend to manage."

Ari glared at him. "Your client—the English royals who want Jerusalem?"

"Forget it," Hancock said with a scowl. "You know I speak for the One World Government. So, let's make a deal now and get on with it."

"How much will you give us for it?" Zev asked.

Hancock looked at Ari. "What will it take?"

"A cash payment," Ari answered, "of fifty million shekels, safe passage north to Jerusalem, and protection for the sites of our buried relations. That should do it."

"You're dreaming." Hancock looked at his watch. "If I leave here without a deal, protection for your departure will be withdrawn. Media coverage will be barred. Keep that in mind."

Ari tapped the table with his fingers. "So you're threatening us unless we bend to your will?"

"Very dramatic," Hancock said. "We are prepared to make a fair offer. Safe passage, and we'll arrange transport by choppers for your sick and elderly."

"Bastard," Ari said through his teeth. "Criminal."

Dove cleared his throat. "So you're willing to pay for a media campaign to make yourself look good? This isn't an offer. It's an insult."

No one spoke for a moment until Rita asked, "Who is paying for this offer?"

Hancock ignored her. "We have some time," he said to Ari. "Let's be reasonable, and see what we can work out."

"That's easy," Zev replied. "Give us your best offer, and this time don't lie about it."

"The security wall alone is worth a billion," Ari reminded him.

"Well, we know you'll disable the software in the wall before you leave," Hancock said. "Best offer? Okay, the safe passage, chopper escort, and ten million shekels to leave everything. Including the furniture and livestock. The concern of leaving graves is a local issue, and should be handled accordingly."

"That won't even pay for the cost of the move," Ari said.

Hancock put his hands on the table and leaned forward toward Ari. "Jew scum. We're taking this place over. Go along, or let me introduce you to the real world. My men outside will come in and terminate every one of you sitting here. I bet the next group we bring in here will sign. After they have to step over your bloody bodies to get to the table."

Silence followed for a moment until Zev finally spoke. "Why? Why are you taking over our land? Forcing us out of the town we built?"

"Because my king wants it for his future Bedouin subjects," Hancock answered. "And so I'm going to get it for him. It's that simple."

"You MI6 whore," Dove said loudly.

"I guess that's fair," Ari said sarcastically. "We should do what you want, or be murdered. Is that about it?"

"Let's just say," Hancock said, "if you people can't be reasonable, an unfortunate accident might befall the lot of you."

"Befall?" Ari asked. "You always talk that way? Try to make everything sound dramatic?"

Rita turned and looked at a corner of the room. She reached her hand out and curled her fingers. Pybar and Smasher stepped forward into the light.

Ari took a phone out of his pocket and dialed as the two enforcers—with their bull necks and arms like piano legs—neared the table. "Moshe, how many of his men are outside?" Ari put the speaker on and set the phone on the table.

Moshe's voice crackled back. "Two outside your building. Two on the perimeter."

Ari didn't hesitate to ask, "Can your men take them?"

"Yes, Commander. Snipers have the two outside in their sights."

"Stand ready." Ari snapped the phone shut and set it down. "Like she's trying to tell you"—he nodded toward Rita—"you could have an unfortunate accident yourself."

Hancock's eyes widened. "You wouldn't dare."

"Why not?" Ari looked at the others. "We've got nothing to lose."

"Please," Dove broke in, "let me do it. I'd rather kill this limey bastard right now than take any amount of money."

It took another half hour to discuss details and throw around insults before they were ready. Then Ari said, "Write it. I've got other things to do."

Hancock pulled a document from his briefcase and laid it on the table. "One World observers will arrive in a few days to ensure compliance." He filled in some blank spaces, and slid the paper across the table for Ari to sign.

Ari moved the paper in front of Rita. "She'll review it."

Rita read the one-page document carefully. She picked it up and shook it. "The money isn't to be paid in installments later." She pointed to the last paragraph. "The full amount due must be paid before we leave."

Hancock looked at Ari. "Half when you leave, the balance a month later," he offered. "That's a good deal."

Ari shook his head. "No, it is not. You'll pay the money before the observers arrive, or we don't let them in."

Hancock picked the document up from where Rita laid it. "Don't be difficult," he said, "or you people will get nothing but trouble."

Ari handed him the pen lying on the table. "We could agree to twenty million shekels paid before the observers arrive, the balance two weeks later in Jerusalem."

"Fine," Hancock said. "We can do that." He made the changes and initialed them.

Ari read the revised document. "Make no mistake," he said directly to Hancock, "we're not giving up our rights to this land. We're simply leaving temporarily until the local area settles down."

Dove nodded. "When we come back, this place had better be waiting for us. We have the right to return to our homes."

Hancock handed Ari the pen and said, "We'll worry about that when the time comes. If you think you can take it back by force, go ahead and try. You know how it works with these people. If a property is left unattended, the previous owners forfeit all rights to it when someone else moves in."

Ari accepted the pen. "That's their culture, not ours."

"Exactly," Hancock said. "So you'll take it up with them."

Ari's lips pressed into a thin line as he started to sign.

"My employers will pay more if you leave the livestock," Hancock offered.

Ari shook his head, signed the paper, kept the copy, and shoved the original over to Hancock. "Now get out of here," he said. "While you still can."

Pybar escorted Hancock out to his car. Smasher stayed by the door. Jacob followed Hancock and his driver to the main gate and reported to Ari.

The group at the table sat for several minutes while Ari listened on his phone. Rita started to say something, but Ari shot her a warning glance, and snapped his phone closed. He stood, and the others followed. "I guess there's really nothing more to talk about so let's get back to the business at hand," he told them.

At the front steps, Ari turned to Dove and winked. "If it's not too late, maybe you could swing by and pick up that box of stuff for Naomi."

Zev leaned close. "We've got to work fast," he said in a low, muffled voice. "We'll work through the night."

"Layla tov, good night then." Ari and Rita waved and left for home. He stayed silent in the car, and she followed his lead.

Ari parked in front of their building, got out, and walked to the passenger side to open the door. They went inside and left the front door unlocked for Dove. Ari turned on a music selection, and sat with Rita on the sofa.

Dove arrived minutes later. Ari met him at the door and locked it behind him before they joined Rita in the living room.

"Let's enjoy a glass of wine and relax," Ari suggested. "We deserve it."

They made small talk while Ari poured the wine. He handed a glass to Dove, and motioned toward the study. "Have you seen my latest collection?"

Dove took the wine. "I insist."

They went in the soundproof room, and Ari closed the door.

"What's going on?" Rita asked.

"Take a seat, Honey." Ari sat in a chair and patted the one next to him. "Dove can explain it to both of us."

Dove set his wine glass on a side table. "It's a new sound-surveillance technology," he told them. "We don't have anything to test for it."

Ari glanced at Rita and saw confusion on her face. "When the negotiator arrived today, he toured our community for almost an hour prior to our meeting. Moshe followed them and he saw the driver install miniature devices in three places along our wall."

"Setting up a triangulation," Dove said.

"For what?" Rita asked. "Can't we remove the devices if we know where they put them?"

Ari shook his head. "We don't want to alert them that we know."

"We think," Dove said, "they've found a way to open a quantum pathway by electrically charging the ions of a given area. Their receiver pulls in the tagged sound particles and restructures the words. It has a range of several kilometers."

"They can pull them in from the air, through walls, everything," Ari added. "Except this room. Activated copper mesh was embedded floor to ceiling during construction."

"We know they have this?" Rita asked.

Dove shrugged. "We think it's still in the experimental stage. Anyway, Shoshona and her crew are shredding documents through the night. Our digging equipment and smart weapons are being taken through the transportation tunnel to the beach camp. Binyamin's men will move the equipment and weapons to the *Gilad.*"

Ari said, "But do we have enough time to complete this before the observers arrive?"

"We do. A couple of soldiers rigged a sort of sled system from the tunnel runners. It's effective. And when Zev is finished setting smart charges in our key buildings and underground bunkers, he'll wire the transportation tunnel."

"They don't know about our tunnels," Ari said, more to himself than to Dove. "We can keep working after the observers arrive if we have to, although I'd rather not."

"I think we'll be ready before they come." Dove sipped his wine. "Matan and Gabriel are part of a special forces team working on disguising the graves we leave. And we're lucky Prime Minister Kiah offered to transport those killed in our recent battle to Jerusalem for burial."

Ari turned to Rita and smiled. "You were great at the meeting."

She looked at Ari, then Dove. "You know we'll never get the second payment."

"Oh sure," Ari said with a wave of his hand.

"Of course we know that," Dove said.

Rita sipped her wine. "You're both taking this better than I ever imagined."

"I'm just looking at the reality in front of me," Ari said. "And accepting it the way it is. I'm following your advice, Honey."

Dove chuckled. "Go ahead. Tell her."

"The reality," Ari continued, "of our latest aquifer report."

"You see Rita," Dove broke in, "our geologists have long watched the aquifer that sits below our community. Our scientists developed a complicated system to measure the water table. We read the data once a year."

"Anomalies in last year's readings caused us concern," Ari told her. "We thought we had a few years to work out this problem, but we knew this day was coming."

"Yes," Dove said. "The designers of Kol Shofar devised a system to link several Negev aquifers together. That was before the conflict started. Without the other Garden projects to link the aquifer systems, the latest report says we'd have to rely on outside water sources in another year."

"And there aren't any," Ari added. "And not enough rain for water catchment either."

Rita set her glass down hard. "So we have to move anyway?"

Ari touched her cheek affectionately. "In peaceful times we would've figured something out. But surrounded by hostile Islamics, yeah, we'd have to move anyway. Except we couldn't afford it before we made this deal."

Rita sat thinking for a few moments. "Do they know about the water table? Our enemies?"

"They have no idea."

"Nor do they know in Jerusalem," Dove said. "And, Rita, you can never tell."

Rita picked up her wine glass. "I never will," she said.

"The Bedouins moving in, and their European backers," Ari said, "have just about enough time to rebuild the mess they made before they find themselves out of water."

chapter 22

TWO INTERNATIONAL REPRESENTATIVES arrived in a late-model luxury SUV for their scheduled day of observation before the move. They arrived in late morning and brought the required cash to Dove's office. Shoshona took custody of the funds while Lilith reviewed and signed the accompanying legal documents to accept the funds on behalf of Kol Shofar.

Ari watched from an adjoining room. With the transaction completed, Ari asked Moshe to give them a tour of the still-standing community room. Ari didn't reveal the location of the underground command and control center or the underground safe housing as he followed along behind them.

After the tour, the officials drove around the grounds for several hours. In the early evening they arrived at Dove's office, declined Shoshona's invitation to spend the night at Kol Shofar, and left for nearby Maccabiah.

Ari received a phone call advising him of their departure at the same time that Dove dropped by. Excuses were made to drift into the protected study.

"Will they come back tomorrow?" Ari asked after he secured the door.

"I doubt it. They said they would, but they saw everything today."

"We're scheduled to leave Passover morning," Ari said. "Big media event."

Dove nodded. "Yeah, that's the plan. Day after tomorrow."

Rita sighed. "This is hard on the families."

"Yeah, the media recording every tear, every humiliation of leaving." Dove shook his head. "It's terrible, but hopefully people around the world will see what's happening to us."

"Naomi and I have an idea," Rita said. "We talked about leaving shortly before dawn instead of the scheduled time of eleven so it'd be easier on the children. By the time the sun comes up, we would be past the east side of Maccabiah where the Islamic neighborhoods are."

"That's true," Ari said. "No one wants the children to endure the jeering and taunting that's sure to happen if we leave when scheduled.

Rita looked at Dove. "I know you wanted the media coverage."

Dove tapped the side table. "I like it. Finish loading after Havdelah sunset ends Shabbat on Saturday night. Leave when it's still dark Sunday morning."

"They'll have eyes in the sky on us," Ari mentioned. "We have to be careful when we blow the military buildings and bunkers."

"And there's more," Dove said. "Moshe tagged the observers and back-traced their signals." He looked at Rita and added, "That basically means Moshe listened to their phone calls."

Ari leaned forward. "What'd we learn?"

"The military transports are coming tomorrow to fly our sick and elderly to Jerusalem ahead of our departure. We knew that. But we learned they plan to take Levi into custody, never deliver him to our hospital in the city."

"We can't let them," Rita blurted out.

"No, we can't," Dove agreed. "I got a coded text message to Binyamin before I came here. He'll send someone. He can't come himself every night. It'd look too obvious."

Within minutes of Dove's words, Ari answered a knock at the door. A medium-height, slight young man with dark-brown curly hair had arrived carrying a fruit basket and a bottle of Israeli wine. The basket was from Binyamin. Ari took the gift card and invited him into the study.

"I'm Jonah," the man said. "We have a plan to help you protect your rescued soldier. But we have to move fast."

Ari nodded, and Binyamin's aide laid it out.

A few minutes later Dove drove Jonah to the temporary hospital. Ari and Rita arrived a few minutes later.

Dove disabled the security camera and covered the web cams while Rita whispered the situation to Sasha.

Levi was barely coherent. Ari waited while a nurse filled a portable intravenous fluid bag and attached the line to Levi's arm. Ari motioned to one of the soldiers standing guard. "Gently," he cautioned when they lifted Levi out of his bed.

With Ari on one side and the soldier on the other, they carried Levi out the front door and into Dove's car.

Rita watched from the window as Ari drove away from the curb with his precious cargo.

Jonah got into Levi's bed and pulled the blanket up around his face before Rita uncovered the security camera lens on the wall.

"I should go with Levi to attend to him," Sasha whispered.

"You have to," Rita agreed. "They might arrest you tomorrow for hiding him. Don't worry about your things. I'll send someone over to take your belongings to Jerusalem for you."

Sasha covered her mouth with her hand and coughed. "I can be ready in an hour. Where am I going?" she whispered behind her hand.

Rita leaned close to Sasha's ear. "Somewhere safe. To the troop carrier *Gilad*."

An hour later, Rita left in Ari's car to pick up Shoshona. They drove back to the hospital. As soon as they entered, Shoshona started shredding files while Rita walked to the car with Sasha.

Sasha climbed in next to Rita and they drove to an area near the security wall's rear entrance. Rita parked and, with night-vision flashlights, they moved under the canopy of trees to the new escape tunnel opening inside the security wall at the now-damaged rear gate.

One of Binyamin's men waited inside. Rita watched while he fastened Sasha's bag onto a tunnel runner. Sasha climbed on behind him, and they sped off, raising a cloud of dust behind.

In the darkness, Rita returned to her car and headed to the temporary hospital to pick up Shoshona. She parked in the drive-way and blinked her headlights once.

"Everything's wiped clean," Shoshona whispered after she got in. "All the medical records. Everything."

When Rita finally walked up the steps of Ari's building late that night after taking Shoshona home, she felt energized. Once inside Ari's quarters, after slipping into her nightgown, she pulled her journal off the closet shelf for the first time since arriving at Kol Shofar.

While waiting for Ari to return, she prepared a cup of hot green tea and sat at the dining table. Opening her journal to the first blank page, she wrote, *"Everything happens for a reason."* She thought for a moment, sipped her tea, and added, *"I love my life, right here, right now."*

The next morning dawned clear in their desert wonderland. *Another exquisite day*, Ari thought. "It would've been a perfect day for planting a garden, or celebrating a holiday," Ari told Rita as she stirred awake. They got up even though it was still early, and he prepared the coffee extra strong.

They spent the morning talking in the living room until twin military cargo helicopters roared in around midday. Ari ran outside to hear them set down beside the community center where the sick and injured waited to be carried to a hospital in Jerusalem.

Ari said shalom to Rita a few minutes later, then left for the hospital to observe the patient transfers.

Shortly before Ari arrived, Jonah slipped out of Levi's room in the confusion. When the One World Government military police came for Levi, Jonah, dressed as a nurse, showed them the empty bed and explained that Levi was already waiting at the community center with the other patients.

Ari heard the commotion in the room and poked his head through the doorway. He feigned ignorance of Levi's whereabouts after reminding them that he was there only to observe. The police finally left.

By late afternoon, those wounded in the revenge attack had been carried away by the transports. Unusual storm clouds rolled in, and Ari headed home feeling relieved that his van was packed and ready. The ominous dark clouds filled the sky by the time he parked in front of his building.

Ari spent a relaxed evening with Rita discussing travel details and going over plans for the early morning departure. Now that he'd accepted the move, he felt almost eager to get on with it.

Dove arrived after dinner with Zev and Monica to discuss final details. Ari invited everyone into the protected study. They sat in padded chairs in a semicircle, with side tables next to the chairs.

"Rita's upset," Ari told them as he closed the door. "I told her it's too late to change the plan. That in a few hours we'll be in motion."

"Rita," Dove pointed out, "Binyamin had to return to the *Gilad*. We can't risk him being arrested on false charges connected to Levi."

"One of us has to stay," Ari added, "until the last resident leaves Kol Shofar before we blow the military buildings. One of us has to lead two hundred soldiers northeast to Be'er Sheva, and on to Jerusalem."

Rita pressed her lips together.

"Besides," he said in a playful voice, "I need someone to drive that cargo van with all my important stuff in it."

Rita finally had to smile. "Okay, you're right." She looked at the others. "He doesn't have anything. Almost nothing. One box of family heirlooms, a few clothes. His military duffel bag."

"It's true," Ari said. "She has more stuff than I do. The van's full."

"So it's settled," Zev said. "Shoshona and Zachariah will lead with Rita following in Ari's van. Dove and I will be right behind you, Rita, with Naomi and the children behind us."

Dove said, "Moshav security will travel embedded in the convoy around families with small children and elders in the middle. A new roadway was scraped in around the blast crater at the main road, so it should be easy going."

"Monica and I will follow with the soldiers an hour later," Ari told them. "There's a One World Gov checkpoint set up past Maccabiah. When we clear that, you'll head north on the main road. I'll take the forces northeast to Be'er Sheva, and pick up the troops there waiting to go to Jerusalem."

Zev cleared his throat. "Remember, we have to keep our attention fixed on what's ahead, not what we've lost."

"If there's nothing else." Dove stood. "Naomi's still packing."

The others stood, said shalom to Rita, and moved toward the door with Ari.

"Commander," Monica said, "thank you for this opportunity to be assigned as your aide."

Ari nodded, they left, and he locked the outer door. He turned out the living room lights, and found Rita in the bedroom setting out her cloth satchel to travel with.

"In four hours I'll be driving you out to the second lead car position at the gate." He wrapped his arms loosely around her. "Are you ready?"

"I am," she whispered in his ear.

The morning darkness hung foreboding and damp when Ari opened the van door for Rita and placed her satchel on the floorboard. Massive storm clouds blocked out the moon. The freezing storm clouds forming in the warm air created sharp cracks of thunder. Ear splitting. It sounded to Rita as if the whole world were exploding as she stepped into the van.

Ari climbed into the driver side, started the motor, and in a few minutes they arrived at the front gate. It stood wide open. Shoshona and Zachariah were parked with several others a short way out on the dirt road, now muddy from the night rain.

Monica drove up in a desert rover a few minutes later. She pulled close to Ari's side and he lowered the window as a light rain began.

"They're lining up the convoy now," she said. "Fifteen minutes."

Ari motioned toward the cars parked nearby. "Go ahead and get some coffee from Shoshona before we go."

Raising his window, he turned to Rita. "I know we still have much to talk about. We will. As soon as we get to the city, things will settle down."

Rita's fingers covered her Star of David necklace. "Ari, don't let anything happen," she whispered.

"What could happen?" Ari leaned closer. "Rita, just so you know, I've got a younger brother named Dan. He's been missing for three years. It's complicated. I'll tell you all about it when we get settled."

"A brother?" she repeated.

He kissed her mouth lightly, flashed a boyish grin, and slid out the car door as two cargo vans pulled behind them. Dove drove with Zev in the first vehicle. Naomi and the children rode in the next. Rita moved over to the driver side as a line of headlights streamed through the gate behind her.

Zachariah inched forward. Rita followed.

A cold drizzle fell from a gray sky onto Rita's windshield. The click clack of the wipers kept her company as she drove past the lettuce fields, now destroyed. Back behind the security wall was the field where she'd learned to shoot with Eyal. And the building where she lived, baked bread, and became friends with Devorah. She smiled, remembering her daily walks in the gardens.

The last year flashed through her mind frame by frame while she followed Zachariah's taillights past the outskirts of Maccabiah. Rita felt a wave of relief when the checkpoint became visible two kilometers ahead.

Twelve parking slots in a row on the side of the road and a temporary metal building served as the official point of entry from the south. Rita pulled into a parking space between Zachariah and Dove. She took a thermos out of her satchel and poured a cup of coffee while she waited.

Dove walked over in the rain and quickly got into the passenger side. "Shalom, Rita. You don't have to drive alone, you know. Zev could drive you for a while, keep you company."

"Thanks Dove, but it's fine the way it is. This way Zev can drive your van and you can drive with Naomi."

Dove didn't look convinced.

"I like driving alone," she added, "and the roads are good."

The corners of Dove's mouth turned up. "It's only been a couple of hours. You miss him already?"

"I'm worried," she admitted. "And yes, it's terrible how much I miss him."

One World Government soldiers, wearing bright blue, crisp uniforms walked to the front vehicles. They came with medium-size dogs and piercing flashlights. A soldier opened the back of

Rita's van. He moved a few things around, then closed the doors and walked to the window. Rita lowered it, and a surly looking soldier pointed his light in her face, then at Dove. The soldier moved back and marked an X with white chalk on the side of her van.

Dove got out and went to Naomi.

Rita tried to settle her mind. The morning sun lightened the sky and the drizzle abated. She felt grateful to be alone, to have this time to think. But her thoughts kept drifting back to the gate, to Ari.

At the gate, Binyamin's fighting men were ready to go. They lined up in rows and waited for the signal to roll through.

"I guess it's time," Ari told Monica. He sat behind the wheel of a new utility rover.

"Is everything done?" Monica asked.

Ari nodded. "Binyamin left me his explosives expert, to be sure. Didn't you hear the boom?"

"Yes, I guess I thought it'd be louder."

"We used new electronic pulse technology," he explained. "We imploded the important buildings, the structures underground, and the escape tunnel."

Monica looked at Ari. "Will we make it past the checkpoint before they know?"

"Sure." He glanced over. "We're leaving hours before their officials are scheduled to take possession."

Ari pulled ahead of the waiting men and flashed his lights. Binyamin's two hundred men in a hundred trucks and desert rovers got the coordinated signal on their dashboard screens.

The drivers of the dozen lead vehicles behind Ari and the designated first five rows of the convoy started their motors. One minute later the next five rows would follow, then the next. Ari's thoughts, for an instant, drifted back to the day he brought Rita to the Kol Shofar entrance for the first time. The day he searched her in Antalya.

The clouds parted and the top of a bright magenta sun appeared above the horizon as Ari drove forward. "Here we go," he told Monica. Two columns of vehicles rolled through the gate onto the muddy road behind him.

When they approached the checkpoint, Ari didn't veer off to the side parking area, but stopped in the middle of the road. The line of vehicles following lumbered to a halt.

A team of peacekeepers performed the searches quickly. When they got the signal to move out, Ari winked at Monica. He knew the peacekeepers were searching for Levi, and they weren't going to find him.

At the next intersection, Ari broke away from the main road to take a less-traveled, more direct route for the next several hours.

They sped nonstop across the desert floor on good roads until the giant metal gates of the Be'er Sheva military command center finally glistened in the early afternoon sun. Ari pulled alongside an identification window, and a stern young guard waved him through as the gates swung open. A soldier stood inside to direct the convoy to a designated parking lot.

Ari drove to the edge of the lot and parked. He turned to Monica. "Maybe we'll get a chance to eat something outside a lurching vehicle."

A jeep pulled up next to Ari and a soldier stepped out. "I'll take you to our commander," he offered. "He's waiting in his office."

Monica stretched in the afternoon sun before getting in with Ari and the soldier.

The area commander, a large, handsome man with dark hair and expressive blue eyes, set the phone down and called out "Shalom" from behind a metal desk in his stuffy, cluttered office. He stood and extended his hand. "Did you encounter any problems getting here?"

"Nothing to speak of." Ari shook his hand and introduced Monica.

Ari didn't mention the abandonment of Kol Shofar. Instead, they made small talk. "Padroski, a Russian name," Ari remarked. It was too obvious to be a question.

Padroski smiled. "My parents were part of the 2010 Russian Jew release program. They met on the El Al flight bringing them here from Moscow. I arrived a year later."

An aide entered and spoke briefly with Padroski.

"We have some time." Padroski looked at his watch. "It'll take a couple of hours to organize the tank crew that's joining you. Let's get some dinner. And, please, call me Paddy. Everyone does."

Paddy took them to a private room off the main dining area. An aide soon brought three prepared dinners on a covered tray. They sat at a table and ate with Paddy while he explained the crisis his unit faced.

"Southern Judea is under constant attack," he explained. "Our contact inside the One World Gov media division advised us that they're going to vote soon to approve an international name change for the Judean Hills back to West Bank for the benefit of the Islamic neighborhoods."

Monica paused, her fork halfway to her mouth.

Ari shrugged. "Who cares what the 'international community' wants to call our land. We know it's the Judean Hills. Always has been. Always will be."

The afternoon sun slid behind the distant hilltops before Ari's convoy was finally cleared to go. The addition of twenty-five Merkava MK-V6 tanks following the convoy would slow them down considerably.

"We have to escort them," Ari told Monica while they slowly rolled out of the Be'er Sheva gate. "It's the safest way, maybe the only way, to get the tanks to the city."

"Commander, do you think we should stay here until morning? We've only got a couple of hours of real light left."

Ari glanced at the setting sun. "It's tempting. But probably safer to go now before enemy surveillance detects our movement here."

Monica settled back against her seat. "When do you think we'll arrive in Jerusalem?"

"We're taking a safer route to stay on good roads. That should put us at the old city gates by around midnight. If all goes well."

They turned north two hours after they left Be'er Sheva and the road became significantly worse. A three-quarter moon rose into view and glistened off the sandy expanse ahead while they traveled at a slow and steady pace.

Monica brought out her thermos and carefully poured a cup of coffee for herself and one for Ari. The quality of the road did not improve when they entered a desolate area of mounds.

"I don't like this section—it's like a maze out here," Ari remarked as he slightly increased the rover's speed.

Strong spring winds blew grit over the roadway, making holes and debris harder to spot in the dark. They drove without incident until Monica suddenly screamed. "Veer off and go around," she shouted.

Ari reduced his speed, but continued to drive straight. "What's happening?"

Monica grabbed the steering wheel and forced the vehicle off the road.

Ari, trusting her, relinquished control and peered into the darkness ahead.

"Stay out of it!" Monica shouted. "Go around this mound." Her face looked pale in the dim light of the dashboard. Ari took the steering wheel and followed her instructions to drive off the road to the left. She turned her head to gaze out her window, her forehead pressed against the glass.

The convoy swung off behind him. Ari completed the detour around the mound of sand and carefully drove back up onto the road.

"Can you tell me what you saw?" He kept his eyes on the road.

"Nothing until it happened." Her voice trembled. "But when we passed it, I smelled burning metal and fuel. I don't know what set it off, but whatever it was saved us. We would've driven straight into it."

Ari remained silent for a few moments, trying to make sense from Monica's words. He glanced out the windows at the dark, peaceful night. "What do you see now?" he finally asked.

Monica turned and looked out the rear window, then turned back. "Nothing now. Only a glow. It's too far back."

Ari drove at a reduced speed to allow the men behind them time to complete the turn.

"What do you think it was, Commander?"

Ari glanced at her. "I'm trying to understand what you're talking about. I didn't see anything back there."

Monica stared at him. "You had to see it," she insisted. "The explosion lit up everything."

Explosion? he thought. His voice became gentle. "Maybe you had a blackout or a flashback."

"Commander, I watched the outlines of the vehicles against the light of that fire."

Ari took a moment, tried to figure out what to do. He'd seen the effects of fatigue before.

White light suddenly flashed in the sky behind them, and Ari saw it in the rearview mirror.

Boom! The sound roared through the night a split-second after the flash, assaulting his ears.

A red fireball mushroomed out of the crater formed by the blast. Ari flashed his taillights to signal the lead drivers behind him, and he hit the emergency stop button that would show simultaneously on the dashboards of the convoy vehicles. Even with advance planning, it would take a good half hour to complete the stop.

Ari pulled ahead on the side of the road and parked, his heart pounding. He grabbed a shortwave radio and jumped out.

The convoy rolled past to a slow stop up ahead, four across, on the roadway.

Men from the vehicles behind Ari jumped out and ran toward him.

"What happened?" Ari shouted.

"Don't know," several shouted back.

The tank squad leader came through on Ari's radio com. "Massive bomb directly under the road."

"Come back," Ari said into the radio com. "What set it off?"

"My last tank in the convoy. It got separated from us. I think he missed the detour because of the sandstorm we passed through. He continued on the roadway and drove right over the bomb, setting it off."

Ari felt a chill go down his spine. Still trying to reconcile what had happened, his mind searched for an answer.

The tank leader's voice crackled over the radio loud enough for the dozen men standing with Ari to hear. "Let's get out of here. This was no improvised roadside bomb."

Ari agreed, and the men with him started for their vehicles, except for the team leader.

"Commander, we never would've made it to Jerusalem. It would've taken hours to sort out the mess and medic the injured. This was meant to ambush us. Trap us behind the burning debris."

Ari agreed. "And without the fighting men and tanks we're bringing to the city, Jerusalem would be weakened."

The man put his hand on Ari's shirt sleeve. "Commander, you saved our lives when you pulled us off the road. How did you know?"

Ari lowered his voice. "Will you keep this between us?"

The man nodded eagerly.

Ari glanced over to his parked vehicle. "An angel told me. *Shechiayanu.*"

The young man's eyes widened. "A miracle," he whispered.

"Let's go," Ari said, and headed for his rover. He jumped in next to Monica and closed the door. His hand trembled slightly from adrenaline flowing through his veins as he put his thumb on the ignition pad.

Ari drove up the road in front of where the convoy had finally stopped. Once he got the men moving, he turned to Monica. "It was a sophisticated bomb—probably military grade."

Monica continued to look straight ahead. "I'd rather not talk about it."

"I understand," he said.

Starlight and the partial moon gave enough contrast for Ari to see the outline of the Judean Hills behind the capital. The landscape changed dramatically when they drove out of the desert onto higher ground.

Ari led the convoy through the last regional checkpoint and into the suburbs of Jerusalem two hours later. The roads were smooth and he finally began to relax.

"Coffee?" Monica picked up her thermos and poured into a cup.

"Todah. I'll have one more."

"Commander." Monica handed him the thermos cup.

Ari glanced at her. "About what happened back there?"

"I don't know what happened," Monica said quietly. "I don't want other people to speculate. I'd rather we didn't have to talk about it to anyone."

Ari nodded.

"I mean, if it showed up in some report somewhere, it could affect my career. I'd have to answer questions. I wouldn't know what to say."

"Before we bury this, could I ask one question?" Ari looked straight ahead as he asked.

Monica looked out her side window. "Okay."

"Did anyone tell you anything? How did you suspect something was wrong?"

"See." Monica's voice became high-pitched. "This is exactly what I mean. I'm sitting here next to you and suddenly a ball of flame and smoke fill the road all the way across. But you don't see anything and then it happens for real."

"Did you hear it explode the first time? Did you hear anything?"

Monica turned to face Ari. "You know, I didn't. But I smelled it."

"I believe you, Monica. And I give you my word I won't repeat this to anyone."

It was close to two in the morning when Ari's procession approached the Jerusalem checkpoint. The soldiers standing guard cheered and waved when the convoy drove through. A driver in his sedan waited inside the city gate to drive Ari and Monica to their temporary quarters. Ari was tired and felt grateful for the ride. *Better than looking for an address in the city at night*, he thought.

Ari handed the rover keys to a young soldier standing ready. He and Monica took their bags and entered the sedan. The driver closed their doors and got in.

"Did the Kol Shofar families come in already?" Ari asked.

"Sure they did." The driver started the motor. "Late afternoon. Big fanfare. Cheering people lined the street. We got most of them settled in by midnight."

They drove to a part of the old city that used to be called the Jewish Quarter. It was now mostly military housing. The driver parked in front of a four-story apartment. He got out and offered to carry Ari's bag.

"No thanks, but I'd like a word."

The driver stepped close and leaned forward.

"Monica is my top aide," Ari told him. "She's important to our cause. Please see that her accommodations reflect that."

The driver stood straight. "She's assigned to general housing for tonight, but I'll put this information in the right hands. A change in her accommodations will be made tomorrow. I give you my word."

Ari shook his hand. "Good man."

The driver waved toward the building. "You're on the fourth floor in the back, Commander. Your name is taped to the door."

Ari picked up his bag and walked through the front entrance doors. He no longer felt the strain of the trip and sprinted up the four flights of stairs.

Music played from behind the door with his name on it. He realized he didn't have a key and started to knock. He tried the door handle first. It was unlocked.

"Rita," he called out as he turned the knob. He opened the door, and soft light streamed past him. She was there, waiting for him.

chapter 23

THE MORNING SUN cast a rosy hue over a bustling Jerusalem as if to welcome the people from Kol Shofar. That first morning, Ari slept in late and then enjoyed sipping coffee with Rita on their balcony overlooking ancient stone walls and streets.

"It all happened so fast," Rita was saying.

Ari poured a second cup of coffee from a nearby carafe. "Is this difficult for you?"

Rita shook her head. "This is magnificent. The most exciting place in the world." She said she felt simultaneously at ease and excited by the city, her first time there after reading about it, yearning to see it, for most of her life.

Ari took a deep breath and let it out. "Yeah, this is something," he said looking out at the view. Centuries-old crowded limestone houses built into a gentle slope led down to a narrow road below. "It'd take a lifetime to learn every secret of this city. I've been here most of my life, and there are still places I've not seen."

"Ari, how long will we be here?"

"We'll find out soon. Tomorrow we meet with Prime Minister Kiah. And the day after, well, I'd like to go see my parents."

"Of course." Rita set her cup on a glass table between the chairs. "I understand and I've got plenty to do here anyway."

"I think you should come with me. No reason to wait."

She smiled and leaned back against the chair cushion. "When will you call them?"

Ari continued to gaze at the landscape. "It's complicated, Rita. I can't call them directly."

"Then, how will they know you're here?"

"Trust me." Ari set his cup on the table. "They already know."

Rita got up and brought out a dish of pastry. "A gift basket of pastries and oranges was here on the counter when I arrived."

Ari thanked her for the coffee and ate a fruit tartlet. "I had a falling out with my parents," he said after swallowing the last bite. "Things may be a bit strained at first."

Rita selected a slice of chocolate cheesecake. "When was the last time you saw them?"

"About a year ago. The time I came back from an op to find you guarding the secret entrance."

"You haven't talked to them since?"

"No need." Ari turned to look at her. "Why?"

She seemed to search for the right words. "If they don't know about me, about us."

Ari took her hand. "It's not about you. My parents wanted me to move to Jerusalem years ago to campaign for the job of prime minister. They didn't agree with my decision to stay in the military and remain at Kol Shofar."

"If you're sure it'll be all right, well, I'd love to go."

Ari squeezed her hand slightly. "It'll be fine. You'll see."

A polished black car from the office of the prime minister arrived in the morning for Ari. He asked Rita to accompany him. Dove was already inside the car.

They drove a short distance through neighborhoods of modern architecture intermingled with ancient stone buildings before the driver pulled into a gated driveway. Using a remote control to open the gate, he barely slowed down when they passed through. The car finally stopped under a vine-covered bamboo trellis. The driver got out and pressed a buzzer on a brown metal door.

A casually dressed aide—a slight man in his mid-twenties wearing clothes that looked too big for him—appeared at the gate to escort them in. The main building was a large two-story structure with a balcony surrounded by gardens and an expanse of lawn. The building, white stone with red stone accents around the door and windows, almost sparkled in the sun. A low, thick security wall enclosed the entire property.

The aide took them through a front room decorated with modern hardwood furniture and a brightly colored wall tapestry depicting a lion roaming a savannah. A library off to the side was their destination. Prime Minister Kiah greeted them from a brown leather chair in front of a wall of bookshelves. A thick floral carpet covered most of the floor.

"Bum knee," he said. "Hard to stand. Please, sit."

Ari had met Kiah just after he took office on the same day the former prime minister was murdered four years earlier. He reminded Ari of a big white-haired bear. He had coarse hair that couldn't be combed to look neat no matter how he tried. Over the years it had become something of a trademark.

Ari said, "Shalom." He looked around and noticed another man sitting nearby. The man wore square-framed glasses perched on his large, narrow nose. *An analyst-type*, he thought.

"My first officer, Pinkhas." Kiah made the introductions while his aide stepped out to return with coffee and sweet rolls.

"I understand you met with Padroski in Be'er Sheva," Kiah said. "So you realize what's happening in Judea, how the fighting weakens our defenses here in the capital."

Ari nodded. "We know the soldiers that were protecting Kol Shofar are needed here."

"Ari," Pinkhas said, "we're sorry you had to lose your community. We appreciate your sacrifice."

"And if only this were the end of it." Kiah sighed. "Unfortunately, more is needed."

Ari exchanged a knowing glance with Dove.

"We have a plan," Pinkhas added.

"We all have a job to do," Kiah said. "Let's talk about the options available to you. We can work out the details later."

"As long as you agree that all Kol Shofar members stay with me," Ari said.

Pinkhas leaned forward. "Let me remind you—you're under the authority of the prime minister."

With everyone looking at Ari and Pinkhas, Rita turned to Kiah. "Perhaps we could hear about the opportunities you've worked out for us," she said, pulling the attention in the room back to Kiah.

"Ah," Kiah said in a pleasant tone, "I've heard about you. The strategist. Moti thinks I should offer you a job."

Ari looked hard at Kiah. "She's not unemployed."

"I understand," Kiah said. "You want to keep her."

"What is the plan for us?" Dove asked.

"A fair question." Kiah glanced at Ari. "You passed by the Judean Hills. Padroski drew you a picture."

"The result," Pinkhas added, "of the fighting in the Judean Hills is that many families have moved to central and northern Israel."

"There's no room for us?" Dove asked. "Is that what you're saying?"

"Not at all," Pinkhas assured them.

"If you want to stay here," Kiah said, "we'll make room for you. We owe you that much."

"You want us to stay here in Jerusalem?" Ari asked.

"That's excellent," Rita said. She got a look of dismay from Ari. "I mean, well, if everyone else . . ."

"Hold on," Pinkhas interjected. "Let's not get ahead of ourselves."

"Hear me out." Kiah held up a hand. "We've negotiated an offer for your entire community with the mayor of Gamla. And only if you're interested in moving that far north."

"Gamla?" Rita repeated. "What would we do there?"

"Not the only place you can go," Kiah said. "Central Israel is still an option."

"Of course," Pinkhas added, "with the now-crowded conditions caused by the conflict heating up in the Negev, the Judean Hills, and Samaria, your community members would be assigned to different areas."

Ari stood. "You call that an offer?"

"Now," Kiah said, "No need for upset. We've just started to explore."

Ari sat on the edge of his chair. "And Gamla?"

"If anyone knows that area, it's you Commander." Kiah leaned back in his chair and looked at Ari. "What they need are families to fill the abundant farmland we acquired in the 2030 War of Independence against Syria during the breakup of Lebanon."

"What would our status be in Gamla?" Dove asked.

"Let me explain," Pinkhas said. "Your people will legally own the land they farm after one year."

"In exchange for what?" Ari demanded.

"This is an extraordinary offer," Kiah said. "This is valuable land. So, of course, it comes with a price."

"Don't you mean," Ari said, "this is probably land without water on the border with Persyria. You want my people for a buffer."

"On the contrary," Kiah said quickly, "we wouldn't want you that far away from us. Isn't that right, Pinkhas?"

"I assure you, this is prime valley land with good water sources."

"What's the catch?" Ari asked.

Kiah shrugged. "We'd rather fill up our best land than leave it unattended. Strength in numbers, and all that."

"Let's get this out in the open," Pinkhas said. "The military unit under your command at Kol Shofar is being reassigned."

Lips pressed together, Ari settled back into his chair and waited. "What will my status be?"

"You'll be on special assignment," Kiah said. "If you decide to move your community to Gamla."

"It's not my decision, it's for the families to decide," Ari said.

"Let's ask them," Rita suggested. "Maybe our people want to move that far north."

Dove nodded. "That's fair."

"Fine with me." Ari stood and extended a hand to Kiah. "I'll get back to you in a few days."

Kiah moved his hand in a downward motion. "Sit. We have news for you."

"News of my brother?" Ari sat.

"Well, no, but this will cheer you. Two of your people arrived a week ago from Paris."

"Devorah and Batya," Dove said.

Kiah smiled broadly. "The very ones."

Pinkhas handed a piece of paper to Ari. "They're in a safe house on the other side of the city at this address. In case our enemy is tracking Devorah's movements, we prefer you don't call them for obvious security reasons. But don't worry, we've arranged a reception tomorrow night for the Kol Shofar leaders and their families. You'll see them there."

The soirée started in the early evening in a grand room at the famous Kjfar Hotel in downtown Jerusalem, and Ari found himself looking forward to it.

Ari and Rita arrived early and found their places among round tables covered in white linen tablecloths with pale blue napkins. Flower arrangements adorned each table and crystal chandeliers glittered, setting an elegant tone.

Ari pulled out a cream-colored, cushioned dining chair for Rita. They waited while servers placed crystal glasses and silver. Dove waved from a nearby family table with Naomi and the children when they arrived a few minutes later.

The room began filling with guests, and in walked Devorah, pushing Batya in a wheelchair.

Ari felt a rush of affection when he saw Devorah. He moved quickly across the room to greet them, kissed Devorah on each cheek, and greeted Batya. Ari took the wheelchair handles from Devorah. "You're seated at our table."

Devorah linked arms with Ari as they walked behind Batya's wheelchair. She whispered in his ear and a look of joy spread across his face.

"Here we are." Ari positioned Batya between Rita and Devorah.

Zev joined them, along with Monica. Sasha and Medad strolled in next, arms linked. Yalon rolled up in his wheelchair with Moshe and Kani to complete the table.

Three flute players on a side stage provided soft background music. White-coated waiters circulated with trays of appetizers. Devorah looked around. "This almost seems like old times."

Ari smiled. He had to agree.

The food arrived, a garbanzo vegetable stew in a braided pastry basket with a spoonful of smooth white cheese on top, served with steamed greens and almonds. The tables soon filled with dishes of olives and baskets of bread.

"We expect you to eat and talk at the same time," Ari said to Devorah. "Tell us everything."

Devorah put her fork down. "Rishon helped us the most."

"He helped me when I traveled through Paris," Rita said. "He's wonderful."

"I don't know how I would've gotten through everything without Devorah and Rishon," Batya told them. "My spine was damaged in the attack and I had to do months of physical therapy after the operation."

Rita smiled at the delicate young woman. "He came back to see you?"

"Every weekend." Devorah looked around. "By the way, where's Jacob? I hoped to see him here tonight."

Rita looked at Ari.

"Jacob's on assignment," Ari answered.

They enjoyed the music and talked through the meal. Out of habit, Ari discreetly studied the people seated around the room.

During the dessert course, Ari wandered from one table to the next, greeting people. The move to Gamla was the topic at every table. Most of the families told Ari they wanted the farmland. The choice to move the Kol Shofar community to Gamla became obvious. Lively conversation and an occasional outburst of laughter filled the room as he made the rounds.

As soon as he could comfortably leave, Ari called for a driver. He hurried Rita to the car after they said shalom to their friends.

"I didn't have the heart to tell Devorah that Rishon is missing," Ari said on the drive home. "I couldn't upset her tonight."

On the steps in front of their building, he wrapped an arm around Rita as they walked. "My brother Dan's in Paris," he whispered close to her ear. "He's been located."

"That's what Devorah told you? That's wonderful."

Ari hugged her tighter. "I told you she'd be happy for us."

They went inside their flat and Ari was overflowing with energy. Rita made herself a cup of coffee. Ari waved her off when she offered to make one for him. She took her cup and joined him at a small, pink marble dining table.

"Let me explain to you why I remained secretive about contacting my family." Ari shook his head slowly. "It's bizarre, really. The political stratagem of wiping out entire family lines isn't new with this enemy, though."

Rita sipped her coffee. "A favorite choice of the Romans, as I recall from my history books," she said. "Starting with Cleopatra, her sister, and their children."

"It's barbaric." Ari ran his fingers through his hair. "But I guess it works. Change the circumstances and you change the outcome."

"You mean, murder the influential families of a culture so it becomes easier to conquer?"

"Something like that." Ari stood and stretched. "In public places, never mention my parents or Devorah by name."

"Should we be talking now?" Rita looked around. "Is it safe?"

"Yeah, the military quarter is retrofitted with copper mesh in the walls and ceilings. The windows are aluminum and fused silicate." He took a deep breath. "It feels good to speak freely. We don't have to go into the den every time we want privacy."

"That's good," Rita said, laughing. "Because we don't have a den."

"We should get some sleep." Ari held out his hand to her. "Are you ready? Tomorrow you meet the parents."

In the late morning, they drove out in Ari's new high-performance government-issued Israeli sedan. "Do you think they know about your brother?" Rita asked as she settled into her plush bucket seat.

"They seem to know about everything." Ari glanced at Rita. "You know you don't have to wear the necklace under your blouse."

Rita touched it. "I thought you said it might be better to let your mother get used to the idea."

"Yeah, I guess you're right." Ari kept his eyes on the road ahead. "Probably better."

They sped through the city gates into the surrounding suburbs. Ari drove on narrow streets and finally turned up a hill leading to a familiar cluster of villas. He parked in front of one villa with garnet-colored bougainvillea growing up stone block walls.

"Ready?" Ari turned off the motor, went around, and opened her door. "C'mon, I'm sure they're getting anxious."

"Are you sure they'll be expecting us for lunch?" Rita picked her purse up off the seat and stepped out.

"Moti sent a courier over last night." Ari pulled an iron latch on the massive double-entry doors, then pushed the door open. "See, it's unlocked. They're expecting us."

They stepped into a tiled entryway full of potted plants. A lion-head fountain in the corner filled the room with sounds of rushing water.

"I'm happy to meet your family," she whispered. "Thanks for bringing me, Ari."

He turned and gave her a wink at the same time his slightly overweight mother entered the room and screamed with joy. She pushed her graying brown hair away from her face and headed straight for Ari. Avraham, a heavy-set man in his late sixties, followed close behind. Ari managed to break free from the hugging and kissing to make the introductions.

"Please, call me Sarah. We don't stand on formality here."

Rita stepped forward. "Thank you, Sarah. I'm happy to be here."

"It's pronounced Sa'RAH," she corrected, and waved a hand toward her husband. "And that's Avraham. Now we should eat while the food is ready."

Ari led the way to a dining room where a table laden with covered dishes stood ringed by six carved wooden chairs with high backs and soft upholstered seats.

For a leisurely hour they enjoyed raw vegetable salads, spreads, cracker breads, olives, and cheeses.

Sarah offered Rita more of her special black-tea fruit juice beverage. "We're happy to meet you." Sarah poured the glasses full. "Do you work with my son?"

Rita glanced at Ari. A smile crept across her face. "Well, yes I do."

Sarah stood, and headed for the kitchen, announcing she would return with cake and coffees.

Rita offered to help, and complimented Sarah on her elegant home.

"Todah," Sarah said. "Oh, I'm sorry, my dear. I forgot you're American. You probably don't know any Hebrew. That means thank you."

Rita returned with the tray. She explained about the Hebrew lessons as she set the coffees on the table. "I've been here for a year now."

"That is so nice." Sarah finished cutting her coconut almond cake at the table. "My son's friends are always welcome here. You come and visit us anytime."

Ari saw a look of upset on Rita's face when she sat. He looked at his mother's smiling face and decided not to ask.

"My father and I were talking about Dan," Ari told Rita. "My parents are as excited as I am."

For the rest of the afternoon they discussed the impending move to Gamla. Sarah and Avraham agreed it seemed to be an exceptional offer.

As the sun began to set, Ari said, "It really is time for us to get going."

"What are you talking about?" Both of Sarah's hands went up and pressed against her cheeks. "Leave so soon? You just got here."

"*E'ma*," Ari said in a gentle voice, "we have responsibilities in the city. This isn't a vacation."

"Still, son," Avraham said, "you could spend the night here and leave early in the morning. Think of your e'ma."

"I don't know." Ari looked at Rita. "What do you think?"

"Then it's settled." Sarah clapped her hands. "You've made me so happy."

"I don't know, Ari," Rita said softly.

"I've already fixed up your old room," Sarah announced. "And the guest room for your friend."

Ari looked directly at his mother. "I don't have an old room."

Sarah wagged her finger at Ari. "The room that would've been yours if you hadn't run off to that commune."

"That's not the point. And Rita's not just my friend, she's my wife." It was the first time he'd said it aloud. He glanced at Rita and her face showed delight, even in the presence of his disapproving mother. He felt like saying it again for emphasis.

"Do you mean common-law wife?" Sarah asked. "I don't see a ring on her finger. I don't remember getting a wedding invitation."

"This is the first time I could see you. I wanted to tell you in person. And I wanted you to meet her."

"You're a commander. You can do anything you want," Sarah said accusingly.

"We were in the middle of the Islamic civil war," Ari pleaded. "The World Court issued a travel injunction against us. We were isolated from the rest of the world for almost a year."

"And you couldn't wait?" Sarah gave Rita a sideways glance.

Ari turned to his father. "Rita's Traditional. We didn't have a formal wedding."

"I think it'll be acceptable for them to stay in the same room," Avraham said, looking at his wife.

"What's next?" Sarah shook her head slowly back and forth. "I can't even think it."

Ari whispered to Rita, "I didn't see this coming."

"Well, what about the ring?" Sarah demanded. "If you claim to be married, where's the proof?"

"I gave her a necklace," Ari answered. "Traditionals sometimes wear a necklace."

Everyone looked at Rita as her face turned a deeper shade of crimson. She made no move to reveal the necklace.

Sarah faced Ari. "Hashem help us. Next you'll tell us you're an Essene. A necklace?" Sarah put both hands in the air, palms up, knocking over a glass of the fruited tea.

"I guess it's time for us to go." Ari pushed his chair back and stood. His face felt as tight as his stomach.

"You can make it up to me," Sarah pleaded.

"How?" Ari slowly sat.

"You're in the city now." Sarah wiped the corner of her eye with her napkin. "We could plan a real wedding with a real rabbi." She wiped her other eye. "If you're sure."

Ari leaned forward. "You mean an Orthodox rabbi after Rita studies for two years."

"Worse things could happen," Avraham added. "It would please your e'ma so much to see you under a *hoopa* breaking a glass."

"Don't hold your breath." Ari stood again.

"Todah for the meal." Rita stood, and started for the door.

Ari said shalom to his parents and followed Rita to the car. They drove a short way before he spoke. "I know how they are and I still didn't expect this. I'm sorry, Rita."

Rita sighed. "Well, I hope your brother feels differently."

"Dan will. I'm sure of it." He fell silent, not knowing what else to say. He was starting to understand why his brother stayed single.

Ari and Rita barely discussed the visit with his parents. Preparations to relocate an entire community became all-consuming for Ari. He pushed everything else out of his mind.

Dove visited Ari on Thursday evening after dinner to discuss details of the move. "Several more families have decided to stay here in Jerusalem," Dove informed them as he sat in an overstuffed chair in the living room.

Ari leaned back in his chair. "I don't understand it."

"Well," Dove speculated, "some have relatives living here, others think they can find better opportunities staying in our capital."

"Maybe they feel safer here than in the north with us," Ari said.

Rita shook her head. "No one knows where safe is anymore. At least here they have extended family and the city's well-guarded."

"Well," Dove said, "Devorah and Batya are coming with us. Batya's helping organize the children. She told Leah she will never marry, now that she's disabled, so she wants to devote herself to the community's children."

"Don't worry, Ari." Rita touched his hand. "Most of the families are moving north with us. Our people are living in cramped quarters and they're anxious to see the farmland."

"I know that's true," Dove agreed. "Naomi told me the same thing. We're still a couple of weeks away from the move to Gamla, though."

"What's the holdup?" Ari tried not to feel frustrated that everything seemed to be taking so long.

"The land transfer application is still being processed," Dove explained. "And the fighting in Judea continues to spread north. It's probably safer for us to travel in groups every few days when we do leave."

"I have to admit," Rita said, "I'm enjoying the luxury of living here. I can see why people might be reluctant to move to a new project again. Life is easy here."

Moti arrived as Dove stood to leave. "I apologize for the late visit," he said when Ari opened the door. "This way we have more privacy."

Ari brought him to the living room and offered a chair. "Tell us," Ari said as he sat next to Rita. "She has clearance. Speak freely."

Moti sat in a chair next to Dove and took a deep breath. "A small, isolated Orthodox neighborhood in Judea near the Jordanian border looks to fall within the next two weeks."

Ari leaned forward. "No."

Moti nodded. "Most certainly this will happen. Half the families have moved already. But we have a plan. It includes moving up your timetable to secure your place in Gamla before the rest of the families begin pouring in."

Dove agreed. "We'll begin sending groups out immediately."

"Are they ready for us in Gamla?" Rita asked.

"They'll make ready," Moti answered. He looked at Ari. "You're being sent to Gamla for a reason. We expect you to report back regularly to us. We've heard rumors that some of the people up there want to arm themselves, like a militia."

"You want me to spy on people? Citizens?" Ari shook his head. "I don't think so."

Moti looked at Ari for several moments without speaking. "No," he said slowly, "we want you to bring them to us. You'll negotiate the breakup of any private group trying to acquire arms."

"I can't do it." Ari said. "I fought in the war of 2030. I won't betray my own people."

"Precisely why you're the right man for the job," Moti pressed.

Ari thought for a moment. "If I say no?"

Moti shrugged. "Informing us about the leadership of Gamla is the price you'll pay. Technically, you're still in the military. You can be reassigned."

"You're threatening us to spy for you?" Dove asked.

"Harsh choice of words." Moti shook his head. "We can do this all night or you can understand what's at stake and help us. We're on the same side."

Ari stood and faced Moti. "I don't like the sound of this."

"Look, Ari, you didn't think we'd let you move away and become a farmer. Be realistic. You're one of us." Moti took a step toward the door and then turned. "Shalom, I can let myself out."

"What are you going to do?" Rita asked after Moti left.

"We can't lose the farmland," Dove said. "We'll lose our community if we spread out over central Israel."

Ari went to the balcony doors and looked out though the glass. "We owe our loyalty to Jerusalem," he finally said. "I think we have to go along. And do everything we can to stay in the truth with everyone involved."

"For all we know," Rita said, "these are baseless rumors."

Ari relaxed and turned toward Rita and Dove. "This feels right. Let's go to Gamla, whatever the terms. The local government there won't be supporting any militia movement. We'll work with the leaders, not against them."

Dove wiped his brow. "Let's start the move immediately before they change their minds."

Ari agreed. "Tell Naomi to prepare the team leaders for immediate departure. The first group can leave in a few days."

"Are you ready to go?" Dove asked.

"We've been living out of our overnight bags the entire time," Rita answered.

Ari grinned. "We never unpacked the cargo van. It's at headquarters underground parking. We could leave tomorrow." *And maybe we should*, he thought.

chapter 24

FOUR DAYS AFTER Ari met with Prime Minister Kiah, one hundred Kol Shofar family members left to form an advance tent camp in Gamla for the people coming later. A planned community next to a large sunflower farm would provide permanent housing by Chanukah. Rita, feeling excited by the move, packed and repacked her travel bag several times.

Prior to the group departure, Zev had arranged a travel blessing from a popular rabbi in Jerusalem as they gathered to leave the comfort of the safe city for undeveloped open land. Ari and Rita drove to a large parking lot next to a national park in time to hear the rabbi speak. Ari spoke with some of the people after the rabbi finished. Then they headed back to their apartment.

That night, Rita sat on an upholstered bench at the foot of the bed and brushed her hair. "We're all packed and we leave in a week," she said when Ari entered. "Not much time left."

Ari reclined near her and explained that he wanted to see his parents again before the move. "I'll leave in the morning and spend Shabbat with them. That should please my mother."

Rita set the brush down, feeling the sting of not being included. "You can't drive on Shabbat. You're spending the whole weekend?"

Ari ran his fingers through his uncombed hair. "I may not see them for a while after the move."

"You're right." Rita shook her head. "Of course you should go."

Ari secured his ankle holster gun in a lockbox on the dresser. "I'll get a vehicle from headquarters and leave our new car here for you."

The next morning Ari brought coffee and a kiss to Rita before he left. When she heard the click of the closing door, she yawned, got up, and enjoyed a leisurely breakfast. Around noon, she phoned Naomi, who said she was busy. Rita set the phone in its cradle. *I don't want to stay here alone*, she thought. *Maybe I should check on Batya.*

Rita drove across town, parked under a trellised carport at Devorah's address, and went to the front of a two-story duplex.

She rang the bell on the first floor, and caught her breath when Jacob opened the door. "What are you doing here?" she blurted out.

Jacob stepped aside for her to enter. "I got back from assignment a few days ago, and Devorah's telling me the latest news," he explained as he led her to the kitchen.

"Rita, how wonderful to see you," Devorah called out from her place at the table. "Join us. We're catching up."

Rita regained her composure and sat across from Jacob. "Where's Batya?"

"Spending the day with Leah." Devorah smiled at Jacob. "We were getting ready to go out to Café Liraz. It's the most popular café in old downtown."

"Another twenty minutes and you'd have missed us," Jacob added. "So glad you came."

"Well, don't let me keep you." Rita stood to leave. "I just stopped by to say shalom and check on Batya."

"You must come with us," Devorah insisted. "This is our farewell with Jacob. Didn't you hear? He's not moving with us to Gamla."

"What?" Rita looked at Jacob. "I thought you had an exemption because of your hero brother."

"No, I'm reassigned to Jerusalem. And anyway, the conflict will end soon, and we'll all be back together again."

"Besides," Devorah said, "it's too perfect. I don't have a car, and Jacob's got some military vehicle. We'll go downtown in your car, Rita. Did you drive here?"

Rita smiled. "We got a new car."

"Okay ladies," Jacob said as he and Devorah stood. "Let's get going before the café gets so crowded we can't get a table. They'll close early today for Shabbat."

Jacob offered to drive because he knew the way. Rita sat in the back seat, leaned forward between the seats to put her thumb on the ignition pad, and they drove off toward downtown.

Parking would've been impossible without Ari's senior-level military pass in the window. Arriving at Café Liraz, they encountered a guard at the door. A rifle hung by a strap over his shoulder. Rita noticed the handgun fastened to his side as he motioned impatiently for her to open her purse.

Rita opened it wide. "I thought the city was completely secure now."

"It is," the guard answered in Hebrew. "And we're going to keep it that way."

"Todah," Rita said as he inspected the contents of her purse.

The serious young man then checked Devorah's purse and Jacob's pockets before opening the café door.

One empty table sat in the far corner. The little round, red table had only two chairs next to it. Jacob insisted Devorah and Rita take the seats while he went to the front counter to order coffee drinks. He returned with a chair and sat with his back to the wall. A few minutes later a short, plump girl wearing a college T-shirt brought three foamy, chocolate-topped mugs filled to overflowing.

"It was chocolate or cinnamon," Jacob explained. "They hate making them plain."

The girl set the coffees and a basket of almond cookies on the table.

The friends sipped the hot drinks and talked away an hour. Jacob entertained them with stories and military gossip.

Rita lifted the heavy white mug to her lips to finish her second coffee. She heard the clinking of glasses and laughter from nearby tables.

Then she saw a flash from the corner of her eye.

Blinding white light exploded in slow motion across the room.

A roar ripped through the air.

Rita's coffee mug flew from her hand as Jacob's hand wrapped around her arm, pulling her under the table. He enveloped Devorah with his other arm and dragged her under at the same time.

Rita's hands moved through the molasses-thick air to shut out the screaming in her ears. Her eyes clenched tight as she hit the floor. Crashing sounds filled the room. She couldn't open her eyes, nor breathe.

Something hard hit her in the middle of her back, forcing her lungs to fill with hot, smoky air. Jacob cupped her face with his hands. He put his mouth on her mouth and forced his breath into her. He held her and patted her back until she coughed.

Rita heard screaming and moaning all around her. Someone was shouting far away. Shouting her name. She tried to move her arms and legs, but couldn't tell if they moved. *Jacob*, she remembered, and reached for his hand.

"Open your eyes, Rita," Jacob shouted again.

Rita blinked. Her eyes burned from the smoke when she opened them. Jacob sat on the floor behind her with his legs extended. One arm held her securely. The other arm cradled Devorah's head resting in his lap. Rita turned and he relaxed his grasp. She saw Devorah and looked up at Jacob.

"She's unconscious," Jacob shouted.

Rita watched his mouth move and understood. She looked down to see blood ooze from a gash in Jacob's thigh where a piece of twisted metal table leg protruded. He pulled the metal out and tossed it aside as a red bloodstain widened on his pant leg.

People ran in from the street and began pulling tables, pieces of walls, and debris off those trapped underneath. Broken glass covered everything. Sirens sounded faint and far away, but flashing lights told Rita the vehicles were right outside the smashed storefront.

Medics hurried in while Rita tried unsuccessfully to stand. A young man in a white uniform rushed over when she raised her arm and waved. She pointed to Jacob's leg. The medic squatted, opened his bag, cut a hole in Jacob's trousers, and began to treat the wound.

Rita pulled herself up to a standing position, braced herself with one hand on the medic's shoulder, and looked around. It didn't look real, everything broken, tangled. A girl about eight years old sat in a chair nearby amid the confusion. The girl looked around, her face white and blank.

Rita took a few unsteady steps toward her. "Sweetie, can I help you?"

The child looked with dazed, glassy eyes at Rita. "Yes, thank you. I can't find my hand."

Revulsion swept through Rita as she looked down to see the little arm ending in a bloody stump. She forced herself to look away, to find a medic.

Through the crowd, a man on the sidewalk saw her desperate wave and ran to help. Rita couldn't speak. She pointed to the child. The man turned and grabbed the sleeve of a medic as he hurried by. Together they carried the girl to an ambulance waiting outside.

Rita sank to the floor next to the girl's chair. Her heart pounded, and her stomach churned. She stayed hunched over, panting.

Men walked by carrying two stretchers. Jacob on one, Devorah on the other. As they passed Rita, Jacob reached out and grabbed her sleeve. The men stopped moving.

Jacob pulled Rita up. The medic waved and a man came running. "Bring her with," the medic shouted.

The man picked Rita up and carried her to the sidewalk behind Jacob. She closed her eyes and tried to shut out everything around her.

Men lifted Jacob's stretcher into the back of a Magen David Adom ambulance and placed him next to Devorah and two others. A woman covered in pulsing rivulets of blood lay convulsing. Rita was lifted in and put on a bench that ran along the side of the ambulance interior. A limp teenage boy lay next to the convulsing woman. Rita gripped the edge of the bench and leaned forward as the ambulance pulled away.

Emergency room doctors began arriving at the hospital when the ambulance pulled in. Devorah and Jacob were taken to intensive-care rooms. A tired-looking doctor treated Rita for cuts, bruises, and a sprained ankle in an examination room now divided into cubicles by hanging sheets. "Your bruised ribs and chipped tooth will have to be treated later," he told her.

An orderly put her into a wheelchair and rolled her to the lobby. She was told to wait for a taxi to take her home. Rita sat in the wheelchair while people rushed past in both directions.

Finally a man entered through the front doors and hurried toward her. "Rita, it's me, Dove." He moved his hand in front of her face.

She looked up. "Dove," she whispered. Tears streamed down her cheeks.

A taxi driver arrived and approached them. Dove thanked him, and sent the man to the counter to help the next person.

"C'mon, Rita, let's get you out of here." Dove pushed the wheelchair to the large glass doors framing the entrance to the hospital. They were propped open for the people rushing in and out. Pushing Rita in the wheelchair, he walked slowly to his car.

Zev ran to them from the street. "I came as soon as I heard about the bomb," he said, panting.

Dove nodded to his nearby car. "Help me get her home."

Zev opened the door while Dove helped her stand and put his arm out to steady her. He gently helped her into the passenger side and sat in the back seat behind her.

A man walking toward the hospital greeted them, and Dove gave him the wheelchair to return. A few moments later they drove through the parking lot exit and onto the main road.

Rita didn't realize her purse was gone until Dove parked in front of her flat. "My keys," she cried.

Dove made a phone call and within fifteen minutes a car pulled up next to them.

The driver rolled down his window. "I'm Michael from headquarters. I've got the master key."

Zev and Dove helped Rita up the four flights of stairs with Michael following.

For protocol, Dove flashed his identification and Michael opened the door.

They helped Rita hobble to a comfortable blue futon sofa. Her moans and groans made obvious her level of pain, even with the medication given to her at the hospital. She stretched out on the futon, and pulled a knitted blanket over.

"I'll call Naomi." Dove took a phone out of his pocket. "You'll spend the night with us."

Rita managed a faint smile. "Todah, but I'll be fine here."

Dove reluctantly put his phone away.

An hour passed before they left her to rest. Her eyes closed, and she drifted off under a haze of medication. *Rita, wake up.* She dreamed Ari was there, talking to her.

"Honey, I'm here," he said softly.

Rita opened her eyes to find morning sun streaming through the olive-green silk curtains covering the balcony French doors. She tried to move but everything hurt. She whimpered and laid her head back on a pillow.

Ari knelt next to the sofa. His breath caught in his throat. "Sweetheart, what can I do?"

Rita opened her eyes and uttered one word. "Coffee."

Relief poured through Ari, almost sweeping out the helplessness he felt when he saw her lying there, bruised and defenseless. He went to the kitchen and eventually returned with two white porcelain cups filled with hot coffee. He set the cups on a glass-topped table in front of the futon.

Rita propped herself up on one elbow while Ari moved close and extended his forearm for her to use as a brace to pull herself up into a sitting position. "Oh!" she cried out. "My left side hurts."

Ari fought back anger and tried to focus only on her.

"It's not bad," she said, managing a faint smile.

When the coffee cooled, he handed her a cup. Using both hands, she raised it to her lips. Rita blinked, and looked around. "It's early."

"Yeah, it's about five-thirty." Ari sat on the floor next to the sofa. "I got here as soon as I could. Dove got through to me around midnight."

She choked back tears. "What about Devorah? And Jacob?"

"Devorah's fine," Ari lied. "Jacob too."

Rita sighed deeply. Between sips of coffee, she described her experience.

Ari set his cup on the table. "The media won't report it until tomorrow, but Dove told me a suicide bomber tried to push his way past the guard outside the door when a teenage girl opened it to leave. The soldier jumped on the bomber and stopped him."

Rita shuddered. "That's terrible."

He heard the pain in her voice. "Yeah, it is. The soldier was only twenty-three."

"Ari, I talked to him." Her voice broke. "He looked in my purse."

Anger crept back into Ari's veins. "There hasn't been a bombing here since we took control of the city years ago. It's supposed to be safe now." He paused as thoughts of revenge filled him.

Rita sipped her coffee. "Can we be in the first group to move north? I don't want to be here any longer than we have to."

Ari drained the last of his coffee and forced a smile. "When do you think you can travel?"

"I don't know." She gazed out the balcony doors. "Soon, I think."

"I'll start a warm bath." Ari stood and leaned over her. "Let's see how you feel after a bath and a real breakfast."

Ari stayed close while Rita slept for most of the day. When Shabbat ended at sundown, Ari started making calls while Rita rested on the sofa. He couldn't get any updates on Devorah's condition, but Dove offered to come over when Ari called him.

"Let's meet tomorrow as planned. Rita still feels weak." He put his hand over the receiver and looked across the room at her. "Not much here to make for dinner. I'll go out and pick up something."

Rita nodded. "I was going to go shopping yesterday after visiting . . ." She tried again but couldn't finish.

Ari ended his call and crossed the room. "This will take some time, Rita. What you went through would knock some people down." He sat on the futon next to her. "I'm sorry. I left you alone." Guilt swept through him as he said it.

Rita shook her head slowly. "I'm okay, really. I'm one of the lucky ones."

Ari closed his eyes for a moment. "I'm the lucky one." Then he said what he hadn't been able to say to her before that moment. "I love you, Rita," he whispered.

chapter 25

STILL WARY BECAUSE of the café bombing, Ari made plans to leave immediately for Gamla. He informed Dove of his decision to drive separately. "For safety reasons," he told him, but the truth was that he hated waiting around for people. Dove was always on time for work, but when the family got involved, punctuality became difficult. *And I do think it would be safer,* he thought.

Ari cradled the phone and turned to Rita. "It's all set. We leave tomorrow morning."

Sprawled out on the futon sofa, Rita slowly sat up. "Good," she said. "The sooner, the better."

A duffel bag with Ari's essentials lay on the floor near the sofa. Smiling, he reached inside the bag and pulled out the small cloth sack with the pull-cord closure. "I kept it with us because it seemed right."

"Ari, I thought you decided to give the coin to a museum?"

"I intended to when I found it. But then Israel annexed Lebanon and formed the district of Gamla. I didn't know what to do when the Gamla Museum opened. I still don't."

"Why not give it to the Israeli Historical Museum while we're here? It must be worth a fortune."

Ari took the coin out of the bag. Feelings of pride filled him whenever he held it. To be a part of something so important, so ancient—those proud feelings kept him going at those rare times when his confidence waned.

"Ari, we can't keep something like this."

Her voice brought him back to the present, and he tried to explain. "I'm just not ready to give it up yet."

That night, as they sat on the bed together, reflecting on their time in Jerusalem, Rita sighed, and her eyes filled with tears. "I don't know why," she said softly, "I feel sad to leave. It's our last night here."

Ari carefully kissed her cheek, and helped her get comfortable under the covers. "It's not *our* last night," he said, kissing her other cheek. "Jerusalem is only a stopover. We're going home tomorrow."

A few hours later, at four as usual, Ari got up. He made fresh coffee and poured all but two cups into a traveling thermos before waking Rita by gently rubbing her arm. "How do you feel?" he whispered.

"I hurt all over," she groaned.

"Take your time, Honey. A cup of fresh coffee's on the counter for you."

With Ari's help, Rita sat up slowly. "Did you say coffee?"

He smiled, went to the kitchen, and popped two slices of cranberry-raisin-almond bread into the toaster.

After an hour, Ari decided they were ready. As he set their travel bags next to the door, his wrist com flashed an urgent message.

"Hold up, Rita," he called out. "Dove's on his way here." He waited impatiently for the next fifteen minutes while Rita sipped another coffee, this time from the travel thermos.

"It's open," Ari called out to the knock on the door.

Dove and a skinny young man with light brown wavy hair and a large narrow nose walked in. "My cousin Rishon," Dove said.

Rita stayed seated next to Ari on the sofa. "Shalom, come and sit with us. What a surprise to see you again, Rishon."

Ari looked at his watch. "Dove, we're supposed to leave now. You, with your family as well." Ari turned to Rishon. "What are you doing here?"

"Rishon's been at the checkpoint for hours," Dove explained. "He's got no identification on him and he couldn't get past the guards. With the heightened security since the bombing, they wouldn't release him until I went and vouched in person."

"Why now?" Ari asked the young man.

"France is falling fast," Rishon told them in a hushed voice. "We've had nothing but nonstop violence for months. Different Islamic splinter groups fought each other for control. Then they joined together and came after us."

"Then why are the police looking for you?" Ari asked.

"I almost got caught falsifying documents at the corporation where I worked. I had to make it look like I stole something ordinary, like money."

"So he traveled here to find me," Dove added. "Well, not really me."

"I thought it was obvious," Rishon said. "I came for Batya. I want to marry her."

Ari relaxed and leaned back. "Well, this is news."

"Are you aware of her medical conditions?" Rita asked.

"I spent every weekend with her for six months. She might walk again. And if she doesn't, that doesn't matter to me. Batya needs someone to encourage her." Rishon smiled broadly. "That's me."

"Do you have a car?" Ari asked. "Do you have anything?"

Rishon shook his head. "I got out with what I'm wearing. I lost everything."

"Devorah's got to stay in Jerusalem for a while," Rita said. "She suffered internal injuries, broken bones, torn muscle."

"That's why Batya's traveling with my family to Gamla." Dove glanced at Rishon. "We'll help him. He can squeeze in with us."

"You're moving to Gamla." Rita clapped her hands and looked at Ari. "Rishon is joining us."

"That's why we're here," Dove explained. "He needs a pass signed by the prime minister's office. It'll take days. We're ready to leave in an hour. You can sign the exemption."

Ari waved his hand. "Why didn't you say so? Give me the paper to sign, and let's get going."

"Does this mean I have your permission to marry Batya?" Rishon flashed a wide smile and faced Ari.

"My permission?" Ari repeated.

"Sure." Rishon leaned forward in his chair. "Batya told me that you're like a father to her."

Ari looked at Dove. "Should I sign?"

"Yes," Dove answered. "Rishon's twenty-five, my dear aunt's only child. May her memory be a blessing. Batya's eighteen. Devorah's all she's got left. These two young people can comfort each other while they build a life together. Naomi and I agree. It's a good match."

"Hey wait. We're leaving the new car here to pick up later. I'm driving Rita in the cargo van." Ari turned to Rita. "What do you think, Honey?"

Rita nodded. "Sure. We'll give them the car for a wedding present."

Ari got the vehicle fingerprint pad out of his bag. He clicked a few buttons, put Rishon's thumb on the biometric pad and said, "Done."

Rishon hugged Ari and thanked Rita. "I don't know what to say," he said quietly, his voice filled with emotion.

"You're part of a community now," Ari reminded him. "We're in this life together."

Dove stood and shook Rishon's hand. "Congratulations are in order," he said.

Ari helped Rita stand.

"A good beginning." Rita linked her arm through Ari's to steady herself. "Our new community's first wedding."

"First we have to get there," Ari said, looking at his watch.

It was noon before Ari and Rita finally pulled out of the garage at the Jerusalem flat. At the northern checkpoint, the guard waved them through, and they headed out on a section of highway hugging the Samarian hills. Ari finally relaxed, and stole a glance at Rita, leaning against a pillow in the bucket seat next to him.

"I'm not asleep," she said.

"Your eyes are closed," he teased.

She glanced over. "How would you know? You're looking straight ahead."

Ari laughed, relieved that she was in a good mood, despite her obvious pain.

Rita carefully leaned down to retrieve the pack from the floorboard. "I'll get some coffee for us."

They drove for a couple of hours while eating the cold breakfast of pita bread stuffed with chickpeas and leftover vegetable salad that Ari prepared earlier.

"We'll make it to the Sea of Galilee by afternoon," he told her. "I'll get fuel when we stop for dinner."

Rita started to reply when they saw several people run across the road ahead.

"What is this?" Ari slowed the car. "They must be fleeing something terrible."

Rita scanned the neighborhoods covering the hills to her right. "Look," she gasped as faint explosions went off behind the skyline.

Ari drove faster, and a few kilometers later the road became a highway. The original road, built by the Romans twenty centuries earlier, circled around Samaria. "I didn't realize the fighting was this far north," he said. "This isn't good."

Ari stopped at a fuel station near the Sea of Galilee three hours later. "I want to push on to the north, if that's okay with you, Honey."

Rita agreed. "We can eat the rest of the packed lunch while we drive."

The sun started its descent as they passed the suburbs and towns of northern Israel two hours later. Rita took a thermos of green tea and the last slice of cheesecake out of the bag on the floorboard to share with Ari. From time to time, Ari asked Rita how she felt. Each time she assured him that she felt all right.

The countryside changed dramatically from sparse vegetation to rolling hills covered in green shrubbery. "It won't be long now," Ari remarked.

They neared a northern checkpoint at what used to be the border with Lebanon. Ari felt good to be there. He pulled up and a stocky blond guard looked over his identification.

"Commander Ari?" The man asking wore casual military clothes and carried only a pistol. "We were told to expect you next week."

"Circumstantial," Ari answered.

The guard made a call on his headset, then leaned close to Ari's window. "Welcome to Gamla. We'll put you up in a town just north of your community farmland." He handed Ari a slip of paper. "This is the address with a map on the back. It's easy enough to find."

Ari thanked him and wished him a pleasant evening.

"Perfect time for you to drive in," the young man said. He raised his hand toward the distant mountains. "You'll see the Gamla."

Ari drove north while Rita studied the little map. The sunset turned the sky ahead crimson behind the mountain range.

"What did he mean, Ari? The Gamla?"

Ari pointed forward. "Look at the outline of the mountain that guards this land. The mountain looks like the back of a big old camel. Gamla means 'shape of a camel' in Hebrew. The first king of Gamla was Alexander Yoni—he lived near where our new community will be. That was close to three thousand years ago."

"A distant relative of yours?"

"Probably not," he chuckled. "But you never know. Anything's possible."

They drove into a small town as the sun gave up and the night sky took over. Ari finally slowed the car in front of a villa surrounded by lush vegetation.

"The map says cottage in back." Ari turned into the driveway, drove past the villa, and parked next to an immaculate-looking stone cottage. He got out and went to check it. No lock on the door.

The long ride left Rita too stiff and sore to walk. He gathered her in his arms and carried her inside, feeling guilty every time she moaned. A lamp glowed in the corner next to a low, plain bed inside an alcove.

Ari got their overnight bags from the van and returned to find Rita sitting at a table in an area between a tiny kitchen and a comfortable-looking living room.

"I'm not sleepy," she announced.

The second thermos, with the green tea, sat in their bag along with a box of matzo crackers. Ari put them on the table. "This is what's left."

"Ari, what did you mean that we're coming home here?" She munched a cracker while he poured tea into two thermos cups.

"I guess I don't really know." He handed her a cup of tea, and then retrieved the Gamla coin from his travel bag. "Ever since I found it, I thought someday I'd be back up here. It felt important, finding this." He held the coin in his open hand and added, "I don't know what it means."

The next day at noon, an official car arrived for Ari's meeting with the leaders of Gamla at the mayor's office. Influential families of the new district lived and worked in a town north of Ari and Rita's new cottage. The ride took about ten minutes.

Ari showed his identification in the lobby, and the driver, an enthusiastic young man with short dark hair, stepped forward. "Shalom," he said through a relaxed smile. "I'll take you to meet the mayor."

They walked down a hallway and into a large room with a thick pale-blue carpet. Zev, Dove, a woman, and two other men sat in padded chairs arranged around a massive clear glass coffee table. Potted plants grew next to a wood-framed window. Colorful landscape watercolor paintings adorned the walls.

Ari pulled a chair next to Dove. "Where's Monica?" he asked while they waited.

"Monica's been transferred to Be'er Sheva."

"Under whose authority?" Ari asked. "I didn't sign anything."

Dove looked at Ari. "A Squad Commander requested her transfer as a liaison officer. Monica asked Kiah to sign it. She said you'd understand."

A smile turned up the corners of Ari's mouth. "Padroski," he whispered.

The door opened, and a large man with silver hair and blue eyes entered with his advisors and walked directly to Ari.

Ari stood and extended his hand. "Pleased to meet you, Mayor Solomon."

Solomon wrapped a big, warm hand around Ari's. With a welcoming smile, he motioned with his other hand toward two sofas facing each other, with padded chairs in a semicircle on either side.

His advisors sat after Solomon did.

They talked for most of the afternoon about current events affecting Israel. The assistant mayor, Colonel Haetzi, mentioned the pressure they felt to allow Slavic Muslims, former refugees in Lebanon, to return from Persyria where most of them fled after Israel moved tanks in and annexed the region.

"We have no intention of risking Israel's sovereignty by allowing our enemy to return," Solomon added. "Persyria won't allow them to become citizens because they're not Arab. That's not our problem."

"That's right," Dove said. "Same problem they had with the former Lebanese government. Jerusalem recommends you set aside a few neighborhoods along the border with Persyria for them. To ease tensions with the One World Gov."

"The party line," Haetzi interrupted in a loud voice. "We've heard it. We're not interested. Gamla is Jewish and it's going to stay that way."

"But Israel's a democracy," Dove pointed out.

The dark-haired woman named Jessica said, "Now, Haetzi, remember, these people are our guests." She turned to Ari. "We don't want our children growing up next to neighborhoods with child brides and honor killings. We don't want our children traumatized by conflict."

Solomon sat studying Ari. "Let's hear what Ari thinks about this mixed neighborhood situation."

"Well," Ari answered slowly, "it works in some parts of Judea and Samaria."

"So you're for it?" Haetzi asked in an accusatory tone.

"I don't know enough yet," Ari shot back, "to be for or against anything. I arrived yesterday."

Zev spoke for the first time during the meeting. "The political leaders in Jerusalem point out that the fighting in Judea and Samaria is instigated by outside agitators."

"Jerusalem should concentrate on protecting their own," Haetzi said.

Ari stiffened. "You're referring to the suicide-bomber outside Café Liraz?"

"Ari," Dove said. "I thought you knew. A bomb went off yesterday at a pizzeria in downtown Jerusalem. Twelve teenagers and two adult workers are dead. Many injured."

Ari shook his head. "I've kept the news off because Rita's so jumpy."

"We heard," Solomon said. "Your strategist was injured in the café bombing incident. We're very sorry."

"She's my wife," Ari said. He suddenly felt tired. *Another bombing,* he thought. *How could this happen?*

Jessica flashed a warm smile. "Give her some time. And, Ari, we're not trying to bring up a sensitive subject with you. We want to know if you're joining us. Or if you plan to move back to the Negev."

Ari looked at the faces around him.

"Let him get to know us before we question his motives," Solomon suggested.

Ari held up a hand. "It's a fair question. In truth, I've avoided it. I came here thinking I'd eventually move back. Now, after what happened to Rita, I really don't know."

"I think we've had enough meeting for this day," Solomon said. "Ari will find his own way. And he'd probably like to go home now and be with his wife. Tomorrow we've arranged a tour of the farmlands we're setting aside for your community."

Jessica's brown eyes pleaded. "Ari, stay awhile. You'll fall in love with this place, as we all have."

Ari nodded, then stood. After rounds of good wishes, Dove and Zev walked with Ari to a long navy-blue car parked outside. He leaned against the car and folded his arms. "I want to live up to the trust extended to me by Kiah's people to rein in the tough guys of Gamla, but honestly, I don't know what's right."

"Our best weapon is to survive." Zev spread a hand out toward the landscaped grounds. "Here, there—it doesn't matter. Hashem will take care of the rest."

"We lost Gamla in 67 to the rampaging Romans," Ari reminded them.

Dove looked toward the distant hills. "But we took their Golan Heights, our Gamla, back during the 1967 war and we took the rest of Gamla back when Lebanon collapsed in 2030."

"Exactly." Ari shook his head. "I don't want to lose anything and then have to wait nineteen hundred years to get it back."

Ari spent the next day resting in the cottage garden with Rita instead of joining the farmlands tour. "We have plenty of time to see the land," he assured her.

Days in the garden turned into a quiet month while they enjoyed a pleasant onset of summer in their cottage. Gamla weather was temperate, with delightful summer rains.

By midsummer, eighty percent of the Kol Shofar population had joined the new Gamla communal farm under construction. Another month passed while Rita healed and Ari learned to relax.

Rita's ankle mended, although she still limped slightly. The café bomb left her with a diagonal one-inch scar on her left cheek, a chipped tooth, and occasional nightmares.

One morning, after a leisurely breakfast, Ari suggested they drive to the countryside. "I can show you the valley where I found the coin." He poured a second cup of coffee and handed it to Rita.

"Let's go today." She raised the coffee cup. "Todah."

An hour later they headed north. "Gamla's largely an agricultural region," Ari explained as they drove past fruit orchards, olive groves, and vineyards.

He turned off the main road onto a lane winding through open land and parked at the edge of a large dairy farm. "This is one of the places I want to show you."

They got out and walked to a seemingly endless wooden fence.

Ari motioned toward the open fields. "This farm wasn't here when we fought the 2030 war. It was only brush, trees, and rocks. Now it's the most productive pasture land in all of Gamla."

Rita looked past the fence to the tall grass, with stately trees scattered throughout. A deep blue pond lay in the middle, with a water sprayer throwing misty shapes up against a sapphire sky lined with distant fluffy clouds. Black and white cows gathered around the pond. A huge black bull grazed nearby.

"This farm," Ari told her, "supplies most of Israel with organic dairy products."

"Is it run by a collective?" Rita asked.

"Actually, a large Orthodox family living in New York decided to contact the government of Israel for permission to live here about ten years ago. The aliyah office offered the family this land."

"This is a big farm for one family to run," Rita said. "They must hire outside help."

"No," Ari said. "I admire them so much. Their relatives from America started joining them after the farm was established. It's a community of family members."

"Does this place hold special meaning for you?"

"A community is more than the sum of its parts, more than a random gathering of people." Ari slid his arm around Rita's waist. "We had a good community at Kol Shofar. We wanted to live and work together; we chose that."

"I think I know what you mean. Each community has a feeling, its own emotional state." Rita leaned her head back to look up at him. "We still have it. We're just in a different place."

Ari sighed. "It feels like the community could slip away. Little by little we're losing people along the way."

"We've added Rishon," Rita pointed out.

"You're right." Ari shook his head. "I should appreciate what I have."

They walked back to the van, arms linked.

The farther north they drove, the more rugged the terrain became. Waterfalls and snow-capped peaks of Gamla were a thrilling change from the stark beauty of the desert. Rita scanned the countryside.

Ari turned into a long driveway winding up to flat-roofed structures built into the hillside.

"This is breathtaking," Rita exclaimed as Ari parked.

"It's a special place. C'mon," Ari said playfully. "I'll show you around."

They ascended a few steps and submitted to a cursory search from the uniformed guard before continuing through the entrance doors. Flowering bromeliads of red, pink, and yellow hung in front of windows on all sides of the room. Potted Boston ferns graced the mosaic tile floor.

"I'm sorry, we're closing now." A well-rounded young brunette greeted them warmly and told them to come back another day. She wore shorts, hiking boots, and a camp shirt with a picture of a waterfall on the front, matching the logo in the lobby.

Ari took his identification out of his pocket, and flipped it open for her inspection.

Exasperated, she looked down at the card. "Oh! Commander Ari. It's you. Of course. I'll give you a tour myself." The flustered woman turned to Rita. "And for you too, Mrs. Commander. I'm Gabriella."

Rita chuckled. "I guess your reputation from Kol Shofar precedes you, Ari. I'm impressed."

"What's Kol Shofar?" Gabriella looked at Ari. "Our hero. The star of the 2030 war."

"Oh please." Ari shook his head. "I just wanted to show my wife the hot springs."

Gabriella pressed a button on the wall, and sliding glass doors opened on the far side. The sounds of rushing, splashing water indicated the direction of the hot springs.

Ari and Rita walked around the spring-fed pool inside a glass-enclosed room filled with dwarf palm trees and hanging vines.

"Was this place built after the 1967 war too?" Rita stopped to run her hand along the edge of a giant elephant fern growing in the ground beside the pool.

Ari smiled, and shook his head. "It's ancient, a natural spring. I knew you'd love it. Our people came here for a thousand years before we lost Gamla in 67. We waited nineteen hundred years to come back for a good soak."

Rita started walking slowly toward the exit. "And the glass building?"

"Yeah, we added the buildings and parking lot after 1967."

They walked out to the parking lot under a starlit night sky. Ari felt a sense of calm and a new purpose. "We can build an even better community up here," he told her. "One without a wall."

On the drive home, Rita rested her hand on Ari's shoulder. "I definitely want to explore the ancient sites in this region," she said softly. "I already love it, Ari. I want to stay. Is that all right with you?"

"I want it too."

When Ari turned at the villa driveway and stopped at the cottage, his headlights illuminated a navy blue car parked nearby.

Dove, Zev, and Haetzi got out of the car. No one said shalom.

Ari opened the cottage door and helped Rita inside. "I see the looks on your faces," he said as the others entered.

"It's the worst, Ari," Dove said in a low voice. "A ruling from the One World Court."

Ari pulled out chairs from the dining table to place around the sofa and padded chair in the main room. "Please, sit."

Rita and Ari sat on the sofa. Dove and Zev took the dining chairs. Haetzi finally sat in the padded chair. He removed a paper from his pocket and handed it to Ari.

"Advance notice of the ruling expected next week," Haetzi said.

"Just tell us," Rita said. "What does this mean?"

"I'll tell them." Dove took the paper. "Jewish persons residing in Gamla and the Golan Heights are evicted. The One World Court doesn't recognize our right to annex southern Lebanon. We'd have to prove Gamla's ancient existence to get an exemption."

"We don't have time to prove anything," Haetzi added. "We have ten days to enter our evidence. They make a final ruling in two weeks. The Persyrian government has made a claim under the Former Occupant Laws. They say taking the refugees from Lebanon is an unfair burden."

"This is nothing new," Dove said bitterly. "The surrounding countries need land for their exploding populations. The last One World census showed eighty-one percent of their populations are under the age of twenty. They average sixty-five people per household. They're crowded and angry."

"We have plenty of ancient sites around here," Zev pointed out.

Haetzi shook his head. "We don't have time to authenticate the northern locations. We need to find one with Hebrew writing. Persyria claims these places are Assyrian."

Rita turned to Ari. "What should we do?"

"Leave as soon as possible," Dove suggested. "These fanatics won't wait a month to take our land. We'd better be gone by the time the court announces the decision. We've got two weeks before a stampede of Jews flee south."

Ari crumpled the paper, and threw it down. "We've lost everything. Again."

chapter 26

THE MORNING AFTER Ari received the eviction news, he arose early and made a plan. Rita got up with him and, a few minutes later, Ari handed her a cup of hot black coffee as she sat in her robe at the dining table.

She sipped the coffee and asked, "The coin?"

"Yes. I'll go to the place I found it in the north and see if I can locate the source. I couldn't explore the surrounding area during the war."

"I thought so. I'll go with you."

"It's very rugged." Ari patted her arm. "The truth is, I can move faster alone. I don't know if I can even find the exact place sixteen years later."

Rita set her cup down. "When are you leaving?" She followed his glance toward the door, saw his backpack and jacket.

"Rita, I have to try."

"I know." She felt fear creep into her heart when Ari stood to leave.

"It's going to take me all day to hike in and find the place, if all goes well. I plan to spend one night camping and the next day searching in that small valley I showed you on our last drive."

Rita nodded. "I'll be ready to go by the time you come back, unless you find something."

"No, I want you to leave tomorrow with Dove and the family. I spoke with him earlier. He and Rishon are on the way over now to drop off an all-wheel vehicle for me to use. I'll leave the van here for you."

"Couldn't we wait only one more day? You'd be back." The anxiety she'd felt earlier came back like a wave crashing against rocks.

Ari sat again. "This place will become a madhouse when news of the forced move is announced. A million Jews will move south in the next two weeks. I don't want you caught in that exodus."

Rita pressed her lips together. "Please, I don't want to leave without you." She couldn't stop herself from saying it.

"It's the best way, Honey. Throw what you want in the van today. Dove and Naomi are driving to their relations in Jerusalem, where they stayed before. Rishon can drive the van, and you and Batya will follow in the car. You'll be safe with them. They plan to leave tomorrow at dawn."

Rita took a moment to let the reality of it sink in. "Ari, where will I stay when I get there?"

"Okay, Honey, this is the tough part. Nothing is going to be available. You'll have to stay with my parents until I arrive."

"Oh no. I'll go along with everything except that. I'll figure it out. Maybe I'll stay with Devorah or Tarah."

"I'll find you," Ari said softly. "You can count on it." He kissed her, a long, lingering kiss, before he left.

Ari pushed the all-terrain rover hard until he approached the last turnoff. He bounced along dirt roads through rocky, brush-covered ground up into a rugged mountainous region until the roads ended. Then he pointed the vehicle due north and headed up the slopes of the old camel's back, the Gamla.

Searching for anything familiar, he drove slowly. He stopped when the vehicle's undercarriage could no longer clear the boulders.

The sun burned overhead while he hiked up a steep path leading to the area he wanted to search. For hours he traversed back and forth in a grid pattern until he found the spot he remembered. At sunset, he forced himself to stop and make camp.

The all-weather field tent popped into shape when he pulled it from its cover. Ari shook out his sleeping bag, set it up inside, and settled in, fully dressed with boots still laced. The smart gun he carried rested under his pillow. He carefully tucked the Gamla coin deep into a hidden pocket inside the sleeping bag and fastened the Velcro top of the pocket.

An hour passed before he relaxed enough to sleep. Small animals rustled brush outside his tent. He listened for unusual sounds, heard none, and started to drift off. A crackling noise outside caused him to sit up, his hand on his gun.

Slowly, Ari unzipped the tent door about halfway and peered out. Nothing looked unusual. A full moon in a sky of sparkling stars cast enough light to see clearly. He poked his head out to see a brushfire starting to flicker a few feet away.

Ari stepped out of his tent, listened, and waited before moving cautiously toward the burning bush. The ground around the small fire showed no signs of disturbance.

"What's going on?" Ari called out. He looked around, put his Glock inside his waistband, and pulled brush away while stomping out the fire.

Movement from behind caused Ari to swing around, reaching for his gun. Five men covered with leaves and brush jumped up from lying prone in shallow depressions.

The strange men with shoulder-length brown hair and full beards, dressed in short brown tunics over loose pants, were so close he couldn't get off a shot off before they rushed in and knocked him down.

When Ari opened his eyes, he lay supine. One man held a baseball-size stone above Ari's face. A teenager with unkempt shoulder-length hair and a scruffy beard pointed a knife at his chest. The other three searched the contents of his tent and back-pack, tossing things about.

The three men soon returned from his tent. One of the men was unusually tall, almost as tall as Ari. The tall man said something and the rock over Ari was thrown aside. The teenager put his knife away and became friendly.

Ari saw his gun under the belt of the tall one. The man motioned for Ari to sit, squatted next to him, and pulled something out of a pouch hanging on his belt. Slowly, his fingers moved back to reveal it. A gold Gamla coin rested in the palm of his hand.

"No." Ari slowly shook his head. "You can't steal that. I will pay you for it. We can make a deal for much more than it's worth. I'll trade my car for that." He pointed to the coin. "Can you understand me?"

The leader grinned and offered the coin to Ari. When Ari took it, the stranger pulled an identical coin out of his pocket.

Stunned, Ari pointed to the second coin. "Where did you find it?" He asked in Hebrew, then English.

The men stared at him while the leader tucked his coin back into his pocket. They jumped to their feet when Ari stood. "We have to go," Ari said. "You show me, help me."

"Go," the tall one repeated. They seemed to know this word.

They walked silently as Ari followed them by the light of the moon for nearly an hour up the mountainside. They finally stopped, and pushed brush from the base of a mound.

The leader pointed to an opening approximately the size of a rolled-up sleeping bag, looked at Ari, and said, "Go!"

Ari hesitated. He studied the man's face in the moonlight. The strange men hunched down and slid into the hole, one after another. The leader looked again at Ari, then followed his men.

The moonlight cast a mother-of-pearl glow on the rocky landscape. Ari bent down and listened inside the opening. The sounds moved away. He pulled the brush close behind him and crawled on his belly toward the men.

The tunnel opened up into a tent-sized room, barely tall enough for Ari to stand. He squinted and tried to see in the dim green light of his wrist com.

One of the men took a stone and tapped four times on the solid rock wall in front of him. Minutes later, a boulder as tall as the men rolled back as though on its own to reveal a vaulted room with a high, domed ceiling. A fuel-cell lamp cast a warm glow from a niche carved high on the wall.

When he entered behind the others, Ari saw two arched openings with lights flickering inside other rooms. The carved room held about twenty people dressed in long tunics, sitting on rugs or cushions.

The tall one led Ari to an old man with a curly gray beard. He sat watching on a large brightly colored cushion. Ari studied the faces of the people surrounding him. Most looked vaguely familiar, with green or light-brown eyes, light olive skin, and dark curly hair.

A woman carrying two pillows approached from one of two connecting rooms. She looked different, young, blue-eyed with light brown hair cut in a modern style.

"Shalom, I'm Tamora, a friend," she said to Ari. She put the pillows on the ground across from the old man and sat. "Please, sit with us. We don't have much time."

"You speak Hebrew," Ari said as he sat. "Who are these people?"

"We'll get to all that. Their language is a dialect of Aramaic. I'll be your interpreter." Tamora spread out her hand, palm up, toward the old man. "*Abba* Santi." Then she gestured toward Ari. "*Abba* Ari."

"How do you know me?" Ari asked. "Why did you bring me here?"

"We know who you are. The men brought you here for a reason." Tamora spoke to Santi, who chuckled through his answer.

"He says all you people who live above the ground are impatient."

"They live here?"

Tamora nodded. "Here and other similar places. Their tribe numbers, at different times, between a hundred and fifty to about two hundred."

Ari looked at the old man. "What tribe?"

"The name means 'The People' in Aramaic," Tamora explained. "In good times they live on the surface. In bad times, they live below. Probably been this way for a couple of thousand years. Maybe more."

Ari took a deep breath. "The air in here is fresh."

Tamora motioned toward the ceiling. "Vented from slant-drilled holes a quarter kilometer away."

Santi said something and waved a hand at Ari.

"You'll sleep here for a few hours because he wants to sleep now. Then he will show you something."

"Look," Ari said. "I don't have time for this. You don't understand what's going on."

Tamora spoke to the old man, stood, and picked up her pillow. "Come with me, Ari. We'll talk in the other room."

He followed her into a similar-sized room and sat on the pillow she offered.

"Who are you, and how do you know me?" Ari asked.

"I'm going to tell you, because we have to trust each other." She sat on her own pillow, across from him. "My parents, Myrl and LaVerna, were former American CIA. My Jewish mother is Semitic and she worked undercover as his Arab wife. My parents were young agents sent here twenty-five years ago to disrupt the State of Israel. Shortly after they began their assignment, they changed sides and fell in love. They faked their own deaths and vanished into the population here. I was born a year later."

Ari sat and talked quietly with Tamora about the situation in Gamla for a couple of hours in the yellow light of the lamp.

"Santi's man has one of the ancient coins," he said. "Is that what you're trying to tell me?"

She nodded. "Santi has a bag of them. He has about ten left. Every hundred years or so, they give one away. Usually to save someone. The one you found is probably one of Santi's coins."

"Even with more coins, I can't save Gamla." Ari's jaw tightened as he spoke. "I have to prove where they originated."

"Santi doesn't know where most of them were found. They've been with his tribe for as long as anyone can remember."

"Why trust me with all this?"

"I told Santi you are the leader of your people, and you do have the gold coin. They want your people on these farmlands. They take food from the corners of your fields without fear of being killed for it. And they call you their distant, impatient relations."

"But he seemed to know me." Ari shook his head. "I don't understand."

"Ari," Tamora said slowly, "think back to the 2030 war. You were injured badly when you led your unit up into this valley sixteen years ago. Your men were the front line. Because of your unit, we won southern Lebanon back from Syria. But you were the only survivor after the ambush."

"I never could explain it." Ari tried to remember. "I was not far from this valley, alone and unconscious. IDF medics found me the next day. And a blanket covered me."

Tamora nodded. "The Israeli Defense Force medics were amazed you were able to dress your wounds before you passed out. They thought you tied a pressure bandage around each arm and on your right leg to stop the bleeding from the knife wounds. You had a broken arm and a crushed shoulder."

Ari stared at her. "How do you know this?"

"You remember the enthusiastic young man who helped bring you here?"

Ari nodded, remembering the knife-wielding teenager.

"It was his father who properly dressed your wounds and covered you. You wouldn't have survived."

Ari looked around. "I'd like to thank him."

"His father died years ago. He was the tall one's brother."

Ari turned to see Santi standing in the opening. The old man tapped a watch on his wrist.

"He wears a watch?" Ari stood with Tamora.

"It hasn't worked for years." She chuckled. "He thinks it's funny to wear time. And he likes the way it looks."

Santi turned and walked toward another opening.

"You better get movin' as my father would say." Tamora slid off her pillow and stood. "Dad's from Texas—brags about it all the time."

Ari hurried after Santi.

"Listen, Ari." Tamora followed him for a few steps. "I know your brother, Dan. That's how this came about. He worked with my parents in Mossad for years. Please don't tell anyone about these people."

Ari stopped. "My brother, Dan? Israeli intelligence? Not possible. I would know."

Tamora pointed to Santi. "He doesn't use a light." She handed Ari her pencil-size flashlight. Ari looked back once, then followed the strange old man into the heart of the mountain.

Santi moved forward through the tunnel system. Hours of crawling, or walking hunched over, left Ari wondering where he was. His flashlight cast an eerie glow as they traveled deeper into dank, uncomfortable places.

"Stop," Ari called ahead to Santi. "It looks to end here."

Santi turned and grinned. "Rest!"

"Yes, but this ceiling is getting low." Ari pointed his pencil light forward. The rock passageway where Ari stood looked smooth. *Obviously carved out,* he thought.

Santi removed a pouch and drank from it.

Feeling his parched lips, Ari began to realize the foolishness of the venture.

They stood at the end of the tunnel for a moment. Santi motioned for Ari to open his mouth, held up his pouch, and squeezed. A thin stream of water shot over Ari's tongue.

The old man lay on his belly and inched forward toward a ledge near the ground. Ari aimed his penlight down and watched him pull himself under. Ari lay down, pointed the light forward, and followed Santi through a horizontal slit in the wall under the protruding rock.

They crawled along the passageway for a long time into a damp corridor, and Ari regretted wasting almost a day on this nonsense. Then the rock sloped upward and became progressively wetter. Excitement filled Ari's tired body when he realized they were probably traveling up an ancient water system. With renewed energy, he pulled himself forward through a rougher section, ignoring the cuts and scrapes he got.

The short jagged area opened into what Ari thought could have been a cistern. Steps carved into the stone led them up the side into a room.

Ari waved his flashlight around the open space. He looked past rocks and mounds of tunnel debris to a partially collapsed archway leading out. They climbed over the obstructions to the arch. It opened around a corner to an even larger room packed with rubble almost to the top of the vaulted ceiling.

The penlight Ari carried illuminated a small area when he laid it on the ground, pointing into the debris. He knelt to clear away some of the crushed rock covering the floor.

They spent twenty minutes clearing a strip of floor under the archway until they unearthed a section of colored tiles forming a mosaic floor. Inlaid blue glass tiles spelled Hebrew words. Many of the tiles were missing, but Ari could make out several Hebrew letters.

A sense of awe came over Ari as he brushed the dirt away with his hand. "What is this place?" he wondered aloud.

Santi squatted, and touched Ari's sleeve.

Ari sat on the ground and pointed the little light toward the ceiling so they could see each other.

Using Modern Hebrew, Santi said, "This is our place. A dwelling for your people and for mine. We are the remnant of a great tribe."

"You speak Hebrew. Why did you try to fool me?" Ari tried to feel angry at the old man, but he couldn't.

Santi sighed. "I put my family at risk by revealing to you our secrets. No fool. I want to know you first before we speak together."

"Tamora? You trust her?" Ari held his light steady and watched Santi's face.

The old man sighed again. "Tamora is like my adopted daughter," he explained. "Our link to the outside world. She came to me and advised me to help you." Santi looked at Ari. "Her parents—they helped me a long time ago."

Ari nodded. "This structure proves we were here. I only have a few days left to get proof of this place out to the world and save Gamla."

Santi tapped his broken wrist watch. "Plenty of time."

"Great. Too bad the clock in the World Court building keeps ticking."

Santi removed a precious gold Gamla coin from the pouch tied to his belt. He climbed over the rubble, which reached to the tall ceiling in some places, and finally crawled back.

Santi stood with Ari at the archway, and looked back toward the debris-filled room. "Ready for discovery now," Santi said. "I put one coin back. We found two here."

Ari gazed lovingly in the direction of the rubble. He believed the Heritage division of the One World Government was nothing more than a highly paid group of criminals who gave themselves the legal right to oversee any archaeological site in the world. After authentication they would likely close it for safety reasons. *To strip it of the most valuable items,* he thought. *I have to let it go. I don't have time to search for artifacts.*

They finished the last of Santi's water before starting the long walk/crawl to the cavern in the mountain where, Ari knew, Tamora would be waiting. Ari pushed hard. He set a cadenced pace, and didn't stop to rest. Santi followed easily. Five hours later they stepped into the cavern room.

Just as Ari expected, Santi's family members, including Tamora, waited with food and fresh water. He washed his hands and sat on the ground with the family in a circle while a woman set a bowl of food on a cloth in the middle. Santi said a blessing while everyone, using wooden ladles, scooped some of the boiled grain, seeds, and root vegetables into individual bowls. Ari ate three helpings.

A middle-aged woman sitting next to Santi served herbal tea after the meal. Ari swallowed a mouthful and looked at Tamora. "I'm not going to make it." He heard his own words as if someone else were speaking.

"Come, a short respite is needed." Tamora led him to a corner of the room where a cushioned blanket lay on the ground next to a pillow. "Rest a couple of hours on my bed. We'll help you, and you'll make it in time."

Ari turned toward Santi and the others. "Thank you for the food. Thank you for . . ." his voice choked.

"It's all right," she said quietly. "You still have several days."

Ari closed his eyes to fight off a sudden dizziness. He sank to the ground and stretched out on the blanket in the cavern sanctuary of the hill people. "I only need an hour or two."

"In a few hours the sun will set," Tamora reminded him. "You can't hike around out there in the daylight." She sat and pulled the edge of the blanket over him.

"You don't understand," Ari said. "I have no illusion my vehicle will be where I left it. I camped close to the Persyrian border. I'll be lucky to walk out in two days to the highway. We still have to get authorities to the site and dig it out enough to authenticate it."

"We'll find a way," she said.

Ari shook his head. "I don't even know how to lead them to the location above ground once I call them in." Tears welled up in his eyes. "I'm too late," he whispered.

"Sleep now, my brother." Tamora gestured toward Santi's family. "We will pray for you."

Four hours later, Ari woke with Tamora kneeling close. He opened his eyes and saw the look on her face. "What?" he asked as he sat up.

"Trouble. Our scouts sighted an enemy campfire a few yards from our cave exit. We can't take a chance on being found."

Ari shook his head. "Whatever it is, I'll get past it." He stretched his shoulders and rubbed his eyes.

She pointed to Santi. "He wants you to wait."

Ari grimaced. "Can't. This is bigger than all of us. How many are out there? I'll kill them. I have to get out." Ari stood, and walked toward Santi.

"Only three." Tamora stood and followed him. "But one of them is a woman."

Ari stopped. "Okay. Is there another way out?"

"Two days through the mountain out the other side," she told him. "Farther from your destination."

Santi stood as they approached.

"We need to make a diversion," Tamora said.

Ari motioned toward the tunnel exit. "Who's out there?"

Santi pointed toward the opening. "We observed a strange new enemy sitting with a man dressed as a northern Arab."

"A Syrian," Ari speculated.

"Maybe," Santi said. "But the other man looks different." Then he said something in Aramaic.

Tamora turned to Ari. "He's willing to trust you to go out. Try to go around the enemy fire. But you'll have to go alone. We can't lead you now."

Santi gave Ari a bag of small, black seeds and a shoulder pouch filled with water. The old man put his hands on Ari's shoulders and mumbled a few words. Then he nodded and sat on his blanket.

The tall man from the tent raid stepped forward. Ari saw his gun in the man's outstretched hand. Their eyes met briefly as Ari reached for his pistol. He put it into his waistband.

Tamora walked with Ari to where the exit narrowed. She handed him a piece of paper and smiled. "A map from the highway to the site. To an above-ground entry."

"*Todah raba*. Thank you so very much." Ari took the map. "I won't forget this."

"*Lo dah vah*." Tamora smiled. "You're welcome."

Ari exited the cave by pulling himself along the ground. The campfire burned a few yards away as reported. Ari worked his way closer.

Laughter wafted over from the three sitting on the ground, each wrapped in a blanket. Ari studied the forms making reckless noise in front of him. *This can't be,* he thought.

One of the men spoke Russian, and Ari stopped moving. Slowly, he drew the gun secured in his belt. *But the woman*, he thought. *She reminds me of* . . .

The woman spoke, and the other two laughed.

"Rita?" Ari stood with a look of bewilderment.

The man dressed as the Syrian jumped up, reached for his pistol, and stopped. "Ari?" Haetzi asked.

Rita sighed, and by the light of the campfire, Ari saw her eyes fill with tears. He walked forward and she slowly stood. "We found you," she said with outstretched arms.

Ari held her tightly for a moment, then sat next to her with his arm draped loosely over her shoulder. "You're supposed to be in Jerusalem," he said. Before she could answer, he turned to the young, platinum-blond man wearing a Russian military uniform and pointed. "Who's this?"

Haetzi had begun putting the fire out. He gathered a bag and slung it over his shoulder. "He's with us now. Shalav's the name. A defector from the Russian army."

Shalav jumped up when he heard his name and saluted Ari.

Ari stood and helped Rita to her feet. "How'd you get here?" he asked her. "What's going on?"

"Oh, Ari." Rita hugged him tightly. "Did you find something?"

"I found an ancient temple, clearly ours." Ari held her close and whispered, "Tell me you have a vehicle."

Haetzi started across the meadow to the trail leading down. "We came prepared. Did you locate the source of the Gamlean coin?"

"It's incredible—everything we need," Ari said. "I even have a map to the location."

They found the narrow goat trail leading down to Ari's original campsite.

"I brought Haetzi up here to show him where I thought you might be," Rita explained as they walked. "We stumbled into a unit from the Russian army on patrol. They took Haetzi and me prisoner, and told Shalav to shoot us."

Ari felt his stomach tighten into a knot.

"I know, Ari," Rita said quietly. "But Shalav's Jewish. That's why he volunteered to come on this mission. He's been looking for a way to defect."

"What do you mean?" Ari glanced at Shalav.

"He killed them, Ari, all five of them. He threw his gun down in front of Haetzi and started begging him."

Ari walked along for a few minutes. "A Russian army unit sits on our border?"

"We'll figure it out when we get back," Haetzi said. "First things first. Look what we brought for you."

They arrived at the place Ari camped. In the moonlight, he saw the gleaming black Thunderbolt III helicopter.

"Let's get to the bird." Haetzi waved his hand and started forward.

"We found your camp," Rita said, "but not much was left. And the car's gone."

Ari stopped for a moment and put his hands gently on Rita's shoulders. "We're going to make it in time. But how did you know?"

"She convinced me to take a chance," Haetzi said over his shoulder. "Knew you'd find something."

They ran to the two soldiers guarding the aircraft, the jet-propelled transport waiting to rush them to the courthouse in The Hague.

"We'd better hurry," the pilot said. "A nasty weather front's moving in fast."

Ari stepped up on the runner and climbed inside after the others. Tamora's map to the ancient temple lay tucked inside his shirt pocket.

"We have enough evidence to present a case, thanks to you," Haetzi told Ari. "Prime Minister Kiah instructed our attorneys to wait at the courthouse. We'll meet them by the front doors."

"The conflict over Gamla will end now," Rita added.

Ari looked out at indigo skies before he closed the chopper door. *This isn't over*, he thought. *It hasn't even started.*

Four days later, amid storm clouds gathering overhead, Ari and Rita descended the black granite steps outside the One World Courthouse. The late-morning sun poured through a hole in the clouds and caught quartz veins running through the granite, throwing shards of light beneath their feet.

Rita smiled up at Ari. "We did it! The court accepted our coin and map as evidence for an appeal. Israel will win."

Ari held her hand as they stepped onto the sidewalk toward their car. "Yes, this is the end of it."

A light rain started as Ari opened the car door for Rita. When she entered, he went around to the other side, got in, and closed the door. Drops started to gather on the windshield and drizzle together into little rivers.

"I hope we make it home before the worst of the storms hit," she said, turning on the heater as he guided the car onto the main highway toward the airport.

He smiled confidently, but in his heart, Commander Ari Alexander knew there was more than just a storm coming. He could feel it. "We'll make it," he said softly. "Whatever's coming, Rita, we'll face it together."

www.ingramcontent.com/pod-product-compliance
Lightning Source LLC
Chambersburg PA
CBHW021303250626
47155CB00002B/346